NOVELS

The Demise of the Soccer Moms ◆ *The Suburban Abyss*
The Hallelujah Horror Show ◆ *Getting Ahead*
Faceless ◆ *An Affair With God*

THE ALEXANDRA MALLORY PSYCHOLOGICAL
SUSPENSE SERIES

The Woman In the Mirror ◆ *The Woman In the Water*
The Woman In the Painting ◆ *The Woman In the
Window*
The Woman In the Bar ◆ *The Woman In the Bedroom*
The Woman In the Dark ◆ *The Woman In the Cellar*

THE HAUNTED SHIP TRILOGY

Alone On the Beach ◆ *Slipping Away From the Beach*
Haunting the Beach

NOVELLAS

Madison Keith Ghost Story Series ◆ *Chances Are*

SHORT FICTION

Reduction in Force ◆ *Maternal Instinct*
Flash Fiction For the Cocktail Hour
The 12 Days of Xmas

Cathryn Grant

BURIED BY DEBT

A Novel

D2C Perspectives

This book is a work of fiction. Any resemblance to actual events or persons, living or dead, is entirely coincidental. Artistic liberty has been taken with Silicon Valley, California, but I got the restaurants right, and that's the most important part.

Dedication

For my daughters — I've written millions of words but there are no words to express the awesomeness that is both of you.

Prologue

TODAY DEVON WOULD receive the official notice of his promotion. It would be accompanied by a very nice salary bump and an annual bonus plan that would allow him to turn the dank pit beneath his house into a first-class wine cellar. Thirty minutes from now, when he walked out of the VP's office, his money worries would be erased. Carrying two mortgages on the house would be history. They'd re-finance and pay off the credit card debt. The value was finally creeping up again now that the recession was more or less over. Everything was good.

He had a smart, gorgeous wife who was as crazy about him as he was about her. His friends kidded that his adoration of Jenna bordered on obsession. They might be right, but who wouldn't be obsessed with a woman like Jenna, with her long, satin hair and her lean body from all that running? Not that she had the gaunt form of a marathoner, she still had lots of nice flesh in all the right spots, and the most beautiful face he'd ever seen.

He strode down the hall, occasionally glancing into the window offices to his right. The view from the fifth floor was dull today, the valley shrouded in early August haze from temperatures that had persisted in the low 90s all week. As he neared the VP's office, he slowed. He paused at the administrative assistant's desk, tapped his finger on the low counter that surrounded it, and grinned. "He's ready to see me?"

She nodded.

Inside the office, Pete was seated on the pale blue sofa. His button-down shirt blended with the sofa fabric, his black slacks stood in sharp contrast. His hair was almost completely gray, but he still looked young. Devon planned to be in exactly the same shape when he was Pete's age.

Papers filled with line graphs and pie charts printed in color were scattered across the low table. Pete leaned back and gestured at the chair on the opposite side of the table.

Devon sat down. "Good quarter so far," he said.

"Revenues are only up three percent."

Devon shrugged. "It's early." He should take charge, get right to the point. They respected that, but it was a fine line between taking charge and barging ahead, breaking the protocol of letting the guy with the biggest title take the lead.

"You're not going to like what I have to say," Pete said.

Devon rubbed his thumb on the cording that ran along the arm of the chair. "I think ..."

Pete held up his hand. "Let me finish. Revenues aren't where they should be. We've decided to take a conservative approach to promotions for the next three quarters. Conservative as in zero."

"I thought it was already in the system," Devon said.

"It wasn't finalized. It'll still happen, just not in the foreseeable future. I know you'll understand. Part of being in upper management is doing what's best for the business."

That was a great way to stop any further discussion. Devon smiled, hoping it didn't look as limp and false as it felt. "Sure. Sure." He stood and shoved his hand in his pocket. "I'm disappointed, of course."

Pete stood and extended his hand. Devon shook it. They talked for a few minutes, exchanging what felt like nothing more than a string of buzzwords. As Devon walked down the hallway, he didn't look out at the haze. He'd been in Pete's office all of three and a half minutes. He'd spent more time climbing the stairs than he had learning that he and Jenna were now in deep financial shit. He'd have to figure out a more effective way to juggle bills and cash. Better yet, maybe he'd think about acquiring another revenue stream. Eventually, he'd get to the next rung on the ladder, but he was tired of waiting for eventually.

One

JENNA PORTER KNEW that if you had money, the San Francisco Bay Area was a terrific place to live. Everything she could want was available, for a price – the best cuisine from nearly every corner of the world, an endless variety of wine, exotic homes, and all the clothes a woman desired. Not that she only cared about money, but lately, cash, rather the lack of it, cast a shadow over everything – her friendships, her ability to be there for her mother, even her love for Devon.

Until seven months ago, she and Devon believed they were well-situated, with a cleverly financed Mediterranean Revival home, hundreds of photographs documenting vacations in Italy, Hawaii, France, and Australia, framed and hanging on the walls, or streaming across the screen saver on their desktop computer. They owned late-model cars, and their home was beautifully furnished. They funded it all with two well-paying jobs in high tech. Their jobs came complete with bonus plans and stock options. The trouble was their stock was handed out in *options to buy*, not ready cash. After Devon's promotion was delayed, huge amounts of red began bleeding through their budget-tracking tool.

If it weren't for Beth's upcoming wedding, Jenna wouldn't be at the Stanford Mall on a Friday afternoon in mid-February. Beth had insisted they shop together for new dresses for the rehearsal dinner. Thankfully, Jenna hadn't been to the mall in months, so there would be a little breathing room on her credit cards. Once Devon was promoted, it would be easy to pay down their debt. It was a temporary setback, he'd assured her.

She popped out of her BMW and walked past the row of parked cars. Directly ahead, a couple stood in front of Fleming's Steak House, framed by the rich oak doors and thick wood pillars. The woman had glossy dark hair, not unlike Jenna's. She wore strappy black high-heeled sandals, a narrow black skirt, and a sleeveless cranberry top. Her arms were folded across her ribs, startlingly white against the red. As Jenna watched, the man grabbed the woman's wrist. He yanked her toward him. The woman's cheeks turned red. She twisted her arm and let out a small cry as he pulled harder. She glanced in Jenna's direction. The dark color of her cheeks spread to her hairline. She let her arm go slack and turned her back to Jenna.

Jenna walked past The Creamery restaurant toward the entrance to Bloomingdales. The couple's tension followed, weighing like a shovel full of mud inside her chest. What were their lives like when no one was watching? She couldn't imagine standing in a public place, displaying all her emotions to anyone walking past. She couldn't imagine Devon grabbing her wrist, twisting until she cried. That would never happen to them. Soon Devon would get his promotion, there would be more opportunities for her own career, including a healthy salary increase once the economy improved and the company stopped being so tight-fisted. She didn't want to ever be standing on a sidewalk trying, and failing, to hide the disintegration of their lives from passersby.

Keeping their debt a secret was exhausting. She dodged questions, avoided invitations to lunch, and trips to the spa. She still kept up her manicures, but this winter had been the first time since she was fifteen years old that she hadn't enjoyed a twice-monthly pedicure. She had her father's second wife to thank for that lifelong indulgence. After Christine introduced Jenna to the hedonistic pleasure of spas, she'd adopted the habit with enthusiasm. She missed her sculpted, painted toenails, but she had to do what she could to help trim expenses.

This past Christmas, she and Devon had scrimped wherever possible, to free up extra cash so they could still purchase nice gifts for their families and friends. They'd pushed most of their credit cards to the max. It was getting more difficult to keep it hidden. Two weeks ago, they'd been forced to fabricate an event with Devon's company so they could gracefully avoid going to a club with their friends, an evening that couldn't have been managed without cash. Recently, she sometimes felt as if she was confined in a steel case, not enough oxygen to breathe freely, the walls only inches from her shoulders, her skin damp. Her pulse accelerated to an uncomfortable level, a rapid pounding that was nothing like the energizing thud she felt after a five- or six-mile run.

She sat on the bench outside of Bloomingdale's. The concrete planter behind her was crammed full of flowering shrubs and annuals. They would all be dead once this brief preview of spring passed and a bout of February frost bit the delicate petals, but for now, the sun was warm on her shoulders and even her large dark glasses couldn't completely block the bright sunshine. She pulled out her phone and shaded it with her hand. Three twenty-five.

When she saw Beth and Allison crossing the parking lot, Jenna put her phone in her purse. Beth's blonde hair was almost white in the bright sun, and even Allison's light brown hair glittered with pale highlights. Jenna glanced toward Flemings. If the couple was still there, would Beth or Allison notice and mention it?

The image of the man's fingers, squeezing and twisting the woman's wrist, gnawed at the back of her mind as if a rat was chewing through the threads of her nerves, preventing any pleasant feelings from making it to her brain. She stood and smiled at her friends.

Beth greeted her with a hug that was too intense. Allison

held her Blackberry in one hand, hugging Jenna with her free arm.

Beth turned toward Bloomingdale's. "Should we start here?" She smiled, exposing the slight overlap of the center bottom tooth over its mate. "I'm so happy you could both take time off work so we can have some girl time."

"Hold on." Allison rolled her finger over the trackball and tapped a message quickly using only her right thumb.

"Can't you tell your office to go away for two hours?" Beth pouted and pulled her chin toward her collarbone.

Allison bent over to shade her phone. Her hair fell forward, hiding her clenched jaw. "This will only take a second."

Beth started toward the entrance. Jenna took a few steps. She paused and looked back. Allison didn't seem to notice they'd walked away. After a moment, Allison looked up, staring past them. Finally, she walked slowly to where Beth stood, holding the door open.

None of them bought anything at Bloomingdale's, but Allison put two Theory dresses on hold. "I like them both, but I'm waiting 'til I see what else is out there." She glanced at her Blackberry. Her hair fell over the side of her cheek, and she tucked it behind her ear.

They strolled through two others stores without trying anything on. They stopped outside BCBGMAXAZRIA. Jenna walked to the window and looked at the display. Although there was plenty more cold weather to come, you wouldn't know it looking in the store windows. They enticed shoppers into thinking spring had already arrived. She was confident she would find something here, and she hadn't used her BCBG card for over a year. Suddenly her mood lifted. It would be good to try on dresses without worrying about the card being declined. She was tired of worrying about every expense. It was the house that weighed them down. They shouldn't have bought something so beyond their reach before Devon's promotion was official. It made her feel slightly ashamed, a vague reminder of her father, always thinking the next big thing was in his hand when it really wasn't. She was annoyed at herself for the comparison. Devon was nothing like her father.

"I can never find anything here," Allison said.

"Let's check it out," Beth said. "You never know."

Inside, Jenna drifted away from her friends. She walked toward the adjacent window where three pale dresses were displayed on slender, muscle-free mannequins. She plucked two dresses off the nearby rack and walked further toward the back.

A sales clerk materialized near her left elbow. "Can I start a room for you?"

Jenna smiled and handed over the dresses. "Yes, thanks."

On the platform in an alcove behind the clerk, a dress that reminded her of an antique gown dyed the color of tea clung to a plastic, faceless figure. The dress fell to the figure's mid-thighs in tiered tulle layers, fluffy, yet still sleek and fitted to her form. It was strapless with a spandex bodice topped by a satin strip. The mannequin was turned slightly, looking out the window as if she longed to escape the confines of her narrow enclosure. In the back, the top layers of the skirt were pulled up to an inverted *V* with longer layers underneath. Jenna imagined her hair flowing over her bare shoulders and back. The dress was a perfect look for the desert with lots of party flair. There was a hint of the 1920s blended with current style.

Despite her complaint that she wouldn't find anything, Allison was again looking at black dresses. Strange, since she already had half a closet full of them, and stranger still that would be her choice for a wedding in the desert, but it seemed she couldn't help but be drawn to clothes that fit her image as an attorney. That was one of the things Jenna loved about her job. Although she couldn't wear this particular dress to work, she had a lot more freedom than her friends to fill her closet with clothes that fit her personality. An attorney and a schoolteacher had their wardrobes dictated by their employers, but an event planner was supposed to look trendy. She felt a prick of sadness for her friends, coupled with gratitude. She turned to the rack near the mannequin to look for her size.

In the fitting room, she didn't bother with the first two dresses she'd selected. If this dress looked as good on her as it had on the mannequin, she knew this was it. She slipped off her silk top, kicked off her heels, wriggled out of her jeans, and unhooked her bra. The dress slid over her shoulders and down her sides like a second skin. She twisted to zip it up the side, adjusted it under her arms, and looked in the mirror. Perfect. It was fitted enough that her breasts looked nice and round without showing so much cleavage she looked slutty. The skirt fell over her hips and glanced across her thighs. Not only did it look great, it felt as soft and light as a summer nightgown.

She turned several times, admiring herself from every angle. She scooped up her hair to see that the dress fit well under her shoulder blades. She let her hair fall back down. It had grown a lot this winter and hung almost to her waist. She poked around inside the dress for the price tag. It must be attached to the seam. She admired herself for another moment before slipping it off.

"How's it going?" Allison said.

"Great. I think I have my dress," Jenna said.

"Show us," Allison said.

She wasn't sure why she hadn't volunteered to show her friends. Usually, they modeled their choices for each other. Maybe she didn't want to rub their faces in it. Neither one of them would be able to pull off this dress. Beth was too full-figured. Allison was too flat chested, and her shoulders were a little boney. Jenna pulled on her jeans and slid her feet into her high heels. She attached the dress to the hanger and pulled out the white card with the price. $378. She sucked in a thin stream of air. That was a lot, but it was so perfect. They could let this balance ride, pay twenty dollars a month or so. It would be fine. She wasn't sure what her limit was here, but it was far more than five hundred, so it would work out great. Better to buy something here anyway rather than a store that still had a balance on the card.

At the checkout counter, Jenna handed the dress to the clerk.

"Is that strapless?" Allison said.

Jenna nodded, but Allison was looking down at her phone again.

"Won't you be cold?" Beth said.

"Not in New Mexico."

"It's not like it will be a hundred degrees," Allison said. "It's March."

The clerk scanned the tag. Jenna handed over her credit card.

The clerk eyed it. "This expired in January. You should have received a new one."

"I don't think I did," Jenna said. "Can you look it up?"

After several minutes, it was determined that Jenna no longer had an active account. "I guess you haven't shopped here in a while." The clerk had a little-girl voice that was eerie coming from a woman who was several inches taller than Jenna.

Jenna shoved the card back in her wallet. She pulled out her Visa. "This one's better. I could use the extra miles." Her neck was damp. She felt Beth and Allison were watching too closely. The clerk swiped the Visa. It seemed almost instantaneous that the machine came back with a message. "I'm sorry, this card is declined," the clerk said.

Jenna's face felt swollen as if she'd been sitting in a sauna. Beth's bracelets tapped against Jenna's wrist. She felt Beth's fingers on her forearm. "It's okay," Beth said softly. "It's for my wedding. Let me buy it for you. My treat."

Bile swam up to Jenna's throat. If she allowed Beth to buy the dress, Beth would most likely tell Michael, maybe even mention it during the rehearsal dinner. She could hear Beth's melodic voice, *Doesn't Jenna look great in that dress? I bought it for her.* Beth might even go further. *Poor thing, she and Devon are struggling right now. Devon's career isn't going the way he'd hoped. I could see how badly she wanted the dress.* Jenna might as well not even have the dress if that was how it was going to be. And Allison would know as well. It wasn't as if Beth was whispering. Jenna would walk out of BCBG with a shopping bag and that fantastic dress, but her friends would be walking silently by her side, pity wrapping itself around her as smoothly as that satin edge on the bodice wrapped across the top of her breasts.

Beth squeezed her arm more tightly.

Although Beth's nails were short, smooth ovals, Jenna imagined talons sinking into her flesh.

"Don't be embarrassed," Beth said. "I really want to do this. I was thinking about it anyway. And now this mix-up reminded me of what I'd planned."

The more she talked, the more humiliating it became. Did Beth really think Jenna believed that? She'd planned no such thing. Unless she'd planned from the start to make sure they all knew what copious amounts of money she had to blow on this wedding. What next? New bathing suits for all? How about Beth paying for a personal trainer so they could all look their toned best? Other brides had done it – instituted enforced diets, so their wedding parties looked as slim and attractive as possible. Not more attractive than the bride, of course.

"I can't let you do that. I'll have to call Devon and ask what's going on. I think it's time we cancel this card if they allow this to happen."

"Please, Jenna."

She knew she couldn't call Devon. And she knew she was making it worse with her lame explanation. Of course the card had hit the limit. Again. The choice was to accept Beth's charity or leave the dress behind. She couldn't do that. She looked awesome in that dress. Maybe this would shake Devon loose, make him realize they couldn't keep juggling, they had to make some serious cutbacks.

She turned slowly and smiled, hoping she looked gracious and confident. "Thank you so much, Beth. That's really sweet of you. I've never heard of a bride outfitting her attendants for the rehearsal dinner."

Beth smiled.

If Jenna closed her eyes, she thought she might see fangs

in that small, careful parting of Beth's lips. "It's so upsetting when things don't function they way they should. I'm sure Devon will set them straight when he calls to correct this."

"I'm sure he will," Beth said. Behind her, Allison nodded.

Two

THE DARK FOYER and kitchen told Allison that Craig hadn't started dinner. She flicked on the light. Her hand shook like it did every time she entered the house in the dark. It annoyed her that a successful professional woman like herself shivered in the dark, her mind stubbornly racing back to her eight-year-old self. It had been a minor incident, really, getting locked out of the house during a power failure. She had no idea why it still troubled her, but she'd never seen such a complete absence of light. Not a star or a streetlight anywhere. She could feel the tears in her throat, even now.

She set her laptop bag on the bench under the panel that controlled the alarm system. The bench was mahogany with curved sides, upholstered in off-white fabric. It was elegant, simple, and comfortable, yet they never sat on it. Sometimes she wondered why it was there – an expensive piece of furniture that was essentially useless. She walked across the foyer and into the living room. Craig sat with his back to her, facing the floor-to-ceiling windows that looked out over the valley. Two glasses stood on the coffee table, their long stems almost invisible in the shadows cast by the miniature bulbs from the track lighting that tended to create a spotlight effect. Under the tiny lights, the red wine glittered like glasses of rubies.

It wasn't that she expected him to fix dinner. She loved to cook, pouring over glossy photographs of fish, pastas, and artfully cut vegetables. Even going to the market was therapeutic. When she watched Craig eat the meals she prepared, there was a sense that nothing else was quite as important as it seemed. But other things *were* important, and it would be nice if Craig would at least start the meal once in a while instead of simply complaining that she worked too much. There wasn't one minute of her seventy-five hours a week at Hammer, Simpson, Lee, and Pimentel that she resented. Every day was an adrenaline rush. And the long hours wouldn't have been any different if she'd stayed with her original plan to become a public defender. It wasn't that she'd chosen the personal injury path only for the money. Somewhere along the line, she'd realized she wouldn't be able to stomach some of the heinous crimes that became routine for a public defender, hardening her into someone who expected the worst of human nature.

"Hi," she said.

Craig turned and smiled. The same shadows that fell over the stems of the wine glasses sliced across his neck, giving his head a disembodied look and making his brown eyes appear almost black. "Successful shopping trip?"

"It was okay. Can you bring the wine into the kitchen, I should start dinner."

"It's Friday night, relax."

At some point, she'd have to tell him that taking the afternoon off to stroll around the mall with her friends meant she'd have to put in a few hours tonight. She walked into the living room and sat next to him on the sofa. He handed her a glass and lifted his in a wordless toast.

Craig was right, she shouldn't be thinking about writing a brief, making sure all the details were buffed like polished wood for her dog bite case. She should be enjoying this man she loved and the view of Silicon Valley they'd worked so hard to earn. Since she was seventeen, she'd wanted to be an attorney. The idea of outsmarting people with her verbal accuracy was endlessly alluring. After five years, the thrill hadn't faded. She loved winning, being right. Sure, it would be nice if she could work a few hours less and still be successful, but that wasn't possible. Not yet.

Craig held up his glass and swirled the wine around the sides. "This is good," he said. "It's the bottle Jenna and Devon gave us for Christmas. That guy sure can manage to find something new every time. I don't know how he does it. We all visit the same wineries."

"He spends more time studying it," Allison said. Devon did have a knack for finding wines that stood out. She'd never checked the prices, but she knew he was willing to spend more on a bottle of wine than she and Craig or their other friends. Of course it was better. She stood, "Come in the kitchen. We can relax while we fix dinner."

"Let's sit here for a few minutes."

"I'm hungry." She set her glass on the table and slipped off her jacket. She reached into the pocket and pulled out a tissue and wiped her nose.

"Allergies?"

She shrugged. "Come with me. Bring my wine." She tucked the tissue into the pocket of her slacks.

In the kitchen she pulled two cooked chicken breasts from the fridge, unwrapped them, and placed them on the glass board she reserved for cutting meat. She pulled a boning knife out of the wood block and ran it through the first breast. It made a clean slice, leaving a strip of chicken as delicate as a flower petal. Planning a Caesar salad for this evening had been a good call. That soft, spring-like quality lingered in the air, even though the early darkness reminded her it was still winter.

Craig went into the breakfast room and put placemats and utensils on the table.

As he lowered the blinds on the narrow windows that ringed the room, Allison heard the wood slats clack against the window frame.

He came back into the kitchen. "Did you find a dress?"

She nodded. "Beth ended up buying our dresses for us."

"That's generous. I guess she can afford it now." He put his glass on the center island and pulled out one of the stools but didn't sit down.

"We had some drama."

Craig took a sip of wine.

Allison ran the knife through the chicken. It dragged as it hit a piece of tendon. She shuddered. The fatty and gristly pieces of meat nauseated her. She cut the offending section off and pushed it to the side. "Can you shred the romaine?"

He got out the lettuce and started chopping, dumping handfuls into the bowl she'd placed on the counter near the refrigerator. "So what's the drama?"

"Jenna's credit cards were declined."

"Huh."

"She picked out a fairly expensive dress and then stood there looking insulted while the clerk told her the store card was expired. Then her Visa wouldn't go through. She acted like it was the clerk's fault there was an issue. After a few awkward minutes, Beth jumped in and offered to pay."

"I'm sure it was a minor glitch."

"I'm sure it wasn't," Allison said.

"How do you know?"

"She looked really pissed. And for all her acting like she was shocked, I had the feeling she wasn't all that surprised. There was something fake about it. But then, Jenna acts like she's on stage a lot, so maybe it was normal."

"Don't say that."

"What? That she's fake? Okay, maybe not fake, she's a princess. She's not used to anyone telling her no. She expects the whole world to work the way she wants."

"Why are you being so catty?"

Allison paused. She rinsed and dried her hands and picked up her glass of wine. She hadn't touched it since that first sip in the living room. She took two long swallows. "I'm not being catty, I'm being honest."

"Wouldn't you be upset if your card was declined?"

"Well that would never happen to me because we pay our bills and we don't buy things we can't afford. Like that ridiculous house."

"Come on, Allie. Don't be like that. I agree, they probably spend money they don't really have, but I hate it when women do that."

"When women do what?"

"Say bitchy things about their friends. You have to accept her the way she is. Otherwise, quit hanging out with her."

"How would that work? Break up our group? Besides, I'm kind of stuck with her if I'm not going to piss off Devon. He'd choose her over me in a heartbeat."

Craig went to the sink and rinsed the knife he'd used on the lettuce.

She hoped that hadn't come out the wrong way – *he'd choose her over me*. It was difficult adjusting to the spouse of someone you'd known since you were ten years old. She understood that you had to adapt if you wanted to keep long-term friendships, and she'd tried, but it was a constant battle. Even though she considered Jenna a good enough friend, it was hard watching Devon lose his mind and his pride around Jenna. After six years of marriage, he still fawned over her like she was some kind of a goddess. Allison could never figure out what kind of hold Jenna had on him, what it was about her that made his adoration border on obsession. Devon personified the cliché of worshipping the ground Jenna walked on. Other husbands weren't like that, at least Craig wasn't. Not that she even wanted that from Craig. It was disgusting. Hadn't women progressed further than that? It was the twenty-first century, women should no longer want to be treated like mythological creatures.

She took a deep breath. The fact was if she didn't want to lose Devon, she needed to keep trying with Jenna. She needed to get control of her thoughts because it was pointless to be so critical. She took another sip of wine. The chicken had left a film on her fingertips, and when she set the glass down, the sides were smeared. Her nose started to run. She wiped her fingers on a paper towel and reached into her pocket for the tissue.

"Do you have a cold or something?"

"No."

AFTER CRAIG PUT the last bite of his salad into his mouth, before he was finished chewing, he poured another splash of wine into their glasses. "I was thinking we should go to Hawaii for your birthday."

Allison took a quick sip of wine as if she was sucking in a drug, needing something to fortify her before she responded. She knew what that meant. His casual lead-in to her birthday – thirty-one years old. In his mind, that meant time to start working on a baby. She took another sip of wine. There was no doubt the ticking of her biological clock was growing louder, more insistent. Craig thought it never crossed her mind, but it did. Monthly. Sometimes weekly. She knew she didn't have many years left, and she wanted children, she really did. It was shocking how fast the time had gone.

"Don't you want to go?"

"It's not that. It's that we'll be gone in March for the wedding."

"That's only four days."

"I know, it's just …"

"Work," Craig said.

"It's close together."

"Are you going to work the rest of your life away? We're young, we should be enjoying ourselves, not working all the time."

"I love my job. And I don't think I work all the time."

"What are you going to do when we have kids? We said once I started my residency …"

"Okay. I know." There it was, right on time. It wasn't like it was new. He was getting impatient. When she finished law school, it seemed she had years to establish her career, but the time went so fast. Somehow she'd thought that by the time she was thirty there wouldn't be as much pressure, that somehow, magically, the hours would be fewer and she'd be able to balance her job and motherhood. Now, she realized that might not be realistic. At some point, she was going to have to make a choice. She coughed. The tickle grew stronger in her throat, and she coughed harder. She picked up her wine glass with her left hand and stabbed her fork into the last slice of chicken.

"Calm down. Every time I even mention kids, you freak out."

"I don't freak out," Allison said.

"You're attacking your food like you want to kill someone."

She didn't want to kill anyone. She felt trapped, that was all. Like she felt when she was twelve and fractured both arms skiing. For over six weeks, her upper body was immobilized in plaster. Most tasks were impossible, and every movement was difficult. She felt the same lack of freedom the closer she got to this birthday, and the next, and the one after that. It was simpler not to think about it. It was better to use the skills she'd acquired in law school, focus on the problem at hand, don't look too far ahead. Don't think of too many things at once or it would be overwhelming.

She stood and picked up her glass. "Hawaii would be nice. I guess you're right if we go near the end of May."

"Don't sound so tired." Craig pushed out his chair, picked

up their plates, and carried them out of the breakfast room.

Allison followed, carrying their wine glasses.

In the kitchen, he pulled open the dishwasher door. "It was supposed to be something fun, something to look forward to. A chance for us to be alone and reconnect."

Reconnect – his euphemism for making love. She poured the rest of her wine into his glass.

"Why did you do that?" he said.

"I need to get some work done."

"It's Friday night."

"I took half the afternoon off. It will only be a few hours."

"You haven't come to bed until after midnight every night this week. You're wearing yourself out. You already sound like you're getting a cold."

Allison didn't say anything. Craig didn't know it had been far later than midnight. Tuesday and Wednesday she'd gone to bed at two-thirty. He'd flip out if he knew that. He fell asleep at midnight and assumed she came in soon after. Last week she'd stayed up until four and gotten up again at six-thirty. She opened the fridge and took out a can of cola. The taste would be sickly sweet after the wine; maybe she'd bring a small bowl of peanuts or something into the office. Something to calm her while she pored over documents, trying to absorb and retain an ocean of details.

Craig walked up behind her and slipped his arms around her waist while she poured the cola into a glass. Pinned between him and the counter, she couldn't move without spilling soda, and she didn't want to hurt his feelings by twisting away from him. She loved her job, and she hated feeling as if she had to constantly choose between it and her husband, between her career and the rest of her life.

Three

JENNA WAITED FOR Devon at the British Bankers Club restaurant. The BBC was a brick structure in downtown Menlo Park, built in 1922. It had been a bar and restaurant since the early 1970s, but before that, it had been the city hall, a library, and even served briefly as a jail. Jenna and Devon and their friends had been drinking and eating at the BBC for nearly ten years. Drinking, mostly. They watched the 49er games in the bar during winter months and sat outside on the patio sipping beer until after dark during the summer.

Jenna had no idea how they would pay for dinner this evening, clearly not with her Visa, but Devon had insisted that despite their lack of disposable income, they had to get out of the house once in a while. When Jenna had pointed out that they'd skipped going clubbing with their friends because they didn't have any cash, Devon assured her things were a bit more liquid now that they'd paid down some of the holiday bills.

The server approached her table for the second time. "You're sure I can't get you anything to drink?"

She put her hand on her water glass. "This is fine, thanks."

She glanced at the vestibule. Devon stood just inside the door. The dim lighting made his dark, wavy hair look even thicker, and the shadow of his beard was enhanced, giving him a hint of danger. She shivered. Devon moved into the bar area, turned, and walked up the two steps to the table where she sat by the window.

"Hi, babe. You look great." He leaned down and kissed her. The tip of his tongue lingered inside her mouth.

He pulled out his chair and the knot inside her chest loosened. The grip of his hand on the back of the chair, the rolled back cuffs of his shirt, and his grin, made her feel happy for the first time since she'd left the mall. The image of her friends, silently watching her cards declined, faded slightly. It didn't seem so bad now that she was gazing at the affection in Devon's eyes.

The server returned, and Devon selected a bottle of Petite Syrah. Without looking at the menu, he asked for bangers and mash. Jenna ordered the curry shrimp. It was an appetizer but large enough to satisfy her. When the server was gone, she said, "Are you sure we can cover this? Maybe we shouldn't have ordered wine."

He reached across the table and stroked her fingers. "Don't worry."

"But how are we paying for it?"

"I have some cash left over from that trip to Chicago a few weeks ago."

"You do?"

"Yup."

"Things are getting worse. We need to figure out more ways to cut back."

"We'll be okay. The promotion will be there in June," said Devon.

He sounded so certain, and yet he'd been certain when they bought the house. He was confident they could afford it once his promotion was finalized. He'd made her feel like a princess when he'd held her hands, put his face close to hers, and whispered, *Is this the one you want?* She knew her pleasure was childish, and of course, the house wasn't a gift, both of their incomes were required to pay the two mortgages, but he'd managed to make her feel treasured as if all he cared about was making her happy.

When he spoke, a thread of confidence wove itself around her ribs, but the moment he stopped talking, she wasn't so sure. There wasn't a hint of doubt in his tone, but what if the promotion was delayed again? "My card was declined this afternoon," she said.

"Really? What card?"

"My Visa."

"Why were you using your Visa to buy clothes?"

"That's not the point. And I had to use it because the

BCBG card was expired. I don't remember getting a new one. Do you?"

He shook his head.

Jenna took a sip of water and waited while the server opened the wine and poured a taste for Devon. When Devon nodded, the server filled both glasses.

Devon raised his glass and waited for her to do the same. She didn't feel like toasting anything. She felt like pouring her wine on the floor. That would shock him. Instead of recognizing how humiliated she'd felt, he focused on which card she'd used as if it was a minor accounting error. None of their cards should be in this situation. It shouldn't matter which one she used. Her friends hardly thought about money, much less worried about it. She and Devon lived in a house worth several million dollars, their jobs brought in a combined income of over a quarter million dollars a year, and yet she couldn't buy a dress or enjoy a dinner out with her husband.

Devon still had his glass raised, oblivious to her hesitation. She lifted her glass and clicked it against his.

"To the most gorgeous woman on the planet," he said.

She took a sip, trying to resist the warmth that soaked her chest when he looked at her like that. His words that would sound false from anyone else, but rang true coming from his lips. She took another sip of wine and set her glass on the table. She pulled the napkin onto her lap. It looked pure and clean, draped across her legs. "It was humiliating."

"It happens to everyone. It could have been a fraud hold for all they knew."

"Just having the expired card was awkward. Then when the *Visa* was declined, Beth offered to pay for the dress, as if she knew I couldn't pay for it."

"That was nice of her. Although it's not like it's a burden for them."

"It made me feel … I don't know. Like a charity case." Those weren't the right words, but she wasn't sure how else to describe it. All she knew was she thought she'd left the pitying eyes of other girls behind when she was fifteen.

During her sophomore year in high school, her sort-of-boyfriend had invited her to a pool party. The other girls, none of them her friends from school, glanced at Jenna's swimsuit, purchased for less than twenty dollars at Wal-Mart, and quickly looked away. She knew they were smirking, prancing around in their obviously expensive bikinis. They knew what her suit had cost, and she knew what theirs had cost. How could you always tell? And why did it matter? She wasn't sure, but it did. They ignored her, and although she knew it wasn't because of her swimsuit, there was something unspoken, invisible that divided them.

After she heard the rumors that followed her boyfriend back from a ski trip, whispers that he'd hooked up with another girl, Jenna was done with all of them. She joined the track team and turned her attention to earning a near-perfect GPA. A good college would transform her into someone who blended seamlessly into a privileged world. A world where she would never be dismissed or worse, pitied.

"We'll get everything worked out," Devon said.

"It's embarrassing when you can't pay for your dress and your friend pays for it as casually as if she's buying you a cup of coffee."

"Yeah, but that's not about you. That's about her and Michael and his family having more money than God. Forget it happened, I'm sure she has."

"You know that's not how women are. They won't forget."

Devon sipped his wine, then moved the glass to the side so the server could put his plate on the table. Devon sliced the bangers into disks. He speared one and scooped up a forkful of mashed potatoes with it.

Jenna cut a piece of shrimp in half. She put it in her mouth and chewed slowly. Sitting at the table made her aware of how her jeans cut into her flesh. Had she slacked off on the intensity of her running lately? Missed more days than she'd realized? Why was she suddenly aware of a few extra pounds? Or was it something else? A sense of exhaustion. Her feet pressed against the sides of her shoes, swollen and longing for the comfort of a cool, hard floor. Her whole body pulled at her shoulders, heavy and bloated. She swallowed a bit of the Syrah. There were a lot of calories in wine, almost a hundred a glass. Maybe she needed to cut down on the amount of alcohol she consumed. But Devon loved wine. It was his hobby, bringing home new finds when he traveled, searching through wine shops, ordering boutique varieties online. He would be so disappointed if she started viewing it as a glass full of unnecessary calories.

"I don't like feeling as if I owe her something. It's bad enough that they're paying for the entire trip to New Mexico."

"If they want to get married in an exotic spot and make a four-day party out of it, it's only fair they pay. And they can afford it."

"I wish you'd told me the Visa was at the limit."

"I didn't know you were planning to use it."

"You still have to tell me. You can't be hiding it."

"I'm not hiding anything," Devon said.

"Not telling me is the same as hiding it."

"It's not. It was an oversight."

"I'm not your employee that you can BS with business-speak," Jenna said.

He laughed." Okay. Sorry. Don't be mad." He scooped up a forkful of mashed potatoes and held it out to her. "Have a taste. They melt on your tongue like butter."

It was impossible to stay upset with him. "I'm not mad, I just want you to stop thinking it will fix itself." She ate the potatoes.

Devon set down his fork. He took his glass, tipped his head back, and swallowed what was left. "You worry more than normal because of how your father is. Our life is completely different. We're not chasing too-good-to-be-true *investment opportunities*. We have great jobs, we have degrees from Stanford. It's all upside."

"If my Visa is maxed out, that's twenty-five thousand dollars, and I don't even know where we spent it."

"We'll get it paid off. With a Director's bonus, I could take that out in one shot."

"But we don't have that *now*." She leaned her elbows on the table. The unyielding surface, even through the padded cover and tablecloth, made her joints ache. "We can't cover our bills."

Devon reached across and took her hand in both of his. He looked at her, unblinking. "We won't end up living in the Jeep, I promise." He winked.

Although she wanted to pull it away, she left her hand in his. Devon acted as if he had a secret stash of money in the basement. The sounds of the diners around them, the music, always too loud on weekend nights, the sudden bursts of laughter, like wild animals bellowing, grew more distinct, drowning her thoughts.

They finished their meals. Jenna drank black coffee while Devon chipped away at a dish of Crème Brûlée. She pulled her box of leftover shrimp closer and tapped her finger on the cardboard. It would be a perfect lunch tomorrow. Before Devon woke up, she'd go for a ten-mile run. That was the great part about the weekends, she could run forever, not caring what time it was, winding her way through the quiet, curving streets, letting her mind drift as easily as the air flowed across her skin. She'd eat a light lunch and skip wine with dinner. If she fasted on Sunday, she might see a loosening of the grip of her jeans by Monday. She definitely didn't want to be feeling this fullness around her middle when they went to Beth and Michael's wedding. She'd be wearing a bikini and dancing in her awesome new dress. She just had to get rid of these three or four pounds that had insinuated themselves onto her body when she wasn't looking. She had to look perfect in that dress. If her friends were paying attention to how great she looked, all thoughts of her credit problems would be erased. Now all she needed to do was erase them from her own mind. Devon wasn't worried. He knew what he was doing. After all, he was the one with the MBA.

He pulled out a credit card and placed it inside the black folder. It was a Master Card she didn't recall seeing before. She drank the rest of her coffee. The server took the bill holder.

"I thought you had leftover cash," Jenna said.

Devon sipped his coffee. "I decided we should save that for other things."

When the server headed back to their table, he was clutching the bill holder like it was an important government document. As he moved closer, she watched his face, trying to figure out whether that was a hint of disdain in the curve of his upper lip. Was he going to hand it to Devon and tell him there was a *slight problem?* Devon would have to use the cash after all. And how did she know he had enough? Maybe that was why he'd decided on the Master Card. Would the server click his tongue at them, or behave as if not being able to pay your bill was a common occurrence?

Finally, the server reached Devon's side. He placed the bill holder on the table. "Thank you," he said. He turned and headed back to the bar area.

Although her throat was no longer frozen, Jenna still had trouble breathing when they stood to put on their jackets.

Four

SINCE HE'D GONE straight to the BBC to meet Jenna, Devon was alone with his thoughts on the drive home. He loved driving his Jeep Wrangler. Even though he wasn't much for the outdoors, never went camping, and had only used the four-wheel-drive function twice, he couldn't imagine driving any other vehicle on a regular basis. He liked sitting up higher than half the cars on the road. In Jenna's low-slung BMW he was too often caught by surprise by some idiot who didn't know how to drive. The Jeep made him feel like he was still in college. He loved stripping off the canvas roof in the summer, riding with the wind biting at his skin. Being part of a global corporation was exciting, but sometimes a guy still had to feel the animal in him, and the Jeep helped with that, although he'd never admit it to anyone.

He didn't have much of a buzz from the wine. When he got home, he'd pour them each a shot of scotch. It might help Jenna unwind a bit more. He hated seeing that scared look in her eyes. It wasn't as if they couldn't pay their bills at all. Tomorrow morning he'd have a chance to look over their cash flow. The weeks were so crazy, it was hard to do more than focus on the job from the minute his eyes opened in the morning. Weekends were an alternate universe, everything slowed down. Even his relationship with Jenna changed on the weekends. Friday night was the transition point, and once she got over whatever embarrassment she'd experienced at the mall, she'd be fine. She'd see it was no big deal – a generous gift. Beth would forget all about it by the time they went to the wedding. She'd probably already forgotten. No matter how packed his schedule was on Monday, he'd call about that store card. Jenna shouldn't have been put in that situation.

He pulled into the long driveway and braked for a moment to admire the house. Built in the late thirties, remodeled in the sixties, then completely gutted and really jazzed up five or six years ago, it never failed to remind him that he was on the right track. The previous owners had lost all their cash in the dot-com bust, forcing them to sell at the wrong time and the wrong price. Even at two and a half mil, he and Jenna had gotten a great deal.

The house was a two-story stucco, pale pink with a tile roof. The doors had glass panels separated by wood frames. Ironwork covered the bottoms of the windows and formed the railing of a narrow balcony off the master bedroom suite. After the remodel, the kitchen was all granite, stainless steel, and cherry. The living room, dining room, and the master bedroom on the second floor all looked out on a black-bottom swimming pool with a small waterfall at one end. A professional landscaper had designed the yard. A service came twice a week to keep the palm trees, lawns, and tropical plants looking lush. That was one area they should think about cutting back. How much different would it look if the maintenance was only once a week? He'd suggest it to Jenna. That would make her feel better. The only flaw in the house, and it wouldn't be a flaw once they got their finances in order, was the basement. Because their house was built in the twenties, basements were still a relatively common feature. It showed the quality of the construction – nowadays a basement added unnecessary costs, as did ironwork and custom windows. The previous owner had planned to transform the basement into a bona fide wine cellar. When he and Jenna bought it, Devon had thought that the wine cellar would be up and running by Christmas, but instead, the economy tanked, and with it their stock portfolio as well as their easy access to cash.

He hated that the basement was a mildewed cave. It gnawed at him whenever he went into the backyard and saw the door leading to the underground stairs. He thought about it every time he bought wine and wanted to put two or three bottles away to save for a couple of years. Everyone knew he was the wine guy. The one who always had the perfect choice, the one with all the knowledge. It was like his emblem. How could a guy who was an expert in wine store it in some small wood rack from Pottery Barn?

The real reason for the house was Jenna. Everything was for Jenna. Sure he wanted his wine cellar, and he loved the place, it was his sanctuary, with lots of rooms – a dedicated weight room, a room with a second fireplace that housed the TV and a comfortable leather sofa, an office, and even a small room where he could display the classic movie posters he'd collected when he was in high school. The house told him he was not only an up-and-coming Silicon Valley business leader, it told him he'd given his wife everything she deserved, and then some. He hated it when she worried. The debt wouldn't be there forever, and it was worth spending the money now when they were young and could enjoy it. Why wait? He wanted her to have a house as beautiful as she was, like a queen in her castle.

He smiled and hit the remote to open the garage.

As he pulled into the garage, he was still smiling. This was how the world worked. It wasn't all about cash, it was about leverage. They had the salaries to get this house, and all they had to do was ride out the slump. It wasn't like they were fifty or sixty years old, thinking of retirement. Having a large debt was what people did, it was how the economy worked. He wasn't going to be like his father, watching every buck, always saying no. He wasn't going to be a man of *no*, he would be a man who said yes to everything life had to offer.

Yes, they were probably more over-extended than they

should be. Maybe he shouldn't be blowing off Jenna's concerns as much as he was. Some of the guys he kept in touch with from high school had a variety of sidelines. Everyone was looking for additional revenue streams these days, whether it was trying to start an internet business or manipulating their stock portfolio on a daily basis. There were also less conventional opportunities.

They'd ride it out a bit longer, juggle the cards more. Of course, property taxes were due soon. Not to mention income taxes. He definitely wanted a drink. It would all work out, and tonight they should be enjoying each other, not talking about budgets and money and business. Tomorrow, or maybe Sunday, he'd take a look at their finances and try to get a better handle on where they stood. He wanted her to trust him. He knew he could handle it.

Jenna pulled her car into the garage as he was climbing out of the Jeep. He hit the remote, and they ducked out as the garage door lowered. They walked to the front door. Inside the entryway, Jenna pulled out the stack of mail while Devon went into the kitchen. She followed, setting the mail on the counter. She carried her laptop bag to the office and returned to the kitchen.

"Want a shot of scotch?" Devon said.

She didn't answer.

"Are you still upset?"

"No. Well, sort of."

He moved behind her and put his arms around her. He

pulled her tightly against him and felt her spine relax and curve into him. "Please don't worry. Let's have a drink and relax. Put it out of your mind. We'll be fine. I promise."

She let him hold her for a few minutes. As he released his grip, she drifted toward the counter and shuffled through the mail – mostly ads and catalogs.

Devon opened the cabinet in the breakfast room and grabbed two glasses. He pulled out the bottle of Macallan and twisted out the cork. He poured a generous shot and a half for each of them. He handed a glass to Jenna and raised his for a toast.

"What's this?" Jenna took the glass in one hand and held up a catalog with the other. *Wine Cellars and More.*

"Just a catalog."

"How did we get on their mailing list?"

"I sent for it." He took a sip of scotch. It was investigative work. Sometimes he got tired of prowling through websites and just wanted a simple stack of paper in his hand with great photographs and advertising copy that led him through the offerings without him having to click back and forth, forgetting where he'd been as he maneuvered through the tangled connections of the internet. No wonder they called it the web.

"We're not doing the wine cellar until we're completely out of debt."

"I know."

"I mean it, Dev. We can't afford it, and we're not going to

extend ourselves even more. Why would you order this now? Why even tempt yourself?"

How had she known he was thinking about ways to get the cellar underway without waiting? She saw through him too easily. Sometimes it was scary the way she seemed to be able to read his thoughts, or at least get the sense of what was on his mind. "I'm not tempting myself. A guy can dream, can't he?" He preferred to take an upside view. You didn't get ahead in the business world by constantly focusing on what could go wrong. Sure, you needed people who specialized in doom, but he wasn't that guy.

"You haven't called a contractor, have you?" She put her glass on the table and crossed her arms.

"Don't you trust me? I said I was dreaming."

"I know how much you want this." She waved the catalog in the air. "It scares me that you sent for this when you know it's a long time before we can even consider it." She opened the door under the sink and shoved the catalog into the garbage.

"Why'd you do that? It's just a catalog."

"It's more than a catalog. It says, *I'm getting ready to move on this.*"

He laughed. "It doesn't say anything. It's a catalog. Come on, Babe. I'm just planning ahead. Once I get that title, we're getting that cellar. You know you'll love it."

"I'll love it when I know it's paid for."

"And it will be." He raised his glass. "Let's enjoy our

drinks and watch a movie." He wandered into the living room. He turned on the light and walked to the large arched window centered between two doors that led to the patio. A few small garden lights didn't show much, but he could see the swimming pool in his mind. When he gazed at the dark yard, the wine cellar was almost as real as the pool. It would be magnificent. All they had now was solid-packed California clay. The structural support of the foundation was still exposed. He wanted Jenna to be excited about their wine cellar. Watching her face as she stared at the cover of that catalog was unnerving. He felt anxious when she was pissed at him. He was doing everything he could. Sure he wanted the wine cellar, but he'd give it up if it upset her so much. Why couldn't she believe he'd soon be a Marketing Director? Did she secretly think he wasn't Director material? Everything about her was so perfect. He wanted her to view him the same way, without a single shadow of doubt or disappointment.

From the first moment he'd seen her, during the spring of his freshman year at Stanford, he'd known he had to have her. It wasn't a possessive thing, and it wasn't just her beauty – a smile that made her look genuinely happy, silky hair the same rich brown color as her eyes, and an excellent body – it was her spirit that captivated him. There was something unattainable about her. He'd first seen her running around the track, long, sleek legs with the graceful stride of a wildcat, outpacing the other women with ease. Unlike those others, she wasn't sweating, pumping her arms, and grimacing as if all that intensity would make her run faster. His pick-up line had been lame – *you sure run fast, I guess there's no hope of me catching you.* She'd laughed. And it wasn't that phony, shrieking laugh that some girls had, but something that came from deep inside. Every morning when he woke up beside her, he couldn't believe his good fortune. Whenever she looked at him across the dinner table, paying attention to what he said, adding her thoughts, he wondered why he'd lucked out.

He set his glass on a small table and stretched his arms over his head. He wouldn't mention the wine cellar again. Not tonight. He wanted to see her smiling, to see her face relaxed, not thinking about the imagined judgment of her friends, and definitely not about clothes. He wanted her to trust that he was going to take care of everything. He wanted her to enjoy their house, their life.

He picked up his glass and walked through the arched opening that led to the TV room. He switched on the light near the side of the sofa and grabbed the remote. The screen came to life. He scrolled through the movie categories. Usually, he preferred thrillers. Jenna liked them too. If he picked a thriller, she'd be more inclined to wrap her arms around him, drape her legs over his lap, but maybe something lighter was called for. He clicked back to the main menu.

Five

AFTER THEY WATCHED a movie and drank more scotch than they should have, Jenna carried the glasses into the kitchen. The tile was cool on her bare feet. For some inexplicable reason, she was always nervous when she carried their wine or scotch glasses down the hall and into the kitchen, afraid they bore some imperceptible moisture that would send them sliding through her hands, shattering across the tile. She set them on the counter and wiped her palms on her jeans.

She turned on the faucet and squirted soap on the sponge. She washed the glasses and dried them with a linen towel, adding a few extra swipes with the cloth wrapped around her fingertips, so the glasses sparkled.

The answering machine displayed a red "1". She hadn't heard the phone ring. She hit the button to replay the message, knowing it was her mother. Everyone else called her cell phone.

Devon came into the kitchen with the bottle of scotch. He kissed her neck just as her mother started speaking.

"Hi, Jenna. It's Mom."

Jenna smiled. She loved how her mother always identified herself as if Jenna didn't know who was speaking the minute she heard Hannah's voice.

There was a slight pause, then, "I have to ask you a favor."

"What does Hannah-banana want?" Devon said.

Jenna stabbed her finger at the pause button. "Don't. I hate it when you call her that. I told you to stop."

"I'm sorry." He moved close beside her and put his arm around her shoulders. He put the scotch bottle into the open cabinet and closed it. "Finish listening to the message. I'm sorry. I got in the habit, and it's hard to stop. Don't look at me like that." He kissed the tip of her nose. "Please. It's just too funny that she has all those banana trees growing in her yard. They're like weeds, and the rhyme, I just can't help that my brain flicks over to that."

Jenna kissed his chin. She sighed and pressed the *play* button.

Her mother's voice continued. "Can you call me? It's kind of urgent. Nothing life or death, but I really need to talk to you. I'll be home all evening. And tomorrow. Bye."

The machine beeped.

Devon moved away from her. "Let's go to bed."

"I should call her."

"Not now. It's eleven-fifteen."

"She said it was urgent."

"She said *kind of urgent*. It can wait until tomorrow. If you call her, you'll get all caught up in her concerns and our night will end on a downer. Come on." He grabbed her hand and pulled her toward the doorway.

"Don't."

"I don't like it when your mother steals you away from me."

"What does that mean?"

"I was looking forward to slipping into bed with my wife, and now your mom's in the way."

Jenna looked at him. What was he trying to say? His voice didn't have the same teasing quality he used when he said *Hannah banana*. She shivered. She rubbed her arms, it wasn't really that cold, but perhaps her circulation was sluggish after sitting on the couch, consuming too much alcohol.

Devon curved his lips into an exaggerated pout. "Come to bed."

"Go on," she said. "I'll be there in a second. I need to wipe down the counter and put the mail in the office."

"You won't call her?"

"No. I'll call her in the morning."

"Promise?"

"God, Devon."

He pulled her fingers toward his mouth, kissed her knuckles, and let her hand go. "I'll be waiting."

She picked up the mail and went into the office. She dropped the junk mail into the trash and put the prospectus for Devon's 401k on the roll-top desk next to the computer table. She pulled the cover over the work area. For almost as long as she could remember, she'd felt like she was the adult and her mother was the child. An only child, Hannah had never held down a job outside the home. Spoiled by her father, she'd gone straight to being a homemaker, and had built her entire self around her husband and children. Despite all of her husband's schemes and plans to find a way to make money without really working, Hannah had been happy just to love him, adapting to their erratic financial situation, playing with her children, and drifting along in her own world, content to know nothing about mortgage payments or insurance premiums or income tax.

When Jenna's father left Hannah, moving in with his new love — Christine — to revel in her wildly confident personality, as well as her lucrative income as a sales vice president for a cosmetics company, that allowed him free reign to pursue whatever "deals" interested him, Jenna had gradually become the mother to Hannah. Jenna had been twelve and Tom, fifteen, when her father *changed residences*, as he put it. Hannah continued drifting through life, a little more listless than before. She didn't get angry, she didn't throw things or shout like Christine did when she didn't get her way. Jenna had never been certain whether it was her imagination that Hannah exaggerated the difference between her and

Christine, becoming more soft-spoken, more hesitant. Hannah didn't seem to mind that another woman paid for her children's college educations. And if it bothered her that Christine went overboard trying to be a mother to Jenna, Hannah never mentioned it.

After her children were grown, Hannah devoted herself to her garden, including the banana trees Devon liked to mock. She baked an endless stream of goodies that she tried to foist off on Jenna and Tom. Most of the baked goods wound up at Jenna's house since Tom was "too far away" in Marin County. Hannah didn't like to drive more than three or four miles from home, and she never drove at night.

During Jenna's daily chats with her mother, she found herself filled with longing. She desperately wanted her mother to be happy. And on one level, maybe she was. It didn't seem to bother her that she would live at subsistence level for the rest of her life, making do with what her ex-husband had determined, without the input of a lawyer, he would provide in support. Jenna's father thought he was generous, still writing a monthly check to Hannah after Jenna turned eighteen. He and Christine paid the mortgage on the tiny, decaying house on an overgrown quarter of an acre in San Jose.

It scared Jenna that her mother accepted all this without any thought that she would be destitute if her ex-husband changed his mind about monthly support if he decided to sell the house. Christine had plenty of money, and without the pressure of having to earn an income, some of her father's schemes had borne fruit, but it was still worrisome that he might get tired of maintaining a house he never saw. The only thing keeping Hannah solvent and healthy was the whim of a man who looked right through her. Why couldn't her mother take more control of her life? A better question was, where had Jenna and Tom gotten their drive to succeed in conventional ways? Neither parent seemed to have contributed a strong work ethic.

Jenna walked out of the office, down the hall, and through the entryway, turning out lights as she went.

Upstairs, the bedroom was dark except for moonlight coming through the doors that opened to the balcony. She paused, and as her eyes adjusted, she saw Devon's form in the bed. On top of the bed, to be more accurate. He gripped the iron bars of the headboard, his elbows bent, the rest of him sprawled, naked. Why was it that women felt ... no, they knew, they had to lay in seductive poses – on their sides, hips angled up in a gentle curve, one leg draped over the other, or on their backs with a knee bent, and elbow crooked with a hand under their heads? Men sprawled. Women believed they needed to display themselves artistically as if posing for a painter or sculptor.

She walked past, headed toward the bathroom. Inside, she closed the door and flicked on the light. The bathroom flooded with recessed light, glowing in a flattering golden hue that made her hair look darker. What she really wanted right now was a nice soak in a very hot tub. Their oval tub was a replica of a claw-footed bath from the nineteenth century, two feet deep. The sloped end provided a comfortable backrest. With bath salts, the steam, and a few candles, she would regain her equilibrium.

She cracked open the door. "I'm going to take a quick bath."

"What for?"

"I feel grungy from shopping. And then sitting at the BBC. I can still smell that aging wood odor."

She held a lock of hair up to her nose as if to prove she was actually noticing the stench.

"I won't notice. There's no such thing as a quick bath."

"I need to relax. And I feel gross."

"You smelled great to me when we were watching the movie."

"Thanks, but I'm taking a bath." She shut the door. She turned on the water, even though Devon was calling, pleading almost, for her to come out and join him, to have a heart, to think of her poor, lonely husband. She laughed. He was so dramatic sometimes. She dropped two lemon bath cubes into the tub. The candles would have to be skipped this time, she wouldn't linger, but she definitely needed to scrub off the grime. She stripped off her clothes and dropped her top and jeans on the floor. She slid out of her panties and bra, clipped her hair up off her shoulders, and lowered herself into the tub. She closed her eyes. The water was still running, gushing out, drowning her thoughts. The heat felt so good and immediately her skin softened, followed by a relaxing of her back and leg muscles.

After a few minutes, she opened her eyes, turned off the faucet, and gazed at the bronze sculpture at the far end of the counter, a gift from Devon on her birthday right after they bought the house. The female figure stood three feet tall. Her hair was draped down her spine, obviously wet. She held a bar of soap in her hand that she was gliding up the inside of her thigh. The figure's eyes were closed, and her other arm stretched above her head, her fingers curved. Devon said the statue reminded him of Jenna, and how sexy she looked when she was bathing. Apparently, he'd forgotten that this evening. She smiled. She stroked her skin, sliding the bar of soap over her legs and swirling it around her belly, letting the warm water wrap around her like a blanket. Making love with Devon would be so much more enjoyable once she was silky clean.

When the water cooled, she climbed out quickly and washed her face and brushed her teeth. Yet another difference between men and women. Devon took a quick shower, if he'd been lifting weights, or had a rough day at work, but he didn't feel the need to prepare in any way to make love. He assumed he was desirable – which he was. No need for cleansing, and flossing, and combing snarls out of long hair. He didn't worry if his feet didn't smell like a baby's, or if his legs had dried skin. He didn't think about the specifics, just the big picture. Sometimes she thought it wasn't fair. Why did women believe they had to shave and moisturize and primp and try to make themselves the most desirable creatures they possibly could?

The funny thing about it was that she enjoyed feminine rituals and accessories. Take that dress today. She couldn't wait to wear it, enjoying Devon's gaze stroking her body, the lightness of being in perfect condition, knowing her legs were long and well-shaped, feeling the weight and softness of her hair on her shoulders and back, wiggling her toes with the nails filed into a smooth cup and painted dark red. She loved it all. She wasn't even sure what she wanted from Devon. More effort? An acknowledgment of all her effort? He constantly told her she was gorgeous, so it wasn't that. She was pretty sure it was the first – she wanted him to put in as much work as she did.

She went into the bedroom and slid between the sheets. Immediately Devon shimmied down and put his mouth around her breast. When he began sucking and tickling her nipple with his tongue, she felt the rest of her tension slide away. No matter what happened, there was always this. Maybe The Beatles were right, *money can't buy love.* All her thoughts floated away as the entire world shrank to her skin, then zeroed in closer, to her breasts. She sighed. During dinner, she'd felt disconnected. Maybe she wasn't the independent woman she thought she was, because deep inside, she feared that she expected him to make more money than she did, expected him to make enough to satisfy her desires, to keep them secure, to pay the mortgages on their spectacular home, and to figure out how to get their finances back on track.

Sure she loved her career, but she didn't feel the same urgency he did to generate the huge income required to live an upscale lifestyle in Silicon Valley. She rolled closer to him and wrapped her legs around his. She lifted herself on her elbow and buried her face in the fine covering of chest hair, letting it brush against her lips and cheeks. As he entered her, all the complaints that tickled at her mind, shattered like a piece of crystal breaking into a million fragments. She pulled him close and enjoyed the sheer power of a man and the shuddering release of all her nerve endings.

After, when he fell asleep, she turned on her side and tried to quiet her mind. All the pleasure of a few moments ago faded too quickly. She pulled his arm around her waist and willed the soft, floating feeling to return. When he teased about her mother, she felt a prick of annoyance. And that last bit, about her mother consuming her. What had that meant? She shivered again. It was nothing. The more pressing concern was their debt. He couldn't keep acting as if they could keep things afloat until his promotion materialized. Tomorrow they'd figure out something.

THE NEXT MORNING, Jenna got up before Devon. She wrapped herself in her terrycloth robe, snuggling into the thick cotton. The house was cold, but she wanted to avoid turning on the heat if she could. She was starting to feel like the people they studied about from the Great Depression, looking for every penny that could be saved.

The air in the office was even colder because the room was its own mini wing, with windows on two sides and glass doors on the third side, opening out to the patio. The windows on one side faced the clusters of towering birds of paradise along the fence, and the other set of windows looked out at the back of the property. She sat on the ergonomically designed desk chair and curled her feet up under her robe. She should have put on socks.

It was only seven, but her mother would be up. Ever since Jenna could remember, her mother was awake at five. When the temperatures occasionally climbed into the nineties during the summer, and the early mornings were like a warm bath, her mother was out in the garden, weeding as the sun poked a tentative finger over the horizon.

Her mother picked up on the second ring.

"Hi, Mom. Sorry I didn't call last night, I didn't see your message until late. Is everything okay?"

Hannah let out a breath so softly, Jenna almost didn't catch it.

Jenna's throat tightened, waiting for her mother to speak. Even though Hannah had said it wasn't life or death, Jenna wished she'd called last night.

The thought of her mother lying in bed, flat on her back, staring at the ceiling for most of the night, made Jenna's chest ache so badly she had to press her hand to her collarbone. If only she could pour some of her confidence into her mother, make her mother start working on a new life instead of silently regretting the one she'd thought she had.

"I did something stupid," Hannah said.

"Don't say that."

"You haven't heard what it is."

"Tell me."

"I need to borrow some money. I hate asking, but I'm desperate."

Jenna swallowed. She could do anything, would do anything for her mother. But right now … she closed her eyes. "What happened?"

"I hired a man to thin the banana trees, clean out all the dead stuff from the morning glory vines along the back fence. He was going to replace the rotten boards …"

"Why didn't you call Tom to help?"

The minute she said it, she knew her brother was not a logical candidate for yard work. "Or ask Devon and me?"

"I know how busy you are. I thought this would be simpler. And I would have had enough to cover it next month. He said he would hold the check until then."

Jenna waited for the rest of the story, knowing the rest of the story before her mother continued speaking.

"He cashed my check two weeks ago, and he hasn't been back. I've been calling several times a day, and all I get is voice mail. And then yesterday, the message said the number was invalid or something."

Jenna pushed the chair away from the desk. She stood, walked to the window, and adjusted the spine at the center of the shutters, angling it to let in light. Except there was no light. The sky was thick with fog, and all that came into the room was a sickly shade of gray. She wanted to ask why her mother wrote the check for the whole amount, or why she hadn't at least post-dated it, but what was the point? Such questions would make her mother feel worse, and it was clear she was already chastising herself, she didn't need her daughter emphasizing her mistake.

"I know I'm an idiot."

"No you're not. Please don't say that."

Hannah's voice dropped to a whisper. "Can I borrow five hundred dollars? I only need it until March fifteenth."

"I can't, I ..." Jenna stopped. Maybe they could be late on a few credit cards. It wouldn't damage their credit too badly to have two or three late payments. "Can't you ask Tom?"

"He'll make me feel even more stupid. I can't. I just can't."

"I don't have any cash to lend right now."

"Why not?"

The tremor of fear in Hannah's voice was like a fist to Jenna's throat. But she couldn't give in, and Devon would never go for it. The only thing keeping Hannah from asking Tom was pride. Jenna understood pride very well, but Tom would be happy to help, and it would be simple for him. He was single, which meant he didn't need to navigate delicate boundaries around a mate's extended family.

"He won't think you're stupid."

"He might not say it, but he'll think it."

Jenna couldn't argue with that. "But you'll have what you need to cover things, and then he'll forget about it."

"It's the asking. The calling him and begging and hearing that tone in his voice that says I should have checked out the guy first. All the things I did wrong."

Jenna angled the shutters back the other way. Now there was a glare, even though the sky was still a pale white sheet, the light had brightened and was making her eyes ache. Maybe it was the scotch and the wine. Probably the wine.

"Please can't you help. It's only five hundred dollars."

Jenna didn't want to tell her mother things were tight. More than tight, they were being strangled. It would frighten her mother, who felt secure knowing that both her son and daughter had devoted themselves to excellent educations, that they had good jobs, and promising careers. In the back of Jenna's mind, she planned that someday she and Devon would have enough to take care of her mother. She wanted nothing more than to break Hannah free of her dependency on her ex-husband. Sometimes Jenna wished she and Devon had bought a more reasonable house, then they could be helping her mother now. Instead, they were saddled with this lavish home and the expanded maintenance costs that went with it. They didn't need such a large place yet, they could have waited until they were a little older, moved up gradually. But Devon had insisted. He made her giggle when he said she belonged in a castle. But what good was luxury if you couldn't really pay for it, and if your mother was crying on the phone because she'd made a mistake and was too ashamed to ask her judgmental son for help?

"I'll see what I can do." The minute the words were out, she was sorry. There wasn't anything they could do, and now she'd offered false hope. Devon would stare at her in disbelief if she even mentioned it. They still had to pay for their half of the upcoming couples' shower for Beth and Michael, and they were also going in on a shared wedding gift with Allison and Craig. She needed to get that straightened out sooner rather than later. She'd buy the gift and ask Allison to write a check. If she did it soon, she could use that cash to help her mother. The problem was, Devon wouldn't agree. "You know, Mom. I shouldn't have said that. We really can't right now and …"

"Why not? Why can't you? Don't make me beg."

"I'm not making you beg. Can you just ask Tom? We have some unexpected expenses here."

"It's only five hundred dollars."

"Please," Jenna said.

"I can't ask him."

"I'll call him for you."

Hannah was silent for nearly a minute. "Whatever you think is best. I hate being a burden, you know that."

Jenna could see her mother's face, damp with tears, her lower lip pinched and shuddering as if it had a life of its own. She wished she was there to offer a hug, to look her mother in the eyes and tell her it was okay. More than that, she wished she could lend the money, wished she could provide an elixir that would transform her mother from the inside out into a woman determined to grab life by the tail, refusing to let go.

Six

RAIN POUNDED THE back patio and thundered across the roof. Devon waited in the living room for Jenna to finish putting on makeup so they could head out to the wedding shower. It was one of those early March storms that's surprising in its ferocity. Wind whipped the palm trees that surrounded the pool, pulling their fronds to the southeast. Rain splattered the surface of the water, making small craters. By this time of year, he was tired of winter. He didn't want any more rain, no more frost on the ground, and no more debt. He was anxious to get moving on the wine cellar, anxious for the end of the fiscal year so promotions and raises would be forthcoming. He should receive news of his promotion in June. July at the latest. He wasn't sure he could wait four more months. The whole thing weighed on him more than Jenna realized. She thought he didn't worry. He didn't really worry, he knew they could keep juggling for quite some time, but he didn't want to be juggling.

"I'm ready."

He turned. Jenna stood at the entrance to the living room. She wore a short skirt and a pink fuzzy sweater that hugged her body. Her legs were bare, and she wore brown boots that reached to the lower curve of her calf muscle. Her hair was brushed back from her face and whatever she'd put on her cheeks and eyes made her glow. Of course she wasn't *glowing*, but she looked great. Happy. He grinned. "I like it," he said. "You're sure you won't be cold? Not that I'm complaining. You look great."

"Maybe a little, going to and from the car, but that's only for a few seconds. You put the gift in the trunk?"

He nodded. He tossed the keys in the air and caught them, "Let's go."

They went out through the breezeway that joined the house and the garage and climbed into Jenna's BMW. After they left their neighborhood, he turned from Oregon Expressway onto El Camino Real.

"Why are you going this way?" Jenna said.

He glanced at her legs. They looked soft and smooth, and he wanted to stroke her skin, but with the heavy rain, he'd better keep both hands on the wheel, for now. "Stopping for wine."

"Allison has that covered."

"I want to get something special."

"Not now. It's not necessary."

"I know it's not necessary, but it's what I do. They'll expect it."

"No, they won't. Not Allison. What she'll be expecting is a check for our share of the food and decorations."

He pulled up in front of Village Wine and turned off the engine. Rain beat on the roof and poured down the windshield.

"It's too wet," she said. "Let's skip it this time. Please, Devon. You know we can't afford it, and no one will notice. Allison already has all the food and beverages."

"They will notice. I always bring something extra. Something different. You don't want them to think we have financial problems, do you? Especially after that thing with the dress."

She sighed. "No, but…"

"Then let's go." He put his hand on the door release. "Are you coming?"

"What about the money we owe them?"

"When are we supposed to give her the check?"

"I don't know, I should have done it last week."

"How much?"

"Seven-fifty," Jenna said.

"Really?"

"It adds up. Food, wine, flowers."

"Okay. Well, we can't write a check today, but I'll figure out something tomorrow. The wine will go on the B of A Visa."

"We can't keep doing this."

She looked like she might cry, her eyes like melted chocolate. Jenna never cried. In fact, he couldn't remember if he'd ever even seen her tear up. She was a strong woman, and he liked that. When he asked her why she wasn't like other girls, she said she'd cried enough when she was a child. Life was too short and what was the point? He put his hand on her leg. Her skin was cold. He cupped his hand and gently rubbed her thigh. "I have it under control."

"I don't think you do."

"We're going to be late. Come with me to get the wine. We can talk about it tomorrow."

"That's what you said three weeks ago after my card was declined. Nothing's changed, and it's only two weeks until the wedding."

"Well Michael's dad is paying for all of that, so nothing to worry about there."

"We need some cash. For small things."

"I'll take care of it."

"How? How will you take care of it?"

He leaned toward her and put his arm around her shoulders. "Have faith in me. I want you to smile, I want you to have a good time at the party. I'll only get two bottles, okay? It'll be fine."

She leaned her head on the inside of his shoulder. He loved it when she did that. It made him feel like he was taking good care of her. "Why don't you wait here instead? I don't want you to get all wet and cold."

She nodded.

He released her shoulders, got out of the car, and bolted to the overhang in front of the wine shop. The store was empty. Not a good day for perusing fine wine if you didn't have to. He'd been surprised at the amount of traffic on El Camino. He supposed people still had a hundred places to go, even if it was the type of day that urged you to stay inside, build a fire, and drink something warm.

The clerk greeted him by name and left him alone to look through the Recent Arrivals rack. He was glad Jenna had agreed to stay in the car. He didn't want her commenting on the prices, pushing him to compromise. It gave him a sick feeling in his gut when she talked about their debt, when she made it sound as if he was creating a dark, frightening world for her rather than the perfect, impenetrable fortress he wanted to construct.

Two events had conspired against him – the economy and the delay of his promotion. He was trying to do the right thing, but all his life he'd swung wildly between two conflicting images. The kid side of him longed to be like his Uncle Steve, a guy who was always returning from or leaving for some exotic location or amazing activity – a safari, a boat trip in the Amazon, climbing mountains Devon had never heard of. *Life is for the young.* That was Uncle Steve's mantra, and he never worried about where the cash was coming from, always had enough to get by. His father's other brother, Matt, was the polar opposite. The guy had millions from the earliest time Devon had become aware of what that meant, and it grew from there because he saved and invested everything.

If it wasn't for unexpected things, like the shower, he could manage the movement of credit from one spot to another. It wasn't like their paychecks were minuscule. But other things kept cropping up – throwing a lavish party euphemistically called a shower, which of course required a gift, purchasing another gift for the wedding itself, and clothes for New Mexico. He had to swallow hard when Jenna had asked if they could manage to extract some cash to help her mother with her latest miss-step.

He still regretted that entire scene. He should have been more gentle, at least shown more concern for Hannah. Jenna knew he found her mother frustrating. She was too needy, and he couldn't understand why Jenna didn't see that. Why was she short on cash again? Why was she asking her adult daughter for money? It was embarrassing, but neither Jenna nor her mother seemed to recognize that. It wasn't that he didn't like Hannah, he simply didn't understand why she seemed so lacking in self-respect. He'd insisted she had to ask Tom for help this time. It was Tom's turn, he'd said, and Jenna couldn't argue with that. He wished Hannah would move closer to Tom and spend a little less time consuming Jenna's mental space.

There was a Pinot Noir he'd read about in *Wine Spectator*. It was touted as one of the best of the year from the central coast with strong sour cherry, black cherry, and blueberry flavors that promised a silky texture. He grabbed four bottles. He'd promised Jenna only two, but there would be twenty people at the shower. He wanted to be sure their closest friends got at least a glass each. Jenna would be upset at first, but then she'd see he was right. There was no point in bringing any at all if he'd be required to scrimp on every glass.

After the bottles were wrapped in paper and put into a double set of bags, he walked slowly to the car. Better to get wet than risk hydroplaning across the sidewalk and dropping four seventy-five dollar bottles of wine. He popped the trunk and laid them next to the gift. He hoped Jenna didn't ask what they'd cost. He slammed the trunk, stepped around to the driver's side, pulled open the door, and fell inside. He looked at Jenna's tiny umbrella on the floor. "I don't know how we're going to get the gift into the house without it getting soaked."

"Allison hired parking attendants. I'm sure they'll have huge umbrellas."

Shit. He hadn't thought of that. He dug in his pocket, hoping he had a few bucks. Only one folded bill, and he knew what that was. A twenty. Oh well, there was nothing he could do now. He'd seen the contents of his wallet when he paid for the wine, so he knew the only thing in there was the hundred-dollar bill he'd been carrying for a week.

He dragged his hand across his hair. Water slid down his

neck. The valet could wipe down the inside of the car, earn the twenty bucks — that would make his day. Maybe it was a good thing. With a tip like that, the guy might mention it to Craig, and they'd know Devon and Jenna were doing just fine.

"You're soaked. You're getting me all wet." Jenna's voice burbled into that giggle he loved.

He leaned toward her and nuzzled her neck.

"Yuck. Don't get my hair all wet."

He straightened in his seat and started the car. He glanced at her. She was smiling. The curve of her lips and the subtle tightening of her cheeks made him feel as if someone had poured a half shot of scotch down his throat. The warmth spread through his chest. The heat made him want to beg out of the shower, head back home, and take Jenna to bed where they could listen to the rain and wrap the blankets around them until they were huddled in a private cave where no one in the world could find them.

He released the emergency brake, but before he put the car in gear, he wiped his hand across his neck, swiped it along his jeans, and then cupped the back of her head and tugged her toward him. He kissed her for several minutes, feeling her relax under his grip. Finally, he eased away from her and pulled out into traffic. If nothing else, he was content that the constantly simmering argument over money had subsided for now.

Seven

THE STREET IN front of Allison and Craig's house was lined with cars. The minute Devon pulled into the circular driveway, one of the valets opened Jenna's door. He held an enormous golf umbrella over the side of the car and waited for her to step out.

"We have to get the gift out of the trunk," Jenna said.

"I'll take care of that when your husband gives me the keys."

Jenna walked under the umbrella to the front porch and waited for Devon to join her. Devon hugged the bags of wine close to his chest as he strolled up the front walk. The size of the paper bag, wrapped around more brown paper bags, told her he'd bought four bottles. The moment of contentment she'd felt during their kiss dissolved.

Allison opened the front door. She wore a black tank top with white pants and black flat sandals. The cloudy light cast a dull shadow on her hair, giving the color an eerie similarity to khaki. Her face was pale and her lipstick almost colorless. "You're late," she said.

"It's five minutes to two," Devon said.

"You were supposed to be here early," Allison said.

Devon held out the bag of wine, "We had to stop. Wait 'til you try this."

Inside, the house looked like a prelude to spring. Allison had decorated with enormous glass vases filled with yellow roses. A vase stood on the table in the foyer, another at the center of the food table in the dining room, and a few more on several small tables in the living room. The living room had large glass doors that folded to the side, making the covered patio part of the room. The patio was large enough for people to stand outside sipping wine without getting thrashed by the storm. The foyer, dining room, and patio floors were all a single creamy shade of Italian tile.

Along with the caterers, a man wiped rainwater off the tile as people entered the house. Jenna hoped the additional cost for keeping the place dry wouldn't be part of what they owed Allison and Craig. She dreaded that conversation, which was sure to come before they left.

Jenna and Devon followed Allison into the kitchen.

Devon unwrapped the wine and set the bottles on the counter. With a smooth insertion of the corkscrew, a firm twist of his wrist, and a sliding out of the cork with its soft popping sound, he opened all four bottles. The wine would be gone before Jenna finished her first glass. Knowing

Devon, it probably cost at least fifty dollars a bottle. She took the glass he handed her and closed her eyes to take her first sip. When she opened her eyes, he was standing closer than he had been when he handed her the glass, his gaze locked onto her. He didn't smile, but his pupils widened slightly, making her feel that he was drinking in her face and it was as delicate as the Pinot Noir. She smiled and took another sip. When he looked at her like that, every nagging, worrying thought slid out of her head.

They wandered into the living room. Devon carried two glasses of wine for Beth and Michael, and then returned to the kitchen to get his own glass as well as one for Craig. Allison returned with him, and the six of them stood in the corner near the entrance to the dining room, their own island, just as they'd been since college. First, there'd been Allison and Devon – friends since elementary school, then Beth and Jenna who had been roommates, living down the hall from Allison. The following year Craig joined the group, and finally, Michael. They were like the parts of an atom, drawn together by their positive and negative charges, clustered into a single entity.

Devon raised his glass. "To eternal love."

"Oooh." Allison smiled and scooped her hair through her fingers, letting it fall around her neck.

Jenna wondered what Craig thought of that move, that comment.

"You say the most amazing things, Dev," Allison said.

"You'd never know you're a hot-shot executive. You're like a poet. If I close my eyes, I can see you reclining by the side of a stream in one of those billowing white shirts, and your hair curled down around your neck and falling into your eyes."

Jenna sipped her wine. Allison sure was chatty. Allison always liked to hear herself talk, it was the legal training, or something. Maybe it was just her personality. But today, her words gushed faster than usual.

Craig raised his glass, clearly not wanting to be outdone, possibly wanting to direct his wife's attention back to himself. "Not that I can compete with that image, but cheers. We're a lucky group."

They held their glasses up and methodically clicked each one. The tone of the glasses touching each other rang in Jenna's ears.

"Great wine, as always," Craig said. "I don't know how you find them."

Devon smiled, and Jenna felt the muscles in her neck relax. Even though Devon's sense of accomplishment would only last a moment, she was glad she hadn't turned the purchase into an argument. When she fixated on the price of the wine, the size of their mortgages, the credit cards, she lost sight of how generous he was. Their lingering holiday bills were evidence of that. He'd insisted they spend a weekend shopping in Carmel. He personally chose each gift for his side of the family. When he saw the sweater with seashells running down the sleeves, he said it was perfect for his mother, a woman who spent every moment she could combing beaches for rocks and bits of shells and polished glass. The sweater had cost nearly three hundred dollars, but all he thought about was the look on his mother's face. "She'll go nuts," he said.

Craig turned toward her. "And speaking of not knowing how you find them. You're looking great today, Jenna."

Her face grew warm. She felt Allison's gaze burn into the side of her head. Why was he doing that? Had Allison hurt his feelings and this was his counter-attack?

"We're all lucky." Michael looped his arm around Beth's shoulders and pulled her close. "Especially me."

Jenna could still sense Allison watching her. She turned and gave Allison a half smile. "Everything looks great. I'm sorry I wasn't here to help you. I kind of thought the caterers took care of most of the set-up."

Before Allison could respond, Craig's voice rose above the others. "I really mean it, Devon. How do you find such great wine? I don't think you've ever brought a so-so bottle." Craig wasn't really wanting Devon to answer the question because he kept talking. "We're so lucky that we can afford all these nice things." He sipped the wine, then stretched out his arm, lifting the glass toward the dining room where a few guests surveyed the spread of food. Craig had a loud voice for a guy that was built like a tennis player, muscular but wiry, blonde hair cut so short on the sides it almost looked like a military cut. "So many people in the world have next to nothing. It makes you stop and think sometimes." He took another sip of wine. "And I'm not only talking about people living in poverty around the world. I see patients every day who're being bled by their insurance premiums or having to pay the bills out of their pocket because they've lost their jobs and insurance. And it's not only the necessities, like health care, either. People in our area who are trying so hard to keep up. Too hard, sometimes. Buying things they can't afford, clothes that are double and triple what they're worth because there's an important name stitched on the inside. They think they'll pay later. Then their health deteriorates because they're so stressed, so tense. It's really sad, don't you think?"

This time, he paused. As if he did expect an answer. Except no one said anything. They all sipped nervously at the expensive Pinot Noir. Jenna hoped Beth would talk about her wedding, or maybe Allison could start chatting again. Anything to fill the extended silence.

Part of her wanted to slap Craig. Or maybe Allison, definitely Allison. She could imagine Allison's tone when she'd told Craig about the scene at BCBG. It was obvious Craig's little speech was an attack on her and Devon. Her head swam with the sudden shift from Craig's gushy compliment to a thinly veiled condemnation of her new dress, the dress she couldn't afford, and everyone knew it. The back of her neck grew hotter. The heat spread to the front and up toward her jaw. She moved, hoping to get a spot closer to the open sliding glass doors. Standing out in the pouring rain, icy water streaking her face might even be preferable.

Three guys stood between her and the patio, so she turned and took a few steps closer to the dining room. Finally, Beth spoke, talking about the schedule for the wedding weekend, starting with a day by the pool and followed by spa visits for all the females in the wedding party.

Jenna went into the dining room and looked at the twelve-foot table covered with food. At one end, there were plates of imported cheeses and tiny crackers. Next were large bowls full of potato salad and pasta, a few trays of sliced meats, and two trays filled with sushi rolls. None of it piqued her appetite, even though she'd eaten nothing but yogurt and an apple for breakfast. She wanted to crawl under the table, hide behind the floor-length cloth, so she wouldn't see her friends trying so hard not to look at her, so she wouldn't feel she could see the words plastered across their minds: *Beth had to pay for Jenna's dress. If the Porters are in over their heads, why is Devon buying expensive wine?*

She wandered through the dining room and into the short hallway that led to the family room. It was cooler. Her body temperature dropped back to normal, although she wasn't sure if it was the escape from the heat of so many talking, wine-sipping people, or the escape from her friends' critical eyes.

The stormy sky outside the floor-to-ceiling family room

windows, combined with burgundy walls and similarly colored carpet with a dark gold pattern, made the room dark but comforting. She settled into a leather armchair. She willed her mind to go blank, to stop thinking about what Craig had said.

"There you are." Devon stood in the doorway holding a bottle of the *pinot* in one hand and his glass in the other. "You disappeared."

"I needed a minute."

"Is something wrong?" He walked into the room and poured wine into her glass.

"That's enough."

"It's good, though. Isn't it? Craig was impressed." He placed the bottle on the table to her left. He sat on the arm of the chair and put his hand on her knee. His fingers were cool on her skin.

"That's what you heard?" Jenna said. "Craig being impressed? He was trying to humiliate us."

"What are you talking about?" He squeezed her knee.

"He was criticizing us. For squandering money we don't have."

"No he wasn't. He doesn't even know. Besides, we're not like that. We can afford everything we have, there's just a cash flow problem right now."

Jenna moved her legs to the left, but Devon kept hold of her knee. She couldn't stand without toppling him off the arm of the chair and sloshing his wine onto the carpet.

Although it was dark enough – all those reds and browns – a wine stain wouldn't be noticed. "He might not know how bad things are, but he sure knows my credit card was declined."

"How would he know that?"

"I'm sure Allison told him."

Devon stood and picked up the bottle. "Let's go back and join the party. Did you see that spread of food? I'm starving."

Jenna set down her glass. "I feel like they're talking behind our backs. I know Allison is judging us." Of course, Allison judged everyone, and she always had. Jenna wasn't sure why it seemed more bothersome now. Maybe because when Allison criticized other people, Jenna felt superior right along with her. In college, when they aced exams, they were equals. When Allison sneered at girls who didn't put forth much effort to look good, Jenna knew the comments didn't apply to her. For the first time, she'd been identified as the weak one, exposed for the others to pick on.

Devon leaned over and kissed the top of her head. "They're not talking about us. I don't like it when you're upset. Please come back with me." He kissed her neck.

She shivered and laughed softly. She stood, picked up her glass, and took a quick sip. It might be fun to get a little tipsy. She'd stop feeling pierced by every glance. Of course, she knew from past experience, that once the buzz faded, she'd feel worse. Everything would return with double the force. But she couldn't sit here all afternoon. And she sure didn't want to turn into one of those women who spoils her husband's fun, sulking until she gets attention, making him walk on eggshells to keep his wife happy.

She held out her glass. "Pour me a bit more. I want to make sure I get to enjoy your great find." She smiled. The wine really was good.

Devon grinned again, but it looked as if he was holding something back. His eyes were dark, maybe it was the blood-red walls and garish gold pattern of the carpet, the water-saturated sky. His pupils were so dilated, she couldn't see the blue in the dim light. Although there was also something vacant in his smile, as if he was smiling for her benefit, but thinking about something else. She hoped she hadn't spoiled his afternoon. Sure, he had his faults, his stubborn optimism and his refusal to think past the present moment, but those were small idiosyncrasies that also had a positive element.

She followed him out of the room, along the hallway, and back into the dining room. Craig stood in the corner, peering over his glasses like a judge surveying his courtroom. Jenna giggled at the odd comparison. She thought doctors, especially GPs, were supposed to be warm and easy-going. She giggled again. She wanted more wine. The feeling of shame had shriveled to something barely discernible deep inside her chest. She bumped Devon's arm, lifted her glass, and he poured a small splash. He leaned over and kissed her quickly on the lips, just long enough to stir up a hint of longing. Then he set the bottle on the dining table and walked over to where Craig stood.

"Since when did you become better than everyone else?" Devon said.

"What?"

"That little speech a few minutes ago."

"What speech?"

"Going on about people who spend too much money. What's all this?" Devon nodded his head toward the over-laden table.

"Well, you paid for half of it buddy. And I'm right. People do spend money they don't have, but I'm not one of them."

"How do you know what people can afford? The only financial statement you have first-hand knowledge of is your own."

Craig shrugged. "I was only commenting on what I see. With my patients."

"What does a GP know about business? About cash flow?"

Jenna shivered. What was he doing? It was bad enough that her friends knew, she didn't want Devon provoking Craig into actually mentioning the dress. The feeling of shame started to swell again. Why had she mentioned it? He hadn't noticed the implication until she'd brought it up. A small part of her might have wanted to see him defend her, to hear him put Craig in his place, make Allison squirm over the snarky comments she'd surely leveled at Jenna behind her back.

"I was talking about the general state of the economy,

about people who are struggling. Don't take it so personally."

From the corner of her eye, Jenna watched Allison move closer to where the two men stood. She'd kicked off her sandals and appeared to be tiptoeing across the tile. Devon also stepped forward. His face was only seven or eight inches from Craig's. Jenna imagined that Craig felt the warmth of Devon's breath, smelled his skin. Craig's back was nearly touching the wall.

Jenna held her glass near her face but didn't touch the rim to her lips.

"You're standing kind of close," Craig said. His shoulders and arms were relaxed, almost swinging, in an obvious effort to adopt a casual stance.

"I want to know why you were preaching about people spending money they don't have," Devon said.

"Why are you so worked up? I was making conversation. Now back off."

Devon moved closer.

From where Jenna stood, Devon's broad shoulders and six foot two frame hid most of Craig's face. She gulped the rest of the wine in her glass. She twirled the stem between her fingers. If she went over and tried to pull Devon away, she'd make it look like she was afraid he was threatening Craig, when he wasn't. Not really. She glanced at Allison. Devon wasn't a threatening kind of guy. As far as Jenna knew, he'd never even been in a fight. Yet, she was thinking of fights. Instinct must be telling her she was afraid Devon was going to punch his friend. She should do something, but she had no idea what that would be.

The rumble of conversation, like distant thunder, rose and fell in the other room. No one else entered the dining room. Allison put her hand on Craig's elbow. Without seeming to move, he managed to extract his arm from her fingers. She let her hand drop to her side.

Craig curled his lips into a slow smile. "Do you want to hit me or something?"

Devon stepped back. He smiled, but it had that same forced look Jenna had noticed in the family room. He turned and walked to the table. He picked up the bottle and lifted it toward the light to check the level. Without turning back to look at Craig and Allison, almost as if he was talking to himself, he said, "You made it sound like you thought I couldn't afford this." He turned and held out the bottle. "There's one glass left, do you want it?"

"I'll have it," Allison said. She hurried back to the other side of the room and picked up her glass from the round mahogany table in the corner.

"I wasn't saying anything about the wine. You misinterpreted. But, wow, don't get in my face like that next time." Craig laughed.

"I'll get everyone to come in and grab some food," Allison said. "Then we can open gifts."

"You scared me for a minute there." Craig laughed again, too hard.

IT WAS DARK when the last guests left. The rain had stopped, but water was pooled in the driveway. The sound of Michael's SUV as the valet pulled it up to the front porch was like a water skier slicing across the surface of a lake. Beth stood on the porch wrapped in Michael's coat, directing the valets to load the gifts into the back.

Allison shut the door halfway and turned to Jenna. "I need to talk to you for a second." She turned and walked through the kitchen, past the caterers who were washing dishes and loading up their equipment.

Jenna followed. She could hear Devon and Craig laughing with Michael in the living room, relaxed and easy as if nothing had happened. How did men manage it? They could come within inches of rolling on the floor in a fistfight or tell their friends to their face that they'd screwed up, but then go on, as close as ever. If that happened with two women, the relationship would be in serious jeopardy. She slowed her pace. She didn't want to know what Allison needed to talk about. She didn't want all kinds of questions about what was wrong with Devon. Even if that weren't on Allison's mind, she would be asking about their half of the cash for the shower. The payment could probably be put off for a few days, but that was all. There was no way Allison would be willing to wait until the wedding.

Jenna lifted her hair off her back. She pulled it forward and draped it over her left shoulder.

The family room was completely dark now. Allison paused just inside the doorway and flipped the light switch. Two table lamps on opposite ends of the couch lit up, and she walked into the room.

Jenna stayed in the doorway. "What's up?"

Allison's eyes looked beady, the pupils small despite the recent darkness of the room.

"Do you have the check, or does Devon have it?"

"How much is it again?"

"So you didn't bring the check, or are you going to write it here? That's kind of awkward right in front of Beth and Michael."

"It would be. But I forgot the checkbook."

"How could you forget?"

Jenna smiled. If she said nothing, Allison would have to speak again. It was best to keep her off balance, force her to carry the conversation, then Jenna could gracefully suggest waiting a week.

"Maybe it's just as well," Allison said.

Jenna raised her eyebrows. "What?"

"That way you can write one check with the seven-fifty for the shower and your half of the wedding gift. I'll look it up." She walked toward the door that led to the office. "I think it's seven-forty-something."

"You already bought the gift?" Jenna said. She slid her fingers through her hair, pressing her hand against her skull. "I thought we were picking it out together."

"You said the Steuben glasses were okay. It was simpler to order online and have them shipped to Beth and Michael's place."

Jenna sat down in the armchair. She *had* said the champagne glasses were fine with her, but it was a casual conversation, and it was so long ago. She heard the desk drawer open. They couldn't even cover the shower expense. Why hadn't she considered that Allison would rush ahead without talking to her? That was exactly Allison's style. Of course, Jenna had hoped to do the same in order to extract some extra cash from the transaction.

Allison returned to the family room. She held out the receipt. "Here it is. Seven-forty-two is your half." The receipt trembled slightly in Allison's fingers. "Aren't you going to take it?"

Jenna grabbed the slip of paper. She tried to look at the total, but her eyes wouldn't focus. It didn't matter. She was sure Allison had calculated it perfectly. She calculated everything with a precision that grated.

"If it's easier, you can drop the check in the mail."

Jenna nodded.

"You looked worried," Allison said. "There's not a problem, is there?"

Jenna stood. "Not at all." Worried didn't begin to describe what she was feeling.

Eight

DEVON KNEW JENNA was upset about him getting in Craig's face. She hadn't said a word during the drive home from the Watson's. He shouldn't have been so intense, should have thought through things more clearly before he zeroed in on Craig.

It's just that he couldn't seem to control himself when someone hurt Jenna, even if it wasn't physical, even if she wasn't all that upset. Something rose up inside him. Blood rushed to his head, and he felt as if the whites of his eyes were glowing red. He stopped thinking about anything except making things right for her.

He hadn't realized Craig was insulting them, but when he heard Jenna describe it, the implication of the words and Craig's tone of voice had taken on a whole new meaning. The guy could be so self-important. Craig thought he knew it all because he was a doctor and therefore had extraordinary insight into the human condition. Well, that was BS. And

Craig was responsible for that sad, scared look on Jenna's face.

Now that he was calmer, now that he'd forced Craig to back down, he saw it differently. He hoped he hadn't come across like a thug, some guy who couldn't control himself. The kind of person who lives like an animal because he doesn't have enough intelligence to live by his wits.

He glanced at Jenna. Her expression was difficult to read, but he was sure it wasn't a happy one, an expression recalling what a great time they'd had or looking forward to the evening. If he could describe it, he'd say she looked blank. The muscles of her face hadn't moved since she'd closed the car door ten minutes ago. She'd pulled her hair around to the side, and it was draped over her shoulder like a scarf. He loved it when she did that. It made her look so exotic, long dark hair lying against her pale sweater. Lots of women chopped off their hair to look more business-like or professional or something. He was happy that Jenna didn't take that view. It was easy to imagine her without the sweater and bra, with her hair covering her breast, except not entirely. She had her hands wrapped around her kneecaps as if she was trying to keep them warm.

He pulled into the driveway, hit the remote, and entered the garage.

Inside, the house was cold. The stuccoed walls had that effect, which was nice in summer, but this time of year, it sometimes felt like the chill of a cave. You'd never know it was almost spring. In fact, Beth and Michael were getting married on the first day of spring. The ceremony was planned to take place precisely at the equinox. He went to the thermostat to kick up the heat.

"Don't," Jenna said.

"It's freezing in here."

"We need to cut expenses every way we can."

"Keeping the house ice cold for the evening isn't going to save more than a few bucks. Besides, you look cold. And the bill isn't due until …"

"I'll put on sweats. Leave the heat off." She turned and sprinted up the stairs to the master bedroom.

Devon went into the office and flicked on the light. He nudged the mouse, and the computer woke up. He'd take a quick look at their budget summary. Not that it was that good of a summary. Half the time he didn't get around to entering what they'd spent in the various categories, so it was hard to tell how things were really going. He knew he should be on top of it more. No guy with a degree in business ignored his personal finances. It wasn't that he ignored them entirely, but he didn't like having to account for all the budget categories Jenna had identified. He preferred big buckets. He had to do enough of that kind of detailed analysis at work. At home, he wanted to enjoy life. He'd planned to get an accountant to manage things once he became a Director. Yet another thing they'd denied him with their rigorous oversight. He'd already waited a year before the delay last summer. Keeping that sense of injustice under check required a lot of effort.

Instead of opening their accounting software, he pulled up a web browser to look at the weather. If it kept raining tomorrow, they could sit down and go through all this. He'd show Jenna things weren't that bad. He should put as much intensity into this as he had into getting Craig to shut up. Watching Craig try to look unfazed while Devon moved in closer than was comfortable had actually been satisfying. The guy tried to look so cool, but Devon could tell he'd been nervous. He smiled. Rain through Monday. He clicked over to the CNN page. The phone rang. He grabbed it without looking at the caller ID.

"Oh. Hi, Devon. It's Hannah."

He switched the phone to his right ear and clicked on a headline hinting at the percentage of Americans who failed to file their taxes each year. He'd avoided looking at their taxes yet, and dreaded thinking what news that might bring. You'd think with their large mortgage they'd have enough to decrease their liability, but last year they'd owed several thousand dollars, and now he'd put off entering the numbers to get a sense of where they stood. There was more than enough time, but he should probably at least take a look before they went to the wedding.

He realized Hannah had said something and he had no idea what it was.

"Hold on, I'll get Jenna."

Hannah was silent.

He carried the phone down the hall, into the entryway, and halfway up the stairs. He called to Jenna, "Your mom's on the phone."

She came out of the bedroom. She looked delicious, wearing white sweatpants and a pale yellow turtleneck shirt. Her hair was glossy as if she'd just brushed it. He should have told Hannah that Jenna was taking a bath, that she'd call tomorrow. Now that he thought about it, he wasn't sure why he'd even picked up the phone. Why was Hannah always inserting herself into their lives? His mother didn't call every day. He understood it was a mother-daughter thing, but still, it was a bit much. It was unnerving, never knowing when she might call, never knowing when Jenna would want to talk to her for half an hour, sometimes more.

He lingered on the stairs while Jenna spoke to her mother. As Jenna moved past him, down the stairs and into the living room, he followed. She sat on the sofa, listening to her mother all the while. Devon sat next to her and then moved slightly to the left and lay down with his head on her lap. He closed his eyes, hoping she would stroke his hair. After a moment, she put her hand on his shoulder but otherwise didn't seem to notice he was there. She hadn't spoken for several minutes. The rattle of Hannah's voice came through the receiver, but he couldn't make out what she was saying. Whatever it was, Jenna didn't seem to have much to say in response.

Finally, the phone was silent. "Didn't Tom send the

check? He said he would."

Hannah started talking again. Devon sat up.

"I'm really sorry, but we just can't right now."

Devon got up and wandered into the kitchen. He opened the fridge and tried to figure out if there was anything interesting to eat. He wasn't really hungry. Just unsettled. He wanted Jenna to be off the phone. Rain tapped the skylight in the kitchen. Orange juice was as good as anything. He grabbed an individual-sized plastic bottle and peeled off the strip that sealed it. He swallowed some then took the juice bottle into the office. He sat at the desk and opened a new browser window and went to one of the sites he'd bookmarked for information about wine cellars. He knew it was out of the question right now, but he liked looking. He couldn't wait until summer. The minute the promotion was official, he'd start getting quotes. It could be completed by fall, and they'd have a party during that warm stretch in October. He'd give tours of the cellar, and the party could be a wine-tasting event. He gulped down more orange juice and looked up. Jenna stood in the doorway. He clicked the button at the corner of the window and closed the browser.

"My mother is in a tough spot."

"Your mother is always in a tough spot."

"Don't say that."

"Well, it's true."

"She's sensitive, and she never had to take care of herself, so it's hard."

He stood and drank some juice to keep from saying something he'd regret. He'd heard this story a hundred times, about her mother's sensitivity. He didn't understand why Jenna didn't get tired of it. Hannah had been divorced for nearly twenty years. He felt that was more than enough time to become self-sufficient. It wasn't that he didn't care about Hannah, but it annoyed him that she didn't appear to be trying very hard. Of course, she didn't have to because she had her guilt-riddled ex-husband to pay the bills and her daughter to provide an endless ocean of empathy. Still, Jenna's tenderness for her mom warmed him more than he wanted to admit. She was the most loving woman he'd ever met. He moved closer and ran his hand down her hair, lifting it away from the side of her face. Her kindness inspired him to be a better person.

"What's the tough spot?"

"She got screwed over by that guy who said he'd dig out the volunteer banana trees. He said he wouldn't cash her check until the work was done. That's why she needed to borrow money a few weeks ago. He not only cashed the check, he disappeared."

"Disappeared how?"

"I guess it was a scam of some sort."

"It's not hard to scam your mother. Why would she …"

"Don't," Jenna said. "Please. Anyway, I asked Tom to help her out, and he did. Although she's upset that he knows she did something stupid."

Devon nodded. Best not to say anything, although clearly Hannah wasn't worried whether her daughter thought she was stupid. Or her son-in-law for that matter.

"She told me she needed five hundred dollars, but she was so embarrassed at the time, she didn't mention the full amount. The check she wrote the guy was for twelve hundred, and she needs another four hundred. Just to tide her over until the next check comes from my father."

"Twelve hundred bucks to dig up banana trees?"

"He was going to clean up the whole yard. Clear the rain gutters. And do some repairs on the house."

"You know we can't do anything."

"It's my mother!"

Devon swallowed the rest of the juice.

"We owe Allison and Craig."

"More than you know," Jenna said.

"What do you mean?"

"She already bought the wedding gift. We owe them for that and the shower."

Devon squashed the center of the plastic juice container. "I was thinking we could go over the bills and the budget tomorrow. See where we can juggle, and leverage what we have. We could cut back the gardener to twice a month or something."

Jenna nodded. "Maybe we can figure out how to help her. Sell some stock?"

"We don't have enough vested right now to make a

difference. And if we did, it wouldn't be to help your mother."

"Why do you say it like that?"

"Like what?"

"With that tone. As if the last thing we would do is help my mother."

"She has a way of creeping into our lives. Like it's our responsibility to bail her out of her screw-ups."

"She doesn't screw up."

"Whatever it is she does. She leans on you too much."

"Wouldn't we help your family, if they needed it?" Jenna walked around him and flopped on the cushioned armchair. She arranged her legs so they draped over one of the arms. She gazed at him with that pouty expression that made her face look like her mother's. He had to look away. It was bad enough that he felt Hannah's presence lingering even after Jenna hung up the phone, but he didn't want to feel like she was sitting right in front of him.

He turned and walked to the door. "They wouldn't need help."

"But if they did."

"I'm not opposed to helping your mother. That's not what I'm talking about it. She has too strong a grip on you or something. I feel like she's in the house, taking part of you away from me. Even when she's not here."

"Are you jealous of my mother?"

"No." He held up the juice container. "I need to go throw

this in the recycling."

He walked down the hall to the side door. He should rinse the container, but it was too much trouble. He went into the garage and dropped it into the recycling bin. The garage smelled like wet concrete and tires. He really didn't want to go back and finish the conversation. This is why it seemed like Hannah was in their house. It wasn't jealousy. It was ... he couldn't think what it was. He wasn't the jealous type. Unless someone was hitting on Jenna. But even then, it wasn't really jealousy because she would never respond to that kind of thing. She made it clear he was the only one for her. But why did her mother take over part of her brain, why did he feel like Jenna wasn't entirely his? If it came down to a choice between sticking with him and giving money to her mother, who would she choose? Him. She would choose him. She adored him. She proved that every day. And yet, her mother lingered, sapping the energy in the room, taking a piece of Jenna's heart.

He went back into the house. Jenna was still draped over the armchair. "Why are you blaming my mother for our financial problems?"

"I'm not blaming her for anything."

"You seem angry. And it's not her fault."

He sighed. This was the problem. Jenna seemed to get this film over her eyes, unable to even see reality when she was upset or worried about Hannah. No one had said anything about blame, and they weren't talking about blame at all, and suddenly this was turning into a discussion of what he thought of Hannah. "Of course it's not her fault."

"Then why do you seem so angry?"

He walked over and tugged on her wrist. "Let's go in the living room. Let's have a glass of wine or something and relax."

He thought she would resist, but she yielded to the pull of his hands.

"I'm not angry," he said. "Actually, I feel bad. I really do. But we can't lend her money. I'm sorry."

"That's why I hate this situation we're in. We should be able to help. Not only lend her money, give her money. She has a hard life, and I don't like it that she's still so dependent on my father."

"So you want her to be dependent on us?"

"I want to be able to help her. We make a lot of money, we live in this amazing house, and I don't want to have arguments about why we can't help our families."

He decided to let that go. There was only one family, one family member, who needed help.

"Like I said, tomorrow we'll work on the finances. Things might not be as bad as we think. There are ways to move cash around. For the short term."

She didn't say anything. He knew she took it as a promise they would figure out a way to help her mother. But it wasn't a promise of anything. All he wanted was to relax and enjoy what was left of their Saturday.

Nine

FOR THREE WEEKS Jenna and Devon had stopped eating out, brought their lunches to work, made minimum payments on the credit cards, and avoided any serious discussion of their debt. They'd cut back on the gardening service. The day after Devon's vague non-promise that they'd figure out a way to get things under control, Jenna was trying to figure out which suitcase she'd bring to New Mexico. She opened one and found a hundred and fifty dollars in the interior pocket. She gave it to her mother. Hannah apologized and handed back the cash. Apparently, she'd explained to Jenna's father the need to keep the yard maintained and he'd coughed up the rest of the money.

Beth and Michael's wedding would take place at the Hacienda del Espíritu in New Mexico, hosted by Michael's father, a dot-com success story who had cashed out his options before the dot went splat. A hundred guests were flown to New Mexico, housed in luxury suites, and would be fed more than any person could, or should, eat.

Jenna and Devon's room, like the others, had a private lanai and a view of gardens filled with cacti and rocks. Their room also featured a bathroom with a Jacuzzi tub and a shower formed by a wall of cubed glass, boasting three shower heads. They could probably fit their entire group of friends in that shower. There was a king-sized bed, a small table that seated four, and a complete entertainment system.

Thursday night they'd eaten alone in the restaurant as other guests continued to arrive throughout the evening. On Friday, the men played golf, and the women relaxed by the pool and munched chips and salsa and guacamole. In late afternoon the women in the bridal party would have a spa session together, and that evening there was a dinner and dance. The wedding was set to take place on Saturday, March 20, at the precise moment of the spring equinox. Beth was convinced that a marriage aligned with the moment of re-birth would ensure a love that would keep blossoming, a fertile marriage, and a life in tune with the universe. Jenna knew this because Beth had explained it in detail, numerous times.

At three o'clock, Jenna scooped up her towel and shimmied into her short yellow dress to cover up her bikini. "I'm going to shower before our mani-pedi."

"Aren't those showers amazing?" Allison said.

Jenna smiled. "I know."

Beth pulled a small towel over her feet. "See you at the salon."

Allison swung her legs over the side of her lounge chair. Jenna waved her fingers and walked quickly along the length of the pool. A few minutes alone would be nice, the constant socializing was draining, but there wasn't time for a run, a shower would have to do.

The path to her suite wound through a garden area with a fountain and flowering shrubs. As she followed the walkway, she heard Allison's flip-flops slapping the stone path behind her.

"Wait," Allison said. "I need to ask you something."

Jenna paused.

"Did you bring the check?" Allison used both hands to tuck her damp hair behind her ears, which gave the impression she was cupping her hands around them so she could better hear Jenna's response.

"Oh … I forgot. I'm sorry."

"You were supposed to mail it after the shower. It's embarrassing to have to keep asking for it."

Jenna felt as if the sun was bearing down directly on her face and neck. Surely, Allison saw right through the lie, or half-truth anyway. She hadn't forgotten at all, owing money was all she'd thought about for the past month. Possibly all she'd thought about for the past year. "I'm sorry. Things have been hectic."

"Is everything okay with you two? I really don't see how

you could have forgotten. We're at their *wedding*. How can you not think about the *gift?* Especially when they're funding all this?" She waved her arm gesturing toward the gardens, then sweeping it up toward the desert and red-tinged Robledo Mountains in the distance.

"I know. I said I'm sorry. I just ... there's been a lot of pressure at work. For both of us, and I have a lot on my mind."

"Come on, Jenna. We all have a lot on our minds. I signed your names to the card. You are going to pay, aren't you?"

Jenna stared at her friend. Allison really thought they weren't ever going to pay? A slight delay and she jumped to the worst possible conclusion. Unless... Maybe Allison and Craig were in debt. It was unlikely, but possible. She shouldn't assume they were the only ones struggling to cover all their expenses. Since Beth and Michael had gotten engaged, since Beth showed up flashing that two-carat diamond, maybe they had all been spending more and more, as if they were drunk on credit and the good deals in the real estate market and their upscale lifestyles and the promise of lucrative career paths.

"I didn't mean to leave you in a tight spot," Jenna said. "I promise the minute we get home I'll rush over with a check. I guess we could even go to the ATM here if you're desperate." It was a risky thing to say. But it would smoke out any desperation on Allison's part. If she agreed, Jenna would know that she and Devon weren't alone. And if Allison blushed and said forget it, Jenna would have shut her up. For now.

"Don't be ridiculous. It's not like we're short on cash. Or can't pay our bills." Allison laughed. "But I don't like being jerked around. And to be honest, after that scene in BCBG, I was a little worried about how solvent you are. Two cards rejected. That's pretty bad, don't you think?"

"I didn't have two cards rejected. The store credit card was a processing error. The clerk said so." Jenna stared into Allison's eyes, daring Allison to challenge her further. "And it turns out, the Visa thing was because we'd made a large purchase and the fraud protection put a hold on it. I hate it when that happens. Don't you?"

"Huh. Interesting. Whatever. As soon as we get back." Allison turned toward the path leading to her suite. "See you at the salon."

Jenna had lost the desire for a pedicure. Right now, all she wanted was to go for a run. Five or six miles in the desert sounded perfect.

BY THE TIME Jenna and Devon headed over to the rehearsal dinner, her equilibrium had returned. She could see in Devon's eyes that the dress had been worth all the grief. She was pretty sure she'd de-clawed Allison with her explanation of fraud protection.

When she told Devon about it, he declared her brilliant. And now he'd declared her the hottest, classiest wife on the planet. Not a bad way to start the evening.

Nearly all the guests turned to look as she and Devon walked through the doorway of the banquet room. She felt her body moving like liquid, loved knowing the dress looked as if it had been made for her. She was so lucky to have a man who didn't feel insecure when other guys admired her. Maybe that was the upside of Devon's endless optimism. He didn't fret about their finances, but neither was he jealous of any attention she received. Instead, it seemed to tickle his ego. And as he regularly pointed out, his wife was not only gorgeous, but smart as hell, and fun. They were both lucky; and she intended to enjoy every bit of their good fortune – eating a fabulous dinner, then dancing until her mind and her body dissolved into the music. But first, an apology to Beth for being late.

As it turned out, she'd over-estimated her ability to gush into Beth's good graces. The start of the dinner had been held for Jenna and Devon.

"I tried your cell three times," snapped Beth. "Where were you? Having sex?"

Devon wrapped his arm around Jenna's neck and pulled her toward him. "That comes later," he said.

Beth wrinkled her nose. "We have a hundred people waiting on you."

"You could have started without us."

"You're in the wedding party."

They'd already practiced the choreography for the

ceremony. This wasn't a true rehearsal dinner, more of a pre-wedding day dinner, so what did being in the wedding party have to do with the start time for the dinner? "I'm sorry, Beth. Really."

"You just wanted to make an entrance in that dress." Beth spat out the words, and although she didn't say it, she might as well have noted that it was a dress she paid for, and the least Jenna could do was show appropriate gratitude for Beth's generosity.

"And quite an entrance it was!" Devon swatted Jenna's butt.

The creases around Beth's nose turned into a full-blown scowl. She wore an ice blue silky sheath, and she looked good. The cut of the bodice revealed the tops of her large, lightly tanned breasts. Her hair, always thick and wavy, blonde with dark streaks, cascaded down her back. It was clear from the red flush on her cheeks that she didn't appreciate being shown up at her own event. This was supposed to be her moment.

Jenna inched out from under Devon's arm. It was one thing to steal the show, it was another to rub her friend's face in it. She regretted that they'd come so late. She smiled apologetically.

"What are you grinning at?" Beth said.

"I said I'm sorry. Tell me how I can make it up to you."

Beth shrugged. "It's too late now." Beth's sisters, her mother, and Michael appeared at her side, waiting for the signal to start the buffet line.

"People are hungry, hon," said Marcy, Beth's eldest sister.

"You'd think that since I bought you that dress, you'd show a little more consideration for my feelings," Beth said.

"You bought that dress, Bethy?" her mother said. "You're such a sweetheart. I don't think there's a more generous girl on the planet."

Michael squeezed Beth's shoulders. "There isn't."

"Let's eat." Beth turned away and pulled Michael after her to the start of the buffet line. Once the other guests saw them filling their plates, the crowd surged toward the tables, and soon a line snaked along the side of the room. The walls were hung with woven blankets and baskets. Pedestals situated throughout the room boasted large pottery vases painted in muted pinks, yellows, and blues. Some looked new. Other less colorful, slightly smaller vases bore cracks and chips that gave the impression of advanced age.

Dinner was a succulent spread of beef and barbecued chicken alongside pasta salads, fruit, freshly baked bread, and liberally flowing wine. As the plates were cleared, a DJ who had been setting up while they ate replaced the harp and classical piano music playing in the background. He jumped right in with three pulsing tunes and by the fourth piece, the dance floor was filled with people.

They danced until they were delirious with their own energy. An hour into the dancing, the sting of Beth's words had faded. After the more sedate members of the crowd had left for the night, the core group of their friends, mostly from college days, danced as if they were a single organism. Beth seemed to have let go of her irritation. She beamed with the reflected love of her friends. Now she was the star of the show, this was all for her, everyone celebrating the beginning of the rest of her life.

When the party wound down at one o'clock, Jenna was confident that all the ugly accusations from her friends were finished. They'd been together for all these years, and it was natural there would be tense undertones once in a while, but overall, they had had great times together. There was no reason that wouldn't continue for the rest of their lives. They supported each other, and they were all on the same trajectory. Watching Beth and Michael get married tomorrow would bind all of them closer together. The alignment with the equinox was an intriguing idea. It would give them all a fresh start.

Ten

BETH WALKED PAST a Saguaro cactus three times her height. Beyond the confines of the resort, some of them reached thirty feet. The sense of proportion helped drain the blister of disappointment from the night before. She needed to remember the hours of fun, not the two-minute exchange when Jenna and Devon showed up late. She regretted her cattiness. She didn't like the animosity, seemingly buried, that had erupted out of her. Why had she been surprised? Jenna always tried, and nearly always succeeded, in being the center of attention.

She continued along the path, calmed by the cacti and flowers and pre-dawn silence.

Chasing her thoughts was exhausting. She wanted her mind to be relaxed, focused on the present moment, drinking in every second of this day. Instead, she was consumed with reassuring herself Jenna was truly a good friend. After nearly ten years, she shouldn't expect Jenna to suddenly become a different person. For whatever, reason, whether it was because Jenna's father had been distracted by his new wife when Jenna was at the vulnerable age of twelve, whether it was because Jenna's mother doted on Tom or something else that Beth wasn't aware of, Jenna had a deep-seated need to be noticed. Friendship meant accepting people for who they were. It was the same as marriage, in some ways. You overlooked flaws, you focused on the good points, you let petty annoyances slide past. If you couldn't love the dark side of a person, you didn't love the whole person. It didn't work to go through life correcting the behavior of others. That attitude was a set-up for constant frustration, and ultimately, loneliness.

Today she was getting married. She shouldn't be thinking about these things. Deep inside, she knew why Jenna's prancing into the dinner late, shimmying in that dress, had gotten under her skin. Most of the time, Beth wasn't overly concerned with her appearance. She knew her hair was beautiful, and she kept it long and cut into layers. She wasn't overweight by any stretch of the imagination, but she didn't have a body like Jenna's. Compared with Jenna, her thighs were a little fleshy, her belly wasn't flat and taught – sitting by the pool, watching Jenna in her white string bikini had driven that fact home. Maybe that was the trouble. It had built up all day.

Michael loved her body. And it was fine. Normal and healthy. She wasn't one of those women who constantly picked over her food, complaining about calories and grams of fat. She enjoyed her life. She ate lots of greens and fruits because she wanted to be connected to the earth, to think about how life all fit together, not because she was trying to knock an inch off her hips. Jenna's appearance shouldn't have anything to do with her life. And it didn't – on any one of the thousands of days she'd known Jenna. But this weekend, it mattered. This was her day. She was supposed to be the most beautiful woman here.

After her walk, her mind was more peaceful. She took a long shower and ate breakfast on the patio outside Marcy's room, surrounded by her mother and her three sisters, warm and content under their love and attention, grateful that she had it all, as they said. The sun, spreading across the mountains, made the desert colors glow. When it started to descend, it would be spring, and she and Michael would be husband and wife.

It wasn't Michael's money that had attracted her. She could care less about that, she didn't need a life of luxury, and it frustrated her when people commented on it. She loved him because he was funny and smart and cute the way he got so wrapped up in his engineering projects, his enthusiasm to find new ways to solve problems. She was already hooked when she found out his father had made millions in the technology industry. What really mattered was that Michael was her soul mate. They envisioned the same kind of life – everything from wanting four children, to believing the desert was a mystical place.

After breakfast, she went with her sisters and Jenna and Allison, to get their hair styled. Beth's hair would be loose, the layers curled around her neck and shoulders and down the center of her back. She wouldn't be wearing a veil, and her dress was simple – pure white, without a train or any of that fussy stuff, just enough décolletage to make Michael smile.

An hour before the ceremony, they gathered in the pavilion that housed a few meeting rooms. The wedding would take place in a large garden facing west, overlooking the desert, the earth a long, unbroken stretch of space bordered by the purplish, green, and gray mountains on the horizon. There would be silence after the initial harp music, and everything would be perfectly timed so that she and Michael promised to love each other for eternity at the exact moment the season changed.

Beth sat in front of the long row of mirrors with her face turned up, trying not to blink while her sister applied mascara.

"Your eyelids are trembling," Marcy said. "Keep still."

"I can't help it. They move all on their own."

"That's not entirely true," Marcy said. "They're moving because you're thinking I might stab you in the eye, and that makes you nervous, and they twitch."

"I can't help what I think," Beth said.

"Don't think at all. It's your wedding day. Everything is exactly the way you planned, and you're one of the lucky ones. You have a guy who adores you."

"Doesn't every groom adore his new wife?"

Marcy shrugged. She moved to Beth's left. "Look up." She stroked more mascara on Beth's lashes.

When Beth's makeup was finished, Marcy drifted outside with their other sisters.

Beth went into the short hallway that led to the adjoining room. She needed a little water so she didn't get thirsty standing outside in the dry air.

From the hallway, she heard Allison talking in a stage whisper, her voice hoarse and strained. "For once in your life, you can stop thinking *me, me, me.*"

"I'm not thinking about myself," Jenna said.

Beth sat down on a bench and waited. She didn't want to walk into a room filled with hostility.

"You were. You always are," Allison said. "This is Beth's day. They've spent tens of thousands of dollars to have all of us here and to create this spiritual atmosphere. Beth was very clear that she wanted harmony."

"You can't dictate harmony," Jenna said. "That's like demanding that someone falls in love with you."

"Great example," Allison said. "Because you can. You can control your behavior, and you can think of other people and how you affect them. It's bad enough you had to have that slutty dress, and then you let ..."

"My dress is not *slutty,*" Jenna said.

"No, the dress itself isn't. But the way you slink around makes it seem that way."

"Why are you being so mean to me?"

"Because Beth is a sweetheart. She'd never say or do anything to spoil one of your celebrations. She's always thinking about everyone else. We have this one weekend where she wants things to be a certain way. It's her wedding and she should be the star of the show."

"It's not a show."

"You turned last night into a show, the way you were dancing, acting like you and Devon wanted to do it right there on the dance floor. I don't know what your problem is. Why you always need to have everyone looking at *you*. Fawning over *you*."

"Fawning?" Jenna laughed.

"When you walk down the aisle, you should be thinking about Beth and Michael. Not about how you look or whether Devon is drooling over you."

"Now you're telling me what I'm allowed to think about?"

"Beth wants a spiritual ceremony."

"Beth can't control what everyone thinks about."

"Why are you doing this?" Allison said.

"I'm not doing anything. I was standing here eating a grape, and you started attacking me. I didn't do anything wrong. So I was a little late. Big deal. If it was so important, they should have started without us."

"You're in the wedding party." Allison's voice was no longer a whisper. Beth wondered if either one of them was considering that they could be overheard. Part of her wanted to go inside and tell them to stop, right now. Tears collected behind her eyes. This wasn't at all how it was supposed to be. This was the happiest day of her life. They were spoiling it, and she couldn't do anything about it. If she went in there, she'd get caught up in their negative energy. If she stayed where she was, they would keep hissing at each other like two wet cats, and their words would get increasingly vicious.

"You came late so you could advertise that you and Devon were too busy having sex to get to dinner on time," Allison said.

Beth couldn't listen anymore. This would get worse and the day would be damaged beyond repair. Once they saw her, once she walked into the room, and they caught sight of her dress, their animosity would melt. All she had to do was breathe and make the tears drip back down her throat, walk into the room with an aura of peace and it would flow over her friends. Allison didn't mean the things she was saying. She must be under even more than the usual pressure at work.

The satin blend of the fabric flowed against her legs like warm water as she moved forward. The softness helped remind her of everything good. She took a long, slow breath. Michael loved her. They were in New Mexico. In a few minutes, they'd stand beneath the endless sky, whispering their love to the universe. Everything would be okay. The soles of her gold gladiator sandals tapped the floor as she stepped through the doorway.

Allison and Jenna turned toward her as if they were a

single creature, standing so close to one another their dusty rose dresses melted into a single swath of fabric. She could see the red in their cheeks flare as they realized they were upsetting her equilibrium, and then fade as they determined to stop arguing.

"You look gorgeous." Allison walked toward Beth and gave her a feathery hug.

"Thank you." Beth smiled.

Jenna plucked a grape off the bunch and bit it in half. Juice squirted across her lip, and she licked it slowly.

Beth turned so they could admire the back of her dress, the waves of hair, braided with thin feathers that emerged then hid themselves as she moved. Suddenly she felt a hand on the skin of her back, the fingers cool and smooth.

"Hold still," Jenna said.

Two fingers slid between Beth's skin and the edge of the strapless dress, pressing slightly against her flesh.

"The facing was up a bit," Jenna said. "It's all fixed."

Beth hadn't noticed she was holding her breath, but now she let it out in a long, smooth stream, releasing all the air until she felt her lungs tight with wanting a fresh breath. She still wasn't pleased. They were going to swallow all that vitriol, bury it deep underground again, and smooth over it so she wouldn't be able to tell, not by a look or a gesture or the choice of a word, that she'd witnessed it. The problem was, she knew it was there. It could be sensed, in the utter decorum of their behavior for the rest of the day and throughout the evening.

It wasn't until that night, when she and Michael were alone in their detached bungalow, bathing in steaming water, sandalwood soap, and the light of four large candles, that she realized Jenna had never told her she was a beautiful bride.

Eleven

IT HAD BEEN three days since Jenna and Devon returned from New Mexico. In that time, Allison had sent five text messages, three emails, and left two voicemails asking for the check. At least electronically, she didn't seem to have any more commentary on Jenna's supposedly bad behavior.

Jenna and Devon discussed it over a dinner of grilled cheese sandwiches – not the best for her fitness level, but a very healthy meal for their budget. There was still no way they could write a check for even half of what they owed. They finally decided on a plan that was a total cliché, but it was all they could come up with – an unsigned check. Jenna would drop off a check with a note of apology. By the time Allison opened the envelope, the Porters would have bought another day. Surely, they could manage to pull fourteen hundred bucks out of their next paychecks, both coming this week. They'd have to defer a few payments on the cards, but their credit was good, so far. The damage would be minor.

Jenna planned to arrive at the Watson's at four when Allison was guaranteed to be at the office. She'd slip the check into a cabinet in the outdoor cooking area. Through the miracle of voicemail tag, she might be able to extract an additional day. She could simply ignore the text messages, although it would be increasingly difficult to explain her lack of response.

When Jenna pulled up close to the Watson's front porch, the cobblestone driveway was still in full sun. She parked her car near the garage, jumped out, and darted around to the side gate. Locked. She backed up and looked at the shrubs surrounding the gate. There must be a way to get over. Or, she could leave the check under a planter on the front porch. Maybe that was a better option. She trotted back around the path that wound past two full-sized lemon trees, pink flowering shrubs, and a bench sheltered by wisteria climbing over a trellis.

She stepped onto the front porch. The door swung open.

"Hi. What are you doing sneaking around my yard?" Allison wore all her usual foundation, shadow, liner, and mascara. Only her lips were free of color. Despite makeup that looked ready for the office, she wore a white cotton camisole with a light green tank top underneath and torn jeans. Her feet were bare. Her collarbone and the knobs of her shoulders were more pronounced than Jenna remembered.

"Hey." Jenna smiled and waved the envelope. "I came to

drop off your check. I assumed you were still at work."

"I worked all night, and we had a deposition this morning, so I came home early."

"Well, here you go." She handed the envelope to Allison with a flourish to cover the tremble that slid along her fingers. "Sorry it took so long."

"Did you sign it?"

Jenna laughed. She held her breath, hoping Allison was too tired to notice her non-answer.

Allison shoved the envelope into the back pocket of her jeans. She turned partially to the side. "Do you want to come in for a glass of wine?"

Jenna backed to the edge of the porch. She took one step down. "I need to run an errand." She hesitated. That might not be the right way to handle this. If she went inside, Allison wouldn't open the envelope immediately. By the time they drank a glass of wine, Allison would have temporarily forgotten the check. Jenna stepped back up onto the porch. "On the other hand, errands are always there, but how often are we both off work early and able to chat?" She grinned. Apparently, Allison had covered up or completely forgotten all the animosity from the wedding. She seemed warm and genuinely glad to invite Jenna inside.

Jenna stepped into the house. The forest green and dark blue stained glass windows on each side of the front door cast their dark colors across the pale tile in the foyer. She followed Allison into the kitchen and around the massive center island equipped with a two-burner cooktop, as well as kitchen appliances for very specific uses – a juicer, a bread maker, a food processor. They went into the breakfast room. Jenna sat at the table and waited for Allison to bring the wine.

While they sipped Chardonnay, Allison talked, her words flowing maniacally from one subject to the next. She related the political intrigue at her law firm, detailing the bio and win record of every attorney from the partners on down ... which people weren't going to make it in her brutal, bloodless world ... which female attorneys would wind up having affairs with one of the partners because they were addicted to power ... which partners were going to destroy the firm if they didn't step up their game. Of course, Jenna knew none of these people. She hadn't even heard half of the names before, so it was difficult to follow the thread.

From there, Allison merged, like she was racing onto a freeway, into the subject of her last physical – three months ago, and her slightly high blood pressure and Jenna probably had healthy blood pressure because she ran so religiously, and Allison wished she had a job that didn't require as many hours so she too could stay in tip-top shape, and all she managed to do was ride her bike around their hilly neighborhood two or three times a month. From there she meandered over to their vacation in the Bahamas the previous spring. While she talked, she scrolled through her Blackberry to show Jenna pictures of her and Craig on the beach, drinking exotic concoctions under palm trees and sipping wine in front of violent sunsets. Pictures Jenna had already seen, but bringing that up might stop the flow, and as long as Allison was talking about other things, she wouldn't think about the check.

After forty-five minutes, Jenna was exhausted. The glass and a half of wine were making her sleepy, and she had to pee. But Allison kept talking. Jenna waited, opening her mouth several times in the hope of asking for a chance to slip down the hall to the restroom. Still, Allison talked on. Finally, Jenna moved her glass to the center of the table and pushed back her chair. Right over Allison's description of the style she was thinking of for decorating *next* year's Christmas tree – all silver and blue – Jenna said, "I have to pee." She stood and walked out of the room. Allison called after her, "And I think the lights should all be white. Or maybe blue and white."

In the bathroom, Jenna turned on the light and took a deep breath. She looked in the mirror. Her forehead was slightly moist. She picked up a clean guest towel and dabbed at her skin. She opened the cabinet door that hid the laundry basket and dropped the towel into it.

After she used the toilet, she washed her hands with apple-scented soap and dried them on the second guest towel. She smoothed the towel and laid it back on the counter. It was a huge bathroom, considering there wasn't a tub or shower – a true powder room featuring a long counter with two sinks and a separate closet for the toilet. She pulled open the drawer. She'd gone through Allison's bathrooms before, this one, and the master bath, when they stayed overnight once after drinking too much during a wine and cheese party. All she'd found in the master bath were birth control pills for Allison, a sedative, also for Allison, and anti-itch cream for Craig.

She never understood why it was so interesting to check out other people's bathrooms. Perhaps it came from being the kid who had so much less than everyone else. She'd first noticed her curiosity when she was a teenager, visiting her sort-of boyfriend's two-story house, palatial compared with her family's 3-bedroom single bathroom home – a cottage, really. His house had a bathroom near the backyard, solely for use when people were using the pool. It was one of five bathrooms, and her younger self wanted to know what was kept in each one. Surely you didn't need that many towels or baskets full of soap and buckets of cleaning products. The most interesting thing she'd found in that long ago hunt through drawers and cabinets while the others were in the pool, was a stash of chocolate bars, tucked under a stack of brand new towels in the upstairs hall bath.

Perhaps most people expected visitors to snoop. Exploring Allison's guest bathroom had been boring, but she couldn't resist the urge to double-check, in case there was something besides soap and Ibuprofen. Besides, it was more interesting than listening to Allison right now. She'd never heard anyone talk so much and so fast without taking a noticeable breath.

The first cabinet yielded nothing. The second cabinet wouldn't open. She tugged harder. Then she saw there was a keyhole under the handle. Who locked the bathroom cabinet? Especially in a bathroom designed for visitors. She slid open the drawers. Was Allison silly enough to lock the cabinet and hide the key right in the same room? The drawer closest to the wall contained an art deco style hand mirror. She turned it over and ran her finger over the swirl of ivory and pink roses on the back. Next to it was a candy tin. She removed the tin and pried it open. Inside was a small silver key. She poked the key into the lock and turned. The cabinet opened. It was empty except for a narrow leather case on the center shelf.

There was a knock on the door. "Are you okay in there?"

"Yes, just a touch of diarrhea. Sorry. How gross, I'm sure you don't want to know that detail, but I'll be done in a second. I must have had too many smoothies this week." She was stunned at how easily the lie slipped out. She flushed the toilet for good measure.

"All right." Allison's voice sounded tense. After a minute, Jenna flushed the toilet again in case Allison was still standing outside. Of course, the tank hadn't filled, but it made enough noise that she was able to unzip the leather case. Inside was a plastic bag containing what looked like a section of a magazine page folded into a rectangle. She slipped it out and turned it over. One edge was tucked inside itself like a miniature envelope. She placed it on the counter and opened the case wider. There was a razor blade with a protective cardboard sleeve.

She lifted out the tiny flap of the envelope. In the center of the paper was a pile of white powder. Somehow, she'd known that's what she was going to find. Was it Allison's manic talking that made her suspect there might be something interesting in the bathroom? Or had she not known until she saw that handmade envelope. How did she know it was most likely speed or cocaine? Had someone told her once that those substances were passed in makeshift envelopes? She really had no idea, she just wondered how long it had been going on and if it was both of them or just Allison.

Her fingers trembled from excitement more than fear of getting caught. She re-folded the little packet and slid it back into the zip-lock bag. She pressed the air out of the bag, sealed it, folded it in half, and put it inside the leather case, zipped that, and placed it in the cabinet. She was just about to turn the key when she realized she wasn't sure what shelf it had been on. She closed her eyes and popped them open quickly to try to catch her brain in its instinctive reaction. The middle shelf. She was ninety-eight percent sure it was the middle shelf. She closed the door and turned the key.

There was a brief urge to take the key. Imagine Allison coming into the bathroom, setting out her little coke-snorting mirror, planning to take a quick hit, only to find she couldn't get into the cabinet. Did that mean Craig didn't know? Or were they both hiding it from their friends? But why wouldn't they keep it in the master bathroom? Maybe the steam from the shower was bad for it. If it got into the plastic baggie, it would certainly dampen the envelope. But come on, a zip-lock bag and the leather case? It must be that Craig didn't know. How many men would look in the cabinets of their other bathrooms?

Jenna walked back to the kitchen, slid onto her chair, and picked up her glass of wine.

"How are you feeling?" Allison said.

Jenna sipped the wine and tried to nod at the same time. She took another sip. Allison's eyes were wide, staring, seeing … Jenna didn't know what, only a face? Or looking deeper, reading something in Jenna's eyes. The absurd desire to put a cloth over her head flashed through her mind as if Allison might be able to peer past the barrier of skin and skull to detect her thoughts. She didn't know what to do, an unusual predicament for her. She wasn't sure if she wanted to ask to be included in Allison's party, sniff up a line herself. Try something new. She was kind of curious. Or should she use this to alleviate the fourteen hundred dollar debt? That would be the most practical use of this delicious new information. There was even the possibility she could do more, suck money out of Allison to help with her own problems. Tell her now, or wait and discuss the possibilities with Devon? If she waited, the cocaine might disappear, and Allison could deny its existence. Damn it. Why hadn't she had her purse in the bathroom, she could have snapped a picture. Sometimes she wondered how people had functioned prior to smartphones. Her mother said, *quite well, thank you very much.* How, indeed, had they blackmailed their friends prior to pocket phones equipped with five-megapixel digital cameras?

She stood. "I think I need to use your bathroom again. I'm sorry." She grimaced, hoping her expression looked embarrassed and slightly pained.

"Sure. I guess you better go home." Allison stood and carried Jenna's empty glass to the counter. She poured another quarter cup of wine into her own and sipped it while Jenna walked out of the room.

Allison didn't look as if she believed the diarrhea story. Why not? It was perfectly plausible. In one respect, Jenna didn't care. She just needed some reason to scuttle back down the hall to the bathroom.

Jenna unlocked the cabinet door and put her phone on silent before she opened the camera app. She took several shots, the leather case, the baggie pulled out and lying on the case on the counter. None of them proved, if Allison denied it, that the coke belonged to her. There was also the chance Craig was the one hiding it. Still, not as likely. Allison was the one who couldn't stop talking, who had changed her behavior. Oh well, even though there wasn't definitive proof, she had enough to make Allison uncomfortable. She patted her finger in the white powder and held it up to her nostril. She sniffed, but the powder adhered to her fingertip. It wasn't enough force, or the moisture of her skin prevented it from being sucked into her nostril. She stuffed the pad of her index finger up as far as she could inside her nostril without sticking her nail inside. She rubbed it inside the cavity and then rinsed her finger. She packed everything back up and locked the cabinet. She felt nothing, but the quantity was so insignificant. The activity had been enough, however, to help her make a decision. For now, she wouldn't do anything. She would tamp down her curiosity over why Allison was headed down this path, especially since Craig so obviously wanted a child. Maybe a last fling before tying down her life forever? Entering that world where your choices no longer felt like your own, everything weighed in light of how it would impact an impressionable human being.

She flushed the toilet, washed her hands, and went back to the kitchen.

"I hope you're going to be okay," Allison said.

"I'm fine. Like I said, too much fruit and yogurt. I tried some flax in it this morning, maybe that was it."

"You're not purging, are you?"

"No."

Allison didn't look like she believed that either, but she didn't say anything else. She walked Jenna to the door, thanked her again for the check, and closed the door. Jenna imagined Allison darting down the hall to check out the bathroom, making sure she hadn't been found out. Well, she could rest easy. For now. Jenna got into her car. The engine kicked over with a satisfying roar, like a male lion asserting his dominance. She sped out of the driveway.

As she approached her own neighborhood, her cell sang out her current favorite song – a line about love lasting beyond the grave – and Devon's face, from a photograph taken on their honeymoon, appeared on the screen. She pressed the button on her earpiece.

"Hey," Devon said.

She smiled at the sound of his voice, still keyed up and anxious to tell him Allison's secret, but not now. Face to face.

"We're going out for dinner. How does Reposado sound?"

"We absolutely can't afford to eat out."

"What if I told you it was a gift," Devon said.

"What do you mean?"

"I got a spot bonus. I get to use my corporate card to treat you to dinner."

She turned onto Willow Circle, slowed, and hit the remote as she maneuvered into the driveway. As always, she felt hugely grateful for her beautiful home, still amazed that it belonged to her and Devon. She admired the pale pink stucco, the ironwork on the windows, and the palm trees, some of them over fifty years old. It was nearly three thousand square feet. She supposed once they had a child or two, it wouldn't seem so large.

"Why aren't you saying anything?" Devon said.

"I was pulling into the driveway."

"So does Reposado sound good?"

"I guess."

"Do you have another choice you'd like better?"

"Are you sure they gave you a bonus? What was it for?"

"Don't you trust me?"

"Yes. I'm just surprised."

"It was for putting up with all the politics."

"Really? They give bonuses for that?"

Devon laughed. "No, it was for making my boss look brilliant with all the insight into customer buying patterns that I put together for his last executive review."

"Well, we probably can't use it for anything else, so dinner would be nice."

FORTY MINUTES LATER they were sitting across from each other at Reposado. The dining area managed to be spacious, open to the second story, but remain intimate with its fine wood tables and chairs arranged with plenty of room between them. Devon studied the wine list like a religious scholar pouring over holy scriptures. Jenna knew it was pointless to interrupt him. He wouldn't really hear her if she spoke. He thought he was surprising her with the kind of evening they hadn't enjoyed for months, but she was the one with something surprising to share.

He requested the wine, a Syrah from the Columbia Valley. After it was tasted and poured, they ordered an appetizer and entrees.

An appetizer was the last thing she needed. With all the rain this month, she'd only been making it out for her five-mile run every other day, at best. The results were obvious when she pulled on her jeans, not quite as prominent when she dressed for work in slacks or a skirt, but she couldn't keep ignoring the extra flesh circling her waist. Before she knew it, the rain would end. She didn't want to be lying around their swimming pool with her gut spilling over the bottom half of her bikini.

Devon lifted his wine glass. "To the hottest woman on the planet."

His toast was lame, but she couldn't help smiling. There was something about his adoration, worship almost, that filled her with warmth. It made her think that their debt didn't matter quite so much. They'd get past it. At least they were focused on it together instead of fighting, or spending money behind each other's backs like some couples did. Even after being married all this time, she felt like their relationship was new, the thrill of getting to know each other burned through her until all the sounds of the restaurant faded to a hum and all she was aware of was Devon's voice resonating through her bones. And it wasn't only physical longing. She was still excited to hear what he had to say, and eager to tell him every detail of her day. She imagined the grin spreading across his face as he heard about Allison and the real secret to how she managed to work such long hours without collapsing from exhaustion.

She let the wine seep through her veins as Devon told her two stories about tension-filled meetings at work that day. His voice trailed off when the server arrived with their appetizer – corn tortillas filled with duck confit.

After the server left, Jenna said, "I had something interesting happen today." She took a sip of wine. "I went to drop off the check at Craig and Allison's."

"Unsigned, right?"

"Of course."

He picked up his wine glass.

"Allison was home."

He set his glass back on the table without drinking.

"But she seemed a little out of it. She said she'd worked all night. She didn't look in the envelope. It was tense for a minute because she asked if it was signed."

"What did you say?"

"I laughed. She didn't seem to notice I didn't really answer the question."

"Then what's the interesting part?" Devon said. He picked up a tiny corn tortilla and took a bite.

"Are you ready?"

He poured a small amount of wine in both their glasses.

"Slow down," Jenna said. "I want my wine to last through dinner."

"Maybe we'll have two bottles."

"No." Jenna took a sip of water. Suddenly water seemed so much more desirable than wine, a substance that refreshed her soul. There was beauty in simplicity, in the basics. Why did she forget that so often? "I used their bathroom, and there's a locked cabinet. I don't know why I never noticed. Maybe it wasn't locked before."

"And?"

"I found the key and opened it, and there was a packet of cocaine in there."

"What makes you think it was cocaine?"

"What do you mean? I could just tell. It was white powder all folded up in a tiny piece of paper inside a leather pouch in a locked cabinet. It sure wasn't bath powder." She pulled her phone out of her purse and showed him the pictures she'd snapped.

Devon ate the rest of the tortilla and took several sips of wine.

"Can you believe it? Allison is snorting coke. Or Craig. But I think it's her. She was super chatty at Beth's shower. And she seemed jumpy at the wedding too. You should have heard her today, she was talking so fast, she hardly took a breath. Now I know how she can work all night and get by with two hours of sleep."

"You're leaping to conclusions," Devon said.

"I know that's what it is."

"Maybe."

"What else would it be?"

He shrugged.

"You don't seem very excited."

"What's there to be excited about? Even if that's what it is."

"Because if we let her know that we know, she'll back off bugging us about the money."

"No."

"What do you mean, *no?*"

"You were going through their things. You don't even know what it is and you should forget that you saw it."

"Why would I do that? This is perfect."

Devon pushed his appetizer plate away. "Can we talk about something else?"

"What's wrong? Don't you see how this could help our situation? When she calls to tell me we didn't sign the check, which she'll do any minute, I'll let her know what I found. She'll be terrified. If Craig doesn't know, she'll be even more worried. But mostly she won't want it to get back to her co-workers. She could lose her job."

"Are you suggesting you want to blackmail one of our best friends?"

"Don't label it."

"It doesn't matter what I call it, and I don't want to talk about it anymore."

"We haven't talked about it. You're dismissing it like I'm some kind of criminal. We have a huge problem when she finds that check isn't signed."

"It's an honest mistake."

"She's not stupid, Devon."

"Okay. But we'll be able to cover it. I'm going to move some stuff around."

"What stuff? There's nothing to move. We've looked at everything."

Devon picked up the bottle and filled her glass.

The wine looked too bright under the lights, shining red as freshly spilled blood. She couldn't enjoy it. The whole thing was making her sick. Thinking back over the past two years, she couldn't even pinpoint how they'd gotten here. Of course, the house was a stretch, but they'd had enough to cover the mortgages and the taxes. They had enough for everything, and maybe that was the problem. Having enough lulled them into spending money without thinking about how it added up. It had been a steady accumulation of lingering bills. It reminded her of last summer when they had the swimming pool drained and re-filled. It had seemed like water was gushing into the pool for hours, nothing but a puddle at the bottom, then she'd looked out, and suddenly the pool was full, a dark, bottomless lake in the late afternoon light.

She pushed her wine glass toward the center of the table.

Devon shoved the metal cone holding the remainder of the tortilla chips out of the way. He reached across and touched her fingers. "I'll figure out something. I promise. But it's better if you forget about whatever it was you found."

"I don't know how you'll *figure it out*."

"Don't you trust me? Don't you know I'd do anything for you?"

Jenna leaned forward. She pushed her glass closer to Devon. "You drink this, I can't have any more."

"We're supposed to be having a great evening, comped by my boss, not arguing. Come on, babe."

"I'm scared."

"Of what?"

"Our friends finding out how bad things are. Thinking we're idiots." The aroma of grilled chicken filled her nostrils, making her mouth water, yet her stomach rebelled against the idea of food. Around them, other couples, well-dressed and pampered from their haircuts to their shoes, laughed and sipped at drinks sparkling with the colors of the spring gardens being planted around Palo Alto – creamy pink, lime green, and the burnished gold of tequila shots. At one table behind Devon, a couple leaned toward each other, the woman's short hair was brushed back from her face that looked clean and free of makeup, her lips smooth and pale pink. Her date's hair was nearly the identical shade of blonde, and his face also looked fresh, unlined. Although their conversation was equally intense, they seemed happy, relaxed, as if they were enjoying the delicate red, blue, and yellow corn chips, dipping them into salsa, occasionally lifting their margarita glasses to their mouths. They smiled and talked with an unbroken flow, surely not worried about how the dinner was really being paid for.

"Are you sure you got a spot bonus?" Jenna said. "It seems odd, all of a sudden."

"That's why it's called spot … on the spot." He smiled. He pushed the wine glass back at her. "This is a great Syrah. Have some more. You'll relax and forget all about these details. And they really are details."

"They're significant details, Devon. We have no cash, we owe fourteen hundred dollars to the Watsons. I'm surprised my phone isn't spitting text messages at me every minute with her pissed off at me for not signing it." There was a knot in her chest as if a clump of hardened refried beans was lodged there, keeping the air from coming up properly, making her breath a thin stream that made the words come out softly even though she wanted to shout. He kept thinking things would be better, that they'd somehow *figure it out*, when there was no way out.

Devon put on his softest smile and tilted his head to the left. "Forget about Allison. Please. I'll take care of her."

"When she sees the check she'll call me, not you. That's why I think using the cocaine as leverage is a great solution."

He leaned back. He pressed his fingers to his temple as if he was upset, but continued to smile. "Leave it alone."

Jenna reached for her wine glass. She moved it back to her side of the table, took a large gulp of wine, and set the glass down too hard. She grabbed a blue tortilla chip and dipped it into the pico de gallo. "Then I don't know what to do, and I don't know why we're eating out when we need money for so many things. You should have asked for the spot bonus in cash."

"That's not how it works."

Jenna closed her eyes. Her face was hot, and she imagined she had bright red splotches on the skin over her cheekbones.

Devon took her hand and stroked her wrist. "Please trust me. Don't you love me?"

"Of course I do. More than anything."

"Then trust me. You have to trust me. When you act as if we're going under any day, or talk about crazy things like blackmailing our friends, it makes me think you don't love me."

"That's not fair. Worrying about an obvious problem has nothing to do with loving you."

"To me it does."

"Why? That makes no sense."

He pulled her hand toward him so her ribs pressed against the edge of the table. "If you love me, you'll stop talking about it and trust that I have things under control."

When he looked at her like that, when he clung to her arm as if he was drawing reassurance from the marrow of her bones, she couldn't speak. She could only think about his eyes, soothing as a mountain pool, and his dark hair, getting a bit long now, curling over his ears. He looked so good, she ached.

Twelve

ALLISON SAT IN the living room, gazing at the glass vase filled with yellow tulips. The vase was thick and sleek, giving the illusion it was dissolving into the glass top of the coffee table. The tulip petals looked creamy and so soft she had the sudden urge to pluck one out of the water and rub it along her cheek. Some days, her ritual of buying fresh cut flowers and arranging them into three vases for the living room, front hall, and their bedroom was the only thing that provided serenity. Or sanity. The flowers weren't always tulips, but they were her favorites. There was something about the perfect color and their short lives that appealed to her. The dark stamen in the center of bright yellow thrilled and frightened her.

She was exhausted, only three hours of sleep again, a six o'clock breakfast meeting and a ten-hour work day after that. On her way to the office, she'd texted Jenna, telling her to come over after work to sign the check. Jenna texted back she was working late, and Allison had replied, *no problem*. She was available all evening, Craig was meeting his brother at a sports bar to watch March Madness.

It wasn't that they needed the money, it was the sheer arrogance, and the ridiculous assumption on Jenna's part that Allison wouldn't notice the check hadn't been signed. She'd noticed right away, while Jenna spent all that time in the bathroom, but she'd decided not to say anything. There was a perverse side of her that wanted Jenna to think she'd gotten away with her silly game. She wondered if Devon knew. Had they planned it together or was this purely Jenna's idea? Did Devon even know they'd agreed to go in together on the cost of the shower and the wedding gift?

For as long as she could remember, she'd recognized that Devon lived more purely in the experience of the moment than anyone she knew. In seventh grade, she'd wondered if he would remember he even had homework assignments if she wasn't around to prompt him to study. All he cared about was what was right in front of him. Of course he'd learned to pay attention to the future, or he would never have made it into Stanford and succeeded in his career, but still, the present dominated his thoughts, so it wouldn't be surprising if he were oblivious to Jenna's plans.

She stroked one of the tulips. They'd been in the vase for two days and were just now opening. She could probably count on at least another day of pure perfection. If only her life could be as simple, as beautiful, as well formed as a tulip.

She had everything she'd set out to achieve, a man who loved her, an amazing career, friends, a beautiful home, financial security. Yet, keeping it all going took so much energy. Using a few sniffs of coke to boost her enjoyment of what she had, to keep her on her toes, had seemed like a great idea when she tried it at an informal office party last summer. The others had drifted away, and it was just her and Cari and Dave, two of the staff attorneys at Hammer, Simpson, Lee, and Pimentel. They said they only did it when they were feeling a slump, when they had to work all night to prep or when they needed to be more than *on* for a client. Plus, they said, it made you feel great, and they'd earned a few perks with all their hard work. Why not kick back and feel good once in a while? It was better than alcohol, which left you feeling fuzzy and slightly sick to your stomach, not to mention adding unnecessary pounds. Coke made you feel alert instead of numb, supremely happy with life. It wasn't physically addictive – the perfect drug – enjoyable in moderation.

She didn't disagree with any of that, even now, but she did feel bothered that she found herself wanting that feeling more often. If she was honest with herself, she wanted it all the time. She had no idea whether Cari and Dave felt the same way, and she didn't want to ask. If they didn't have the same escalating craving, mentioning it would expose her weakness, her lack of control.

The coke took away that subtle, steady pressure from the

world at large, the realization that every day she marched further from her twenties and closer to the end of the line for making a decision about having a child. Not making a decision, really. She knew she wanted a child — children — but she hadn't anticipated how quickly the turning point would come. Craig kept up his steady stream of comments, asking her to at least give him a date for when she thought she might be ready. His nagging to scale back on her work hours was subtler, but she got the message like a smack across the cheek – she couldn't work these hours and raise children, even with their agreement to share parenting equally. Something would have to change, and she wasn't ready for that, wasn't ready to let everything she'd worked so hard for just fade into the corner of her life. Once she scaled down, she'd never get it back.

Merely thinking about it made her lungs tighten. Her spacious living room opening out to the patio and the view of the valley, the long hallways, the sweeping staircase, and soothing rooms of her house in the hills of Los Altos felt constricting. The walls seemed to move closer, narrowing her options every day. It was terrifying. Cocaine lifted her brain above all of that.

The doorbell chimed. She jumped up. The corner of the coffee table gouged her shin. The inch-thick vase stood solidly in its spot, and the tulips remained motionless. She rubbed her shin and felt the torn skin, but no blood.

When she opened the door, Jenna was standing at the far

side of the porch as if she'd pressed the bell then inched back, ready to run away if the door wasn't answered immediately. She wore silk charcoal slacks and a pale pink blouse. Her hair was woven into a single braid that hung over her shoulder as if she'd placed it there for effect. Her pumps with three-inch heels were the identical color of her pants. Her expression was smug. Didn't she feel any shame? She owed fourteen hundred dollars, and she acted as if the issue was a simple payback of borrowed change. When Allison first met Jenna, she'd liked her. She still did, most of the time, it was just that over the years, Jenna's desire to be the constant center of attention wore on her nerves. More truthfully, it was Devon's near-worship of her that was tiresome, sometimes to the point of nausea.

"The check's on the kitchen counter." She opened the door wider.

"That's not a very friendly greeting," Jenna said.

"I'm tired. I worked all night. And I don't like it that I've had to beg you for money when we agreed up front that we'd do this together."

"You haven't had to beg." Jenna stepped into the foyer.

Allison closed the door and went into the kitchen. The tile was cool on her bare feet and took away a little of the edginess. "I shouldn't have had to ask at all," she said. "You knew you owed it, and you should have had the check ready the day of the shower."

"I didn't know you'd already bought the gift."

"The gift wouldn't have been an issue if you'd been on time with your share for the shower." She stopped at the counter where the check lay like an island of pale green in the center of the blue granite. She picked up the pen lying next to it and handed it to Jenna.

"It was an honest mistake."

"I don't think so."

Jenna turned the pen over, twisting it through her fingers. "How is everything going?"

"Fine."

"You've been really nervous lately. Super chatty," Jenna said.

"Really?"

"Not today, but at the shower. Yesterday."

"I don't know what you mean. Can you please sign it? I'm not up for socializing."

"I'm wondering how you're doing, overall."

"Everything's great."

"I found the coke in your bathroom, you know."

"Are you going to sign the check?"

"I thought you'd be more concerned that I know you're snorting cocaine than about making sure you get your money."

"You owe us."

"Are you strapped for cash?" Jenna said.

"Of course not. I just think you should pay us what you owe instead of playing games."

"I'm not playing games. I'm concerned. About the cocaine."

"Sign the check. There's nothing to discuss even though it sounds like you were snooping in my cabinets."

"We all do it."

"No, you apparently do it."

"What about the coke?" Jenna said. "Aren't you even a little worried? If people knew, it could ruin your career. Does Craig know? Or does he use it too? That would be really upsetting, knowing a family doctor was using cocaine. Although it's hard for me to imagine that, since he's so into healthy eating, and sports and all."

Jenna grabbed her braid, ran her fingers over the strands of hair and then tossed it over her shoulder. The movement made her long silver and turquoise earring swing against her neck. She managed to look both nervous and supremely confident. She placed the pen on the counter and folded her arms. The motion exposed her left hand. Her diamond glittered even though the room was growing dark as the sun settled toward the valley.

"Quit stalling. I want to lie down for a ten-minute nap before I start dinner. And I want to put this behind us."

"I was thinking ... even though we owe you money, since I know about the coke, maybe we can forget both things."

Allison looked at Jenna, waiting for her to smile, or blink, or something. Was Jenna actually trying to blackmail her? Because that's what it sounded like. All this time, she'd wondered whether Jenna knew what Devon was up to. She was pretty sure he hadn't mentioned his little side job, his extra revenue stream, but she hadn't been certain. Now it was clear that Jenna had no idea he was supplying the cocaine. It wasn't like he was full bore into dealing drugs. As far as she knew, she and three of his other friends from high school were Devon's only customers. Or clients, as he liked to call them, wanting to downplay the illegal aspect, and fantasize to himself about providing a necessary service.

It had happened last fall at their annual Halloween party. Allison had slipped out the front door and gone to sit in her car to take a quick hit. She'd wanted to avoid drinking that night, she had a court appearance the following morning, but she still wanted to have fun, keep her energy level high. And let's face it, she wanted those blissful feelings of all being right with the world that came with a tiny scoop of powder up her nose. No harm, no foul, no one hurt. No needles, no vomiting, no addiction. Just an energized happiness that helped her focus on the good things she had instead of the stress or the hassles or the disappointments. She had looked up and seen Devon outside her car window, grinning.

"Busted," he mouthed.

She leaned over and opened the passenger door. He walked around the back of the car, climbed in, and pulled the door closed.

He told her not to worry, it would be their secret. Isn't that what childhood friends were for, keeping each other's secrets? She'd still worry. If Craig found out, if the more conservative members of her firm knew … Then Devon removed that worry by putting himself right into the middle of it. "I don't know where you're buying, but I can help you with that. Scott Miller, remember him? Nerdy guy who wanted to start the baseball pool and skim a commission off the top during Junior year of high school?"

Allison remembered. She supposed people didn't change all that much. Someone who wanted to take a *commission* in a baseball pool could easily transition to dealing drugs.

"He's been asking me if I wanted to make a little extra cash supplying coke. Nothing big, not getting in deep, but something minor, as needed. Flying under the radar, too small-time to ever interest law enforcement."

"That would be awkward, buying it from you," Allison said.

"It's safer. You know you won't get anything bad, and you know I'm not going to do anything too risky."

That night, their friendship had shifted slightly. They weren't only supplier and customer, they were friends with a secret. He'd been right. It eased some of her fear, knowing he would be careful, not having to explain a text or a phone call from a stranger. It almost made her feel like she and Devon were best friends again, before Jenna entered the picture and turned him into a bit of a sap.

She loved that Jenna knew nothing about the coke. She guessed that Devon knew nothing about Jenna's blackmail plan either. She laughed at the expression on Jenna's face.

"What's so funny?" Jenna said.

"Are you trying to blackmail me?"

Jenna licked her lips. She smiled, but her mouth was still stiff around the edges. "That's kind of extreme."

"I don't think it is. You want me to forget you owe us money and in return, you won't tell anyone you *think* you found cocaine in my bathroom cabinet."

"It makes sense."

"Sign the check. I'm tired of this."

"Aren't you worried I'll tell someone?"

"Who would you tell? Devon?" Allison laughed again. More of a harsh, barking laugh, which she regretted because she didn't want Jenna to wonder why she was so unconcerned. This was too much fun. Knowing his devotion to Jenna might have a splinter. It wasn't that she wanted their marriage to fail, but it would be nice for Devon to be more normal again. He acted as if he'd just met the girl of his dreams. It was embarrassing.

Did Jenna really think she was afraid of a weak attempt at blackmail? She wasn't afraid of anything. Or at least not many things. Only one thing, really — her complete inability to overcome her terror of the dark. It surfaced when she least expected it. She walked to the wall near the breakfast room and flicked the switch. Light poured over the center island, making the blue look brighter, reflecting off the pine cabinets.

She could still feel the unrelenting blackness of that night. Their parents had been out for the evening. Her sister, feeling the power of being left in charge, sent Allison outside in the rain to get a Barbie doll she'd left on the back porch. Although her sister no longer played with Barbies, it had been a favorite. In an extreme coincidence, the electricity went out just as her sister locked the back door. The sky was thick with black clouds. Not even the shadows of the patio furniture were visible. She cried and pounded on the door, kicking the frame until her toes were pulpy. She'd been outside in the dark for nearly an hour before her sister relented. The darkness was terrifying, yes, but it had been her sister's cruelty that kept the haunting memory alive. She couldn't remember what additional threat her sister had whispered that prevented Allison from ever telling their parents.

Jenna tipped her head to the side. "What's wrong?"

"Nothing."

"Does Craig know what you're doing?" Jenna said.

"I don't want to discuss it. Quit wasting time."

Jenna took a few steps back and put her hand over her mouth. "I can't sign the check today."

"Why not?"

"We have a little cash flow imbalance right now. That's all. My mom had some problems, and we had to help her out."

"What's wrong with your mom?"

"She had some unexpected expenses. That's all."

"When will the cash flow problem be resolved?" Allison

said. Jenna was clueless. What was Devon doing with the income from his coke sales? Was he funneling that somewhere else? If they had a *cash flow* problem, Jenna clearly didn't know how bad it was.

"I don't know. Can't you wait a few weeks?"

"Why did you come over here if you knew you couldn't cover the check? Why didn't you call and tell me?"

Jenna stared at her but said nothing.

"Oh, I get it. To blackmail me."

"Please don't be like this. We're sort of trapped, there's nothing I can do."

Allison leaned against the edge of the counter. Jenna had no idea what it meant to be trapped. "Call me in a day or two and let me know when you can sign it." She walked to the kitchen door. Without turning, she said, "I don't mean to throw you out, but I really am tired. I need to get some sleep if I'm going to make it through the evening."

Jenna followed her into the foyer, walked past her, opened the door, and didn't turn back until she reached the edge of the porch. She turned slowly. Her braid moved across her shoulder like a serpent. "Think about what I said. We can help each other out. I thought we were close friends and isn't that what friends do?" She stepped down and walked along the curve of the driveway to her car. She hit the button, and the car beeped its readiness for her to open the door. She swung the door wide, scraping it on the Mexican sage that grew along the interior curve of the drive.

Allison closed the door and went into the kitchen. She filled a glass with ice, opened a can of cola, and poured it over the ice. She walked through the living room to the patio doors. The temperature was falling quickly now that the sun had dropped below the horizon, but she needed to gulp down some fresh air as much as she needed the shot of caffeine from her soda. She opened one of the doors a few inches.

What kind of woman blackmailed her friend? The kind of woman who was desperate. Or the kind of woman who was used to getting everything she wanted. But over a wedding shower and gift? She settled on the sofa and sipped her drink. She wasn't sure yet if she'd tell Devon. She also wasn't sure how long she planned to wait to force the signature on the check. She might be able to turn this around so she could get a few grams for free.

For the first time in a year, or more, she didn't feel quite so trapped. It made no sense because it was completely unrelated to the things that made her feel cornered – her biological clock, her growing desire for cocaine – but the idea of having choices, even in something so petty, made her feel she could move around a bit. She felt as if she'd been closed in a small, dark space, unable to stretch her arms over her head, unable to see, fear pricking at her stomach like a needle. Now she could extend her limbs in any direction, feel blood and oxygen traveling through her muscles. It was a terrific sensation. She wondered how long it would last.

Thirteen

WHEN JENNA WOKE on Saturday morning, she heard splashing in the swimming pool. It was surprising that she hadn't noticed that Devon was awake. Usually, she felt the absence of his body within moments of him leaving their bed. She turned over to face the round pewter clock on her nightstand. Its white face and large black numbers were easy to read even when the light was dim. Six-forty-three. She touched the silky metal casing. She loved that it looked like an antique, even though she'd found it at Pottery Barn.

She closed her eyes. Yesterday's conversation with Allison rushed to the surface of her mind. Allison's lack of concern had been baffling. Allison hadn't blinked or indicated with any movement of her body that Jenna's knowledge of her coke habit made her uncomfortable. She'd laughed, not once, but several times and Jenna still couldn't figure out whether or not it was nervous laughter. Something told her it wasn't. The tone was more cynical as if she knew something Jenna didn't. Maybe Craig did know and was okay with it. Maybe everyone at her firm was using some kind of drug to delude themselves into thinking it gave them an edge. Whatever it was, Jenna had been so certain her plan would work, and now she felt like she was in a worse position than ever. It was sickening to know that she'd tried to coerce Allison without getting Devon's agreement first.

The splashing had stopped, so either Devon was floating on his back, watching the morning light shift across the water, or he was out of the pool and would soon be back in the bedroom. She'd wanted to go for a run before they did their errands, so she'd best haul herself out of bed and wrap herself in spandex before he came into the room, eager to start the day. For her, everything was an effort lately. Tasks as simple as the necessary trips to the dry cleaner and the pharmacy were demoralizing because each one meant a transaction on a credit card that was precariously close to the limit. Whenever a clerk swiped it more than once because the machine hadn't read it correctly, or the machine took a few seconds longer than normal before printing a receipt, Jenna froze, knowing she didn't have another card that offered a better option.

She sat up and pushed the covers off her legs.

In the bathroom, she pulled her shorts and sports bra off the hook on the back of the door. She tugged on her clothes and brushed her hair into a ponytail, then braided it and added another elastic tie near the tip. She stepped back to check her reflection. The thin lip of flesh that had been forming at the waistband of her shorts had disappeared. The extra mile she'd added the last few weeks had done its job. Or maybe it was the result of fewer dinners out.

As she sat in the armchair near the balcony doors, tying her shoes, Devon's bare feet thumped on the stairs. He appeared in the bedroom doorway, his hair wet, but the rest of his skin smooth and dry. He held his towel balled up in his left fist. "How long are you going to run?"

"At least six miles. I was thinking about going for ten."

"After we get groceries, I wanted to get some new air mattresses. I think they both have leaks from sitting around all winter."

"We don't need those until summer."

"But it's warm enough to swim, and I like to float around when I'm done."

"I know that, but we can't afford it. You should be thinking about how we're going to cover that check."

"I said I'll handle Allison."

"How?" Although she wanted him to manage Allison, she really needed to tell him what she'd done. Later. Over lunch, or this evening. She didn't have to do it right this minute.

He looked gorgeous standing there. He hadn't moved from the doorway, and the darkness in the bedroom made his skin look tanned. His hair fell over his brow. She wanted to sweep it away from his eyes. There were a few drops of water on his upper chest, drawing her attention to his nicely shaped shoulders, and down to his arms and sides, every part of him luring her to touch him, to feel the strength in his body. "I guess a few air mattresses won't cost that much. It's just Allison … my mother."

He moved toward her and kissed her lightly on the lips and then on her earlobe. "It'll work out. I can get Allison to wait a month or two. I promise. Enjoy your run." He ducked into the bathroom, and a moment later she heard the shower water pounding the floor.

WHILE THEY WERE putting groceries in the trunk, Allison's image appeared on Jenna's phone, accompanied by a furious vibrating. Jenna let the call go to voicemail, but the knot of worry returned to her intestines. The voice mail alert popped up on the screen. She shoved the phone into her pocket and lifted the last bag into the trunk. "Allison just left a message," she said. "What, exactly, are you going to do and when are you going to talk to her?"

"I'll call her tomorrow."

They got into the car and left the parking lot. She let the sway of the car move her from side to side, as if the car was rocking her, trying to calm her, as it followed the curves of the road. If she relaxed her shoulders into the shape of the seat, kept her hands loosely folded on her lap instead of clutching the sides, she felt as if she and the car were a single entity.

They pulled into the driveway. A few raindrops splattered

on the windshield. Devon pulled into the garage, and they carried the groceries into the house and proceeded to fill the refrigerator drawers with plastic bags of vegetables and fruit, including the first strawberries of the season.

Her phone vibrated against her hipbone. She pulled it out of her pocket. There must have been a call while she was lifting the groceries out of the trunk and she hadn't felt the vibration, because the screen indicated three missed calls and one voicemail. "Third call from Allison," she said.

Devon pulled open the crisper drawer and dropped in a bag of salad greens and two red peppers. He closed the drawer. "I guess I should call her today."

"You think?"

Jenna set her phone on the table and went upstairs to the bedroom. She kicked off her sandals and flopped onto the bed. She was thirsty but had no energy to get up again. A nap might be nice. She really needed to tell Devon about her failed blackmail attempt before he called Allison. But she doubted he was rushing to do that right now. She closed her eyes.

WHEN JENNA WOKE, the house was silent. She got up and walked down the stairs to the living room. Empty. "Devon?" She went into the kitchen and saw a blue sticky note next to her mobile phone. *Went to the wine shop. Don't worry, it's not a problem.*

She crumpled the note and dropped it into the trash. Of

course it wasn't a problem. Nothing was a problem. Everything would be fine when the promotion came through. Until then they would juggle and shift and shuffle as if they had twenty decks of cards to play with. She grabbed a bottle of lemon-flavored sparkling water and twisted off the cap. Her muscles felt so slack she almost wanted to go for another run. It would clear the fuzziness from her brain and force her constant thoughts of Allison to subside. She picked up her phone, no missed calls, no text messages. That was a good sign.

The doorbell rang.

She walked into the entryway. She paused to take a long swallow of water. The entryway was narrow with an arched opening to the living room at the end. In front of her, the staircase made a tight turn and climbed steeply to the second-floor landing. The area wasn't as spacious as modern entryways, but she didn't care. The rust colored tile, in sharp contrast to the white plaster walls, made it feel spacious enough. She loved her house, the blend of old and new, the care that had been taken to modernize the kitchen and bathrooms without losing the character. Despite the burden of their debt, she needed to step back and remember what they had. So what if things were tight right now? It wouldn't be forever, and in the meantime, they had this beautiful home to enjoy, the swimming pool, good food, and each other. Most of the things she loved, she could do for free – her daily runs around tree-lined streets, cuddling with her husband, and eating healthy dinners on their back patio. She was making a big deal out of nothing. They'd get past this. So what if their friends occasionally whispered behind their backs.

She opened the door. Allison.

"Hi." Jenna took another swallow of lemon-flavored water.

"I'm here to have you sign the check."

"Devon was going to call you."

"He called, but I missed it."

Jenna looked past Allison. "Where's your car?"

"I rode my bike. I needed to burn off some energy."

"I'm sure." Jenna turned and walked to the living room.

"Why did he call?"

"He was going to talk to you about the money."

"Oh. Well, I decided I can't wait. You agreed to split things, and it's not right that you're stringing us along."

Jenna set her bottle on a coaster. She sat on the edge of the cranberry leather armchair and looked up at Allison. "We can't cover the check."

"You have to."

"Are you not listening? We can't."

"Things can't be that bad," Allison said.

Jenna felt as if Allison was going to peel off every single article of clothing until Jenna was completely naked, unable to hide anything from those staring, steel-colored eyes. "We canceled our gardener and housekeeper," Jenna said.

Allison glanced around the living room as if she expected to find evidence of dust piling up on the base of the lamp or along the mantle.

The sound of the side door opening and closing filled the silence. Jenna stood, longing for Devon's presence as if she hadn't seen him in months. Devon appeared in the archway. "Hi, Allie."

When people called Allison by the shortened form of her name, she corrected them sharply. That she let it slide with Devon was proof that he could manage her.

"Jenna's giving me the runaround about the money you owe for the shower and the wedding gift," Allison said.

"I'm not giving you the runaround. I told you we have a cash flow issue right now. My mother ..."

Allison held up her hand.

Devon looked at Allison. "Chill out. You know we're good for it."

Allison dropped her arm to her side. She heaved a loud sigh.

The landline rang. Jenna stepped around Devon into the entryway and went into the kitchen. She saw the display and picked up the handset. "Hi, Mom." Usually, she felt a warm glow of pleasure when her mother called, but this call felt more like a reprieve.

Her mother's voice was soft, breathy. "Hi, Sweetie. Can you drive me to the pharmacy? I need to get my prescription and pick up a few other things. If it's not too much trouble."

"I'm kind of in the middle of something." Really, she wasn't in the middle of anything she wanted to remain in the middle of. This might be a perfect escape route. Besides, she hadn't spent time chatting face to face with her mother in several weeks. It would be nice to catch her up on the latest gossip at work. Her mother's eagerness to hear about the nitty gritty details of Jenna's co-workers' lives was entertaining, and with her mother, there was no risk that sharing a juicy secret would come back to bite her professionally.

"It's starting to rain again, and I need new wiper blades. The one on the driver's side has a big section that's torn, and I can't really see. In fact, I'd like to pick those up too. Maybe Devon can put them on for me? We could stop for a glass of wine."

"Sure. Okay. I'll be there in twenty minutes. I just want to change into my boots."

Jenna returned to the living room. She couldn't tell where the conversation between Allison and Devon had progressed to but didn't want to find out. "I need to drive my mom on some errands. I'll be back in about two hours."

Devon nodded.

Jenna jogged up the stairs. She really did like Allison. They used to be close, despite Allison's extreme work schedule. When Allison was in law school, Jenna sometimes quizzed her before exams. Allison said that even though Jenna wasn't familiar with the material, she was the best study partner because she didn't give hints on the rare occasion when Allison hesitated over an answer. It must be the cocaine that had made Allison so acerbic. Allison needed help. Once they were past this money thing, Jenna would persuade her to start running to deal with her stress. They could even run together one day a week. They'd feel like friends again instead of debtor and creditor.

Fourteen

ALLISON WAS SURE Jenna wasn't coming back. Settling onto the sofa, she pried off her athletic shoes and lay on her side, propping herself up on her elbow. "Well, Dev. What are you going to do? It looks like Jenna is driving you to bankruptcy."

"It's nothing like that. Quit harassing her."

"You know what she tried to do, don't you?"

Devon edged into the room and sat on the arm of the sofa.

Allison pointed her toes toward him and smiled. "You don't know, do you."

"I'm not sure."

She laughed. "Blackmail."

"What?"

"Your beautiful wife tried to blackmail me. And I know it was all her idea, because why would you try to blackmail me about something when you'd be in more trouble than me?"

"What did she say?"

"You don't like being in the dark, do you. Well, neither do I. This wouldn't have happened if you'd just told me. It's like we're not even friends anymore. The longer you're with her, the further you drift away."

"That's how it is when you're married."

"Not when we used to be best friends."

"We're still friends."

"*Best* friends."

"You have Craig, I have Jenna. And we hang out just as much," Devon said.

"Why did you let her think she could extort money from me?"

"Don't make it sound so criminal. I told her not to mention it, but I guess she didn't understand why."

"Ah. So you are keeping secrets. Apparently, your additional revenue stream still isn't enough to allow you to pay your bills."

"It's temporary. I never expected my promotion to be delayed this long. In a few months ..."

"A few months is a long time when your cards are maxed out, and you owe your friends money."

"Our cards aren't all maxed out."

"That's not what it looked like when we went shopping before the wedding. Jenna had two cards declined before she admitted defeat."

Devon's eyes glittered. His breathing was too loud. He

stood and walked to the narrow window between the two sets of doors that opened onto the patio. The burgundy drapes were only partially drawn. He pushed them to the side, then ran his fingers down the fabric as if he was testing the strength of the weave.

"Don't look so morose," she said.

"None of this is Jenna's fault."

"Of course not."

He turned. "Give us a few weeks. We'll get it sorted out," Devon said.

"Why didn't you ask me that earlier? Why did you let her keep playing games with me?"

"I don't know." He let go of the drape.

"There's one way you could make up for it." She swung her legs over the side of the sofa and hopped to her feet. "How about a freebie. You and I. We could talk like old times. Jenna said she'd be gone for a few hours."

"I guess so."

"You have other customers, right? You can cover it. Not a lot. A line or two. Three would be quite nice, don't you think?" She walked over to the window and grabbed his wrist. "Come on. Where do you keep it?"

"In the cabinet near my side of the bed."

"Isn't that a little risky?" She felt a small thrill run through her nerves. She knew it was disloyal to Craig. She loved Craig more than anything, but she and Devon had been friends longer than forever. She didn't see why men and women couldn't still be friends when they were married. It shouldn't be any different than when they were single. Sometimes it felt like Jenna had moved in and sucked out Devon's soul. Knowing the coke was in the bedroom and that Jenna was being kept in the dark was very satisfying.

"She doesn't go in that cabinet. If I kept it in the office, she might stumble across it."

"How do you know she doesn't go in there? She snoops through my bathroom cabinets. It's not a stretch to think she checks out your things."

"It's buried inside a tissue box."

Allison laughed and tugged harder on his arm. "You're so clever. Let's go."

He resisted as she continued pulling at his arm, but after a few steps, his pace picked up, and he followed her up the stairs to the master bedroom.

The room was large with a fireplace on one wall. The drapes that covered the doors leading to the balcony were pulled closed, leaving the room in semi-darkness. The air was cool and smelled like coconut and something fruity – oranges maybe.

Devon went to the nightstand on the right side of the bed and opened the cabinet. He pulled out a blue floral box of tissues and yanked out the tissue poking through the cellophane. He reached in and lifted out several more tissues in a neat stack and then pulled out a baggie containing five separately wrapped packages of cocaine. He removed one of the packages and a razor blade wrapped in foil. He left the plastic bag on the bed.

In the bathroom, Allison pushed the bronze statue closer to the mirror.

"Don't touch that." Devon pulled a small mirror out of the drawer, set it on the counter between the two sinks, well away from the statue, and placed the tiny package and razor blade on top.

"You're joining me," she said.

"I shouldn't be consuming the inventory."

"It's a small amount. You'll make it up in sales to me."

Devon opened the packet and scraped a small bit of powder onto the mirror. He unwrapped the razor blade and chopped the powder. He stroked the blade along the pile, separating it into four lines. He pulled out his wallet and removed a twenty-dollar bill. Once the bill was rolled in a tight tube, he handed it to Allison. "Ladies first."

Allison giggled. She calmed herself so she wouldn't accidentally blow the powder off the mirror and lose precious milligrams. She held the bill to her nose, breathed in the smell of money, then removed it. She let out all her breath, then held it up again, bent over the counter, and drew one of the lines into her left nostril. The drug shot up into her sinuses. She closed her eyes and smiled. After a moment, she put the rolled bill to her right nostril and took in the second line. She handed the bill to Devon. "Your turn."

Devon inhaled the remaining lines with two sniffs. While

he rinsed and dried the small mirror, Allison stroked the statue's arm. It was over three feet tall, a nude woman running her hand down the inside of her thigh. "I've always wondered, why does Jenna have a statue of a woman playing with herself?"

"She's not playing with herself." Devon looked at her reflection, frowning.

"I bet it wasn't cheap. She sure knows how to spend money."

"I bought it for her birthday."

"Oh."

"It reminds me of Jenna," he said.

Allison rolled her eyes, watching herself in the mirror, smiling at her mock horror, and feeling the drug rush through her, making her alert, filling her with a sense of benevolence, even toward Jenna.

"She looks like a goddess," Devon said.

"Oh come on." She pinched the figure's nose.

"Stop grabbing it like that. And quit talking about Jenna like that. I thought she was your friend."

"Of course she is. But a goddess? You realize how ridiculous that sounds."

He put the mirror in the drawer. "That's how I feel."

Allison ran her finger down the statue's neck, between her breasts. She pinched the left nipple.

"Don't!" Devon grabbed her arm and twisted it away from the figure. "Why are you like this?"

"Ow. I'm not like anything. It's kind of gauche, that's all. And calling someone a goddess is a little extreme. You're obsessed. She's taken over your brain so that you aren't even normal anymore." She pinched the right nipple.

Devon pushed her sideways with his hip and grabbed the statue off the counter.

She laughed. "Don't get so upset. It's a hunk of metal. It's not Jenna herself. Because if it were, she'd be facing the other way, wiggling her ass at you like she does with all the men, and then you wouldn't be able to think straight. Although I'm not sure ..."

"Don't say that!" His face was pale, then flushed red as he swung the statue over his head.

She felt the bronze weight thud into the top of her shoulder.

DEVON FELT SICK as Allison collapsed under the force of the statue. "Oh, shit. I'm sorry." He realized he was talking to himself because Allison's eyes were closed. "Oh, God." He set the statue on the counter and squatted near Allison. She wasn't dead, was she? She couldn't be dead. He picked up her arm and felt around her wrist, not really sure how to take a pulse. It seemed like there was a gentle throbbing, but he couldn't tell whether it was Allison's or his own. He pressed his fingers under her jaw and felt blood pumping but still wasn't certain if it belonged to her or him.

He sat down on the bathmat. What the hell was he going

to do? She couldn't be dead. He should call 9-1-1. What would he say? How would he explain why they were in the bathroom? He could say he found her in there, she'd excused herself, and when she didn't return, he went to check on her. He had to put away the coke and tissue box first. No. Why couldn't he think logically? The coke wasn't the problem, it was Allison's unconscious body.

He reached up, straining across her motionless form. He yanked open the drawer and pulled out the mirror. He held it over Allison's nose. A faint spot of moisture appeared. He held his breath, pulled the mirror away, wiped off the damp spot and put it back near her nostrils. More vapor. He sighed, shoved the mirror back in the drawer and slammed it closed. What if her neck was broken? Should he move her? He should call 9-1-1. The longer he waited, the fewer options he had.

He looked up at the bronze figure. It looked perfectly fine, cool and serene. He stared at Allison's immobile face. Surely there would be horrible bruising, maybe even more damage – internal bleeding. He couldn't pass this off as a friend slipping in the bathroom, even if he went to the trouble of running the shower and getting some water on the floor.

He was taking too long. He couldn't keep waffling. He could wait until Jenna got home. God, he was disgusting. Jenna deserved better than this. She didn't need a husband who struck a woman because she mocked him and then waited for his wife to tell him what to do.

He'd liked Allie from the first day her family moved in next door. She teased and taunted him. He liked it that a girl could kid around like a boy, that she didn't cry when she was hurt. Even in junior high, she kept up with him when they raced their bikes to the creek in the open space preserve a few miles from their neighborhood. Allie was right. They had been best friends.

He didn't want to stand up and see his face looking back at him. What kind of guy wailed on his childhood friend because she made fun of a statue? He had to think. Had to do something. Sitting on the bathroom floor until Jenna came home was not the answer.

Allison sighed. Her leg moved, straightening somewhat.

She would be so pissed. Would she try to punish him legally? He owed her and Craig over a thousand bucks. He was supplying her with cocaine, and his wife had tried to blackmail her. Now this. He had to think, but his thoughts slid around like uncooked egg on a tile floor. Maybe it was the coke.

Another sigh escaped from Allison's lips, and they remained partially open. Oh God. He jumped up and stepped into the bedroom. He jerked his head, looking around the room, not sure what he was looking for, a thought brewing below the surface of his conscious mind, that he had to get her out of here, had to buy himself some time to think about how he was going to correct the situation. Jenna's bathrobe was tossed over the back of the chair in the corner where she liked to sit with the doors open on weekend mornings in the summer, tossing seed to birds on the balcony. She got them to come right up to the threshold. He teased her that someday they were going to hop right into the bedroom and then what would she do? He grabbed the bathrobe and yanked the silky cord out of the loops.

Back in the bathroom, he turned Allison on her side. She moaned, which startled him. The silky belt wouldn't do. He ran downstairs to the utility room. He grabbed a coil of rope out of the cabinet and a roll of duct tape. He hurried back up to the bathroom. He wound the rope around her ankles and tied five knots. It was the rough, scratchy kind, but it was only temporary. Damn. Scissors. He reached up and fished around in the drawer. He used Jenna's tiny nail scissors to gnaw at the thick tape. After several minutes he realized it would have been faster to run back down and get something heavy duty, but he was halfway there now.

Once her wrists were taped he straightened up, panting. He hadn't exerted himself, but the rush of adrenaline made his heart pound. He had no idea how he would find his way out of this mess, but he didn't have time to think about that right now. He glanced at the bedroom clock. Seven-twenty. He should still have a little more time. He stared at Allison, unable to focus his thoughts. He picked up the tape, gummed the scissors through until he had another piece, and patted it over her mouth.

He thudded down the stairs to the kitchen, grabbed the key to the basement padlock. He went through the living room and outside to the basement door that opened at an angle from the side of the foundation. He opened the padlock and lifted the door. Seven steps led down to his future wine cellar. He went to the small wooden shed where they kept pool supplies and grabbed a stack of towels. He went down the steps, found the nut tied to the light bulb string, and yanked on it. The basement smelled clean, and there was no moisture despite all the rain. Once they started work constructing it into a wine cellar, the floor would be finished, probably with tile, or maybe hardwood. He wasn't sure what was best, he'd have to look into that. He placed two towels on the dirt and folded one into a pillow. She would be okay until he could think this through.

When he returned to the bathroom, Allison was still unconscious. He squatted as if he was lifting weights, slid one arm under her shoulders and the other behind her knees, and lifted her like a baby. She was lighter than he'd expected. He turned sideways to maneuver her through the bathroom door and then again out to the landing. Edging his way down the stairs was tricky since he couldn't see his feet and her body felt heavier trying to walk down. He went through the living room to the open back door. It was a relief that it had stopped raining and the pavement had dried enough that he didn't have to worry about slipping. Once he reached the bottom step in the basement, it was only a few feet across the hard-packed dirt to where he'd arranged the towels.

He squatted and laid her on the towels, covered her with two more, and stood. She hadn't moved. Looking at her sleeping face gave him pause. He knew with a deep, nagging tremor that this was making his problems infinitely worse. Yet, what other choice was there? He should call the paramedics, he should ask Jenna what to do, he should stay here and make sure she woke up. When she woke would she start moaning? Of course she would. Could she manage to make a sound loud enough to be heard in the house? There was no way to check. He'd have to hope that between the duct tape and the flooring and insulation, no sound could filter out.

He turned off the light. Allison had been terrified of the dark when she was a kid, but she must have outgrown that. Had he outgrown his own childhood fears? To be honest, he didn't remember having any. He'd been a happy kid. If there was a fear, it was that he'd turn out like his father, miserly and always spoiling everyone's fun by announcing what they could and, mostly, could not, afford. He turned the light back on, went up the basement stairs, closed the door over the opening, and inserted the padlock.

Inside the house, he collapsed on the living room sofa. He'd have to find a way to get back down to the basement later tonight. He'd have to give her food and water. Not to mention figure out how she was going to relieve herself. He'd bring blankets too, so she was well covered and had more padding. He might want to think about giving her some Vicodin, there was some in the bathroom cabinet from the time Jenna got a bad sprain running in the foothills.

He must be out of his mind. He should go down there now and untie her and call for help. How long would it be until Craig got in touch, asking if they'd seen her? The bike. She'd ridden her bike over. He jumped up and ran through the entryway to the front porch, leaving the door swinging open behind him. The bike was under the portico between the house and garage. There was nowhere to put it that would guarantee Jenna wouldn't stumble across it. Even covering it with a tarp in the garage might attract her attention. He wheeled it around through the side gate and unlocked the cellar door. He hoisted the bike on his shoulder and carried it down the stairs. Allison was still asleep. Was it called sleep when someone was unconscious? Was the length of time she'd been out considered dangerous or was it normal? How could there be so many things he knew nothing about? This was his last chance. He could still untie her and carry her back, but the thought of facing Jenna any minute, explaining what he'd done, was worse than thinking about what might happen later.

He went back around the side of the house and glanced at the neighbors to his right. He felt like every step he took demonstrated his stupidity – looking for observers after the fact was proof of that. The fence had lattice at the top, extending the height of the fence to over six feet. It was laced with vines on the neighbor's side and lined with giant birds of paradise on his side. The property behind was ringed with pine trees, and the house across the street had a brick wall topped by iron fencing. Large shrubs grew behind the wall. It appeared that he was safe from curious neighbors.

He returned to the kitchen and took the scotch out of the liquor cabinet. He poured two shots, leaving the bottle on the counter.

After he settled on the sofa and put his glass on the coffee table, he pulled off his shoes. Only a single floor lamp was turned on. While he'd been busy, it had grown dark outside. He couldn't see any mud or dampness on the carpet, but he turned over his shoes to check the soles. They looked clean. Once again he was checking for mistakes after it was too late. Everything he'd done today was a mistake, but there was no other choice.

Her Blackberry. She always carried it. He felt around the cushions of the sofa. He slid off, laid on the floor, and shoved his arm underneath the sofa. Where would she have left it? She never went anywhere without it. He raced up the stairs and into the bedroom. It was lying on the nightstand. He powered it down, removed the battery, and stuck it inside his work boot in the back of the closet.

When she woke up he would beg her forgiveness, remind her of good times. She'd get over it, especially if he offered her free coke. Of course, that would push his financial situation to the breaking point.

ALLISON HAD AN ache that ran from her neck to her hip. It was difficult to breathe. Something covered her mouth. She tried to lick her lips. What was wrong? She opened her eyes. What the hell? She couldn't move. She twisted and tried to sit up. Her ankles were tied, and her wrists felt glued together. The only thing she seemed to be able to do was blink away the tears from the pain and roll from side to side. But no matter how hard she strained, she couldn't maneuver herself into a sitting position.

What had happened? She closed her eyes, pressing tears out. The tape across her mouth pulled at the skin of her cheeks. She took deep, wheezing breaths through her nose. Trying to cry out was pointless, all that emerged was a strangled squeal, like a pig.

Instead of seeping slowly into her brain, the memory smacked against the inside of her skull the same way Devon had smacked her with that ridiculous statue. *A goddess.* The guy was sick, his brain taken over by Jenna and whatever it was that drew him to her. The idea that he would do something like that, like this, was almost worse than the pain along the entire left side of her body. She rolled onto her back, hoping it would relieve the pressure. He better not have damaged anything. What the hell did he think he was going to do? Why would he tie her up like this and throw her ... where?

She was in a cave, a single light bulb hung from the

ceiling, and she was lying on towels. The room smelled like dirt. The only thing that kept it from being a cave was the wood framing. Of course, his future wine cellar. And she hadn't even been able to enjoy the coke. It was absorbed into her body now, the rush over. Possibly a little tingle still, but how could she tell? God damn him. He must have been scared after he hauled off and hit her. This was his solution? If she didn't feel like kicking him in the balls, she would laugh. Or cry.

No. She would kill him. They were having fun, sniffing a little coke, best friends, like it used to be. All she'd done was kid him about worshipping Jenna. He used to love it that she teased him, he said she wasn't like other girls, super sensitive, unable to take a joke. She gave it right back. Now, the Devon she'd known was gone. She made one teasing comment, and he bashed her with a hunk of metal? There was no longer any point in being friends. Instead of feeling bad for hurting her, knocking her unconscious, he decided to tie her up, wrap duct tape around her, and dump her in the basement. It was humiliating and painful. She was scared to death.

Apparently, he was going to keep her here until he figured out what to do. If he thought that would make her compliant, he didn't know her at all. Craig must be frantic. She had tons of work to do. She would kill him. She wasn't sure how, considering her situation, but she would. What if he waited days before coming back? Surely he wouldn't.

As if something ripped loose inside, all her rage dissolved

and she started to sob, although even that was difficult with her mouth sealed shut. She willed herself to stop. If her nose clogged up, she would have serious trouble breathing.

Still, the tears came as her mind raced from the eventual need to pee to the light bulb, wondering how much life it had left. If it went out, she would die.

Fifteen

THE HOUSE WAS dark when Jenna pulled into the driveway. She pressed the remote and drove forward. She enjoyed the cozy feeling of knowing she was home, tucked safely into the confines of the garage. It surprised her that every time she pulled in next to Devon's Jeep, she felt content, knowing he was there, waiting for her, that he'd always be there. Years ago, before they lived together, she'd had the same bubble of happiness when she came home from work and saw the dark blue Jeep parked in front of her condo.

She pressed the remote again and went through the portico to the side door. The hallway and office were dark. A single light glowed from the kitchen, and she could see a faint bit of light spilling out of the living room. "Devon?"

"In here," he called.

The only light in the living room was the floor lamp at the opposite end of the couch from where Devon was seated.

A scotch glass with a half-inch of dark gold liquid in it sat at the edge of the coffee table. Jenna walked into the room and nudged the glass back from its precarious spot. "Why are the lights out?"

"I didn't notice it had gotten so dark."

"How could you not notice?" She set her purse on the floor and leaned over and kissed the top of his head. His hair was soft on her face.

"How did things work out with Allison?"

"Fine."

"What does that mean? Did she back off?"

"I think so."

"So she'll give us some breathing room? For how long?"

"I don't know."

"What's wrong?" She sat next to him and leaned her head against his shoulder. She wriggled closer, nestling the top of her head against the side of his neck. She slid her arm around his waist. After a moment, he lifted his arm and draped it around her shoulders, but he didn't seem aware of her presence. She scooted away. "Was it humiliating? Explaining things to her?"

"No."

"Then why do you seem so down?"

He picked up his glass. "I'm going to have another shot. Do you want one?"

"No. I had two glasses of wine with my mother. Now I'm hungry."

"I'm not."

"Ok. I guess I could have the leftover fettuccine. But you shouldn't drink and not eat anything."

"I'm not hungry right now. Maybe later."

"Aren't you going to tell me what Allison said? I want to know how much time we have and whether you got her to understand she can't change her mind every two days."

"In a minute." He turned and walked out of the room.

She leaned back. Things must have gone badly. Otherwise, he would explain the details, he'd be assuring her there was nothing to worry about, that he had it under control. He was gone longer than it took to pour a shot. When he returned, he carried the half-full bottle.

"You're sure you don't want some?" Devon said.

"Is something wrong?"

"I need to tell you some stuff."

"And I need a drink for that?"

"Maybe."

"What happened?"

Devon set the bottle and his glass on the table and left the room. He returned with a glass and set it next to his. He uncorked the bottle, poured a bit into the second glass, and handed it to her.

She raised her glass for their ritual toast, but he ignored her and took a sip of his drink. "I hate having to tell you this," he said, "and I hope you're going to forgive me."

She ran her finger around the rim of her glass. She hadn't

really wanted anything to drink. She was only doing it because it seemed to reassure him that they were on the same team, that she would support him in whatever he was going to tell her.

"I don't know where to start," he said.

"Just say it."

"When the promotion didn't go through I didn't know how we were going to manage the mortgage and all our other expenses."

She ran her finger around the glass again. The crystal let out a sharp hum.

"Don't do that. It gives me the chills."

She leaned back on the couch, leaving her drink untouched on the table.

"Scott Miller," he said. "Remember him? He came to our wedding. I knew him from high school."

"I think so."

"I ran into him last summer when I first heard my promotion might be delayed. He said someone like me could make easy cash."

"You didn't get into some pyramid thing, did you?"

"Do I look stupid?"

She shook her head. She'd never thought that. He was just too optimistic, lacking the capacity for worry. It wasn't that worry was a positive trait, but not having any sense of concern for the future ... no, that wasn't right. He thought about the future, but he assumed it would always be good.

The promotion would always be there, the raise would be more than anticipated, the stock market would trend up, or at least the investments they chose would run counter to the market when it was down, and better than the market when it was up. They'd be flush before the mortgage rate on the house was due for renewal. Nothing but the best possible outcome, as if imagining it would make it so.

"Anyway, Scott said that because I associate with people that have a lot of money, people that want to have a good time and can afford it, there was income potential. People who don't need to just drink beer like the average Joe to change their mood, but people who can afford a classier high. People who can afford cocaine."

Jenna picked up her glass. "What are you saying?" She took a tiny sip and set the drink back on the table.

"I didn't want you to threaten Allison ..." he coughed. He swirled the scotch in his glass, then held it to his lips and swallowed the rest of it in one gulp. "The reason I didn't want you to threaten her about using coke is because I'm the one selling it to her."

For a moment, Jenna wondered if her pulse had stopped. Her muscles were stiff, even the thoughts seemed to have paused in her head. She should be angry, scared, so many things. She should say something, but her mind refused to come up with any words.

"I know it wasn't very smart, but having the cash helped."

"It obviously didn't help enough," she said. That was not

what she wanted her first reaction to be. The problem was, she couldn't think. There was nothing there beyond the numbness, the sensation that her life had stopped moving. The darkness in the house, and outside the windows, wiped out the rest of the world. She stared at her glass. She wanted a drink, but couldn't find the strength to reach forward.

"Why aren't you saying anything?" He rubbed his jaw.

"What is there to say? You could go to prison."

"I won't. I won't get caught. That's the beauty of it. I'm not involved with serious dealers, and the people I'm supplying have a lot more to lose, so it's not like they're going to do anything or get caught themselves. And they use it in moderation because they don't want to damage their careers. They're not addicts."

"Everyone who uses chemicals is an addict. Heck, we're addicts because we can't go a day without coffee."

"Yes, we could."

"Have you ever tried? I did, once. The headache was so wicked I had to keep popping Excedrin." She paused. She couldn't believe she was talking about coffee. "What were you thinking? Are you still doing it? Of course you are. How many people?"

"Allison and three guys at work."

"Great. So you're not only committing a felony, you're risking your job at the same time. Why would you think that a person who thinks snorting coke is a good idea will be cautious? How can you trust them not to tell two other people and then they'll tell people? Half your office might know."

"No, they wouldn't say anything."

"How do you know that?"

"Because it would hurt them more than me."

"People don't think. They can't keep their mouths shut. And why are we even talking about this? It's not like getting caught is the only issue. I don't understand why you would risk everything we have."

"Because we needed cash. Your mother ..."

"Don't blame my mom for this. She has nothing to do with it."

Devon's eyes glittered. He set his glass on the table and dribbled more scotch into his glass.

"You don't need any more," Jenna said.

"I do."

She picked up the cork and used her other hand to gently lift his fingers away from the neck of the bottle. When he didn't resist, she pulled it toward her and stuffed the cork inside. She picked up her glass and held it with both hands. She leaned back and cradled the glass in her lap.

His eyes were even shinier now. "I'm sorry. I'm so sorry. I wanted this house for you, for us. We should have waited until the promotion was a done deal. I'm sorry. I'd do anything for you, and I thought this would help. I thought it was worth the risk. I love you so much."

She put her glass back on the table, got up, and walked

around to where he stood. She moved up behind him, wrapped her arms around his waist, and rested her head between his shoulder blades. "I know you do."

For several minutes, neither one spoke.

"Is that how you got Allison to back down?"

His shoulder blades shifted as he nodded his head.

"How did you leave it?"

"What do you mean?"

"Are they going to wait until summer for us to pay them back? Are they going to forget it completely?"

"I'm not sure. At least for now, she won't bring it up again."

Jenna pulled away from him. "How did you leave it, then? Does Craig know about any of this?"

"Are you kidding? Mr. Straight-and-Narrow, I-never-do-anything-wild-and-crazy?"

"But do you know that for sure? That doesn't mean he hasn't figured it out."

"He doesn't know."

"So how did you actually get her to agree to wait?"

"I told her I'd give her some coke for free."

"How can we afford that?" The minute the words were out, she realized what she'd said, what her mind was really doing below the frozen surface. No matter what happened, it was *we,* would always be *we.* She couldn't believe he'd done something so risky, and yet, he'd done it for her. She moved against his back again, holding him more tightly this time, pressing her cheek against his spine, slipping the tips of her fingers into the waist of his cargo shorts. Holding him was her own drug, it made her feel whole. She couldn't imagine letting go. He was trying. He was so happy and so sure that things would work out. It was addictive in itself, the way he expected the best. He was always charming, always in a good mood. "You didn't use it, did you?"

"Once or twice."

"Why? Why would you do that? No matter what Allison thinks, or what your buddy says, or how any of these people think they can control how much they need, it's a dangerous drug."

"It's not a regular habit. I tried it out, that's all."

"Only once or twice?"

"Maybe three times."

She squeezed tighter. "Are you going to stop now?"

"It wasn't that much. Really. You have to believe me."

"I meant stop selling it," Jenna said.

"We need the cash."

"We don't. We'll figure out something else. Maybe sell one of the cars. I could take the train to work. Or you could ride your bike."

"That's too much hassle," he said.

"We could do something."

"I can't think about it right now."

They should be making a plan. For all her admiration and love of his sense of confidence, it formed an impenetrable shell. How could he refuse to think about it? Now that she knew, she couldn't imagine thinking about anything else. They needed to talk it through, make sure they slowly got Allison relying on someone else. She didn't like Allison's proprietary attitude toward him, clinging to the years she'd known him when Jenna wasn't around, acting as if that gave her some inside track, a hold on him that Jenna couldn't break. Devon didn't see it that way, but she still didn't like it. Now, she had to find a way to not only get the money paid back but also stop the drug sales. Only when both of those things happened would she loosen Allison's grip on him. Or at least part of it. She'd never be able to erase those years, never be able to insert herself into those memories, but at least she could keep Allison from dragging him down with her.

If Allison hadn't decided she couldn't do her damn job, or whatever her problem was, without using illegal drugs, without destroying her health and potentially her marriage, threatening the very career she was trying to prop up, Devon wouldn't be in this position. She was certain he would never have pursued it if he didn't have an easy, needy customer like Allison. He wouldn't have had the blatant lack of fear that allowed him to approach other people. Allison probably convinced him it was safe because she was his best bud, that she would never tell anyone, and so he was lulled into thinking it was a good idea. What was it about the people you'd known as a child that made you think they were smarter than everyone else, that they couldn't be wrong, couldn't make terrible mistakes? People from your past lived their whole lives in a misty cloud of innocence.

She pulled away and went back to the couch. "You have to think about it. Right now. That's how you got in this situation. You need to tell Allison to find someone else if she really thinks that's what she wants to be doing – snorting her life away."

"She's not snorting her life away."

"Why is she even doing it? She's risking her job, maybe her marriage. For sure her health. I guess that means they aren't having kids for a while. Even though Craig talks about it all the time as if it's going to happen any day."

"It's not like she's addicted."

"I'm sure."

"Lots of people do it. Several people in her office are into it. For the edge."

"If anyone thinks it gives them an advantage, they're deluded."

"There is this surge of excitement, a feeling that you're more confident, less worried. You feel as if everything is right with the world."

"When are you ever worried?"

"It happens." He grinned.

She picked up her glass and sipped the scotch. It burned her lips, then slid down her throat like a thick blanket, and eased its way up to her brain. She waited while some of the tension dissolved under its effect. It was unbelievable that smart, well-educated people truly thought a drug could improve their performance. How could you be so intelligent and so brainless at the same time?

Devon's phone vibrated on the coffee table, the sound of someone rattling a spoon against the inside of a glass. He grabbed it. "Shit."

"What's wrong?"

"It's Craig."

"So?"

The phone continued shuddering.

"Aren't you going to answer? Or are you worried she told him and he's pissed at you?"

He didn't speak for a moment. Then in a quiet voice, he said, "Yeah."

The phone went silent. He continued to stare at the screen. "Four text messages from Craig," he mumbled. The phone vibrated again. He swiped his thumb across the screen and held the phone to his ear. "Hey, Craig. What's up?"

Jenna sipped her drink while Devon listened to Craig. The sound of his voice was louder than normal, but she couldn't make out his words.

"Don't know," Devon said. "No."

What was going on? Devon's voice sounded almost harsh as if he was angry at whatever Craig was saying.

Devon was silent while Craig was clearly going on at length about something.

"I said I don't know." He paused. "Will do." He clicked

off the phone and shoved it in his pocket. He picked up the scotch bottle, yanked out the cork, and poured until his glass was a third full of the dark gold liquid.

"That's too much. What's the matter?" Jenna put her glass on the table. She reached for Devon's while he was shoving the cork back into the bottle. "What's wrong?" she said.

"Nothing. Craig was wondering if we'd seen Allison."

"Why?"

"She hasn't come home yet," Devon said.

"Really?"

"She probably stopped somewhere else to take a break. Maybe she's out of shape," he laughed.

"But it was raining again."

"He wanted to know if she was with us. I said she's not. With us."

"Did he know she came over here?"

"I don't think so."

"Where else would she have gone?"

Devon walked around the table and sat beside her. He set his glass down and put his arm around her shoulders. "Who knows."

"Is he worried?"

"Of course he is, but she'll turn up."

"I hope she's okay. What if she's hurt and goes to the hospital and they do blood work and find cocaine? What if Craig finds out and she tells him you sold it? You know how he is," Jenna said.

"That's a lot of *what ifs*. Don't worry. Let's focus on what we can do if I'm gonna quit selling this stuff. Maybe we should take money out of our 401k's."

"That's crazy. It'll make things worse. Think about the taxes next year," she said.

"By then I'll be a Director."

Jenna picked up her glass and took a sip. It was almost empty. She was tired, anxious to eat something, take off her clothes, and slip into bed. Despite her slow sips, she'd downed the alcohol too fast. On top of the two glasses of wine, it made her brain spongy. Maybe it was fear. Maybe it was hurt that he'd hidden this from her. What other secrets was he keeping?

Sixteen

THE MORNING LIGHT glared through the remaining clouds as Beth pulled into the Porter's driveway. The first glimpse of their house always caught her off guard. Built in the twenties, it seemed taller than two stories, with lots of long, narrow windows fronted by grille-work. It was painted a shade of pink that made her think of Pepto-Bismol. Although she'd never say those derogatory words out loud, and it wasn't really quite that pink, the thought refused to go away. The house was truly beautiful, but she couldn't get past that color.

She felt awkward, dropping by on a Sunday morning without an advance text message or call, without an invitation. Who did that any more? When her grandmother was young, maybe even when her mother was Beth's age, neighbors and friends dropped by to visit, or at least that's the way Beth imagined it. Now, people left a message on one social network or another. They called, sometimes. Even though she was quite content with her life, she sometimes wondered if there hadn't been some things that were better before she was born. Maybe those things still happened outside of Silicon Valley, or outside of California, or in other parts of the world. Maybe it was only her group of friends and her neighborhood where people behaved like this, locking themselves away. In college, she'd been deluded into thinking the world was more social. She and her friends dropped by each other's dorm rooms multiple times a day, treating them as second homes.

She turned off the engine and sat for a moment staring at the bilious pink. Jenna loved it. She thought the color highlighted the character of the time period when the house was built. The property was landscaped with tropical plants – birds of paradise and various types of palm trees, including two coconut palms that stood on either side of the driveway, bending toward each other as if they wanted to mirror Devon and Jenna's magnetic attraction. Sometimes the trees left her wondering if she and Michael had the same kind of magic that Devon and Jenna seemed to possess. Those two couldn't keep their eyes or their hands off each other. Devon constantly had his arm around Jenna's waist, or she was hanging on him like a groupie. When they weren't clinging to each other, Beth often caught Devon staring at Jenna with such adoration, she knew their devotion wasn't faked. She could see in his eyes a complete lack of awareness of anything else around him. The dilated pupils and his seeming isolation from any peripheral sound as his gaze locked on Jenna while she talked or laughed, was one of the purest, truest things she'd ever witnessed.

She thought she had the same thing with Michael, but she wasn't always one hundred percent sure. It would miss the point if she asked him, or anyone else, whether he stared at her with such unvarnished infatuation. On the other hand, that kind of intensity was destined to fade at some point. And did she really want that? She wanted real love, the kind that lasted all the way through sagging flesh, and crepey skin, straight to death. All the same, if she was honest, she envied Jenna. She hated herself for that, but she did.

The doorbell was too loud, amplifying her fear that she would face an unwelcoming response from Jenna or Devon. It was possible they weren't home, or wouldn't answer. She wasn't sure if she felt a sense of foreboding because she was intruding, because she knew she was being nosey, or because she had an all-consuming sense of unease after Craig's phone calls. Craig hadn't actually been crying when she spoke to him last night, and again half an hour ago, but she heard a quaver in his voice that said tears weren't impossible, that he was exerting every effort to keep himself from losing it. When he hadn't heard from Allison all night, he'd called the police. Their response had been limp, saying they had no reports of bicycle accidents and was he sure she hadn't spent the night with a friend or relative?

Beth suggested they all get together, go in force to the

police and persuade them something was very wrong, but in Michael's view, the police were probably right. Allison was with a friend, or she and Craig had a fight, and she was punishing him by not calling. *Didn't that sound like something Allison would do?*

Michael had a work project that absolutely needed to get some forward momentum this morning, he said. But if it made her feel better, she should join forces with Devon and Jenna, it couldn't hurt anything.

She pressed the bell again. The tops of her feet were warm under the thick leather of her Birkenstocks, but her toes were cold. She curled them slightly and folded her arms around her rib cage, pulling the sleeves of her sweatshirt over her knuckles. It was only nine. As soon as the sun climbed higher, she'd be appropriately dressed, but right now she wished she'd worn jeans instead of a skirt.

The deadbolt turned, and the door swung open. "Beth! What are you doing here?" Devon said.

Beth shivered. She'd expected him to be surprised, to act startled, but his voice sounded almost brutal as if he hated her. She waited for him to apologize. Instead, he stared at her with hard, slightly red eyes.

"Have you talked to Craig?" Beth said.

Devon leaned against the door so his weight pushed it toward her as if his desire was to close it in her face rather than answer the question.

"Last night, why?"

"Allison didn't come home all night."

"Really?"

"You're not surprised? You're not scared?"

"I'm surprised, and kind of worried."

"You don't sound like it. Can I come in?" She inched closer to the door.

"Why?"

"It's cold out here." Why did she have to explain? Why did she even have to ask? He should have immediately invited her in. Instead, she got the feeling he wanted her to change her mind about talking to him, to hurry back to her car and leave him alone.

"Oh, right." Devon stepped back and made the opening a few inches wider, forcing her to turn partially to the side and squeeze herself through the narrow space. The entryway wasn't any warmer than the porch, and she shivered as he stepped around her to close the door. Was it the air in the hallway making her cold, or was there something about the door closing behind her, Devon's obvious lack of desire to invite her inside the house, or something else that made her bones feel laced with ice. "Craig is nearly hysterical," she said.

"He wasn't when I talked to him."

"Of course not, Allison hadn't been gone all night. He's called her parents and her sister. He called Cari and Dave from her office, and none of them have heard from her since Friday. She went for a bike ride while Craig went to the gym. When she didn't show up by five, he was pretty worried."

"Did he call the police?"

Beth walked past him into the living room and sat on the sofa. She looked out at the backyard, past the patio furniture at the swimming pool. The black bottom made it dark as a lake. The waterfall that usually tumbled over the pile of rocks wasn't running. The automatic cleaner wasn't moving either. It floated on the surface, its white arms stretched out like a dead octopus. She turned to face him. "Yes. But they wouldn't do much because she hasn't been missing long enough."

Devon leaned against the curve of the arched opening. He stared past her as if he was also considering the dark water.

"What should we do?" Beth said. "I can't believe this is happening."

"I'm sure there's an explanation."

"How can you be sure?"

"If there'd been an accident, we'd know," he said.

She wished he would come into the room and sit down. It seemed as if wasn't alarmed that Allison was missing. Allison could be lying in a ravine, unconscious. Or something worse. Imagining those scenes would generate negative energy, but she couldn't stop.

"So why did you come over?" Devon said.

"We have to do something."

"There's nothing we can really *do*," he said.

Jenna appeared in the doorway behind him. "Nothing we

can do about what?"

Beth waited for Devon to tell Jenna the news. Instead, he continued his blank stare at the swimming pool. He ran his hand along the plaster inside the arch, stroking it as if he'd been sanding the surface and was feeling for rough spots that needed additional attention or a finer grain of sandpaper.

"Nothing we can do about what?" Jenna repeated.

"Allison is missing. She went for a bike ride yesterday afternoon and never came home," Beth said.

"All night?"

Beth nodded. She leaned forward, pressing her elbows on her knees. Her hair fell over the sides of her face. When she spoke, her words echoed inside her skull. The table in front of her was smooth and dark. At the opposite corner was a faint ring from a glass, a sticky residue like sap.

Devon moved out of the archway and disappeared from Beth's view.

"Where are you going?" Jenna said.

"I was getting ready to lift weights when the bell rang."

"How can you think about working out?" Beth said. "We have to do something to help Craig." What was wrong with him? Usually, Devon was eager to be helpful.

Jenna remained in the doorway. "I hope she's okay. But I suppose Devon's right, actually. There's not really anything we can do."

"We have to try," Beth said.

"Try to do what?"

"We could call around. Maybe call the stores she shops at?"

Jenna frowned. "She's been gone all night, I doubt she's in a store."

"I didn't mean she's in a store now, to ask whether anyone had seen her."

"Shouldn't we let the police do that?"

Beth swallowed. This was the kind of thing you heard on the news, not something you ever thought you'd live through. "She could be ..."

"We don't know anything. There could be a lot of explanations."

"Like what?" She sat up straight, eager for reassurance. Maybe she was over-reacting. She shouldn't leap to the most horrible possibility. But there was nothing that explained Allison being gone all night. No matter how hard she tried to be positive, to send out calming energy, all she felt was panic and that persistent sense of unreality. A woman didn't simply wheel a bicycle out of the garage, hop on, ride through a neighborhood like this one, and never return.

"Maybe she needed time away. She's been wound pretty tightly lately, don't you think?" Jenna said.

"I suppose. But you don't go off on your bike to get time away. And she would tell Craig, I know she wouldn't leave him frantic like this. You should have heard his voice."

"I can imagine," Jenna said.

"Aren't you going to sit down?"

"I don't see what we can do."

Beth rubbed her legs. Her kneecaps felt like blocks of ice. Jenna's voice was so cold. A normal reaction would be more like hers, wouldn't it? Of course, there was nothing normal about this situation. It seemed Jenna had the right idea, staying on her feet, not sitting where every anxious thought could pool at the base of your skull and send that jumpy, twitching desire through your body, making you feel as if you wanted to hurl yourself against something. She supposed Devon had the right idea after all, the repeated, steady motion of lifting weights, contracting and extending fibers, the calming effect of exertion. "We could go over and stay with Craig. Keep him company until the police come by to take their report."

"That seems dramatic. I'm sure there's a logical explanation."

"You keep saying that, but you haven't suggested anything."

The clang of metal echoed from the room at the other end of the hallway.

"Okay, maybe there isn't an explanation, but I still don't see what we can do," Jenna said.

"We should go to the police station and demand that they start looking for her."

"How do you know they aren't?"

Beth wasn't sure. They'd taken Craig's information. They'd said they would come over and talk to him, get a photograph. Surely they had time to look for a woman who had gone missing. It wasn't as if there were murders and drug deals happening on every corner around here. She inched to the edge of the sofa and stood. She pointed at the ring on the table. "There's something sticky there."

Jenna didn't look at the spot. "I'm sure she'll turn up."

Beth walked toward the archway and into the front hall. "I don't know how you can be so unconcerned. Both of you."

"I'm not unconcerned at all. I just don't know what we can do."

"But you don't seem that upset."

"Of course I'm upset. All I'm saying is that Allison has been jittery and tense and a little bit manic lately. I don't think something sinister has happened to her, like getting assaulted or murdered. The times when a random stranger grabs a woman and hurts her or something are rare."

Tears rushed into Beth's eyes. She couldn't wrap her mind around the idea of Allison, knifed or strangled, lying in a ditch or buried in a shallow grave. If it were true, wouldn't she *know*? "You don't think she's dead, do you?"

"No, but it seems like you do." Jenna pulled her hair over her shoulder and combed her fingers through it.

"No I don't," Beth said.

"Then let's wait and see what the police say. Or if we hear from her."

"You haven't had a chance to absorb it like I have. When

it's been circling in your mind for a while, you'll start to realize there's no explanation."

"There has to be. Do you want a coffee?"

"No thanks." Beth put her hand on the shelf of a small alcove in the wall that held a tiny ceramic vase. She always wanted to touch the delicate lip at the top, but it looked like even the brush of her fingertip would make it wobble. "The last thing I need is caffeine," she said.

"Some herbal tea?"

Beth shook her head. She couldn't behave as if nothing was wrong, as if Allison would suddenly reappear. It was so typical that Jenna was putting on an act of confidence. She seemed to relish the role of the opposite, teary when others were dry-eyed so that only she appeared to have emotions, or staying calm when others were upset, making them look foolish and hysterical. Or maybe it wasn't that at all. Maybe Jenna was too concerned with herself to seriously consider the possibility. Or, maybe she knew where Allison was. "When did you last see her?"

"What does it matter?"

"Why are you avoiding the question?"

"I'm not. I don't understand why that matters."

"That's what the police will ask."

"I'm sure she'll turn up before the police get that involved."

"They're already involved."

"Yes, but ..."

"That's how they figure out where someone might have gone off their normal course, by finding out who saw them last. Then they can figure out where they were when they disappeared."

"Well, we already know that," Jenna said. "She was riding her bike."

"But where?"

"Why does it have to be anywhere? She went for a ride. To get exercise."

Was it Beth's imagination that Jenna's gaze shifted slightly, glancing at Beth's hips, a little bit of flesh spilling over the top of her skirt? "I suppose I should adopt your attitude," Beth said. "I'll assume there's a logical explanation. That she'll turn up."

"Call me if you hear anything," Jenna said.

Beth nodded. "Same here. If she texts you or something." She opened the door and stepped outside. Somehow it didn't seem appropriate to say *goodbye* as if this was a casual visit. As if she had had a cup of coffee as if it were a normal day.

AT HOME, MICHAEL sat at the kitchen table. He closed his laptop. "Did Jenna and Devon have any thoughts on where she might have gone?"

Tears swam across her eyes at the hint of fear in his voice. Talking to the Porters had been surreal. She felt as if they weren't even discussing the same subject. Both of them were so detached, so … not there. Devon's monotone and vacant stares, Jenna's calm approach that managed to dodge providing any specific suggestions or an answer to Beth's question. Something wasn't right, yet she couldn't define what that was. Everyone reacted differently to shock. Did someone who was in shock decide that lifting weights was the best use of time? Even if you knew you couldn't do anything, even if you were completely aware of how helpless you were, didn't you at least have an irrational desire to try? Didn't you verbalize your concern, instead of brushing it off as if nothing was wrong?

Twenty hours since anyone had seen her. With nothing but her bicycle and whatever she'd worn for her ride. Perhaps she'd taken a bottle of water. She wasn't going to simply turn up. Beth put her hands over her face as if she could stop the tears from flowing.

Michael stood and walked across the kitchen. She leaned against the counter near the sink, wanting to run the water and wash her face, but she had no strength to turn the faucet. He pulled her gently away from the counter and leaned over her. He wrapped his arms around her waist and pressed his hands flat against her back. She cried harder, letting herself go now that he'd confirmed she wasn't over-reacting. He placed his hand on the back of her head. That was what had been so off about Jenna and Devon – they made her feel as if she was behaving oddly. As if she was the one who didn't make sense.

There was only one explanation for their nonchalance.

Suddenly, she stopped crying. They must know where Allison had gone. Either they'd talked to her or seen her. When Craig had called to tell her Allison was gone, she'd felt like someone had punched her in the stomach. But the Porters didn't react that way at all. The only question was, what did they know? Maybe she'd left Craig, and they knew the details and were under strict instructions not to say anything. Poor Craig. That thought was almost as painful as thinking Allison had been murdered. To think she would leave him without an explanation. That she'd tell Jenna, or Devon, or both. But that didn't make sense. No one left her husband by riding away on a bike.

Where could she have gone? And what had she told the Porters?

Seventeen

JENNA TOOK A bottle of plain sparkling water out of the refrigerator. She twisted off the cap and poured half the contents into a glass. She pulled the small bamboo cutting board out of the drawer and tucked it under her arm, grabbed a knife, and went through the living room to the patio. It was almost too hot to sit in the sun, but the house felt chilly, and right now, the idea of heat on the back of her head was enticing.

She set her things on the tiled drink table in the section of the patio where the morning sun reached under the roof. The lemon tree at one end of the pool had grown at least two feet taller since they'd bought the house. No matter how often she harvested the lemons, there were always more. She wished she liked lemonade. She plucked off a lemon that was so large she couldn't close her hand around it. She carried it to the table, sliced it in half, cut off a thin disk, and sliced that in half. She dropped a piece into her glass.

Devon was still lifting weights. She hadn't spoken to him since Beth left. She'd wandered around the house, spent a few minutes bemoaning the state of her toenails that already had a chip in the polish since her pedicure in New Mexico. She'd touched up the chip with a dab of Techno Girl polish, but the shade of pink wasn't a good match. Then she'd tried to surf through *The Chronicle Online*. It was the second time that morning she'd tried to read. None of the stories held her interest beyond the first two lines. She'd read it all before – a restaurant that infused new meaning into traditional Italian food, a bar offering live music that compelled you to get up and dance, summer clothes that went from office to evening-wear – *on a budget*. She laughed when she read that and clicked the window closed.

She'd left one of the doors open, so Devon would know where she was when he finished working out. It was nearly noon. They'd had poppy seed bagels and cream cheese for breakfast, and she was getting hungry. The sparkling water would satisfy her for a while, but she needed to think about fixing lunch. Before the debt started to eat away at them like gophers chewing plants from the roots up, they would have gone out for lunch on a Sunday afternoon, wandered around the mall, or gone to a movie. But now … She took another sip of water, annoyed that the slice of lemon bumped against her lip like it was trying to get her attention. She set the glass on the table and closed her eyes. The yard was too quiet without the rushing sound of the waterfall. That was what made the black-bottomed pool so interesting, it made the yard feel lush and tropical. It wasn't as if it cost that much to run. The water was negligible, but the pump required electricity, and they'd agreed to do everything they could to lower their bills.

Devon's voice startled her, too loud, from inside the living room. "Why are you out there?"

"I wanted to sit in the sun."

"Come inside."

"Why?"

"It's time for lunch."

"In a minute."

He grabbed the edge of the door. "What are you doing?"

"I'm not doing anything. I'm enjoying the sun."

"It's supposed to rain."

Pale gray clouds lay across the tops of the foothills, and thinner streaks of white clouds crossed the sky. "Not for a while," she said. "And it's warm."

"Come on. Let's eat."

Jenna crossed her legs. That spot where she'd touched up her toenail was going to annoy her. All she could see was the uneven surface, the mismatched color. She'd ruined the pedicure, but what was she supposed to do? Walk around with a big chip? It didn't really matter, her toes were covered at work, but it upset her to look down and see the flaw staring back at her. "I wanted to relax for a minute."

Devon hadn't moved. Now he had both hands on the

door, gripping it as if he wanted to yank it off its hinges. "Please come inside. I'm really hungry."

She uncrossed her legs and stood. She left the lemon on the cutting board, picked up the knife and glass, and walked to the back door.

"Can you grab the other stuff?" She nodded her head at the table.

"Later."

"I thought you were worried about rain," she said.

"Why are you so calm?" he said. "I thought you'd be upset about the … the drugs. About Allison disappearing. About Beth buzzing around trying to start a search party."

"It's all too much," she said. "So many things are wrong, I can't think about any of it." She stepped into the house, set her glass on the table, and went back outside to pick up the cutting board and the lemon.

In the kitchen, she opened the long cabinet next to the fridge. There was a box of potato leek soup. She set it on the counter and turned to Devon who hovered behind her like he couldn't let her out of his sight, had to track every movement.

"How about soup and …" She opened the refrigerator door. There was a block of cheddar cheese and a bunch of grapes that still looked fresh. "Cheese and fruit?"

"Fine."

"What's wrong with you?"

"Aren't you wondering what Beth is going to do?" Devon said.

"There's nothing she can do. It's unsettling, but I'm sure there's an explanation. Allison probably wanted time away. Maybe she's partying. It's not like this is a dangerous area with lots of violent crime." There was something about Beth's tendency toward drama, toward always wanting to lead some type of group action that stirred up Jenna's desire to over-react in the opposite direction. "She's assuming that Allison was murdered. It's more likely she's off somewhere working and didn't bother to tell anyone. What do you think happened?"

He reached up to the cabinet to her left and pulled out two yellow-glazed pottery soup bowls. He set them on the counter and popped open the plastic spout on the box of soup. Jenna took the cheese to the center island and unwrapped it. She pulled a knife out of the wood block and pressed it through the cheese.

While the soup heated, Devon stared at the tinted microwave door, as if the intensity of his gaze would speed the process.

"Do you think she went to a party?" Jenna said. "You know, because of the cocaine? What happens if you over-do it? Do you pass out? Do you think she's in trouble?"

"Of course she's in trouble. She didn't come home all night."

"Should we have told Beth she was here yesterday?"

"I didn't see the point."

"Me neither," Jenna said. "We really couldn't. It would

seem like we were lying since you didn't mention it to Craig. I'm sure it doesn't mean anything. I have a feeling there's a simple explanation." She laid the slices of cheese on an oversized plate, lining them up along the rim so there was room for the grapes in the center.

"It's good we were thinking the same thing," Devon said.

"We're always in sync." She smiled, but the words didn't make her feel quite as good as they would have before last night. Before she knew Devon was selling drugs. Before she knew he was hiding things from her. Whenever that thought had come to her during the night, she'd pushed it away and reminded herself he'd been trying to take positive action. He felt helpless. She got that. She should have been more sympathetic instead of always complaining about their debt, worrying out loud, making him feel as if he had to do something, anything. Still. Selling cocaine? It was a momentary lapse of sanity, that's all. They'd find their way out of it. "I hope it wasn't a mistake not to mention she was here."

"Why?" Devon said.

Jenna carried the cheese and fruit plate to the table. Devon lifted the second bowl of soup out of the microwave and set it on the placemat.

"What if something is really wrong? What if the police start looking for her and they ask us questions?"

"Are you afraid to lie to the police?" He slapped her butt.

Jenna laughed and elbowed him.

"As long as neither one of us mentions it. Besides, why would it even matter that she dropped by here?" Devon said.

"I don't know. Maybe something really bad happened." She didn't want to think like that. Partying seemed the most likely explanation. Beth had been quite annoyed when Jenna had been unable to come up with any ideas about where Allison might be, but she couldn't very well mention Allison's new pastime. "It doesn't really matter, I guess. It's not like we know where she went."

They sat down. Jenna reached for a piece of cheese at the same time as Devon. His fingers touched hers, and he moved his hand away. Jenna picked up a slice and nibbled on it. She studied the side of his face. His jaw was covered with bristle. When she was this close, she could see the individual hairs, thick and aggressive, like miniature soldiers standing guard. When he hadn't shaved for more than twenty-four hours, the shadow changed his appearance so that he seemed more of a gangster or biker than a marketing executive.

"Aren't you going to eat? I thought you were starving?"

He picked up his spoon. "We should go bowling this afternoon, see a movie. We need to get out of here."

Jenna laughed. "I don't think so." She bit at the skin of a grape and peeled off a strip with her teeth. "When they find her, I mean when she comes back. You're going to tell her you're not selling the cocaine anymore, right? No matter how much we think we need the money?"

He moved his head slightly.

"Is that a *yes?*"

"What do you think Beth is going to do?" Devon said.

"Why do you keep asking me that? I suppose she'll call all of our friends. I should have offered to help. I was still kind of numb from what you told me." She smiled so he would know she wasn't angry, that she understood why he'd done it, that she'd help him correct the mistake. She ran her finger down his forearm, wrapped her hand around his wrist, and held it there for a moment.

"Do you think the police will talk to her friends? Her co-workers?" he said.

"Why are you assuming she won't turn up?"

"I don't want it to come out about the coke. Some of her co-workers do it. If the police find out she was into that ..."

"Oh." She hadn't thought of that. In reality, she secretly hoped that it would come out. That Allison would get so caught up in her own troubles, that she'd be so swallowed by her own shame, she'd no longer have time to hound them about the money. It wasn't that they'd never pay it back, all they needed was a little extra time. A few months. A small part of her wanted to see Allison punished, now that Jenna knew Allison and Devon had been more than happy to keep secrets from her. She blamed Allison for that. Devon was only trying to fix their debt problems, in whatever misguided way he could think of, but if Allison weren't buying, he wouldn't have been selling. If Allison were a true friend, she would have insisted Devon tell Jenna what was going on.

After they finished their soup, Jenna stood to clear the plates. Before she could stack the bowls, Devon pushed out his chair and blocked her way. "Why don't you relax. Go for a run."

"I just ate."

"Then go read a magazine. Or call your mom. I'll clean this up."

"Okay." It wasn't that he never cleaned up the kitchen alone, but he seemed eager for her to leave the room. Maybe she was imagining it. Nothing felt normal. She was most likely reading into every word, every gesture. She wandered out of the kitchen and went upstairs. She should look for another shade of polish and fix her toenail, hopefully without having to paint an additional layer on all of them.

HER TOENAIL WAS still tacky and looked more mismatched than ever when the doorbell rang. If she walked with her toes curled up, she could make it across the bedroom carpet.

The bell rang again.

"Devon! Can you answer the door?"

The house was so quiet she heard or rather felt, that faint ticking sensation at the base of her skull. She was never sure what caused it. When she was a child, she'd assumed it was her brain working. Now, she realized it was probably tight muscles or tendons in her neck or some kind of over-sensitivity. She hobbled through the bedroom and into the hallway. Once she reached the hardwood floor outside their bedroom, she could walk down the stairs without forcing her toes into an awkward position.

She opened the front door. Craig.

"Hi. Did Beth call and tell you?"

Jenna moved back. As Craig stepped into the entryway, his shoulder bumped the doorframe, and he stumbled slightly on the woven rug in front of the parson's bench.

"She stopped by." Jenna closed the door. She wrapped her arms around Craig's shoulders, trying not to fixate on her vulnerable toenail, making sure to keep her feet back so her toes didn't brush against his work boots. His wiry body felt tighter than ever. He smelled like fabric softener, buried deep in the fibers of his cotton t-shirt. While she held him, Craig left his arms at his sides. It seemed as if he'd stopped breathing. She let go.

Craig sucked in air like he'd swum the length of the pool underwater. "It smells different in here."

"Different, how?"

"I don't know."

She smiled. "Well, I didn't know our house had an odor. When it gets warmer, it sounds like we need to leave some windows open overnight." Were they really discussing the smell of the house, as if Allison was in the other room?

"I didn't say it smells bad, just different than usual," Craig said.

"Do you want something to drink? Coffee? A beer?"

"No."

"Water?"

"No."

"You should have some water," she said. "You can't let yourself get dehydrated."

"Did Devon tell you I called last night?"

"Yes." Jenna went into the kitchen and got two glasses out of the cabinet. She filled them from the refrigerator spigot and carried them back to the entryway. She handed one to Craig. "Come on in." She walked into the living room. After a minute, he followed.

"Did you talk to her, or see her yesterday?" Craig said.

"No." She was relieved she had her back to him. She turned and took a sip of water. She ran her finger down the side of the glass.

"So you didn't hear from her at all? She didn't text you?"

Jenna shook her head slightly. "What did the police say?"

"They took information, but they won't really do much right away unless there's an obvious indication of a crime."

"She didn't leave a note?"

"No. Something's wrong. I don't know why they need to have proof of a crime. She didn't see any of her friends or her family, so obviously, something is wrong." His voice grew tight as he spoke. He stopped abruptly. He took a long swallow of water. He lifted the glass when he was finished. "Thanks for this."

Jenna gave him a tiny smile. "There must be someone ..."

"No. There's no one. I tried her parents, her sister, and everyone at her firm."

"Could she be working on a secret case?"

Craig rolled his eyes. "Where's Devon?"

Jenna glanced toward the entryway. Where was Devon? "I don't know," she said. "He was here a few minutes ago."

Craig stood and walked to the living room doors and looked out. His shoulders trembled. He straightened his back and turned. "You're sure you haven't communicated with her at all? You're practically her best friend."

She wanted to laugh but managed to swallow instead. That was a sad commentary if he really believed that. Lately, she wondered if Allison liked her at all. "I don't know where she could have gone."

"Someone took her."

"Don't say that," she said.

"What else can it be?" He put his glass on the table and looked out the window. "There he is."

Devon walked around the edge of the rocks, devoid of their waterfall, and across the slate that surrounded the pool, flowing seamlessly into the patio area. He opened the door. Craig moved back, and Devon stepped into the living room.

"Where were you?" Jenna said.

"Looking around the yard. Checking out the weed situation since we let the gardener ..." He slapped Craig's back. "Sorry. Any news?"

"No," Jenna said. "Craig called people from her office."

She'd thought for sure that was the explanation, that Allison had gone to a party with her friends, that she hadn't planned to stay long but got high and lost track of time. Or something like that. She surely hadn't been abducted. She couldn't imagine how, or why that would happen.

"She's gone," Craig said.

"They'll find her," Devon said.

"What if she's …"

"Don't even say that," Devon said. "Don't think it."

"Well, where could she be?"

Startled by the volume of his voice, Jenna put her hands over her ears.

"Chill." Devon patted Craig's shoulder. "She'll turn up."

"Missing people don't simply turn up."

"Sure they do," Devon said.

She glanced at Devon. He squinted at the yard as if he'd dropped something near the pool and was trying to spot it. "He's upset," she said softly.

"Upset doesn't begin to describe it." Craig spat out the words like a soggy wad of tobacco that he'd kept under his tongue for too long. "I didn't sleep all night. The police don't do anything, my friends don't do anything. My life is coming apart, and no one seems to recognize it."

"What should we do?" Jenna said. "We feel helpless."

"You could stop being so calm."

"That's not fair," she said.

Craig shrugged.

"We're trying to help you stay rational. It doesn't help Allison if you lose it," Devon said.

"I am losing it! She could be dead already!"

"I'm sure she's not dead," Devon said.

Jenna stared at him. Of course, they wanted to reassure Craig, but it was better to be ambiguous.

"Don't patronize me. Allison is the most responsible person I know. She would never just wander off, never go somewhere without telling me. You know something's wrong, and you can't make me feel better by pretending you're confident she's okay."

"Did you two have a fight?" Devon said.

Craig turned and stalked to the arch leading to the entryway. "What are you trying to say? That she left me? No. She didn't do that. She wouldn't do that."

"So you did have a fight?"

"You're an ass." Craig backed into the hallway. "It smells different here. And I just realized why."

Jenna put her glass on the table. She heard the patio door rattle as Devon leaned against it.

"I smell Allison's perfume."

Devon walked across the living room, seeming to take several minutes to negotiate the wide expanse. No one spoke. When he reached Craig's side, he said, "I didn't mean to be a jerk. I know you're upset, man. It's not that we don't care." He lifted his hand as if he intended to thump Craig's shoulder again, then let his arm fall back to his side. He lifted his hand again and ran his palm along his jaw, scrubbing as if he wanted to get rid of the bristle. "You think you smell her perfume because you're wound up."

Craig backed further out of the room, taking strides impossibly long for a man not watching where he was going. As if by instinct, he stopped a foot short of the front door. "Maybe," he said.

Jenna sidled up next to Devon and looped her arm around his waist. "It could be I've worn the same scent as Allison from time to time."

"Since when do you wear perfume?"

"Maybe not perfume, but body wash, lotion, stuff like that."

Craig opened the door. "You," he lifted his chin toward Devon, then Jenna. "Both of you are acting strange. I think you know where she went."

"We don't. Really," Jenna said.

"If you know anything and you're not telling me ... I'm worried sick that she's ..."

"We don't know anything." Jenna wished desperately that Devon would help her out. She felt absurd, repeating the same thing over and over until it was sounding false by its very repetition. Why wasn't Devon helping?

Craig flung the door open. The doorknob crashed into the wall, and the door swung back toward him. He put up his hand and stopped it from hitting him. "If you hear from her, or remember anything she said, call me."

Jenna squeezed Devon's waist, digging her fingers into his flesh, afraid to speak.

Without closing the door, Craig walked across the porch and along the driveway to where his Mercedes was parked, the front end touching the leaves of the agapanthus that bordered the drive.

When his car disappeared past the neighbor's oak tree, Jenna let go of Devon and closed the door. "I guess we made a mistake."

"No we didn't."

"It's no big deal, we should have told him she was here." She leaned against the door and looked at her toe. She hadn't been aware of it the entire time they were in the living room, and she hoped there weren't carpet fibers caught in the polish. It looked okay, but the entryway didn't have enough light to tell for sure.

"He didn't smell perfume," Devon said. "He's imagining things."

"Does that matter? If he thinks he did, then he's not going to trust us. Which isn't fair, because we don't know anything. We didn't do anything. Well, you sold her the cocaine, but that's a whole other issue."

Devon turned into the hallway that ran past the dining room to the wing that housed the office and workout room. "I'm going to look at our taxes," he said.

At any other time, she would have been pleased that he was thinking ahead. But now, for some reason, she wasn't happy. The sudden decision to review their taxes felt like an excuse. As if he was trying to escape, although what he would be trying to escape from, she had no idea. "Can't we watch a movie or something? Don't forget I'm leaving for the trade show tomorrow. It would be nice to cuddle up and forget everything."

Devon smiled, although he seemed to be looking past her. "In a few. After I spend thirty minutes on this." He went into the study.

Jenna sniffed the air. She didn't smell anything. She walked into the living room sniffing harder. There was no hint of Allison's perfume. Or was there? By now, she'd been breathing so hard and was so acutely aware of the temperature of the air and the difference in texture between the hallway and the living room, she wasn't sure what she smelled.

Eighteen

DEVON BOLTED UP in bed at five-thirty on Monday morning. Adrenaline rushed through his veins. This would be a tricky morning. He hadn't been down to the would-be-wine-cellar to check on Allison since yesterday afternoon. He'd brought her a peanut butter sandwich, a bottle of water, and some Vicodin. It had been tricky getting all that pulled together with Jenna in the house, with Craig dropping by unannounced, but he'd managed.

When he was down there, he'd helped Allison pee into a small bucket then hosed it out near the back fence. Getting her to eat had taken a long time. Every few minutes she seemed to forget that she was chewing. He had to get food into her because he couldn't risk leaving her mouth un-taped when he left her. She promised not to scream, but Allison was not a woman to be cowed easily. Despite her drugged condition, he worried she was simmering, biding her time.

He had no idea how the hell he'd managed to get himself

in this situation. How was he going to let her go without her ruining his life? He pushed the thought out of his head. Deal with the current problem. Figure out the details and resolve issues as they arose. Right now, the biggest problem was getting food to her, he didn't want her dying on him. Although, in some ways, that would resolve a lot of problems. He shuddered violently.

Jenna turned over and put her hand on his leg. "What's wrong?"

She said it in a lazy way as if she didn't think anything was truly wrong. Her voice was rough. He liked that sexy tone that came moments after sleep ended. It calmed him, and he stopped shaking. What kind of monster was he, with thoughts like that? Keeping a woman tied up in the basement? Food for Allison. He had to focus. He kicked the covers down to the foot of the bed and rolled to a standing position.

"Why are you getting up?" Jenna said.

"Lots to do this week. I need to get an early start."

"I kind of thought Craig might call during the night."

"Huh. I guess that means they haven't found her. But that could be a good thing, right? They didn't find a body."

"Don't say that."

"Why? That's what everyone is thinking," he said.

Jenna got up and walked to the bathroom.

"Go ahead and shower first," Devon said. It would be better if Jenna left for work first. Dealing with Allison might take longer today because there was no way to predict what her mood would be. Yesterday she'd been meek. She hadn't talked much and was willing to eat, but he couldn't count on that lasting. He needed Jenna out of the house. Of course, later this morning Jenna was leaving for her sales meeting in Vegas, so for the next few days he'd be able to take care of Allison without distraction, and concentrate on finding a solution.

After they'd showered and dressed, they stood at the center island in the kitchen, drinking coffee and eating toast. When they were ready to leave, Jenna wheeled her suitcase down the hall and out the side door. They stood in the portico, and he put his arms around her waist, pressing her hips and lower back against his body. Her mouth was so soft and welcoming, for a moment he thought he might cry. If she knew what he'd done … He pulled away and opened the side door into the garage. Jenna walked around her BMW, climbed in, and popped the trunk open. Devon put her suitcase inside, closed the trunk, and hit the button to raise the garage door. She started the car and backed out. She slid her sunglasses on. She gave him a little wave, then lifted her hand, palm up. He knew she was wondering why he wasn't getting in the Jeep. He waved vigorously and fumbled with the doorknob as if he was locking the side door. Still, she waited. Slowly he walked to the Jeep and got in. He looked in the rearview mirror and watched her back up to the end of the driveway. She stopped. It was their habit to pull out of the driveway one after the other. He backed out of the garage and hit the remote. He heard the acceleration of her engine as she pulled onto Willow Circle. He waited a few minutes, then turned off the engine and went into the house through the front door.

A few crackers and a small can of tomato juice would have to do for Allison's meal. He didn't have time to wait while she picked her way through a sandwich like she had yesterday. His hand shook when he opened the door to the back patio. There had to be a way to persuade her to keep his secret so he could let her go. Some kind of deal in which he vowed not to betray her use of cocaine if she forgave him. Couldn't she give him that? Surely after a lifetime of friendship, she must know he was a good person. It had all happened so fast. It was an accident. She'd said such bitchy things about Jenna. Allison must see how she'd hurt him.

That might be the trick. He would show her how wounded he was, how much he cared for Jenna, how desperately he needed Allison to understand that. He'd appeal to Allison's maternal side, that thing in all women that kicked in when something or someone was suffering. He saw it in Jenna all the time, how she hated it when she came upon a dead bird. It was the thing that made her sob when some dumb squirrel ran across right in front of a car and got squashed. It was sad, the loss of life, the furry animal suddenly gone, but still. Why did animals do that? Didn't they have any fear of something larger and louder than themselves? Why did they have to be so stupid?

He unlocked the door that led to the basement and made his way down a few steps before turning to pull it closed behind him. He'd forgotten how dark it got when the door was closed. Old construction was solid, the wood planed to perfection, no gaps around the doors that allowed light to seep inside. Everything sealed tight. Maybe he shouldn't have turned out the light the last time he was down here. But he'd decided she would sleep better in the dark once the Vicodin kicked in. The air was stale and dry. It entered his nostrils like something solid, stirring up the urge to sneeze, tightening his throat so he found himself breathing hard as if he'd climbed up a flight of stairs rather than down.

He waved his arm in the air, feeling for the nut tied to the string dangling from the bulb at the center of the space. That would be another addition to the cost of construction. Was there already wiring to allow for good lighting? He doubted it. His hand brushed against the string, and he grabbed at it. Nothing. It must have been a cobweb. He waved his hand again. Another example of not thinking ahead. He should have left the door open until he turned on the light, or brought a flashlight. "Sorry, Allison, it's taking me a minute to find the string for the light."

The room was silent.

Shit. Why wasn't she making any sound? He expected a groan, a whimper, something. Hopefully, she was asleep, not unconscious. Or worse. He waved his arm, turning in circles until finally he felt the string and yanked hard. The area around him filled with light, and he saw Allison had herself burrowed under the blankets and towels, so all that was visible was her hair, plastered on the ground. He set the juice and crackers on the edge of the towel and touched her shoulder. She moaned and twisted the upper half of her body to the side. He imagined it wasn't very comfortable sleeping on hard-packed dirt. He should have thought to bring a sleeping bag. No. What was he thinking? He wasn't setting up camp down here. This was temporary. A day or two at most.

Allison's hand poked out from beneath the blankets.

He released his breath. She was okay. Still doped up, which was good. It was a delicate balance between keeping her quiet and non-combative and making sure she ate something. If she was too groggy, it was difficult to get her to even sip water and swallow more tablets. He bent over and lifted the corner of the blanket covering her head. He pulled it down past her shoulder. Underneath was another blanket. He pushed that away from her face. Her breath was shallow, and although she'd moved her hand earlier, there was no other movement, not even a twitch of her eyelids or a tremor in her lip.

Part of him didn't want to wake her. It was easier to let her sleep, but he should get her to take some more Vicodin. He prodded her shoulder, trying to get her to roll onto her back so she would start to wake before he helped her to a sitting position. Had he given her too much the day before? He'd been wound up from all the activity, Beth dropping by, worrying and fretting that they had to *do* something. Craig already talking to the police, and now that Allison had been missing for two nights, the cops would start asking questions of her friends and co-workers, neighbors and family. This could get out of control very quickly.

He shook her again. Once he was in the office, he'd close his door and do some serious thinking about how he was going to fix this situation. This was his last chance, with Jenna gone for a few days. He had to stop giving himself false reassurances that he'd think about it "later". There was no more "later". He shook her harder. She moaned, and a thin bubble of mucous appeared at the tip of her nose. It popped and settled onto her skin in a damp spot. He dabbed at it with the edge of a towel. She shuddered.

This was no good. She was in too deep. He'd have to come home at noon.

Her skin was dark red, almost purple around the edges of the duct tape sealing her mouth. He knelt down and peeled it carefully away from her face. Seeing her like that was too much, he'd have to trust she wouldn't scream. As long as the Vicodin was in effect, it shouldn't be a problem.

He climbed the stairs, went out, and locked the door. He glanced at the fence between their house and the one next door, closest to the basement. The backyard was quiet except for some songbirds, gleefully shouting their pleasure at the cloudless sky. Good for them. He wished he had something to sing about. Anything.

Inside the house, it was eerily quiet as if the house itself was waiting for something to happen. Any moment there would be a scream, Allison's voice shrieking past the barrier of dirt and plaster, letting the entire neighborhood know that a monster was keeping her captive in what was little more than a cave.

He trudged up the stairs to the master bathroom to wash his hands. It wasn't that they were dirty and needed scrubbing, but walking across the dirt floor, the grit scraping the soles of his shoes, had made him feel disheveled. He dried his hands and went into the bedroom. This was as good a time as any to try to figure out what to do with the coke left in his nightstand. He had one more delivery to his buddy at work, he could do that today, but there was still some left that had been planned for Allison. He considered offering it to her in the basement. That might make her look on him more favorably, or make her consider how much she needed him. Sure, he'd promised Jenna he would stop selling, but that didn't have to be right away. That could happen after he got the rest of this mess sorted out. Right now, he needed a more secure storage place in case the police started poking around. It wasn't that they would leap right to a search of their house, but who really knew how they did these things. He had no experience with police investigations and it was too risky to leave it sitting around where the most casual activity could expose it. It had been careless leaving it there all this time, blissfully assuming Jenna would never have an inclination to open the cabinet.

The nightstand had a drawer at the top and two shelves covered by a door. On the top shelf, he had a thriller he'd started reading before he got his iPad and switched to eBooks. The bottom shelf contained a wood box his parents had given him to hold coins and keys, but he kept all that stuff in the office, so the box was empty. Balanced on top of it was the tissue box that hid the packages of cocaine. He pulled it out and removed the plastic bag. The trouble was, where would he keep it? If the police did come to the point where they'd search the house, nowhere was safe. He could take it to the office. There was a cupboard with a locking door over his desk.

The doorbell chimed. He shoved the tissue box into the cabinet and slammed the door closed before he even had time to think about who might be there. A solicitor that saw your car in the driveway? A neighbor who'd seen the same and wanted to ask a favor? Proselytizers? He walked to the bedroom door and paused. There was no reason to be concerned. It was only eight-fifteen. Somewhat logical that he might still be at home.

He went downstairs and opened the door. Beth stood at the edge of the porch. The deep shade that covered the porch until mid-day made her eyes appear as empty sockets, yet he could feel her staring at him. "Hi," he said.

"I'm on my way to the gym, we have a teacher in-service day."

"Oh."

"I was surprised to see your Jeep in the driveway."

The first words that rose to his lips were that he was running late, but fortunately, he stopped before he spoke. He'd already told Jenna he wanted to get an early start today. This might be a sign he was starting to think more clearly, pausing before blurting out the first phrase that popped across his mind. "I forgot the power cord to my laptop and had to come back home." He smiled, impressed with his smooth solution. That answer would make sense to Jenna if Beth mentioned her impromptu visit. "So what did you want?"

"I don't really know," Beth said. "I saw the Jeep, and it seemed odd. You were so distracted yesterday. I guess I was worried that something's wrong."

"Nothing's wrong." He smiled, feeling more confident now.

"You weren't laid off, were you?"

"Of course not."

"Why do you keep grinning like that? It gives me the creeps."

What was the matter with her? Who reads something sinister into a simple smile? It seemed she was so freaked out by Allison's disappearance, she was reading into everything. "Didn't mean to scare you," he said.

"Well, you are. Do you know where Allison went on Saturday?"

"We already told you no."

"I wanted to make sure. Something doesn't feel right."

"What could there possibly be that doesn't *feel right*?" he said, leaning more heavily than he should have on the last two words.

"You don't seem that upset."

"Of course we're upset."

"You're both really ... detached."

"We're not." He shouldn't have to stand here and explain himself to Beth. All he was doing was feeding her paranoia. Of course, it wasn't really paranoia. She was right. Did she have some kind of sixth sense that let her know they were hiding something? She was into all that mystical stuff, the equinox and being married in the desert. Yoga. Who knew what else. He shoved his hands in his pockets and leaned against the doorframe. He was being overly panicked again. Of course, she didn't have any special insight. It was his fear speaking, creeping up from his gut where it had been sitting like a tiny black spot since the situation with their debt had escalated, multiplying out of control like cancerous cells after he'd locked Allison in the wine cellar.

He wondered if Craig had mentioned the perfume to Beth. Probably not, or she would have said something about it. Time to take the offensive, or she'd stand on their porch all morning, staring at him with those dark holes where her eyes should be. If she thought she could force him to reveal all his secrets simply by staring at him and not speaking, she was wrong. "What do you want, Beth? I need to get to work. I don't know why you keep hovering around as if your worrying is going to make Allison reappear."

"All you can think about is work?"

"You're going to the gym!"

"I have to get rid of this stress. I'm scared to death something happened to her."

"Of course something happened to her. But she probably made that *something* happen all by herself. I'm sure she'll have an explanation. She probably needed a break from Craig."

"She wouldn't leave without telling her friends."

"How do you know?"

"Because I know."

"I can't do anything for you. I have to get to work." He stepped onto the front porch and pulled the door closed behind him. When he turned to lock it, he realized he wasn't sure whether the tissue box was still on the bed. Had he stuffed the plastic bag back under the tissues, leaving a few poking out of the opening so it looked normal? He couldn't remember. He'd have to check when he came home for lunch. He couldn't go back and get it now with Beth breathing down his neck. What did she think she was going to accomplish by going around asking people if they were upset, trying to think of something to *do* to help bring back Allison? There was nothing she could do. He, of all people, knew that. He laughed.

"Why are you laughing? You sound like a maniac."

"Laughing doesn't make me a maniac." He pulled his key out of the deadbolt and moved closer to Beth.

She stepped back, putting one foot down on the path behind her.

Devon waited.

She stepped to the side of the path. "No one laughs like that when one of their closest friends has disappeared into nowhere."

"How do you know how people react?" He walked past her and went to his Jeep. He opened the door. "Can you move your car so I can get going?"

Beth stayed rooted to the spot at the side of the path. She looked like she was made of stone, surrounded by agapanthus and two small fruitless plum trees, their leaves almost black in the shadows surrounding the front porch. Her skin was nearly colorless, and although he could see her eyes now, they were impossible to read.

"I'm not going to sit around and wait to find out Allison is dead, and then find out I could have done something. When a friend is missing, people are scared. They don't laugh at inappropriate times and act more worried about work or shrug it off. Even if all they do is put up flyers, they *do* something."

"Do you have flyers you want me to put up at my office?" He knew his tone was dangerously sarcastic, but there was no stopping it. Beth fluttering around like a butterfly, flapping her insubstantial wing at his cheek, throwing her body at something she couldn't even see, was stressing him out. There was only one thing occupying his attention right now, and that was getting to the office, closing the door, and trying to work out a plan. He had to have a plan. He laughed again. How often did Jenna tell him to think more about the future?

"What's so funny?"

"Nothing. I'm tense, and I guess it's coming out as a laugh. Sorry if you find that disturbing. Not everyone responds the way you do, Beth. Thinking of flyers and criticizing other people for how they're behaving isn't going to accomplish anything." He walked back to where she stood. "Get a grip and stop assuming the worst."

She folded her arms across her chest and lifted her face as if she was trying to look him right in the eye, which of course she could not because she was at least eight inches shorter than him. Usually, she was so sweet, so unwilling to make waves. Had she changed since she'd married Michael? She glared at him like she knew he'd done something wrong. But he hadn't. Yes, it was wrong that Allison was locked up and drugged like an animal in a cargo transport, but it wasn't his fault. The whole situation had spiraled out of control before he had time to realize what was happening.

"I'm not assuming the worst," she said. She unfolded her arms. "But you're acting like you think this is no big deal. And when you keep laughing for no reason, it's unnerving." She poked her finger at his solar plexus. "If we weren't standing on the driveway in plain daylight, I'd be scared to be alone with you right now."

He laughed. "Whatever. Now move your car. I'm late." He grabbed her wrist and pulled her along the path.

"Let go of me."

His keys were in his hand, so his fingers only half circled her wrist. He twisted harder and tried to pull her toward her car. She was pissing him off, acting as if she knew he'd done something wrong. There was no way she could know. His own guilt and the sense that he'd backed himself into an impossible corner was causing him to over-react, yet he couldn't stop himself.

She refused to budge. He yanked harder. His key scraped the tender skin at the back of her wrist.

"Stop it! You're hurting me."

He let go of her. "Don't exaggerate."

"I'm not." She held up her arm. A thin, red line ran across her wrist. "You made me bleed."

"You're not bleeding. Calm down."

Beth blinked slowly. She turned and walked to her car, got in, and backed out of the driveway.

DEVON ARRIVED HOME from work at noon and went straight to the master bedroom. He took the tissue box out of the nightstand where he'd stuffed it after all, removed the plastic bag with the coke and the razor blade, and shoved it into a white bag with the company logo stamped on the side, a giveaway from the last trade show he'd attended. He carried the bag to the car and shoved it under the driver's seat. Tomorrow he'd go in early when no one was around and stash it in his office.

The thought of dealing with Allison right now was too much, especially after the unsettling encounter with Beth a few hours earlier. He'd realized the minute she left that he'd allowed her to provoke him. She'd give a full report to Jenna if she hadn't already. He went into the kitchen and got the bottle of scotch out of the cabinet. He set a glass on the counter. He poured a generous shot and took it into the living room. He settled on the sofa and stared at the brown and red abstract painting that dominated the wall across from him. For all the times he'd sat in this same spot and stared at the painting, he realized now for the first time that the red looked like streaks of blood. Of course, it wasn't a huge leap to think of red paint as being similar to blood, but he was startled by the thought. He continued to stare at the painting, thinking of that line of blood on Beth's arm. It was nothing, but not only would she dramatize the incident to Jenna, he should also expect a call or a visit from Michael telling him to keep his hands off his wife.

How had everything gotten so fucked up? He lifted the glass and took a long swallow, enjoying the burn on his lips and tongue, the heat as the liquid flowed down his throat. He'd thought about the Allison problem all morning without success. Then, on the drive home, he'd remembered the concept of Stockholm Syndrome. The solution might be to keep her longer instead of letting her go. Get her to the point where she was dependent on him and beholden to him. The only problem with that was still how to explain her absence once he released her? He supposed she could say she'd needed time away. But she hadn't taken any clothes with her, not to mention the fact she'd left on her bicycle. Making her completely dependent on him had seemed like a promising idea while he was driving, but now, he realized it was vapor. He was as trapped as she was down in the basement. He swallowed the rest of the scotch.

He'd never felt so alone in his life. Could he keep her there for months? It wasn't as if they could afford to start fitting it out as a wine cellar any time soon. But the thought of his own stress, worrying every day that he'd be caught, made that an impossible solution. Was there some kind of drug he could give her that would make her forget everything that had happened? He'd have to research that. He could drive her somewhere and release her, let someone find her, and they could assume she'd .... What? Assume what?

He picked up the glass and slammed it down on the table. Why was this happening to him? He wanted to hurl the glass at that painting, mocking him, making him think of blood. The paint strokes were thick and rich, some areas bright red, others darker, flowing across the brown that now looked like the living room carpet to him, which of course it did, since they'd bought the deep, chocolate carpet to tie with the background color of the painting.

He went back to the kitchen and poured a partial shot. Another sip warmed his brain and made him feel a little calmer. Maybe he would just do nothing. That had worked for most everything else in his life. Sometimes, if you waited for things to unfold, they worked themselves out. He wasn't sure how that could be in this case, but there was no other choice right now. He couldn't release her and have her destroy his life. At least while Jenna was gone for the rest of the week, he could relax. He wouldn't be thinking every minute how to get down to the basement without Jenna noticing, and his mind would kick into gear. The solution would come to him. He swallowed the rest of the drink. As much as he longed for Jenna when she was gone, feeling as if part of his body had been ripped away, leaving him as half a person, this time it might be good. He needed some breathing room. Once he had that, everything would work itself out.

Nineteen

FOR THREE AND a half days in Las Vegas, Jenna's only contact with Devon had been late at night, lying in bed, whispering into her phone.

All day Tuesday she'd worked on the final arrangements for the evening event – a party for customers and corporate partners with live music and casino games. Wednesday and Thursday had been consumed by logistics for the golf tournament and banquet. She loved organizing events, mingling with the attendees and watching them party, resolving any problems that arose.

It felt great to be dressed up again after weeks of spending most of her time at home. Sure she wore slacks and skirts to the office every day, but she enjoyed the chance to go for more drama – higher heels, thicker lines around her eyes, darker shadow, and earrings that dangled to her shoulders. Not that she looked cheap. It was the opposite, she looked awesome the night of the welcome party. Despite having to wear clothes from last year's event thanks to her non-existent clothing budget. She'd worn black silk pants that were narrow at her ankles, black patent leather pumps with four-inch heels, and a black top with silver straps and trim. She would have liked to wear her silver high-heeled sandals, but she couldn't very well do that without a pedicure.

As she'd moved among the guests at the welcome party, she'd managed to forget everything that was going on at home. For three glorious hours, there hadn't been a single thought of the balance on her credit card or about who was to blame and who owed what in terms of both cash and friendship. She hadn't thought about the fact that her husband was selling drugs to make ends meet. And she hadn't had a single thread of concern over Allison's disappearance. Maybe that made her a bad friend. But she was frankly tired of Allison. Friends should be more forgiving. Of course, she hadn't been very generous with sympathy once she found out Allison was snorting cocaine.

Since Monday afternoon, she'd felt like her old self, smiling, laughing, enjoying life. Now that it was over, she suddenly had too much time to think, and she wanted to hang on to that Las Vegas buzz that had a way of consuming all her senses.

After the final dinner, she'd planned to go to the cocktail lounge. She'd listen to loud music and have a few glasses of wine with her friends — Kate, who had given birth to her first child seven months ago, was eager for fun without responsibility; and Julie, recently divorced was *definitely up for a good time*. Jenna couldn't believe both of them had bailed on her. Kate wasn't a surprise, she decided to go to her room and sleep, something she didn't get much of at home. Julie had a migraine, so there was nothing that could be done, but Jenna didn't want to sit in her room and watch her mind race in circles. It was better to keep busy, stay around people. The thought of a few hours at a blackjack table was appealing, imagining herself acquiring extra spending money, but she supposed it was true that it took money to make money. Even here. She could still relax in the lounge, let the too-loud music thump through her head.

The minute she pulled her card key out of the lock and pressed down on the door handle, her phone rang. Devon's face popped up. She let the door fall closed and dropped the card onto a small table to her left.

"How'd it go?" Devon said.

"Good. Everyone was really pleased. Any word on Allison?"

"No. I miss you."

"I miss you more." She kicked off her shoes and sprawled in the chair next to the cabinet that held her clothes and the TV. She'd wear flats when she went to the bar, change into jeans.

"I want you," he said.

"Me too."

"Things have been difficult."

She didn't want to ask why. She didn't want to hear about Craig's despair or Beth's panic. Since Monday, Beth had sent seven or eight text messages and left three voicemails asking Jenna to call right away. Beth should understand that when Jenna was at an event, she was working 24-7. Now that her thoughts were yanked back to the Bay Area, Beth's most recent message poked itself into her mind. Beth had said in a rather icy voice that she needed to talk to Jenna about Devon's behavior. Her final words had been, *He's scaring me.*

"Did you get into some kind of argument with Beth?" Jenna said.

"Did she call you?"

"Three times. She left a message about you being scary." Jenna laughed. Saying it out loud helped. The last person on earth who would be considered scary was Devon Porter, with his easy grin and blue eyes. He looked playful more than anything.

"Have you talked to her?" Devon said.

"No. What happened?"

"She came over. The day you left."

"You didn't mention it."

"I didn't think it was that big of a deal, but then she had Michael call me." He laughed. "That guy is protective."

"Aren't all men? What *happened?*"

"She got all spun up about the fact that we aren't more concerned about Allison."

"We're concerned."

"I guess we should be panicked. Anyway, she wouldn't let it go. And she was blocking the Jeep. I asked her to move a couple of times and she wouldn't. So I grabbed her, and my key scratched her arm."

"You're kidding."

"I guess she didn't like me grabbing her. Michael was pissed, although I think I got him calmed down."

"Why did you grab her?"

"Don't you turn on me too. Please, Babe. I need you more than anything."

"I'm not turning on you. You should have asked her to move."

"I *did*. Multiple times."

"Is everything okay now?"

"It appears to be with Michael. Who knows about Beth. Anyway, if you talk to her, tell her to chill out. It was an accident."

Jenna wasn't sure what to say. It was difficult, impossible, to picture Devon grabbing anyone. Although ... she remembered the tight muscles at the back of his neck, the surprising aggression she'd sensed that afternoon at the wedding shower. She didn't think she'd describe him as scary, but it had been ... disturbing. A facet of him she'd never seen before and hoped to never see again.

"I hate it when you're gone," he said. "I hate sleeping because even when I'm asleep, the bed feels empty. I have dreams about not being able to find our house, and when I wake up, I don't know where I am because the bed doesn't feel right. It's cold."

She felt the warmth of his words over the phone, the tenderness like something tangible, floating over the air, flowing across her skin. "I don't like it either. I hate that you're not there when I wake up in the morning."

"Something else happened. The cops came by."

"That's not surprising."

"It surprised me," he said.

"We knew it would happen sooner or later. I wonder if something terrible really happened." She swallowed, but it didn't help the tightness in her throat. She should be worried sick about Allison. No one simply disappeared for … how many days had it been? Five days. No one could say the words they were all pushing to the backs of their minds. That she was dead, murdered and lying in a ditch or a warehouse or a shallow grave. Possibly drifting along the ocean floor. She shuddered. It wasn't helpful to let morbid thoughts take root. Maybe Devon wasn't the only one Allison was buying cocaine from. Maybe there was someone else, some guys who weren't so nice. The idea made Jenna feel like she'd been jarred awake from a nightmare. What had Devon gotten himself involved with? Selling drugs wasn't some casual side business like selling collectibles on eBay. It was dangerous, filled with violent people, gangs and thugs, the Mafia – the types who would do anything to protect their business. Just like her and Devon, lying and trying to blackmail Allison, anything to shore up their precarious financial situation. Was everything about money in the end? "So what did they say?"

"They ran through a list of questions that sounded like a script. *How long had I known her, when was the last time I saw her, did I have any thoughts on where she might have gone.*"

"When did you say you last saw her?"

"At the wedding."

"It scares me, lying to the police."

"We have no choice."

They'd had no choice but to let the gardener go, no choice but to eat at home, no choice about getting a pedicure. The words echoed through her mind, *no choice*. If the police returned, there would be more lies to cover the first one. "What did you say about where she might have gone?"

"I said I had no idea. I hinted that maybe they had a fight. Craig was pretty rattled, it makes sense he wouldn't want to tell us if they had a big argument."

Jenna was suddenly cold. She tugged the throw pillow out from behind her and placed it over her feet. It fell off. She curled her legs up into the armchair, but there wasn't enough room to sit comfortably. She shifted the phone to her left ear. She stood and walked to the thermostat to adjust the fan down to the low setting. "Do you think that was smart? Adding another lie?"

"It wasn't a lie. They asked what I thought, and that's what I think."

She couldn't argue with that. Still, it felt like a lie. Not a lie precisely, but deliberately misleading, sending the police along a different track so they wouldn't focus on trying to find out whether Devon's other statements were truthful. They had no reason not to believe him. Yet. "Do you think it will come out that she was using cocaine?"

"Why would it?"

"I'm scared."

"Why?"

"What if she was at some party that took a bad turn, what if she was involved with a lot of other people we know nothing about? And the police start looking into her life, and then they find out she was buying drugs from you."

"That would never happen."

"You don't know that."

"I have worse things to worry about than a bunch of questions from a few cops who have no idea where she is."

Devon's voice was loud. She pulled the phone away from her ear. "Why are you shouting?"

"I'm not shouting." His breathing was strained as if he'd run up the stairs.

"What else are you worried about?" she said.

He was silent.

"Devon?"

"I meant the debt, making sure I perform at work. Paying our taxes."

"Oh. You sounded almost angry."

"Sorry. I miss you so much. I wish you could come home

tonight. I need to hold you."

Jenna smiled. "In less than twenty hours I'll be there."

"I'll be at work when you get home."

In the past, she would have suggested a dinner out, but that was impossible. Instead of spending money to celebrate being together after being separated, all they had was each other. That might be a good thing.

"What are you doing tonight?" Devon said.

"I was supposed to go out with Kate and Julie, but they bailed on me. I'm going to go get a glass of wine, maybe a little something to eat."

"Okay. Well, have a good time. Don't let any guys hit on you." He laughed.

"Are you trying to rush me off the phone?"

"I just have stuff to do. Taxes."

"How is it looking?"

"It's too soon to tell, I'm still entering everything."

AFTER JENNA HUNG up and changed into her jeans, she felt unsettled. Devon's lie to the police and the confrontation with Beth sat in her stomach like soap sitting unused in a dish for too long, the scum hardening and adhering to the sides. A glass of wine would be nice. Something with more quality than what was sitting in the mini fridge in the hotel room. Two glasses of wine would be even nicer. She would order a small plate of crab cakes or something to go with it. Never before had her corporate credit card given her such a sense of freedom. She almost felt lighter as she moved around the room.

She slipped on a pair of ballet slipper flats, transferred her credit card, room key, and lip-gloss from her computer bag into a narrow purse with a long strap. She moved the setting on the thermostat up to seventy-two, so the room would be cozy when she returned and turned off all but the light in the entry area.

The Luxor offered six restaurants on various levels and a number of bars. On the casino floor were two lounges. One boasted large screen TVs showing a basketball game. She wound her way past the blackjack tables and down a row of slot machines to a third, smaller, bar area. Only five people were seated at the bar, two couples and a woman in a lime green dress studying the Keno results posted on the screen overhead. There were ten or twelve small tables, only a few of them filled. Jenna pulled out a chair and sat down with her back to the bar, facing the casino.

A waitress with skin so pale she looked as if she didn't exist outside the dark, timeless world of the casino, took Jenna's order for a glass of Kendall Jackson Chardonnay, the best one they had, and an order of egg rolls.

The wine arrived quickly. Jenna took several long sips, which immediately blurred the edges of her thoughts about the ruptures in her life back home. She set the glass on the table. The wine smelled crisp and clean and tasted like citrus. She leaned back in her chair and closed her eyes.

Along with her egg rolls, the waitress delivered a second glass of wine. "I didn't want a second glass yet," Jenna said. Had she mentioned she'd be having two glasses? For a moment, she wondered if the waitress had read her mood, or maybe everyone who came in here had the same mood, so reading it wasn't that difficult.

"A gift from the man in the corner."

The waitress didn't nod or gesture to indicate who she was talking about, but there was only one table with a man alone. "No thank you. I want a second glass, but not yet, and not from him."

"He figured you'd say that and he told me to tell you *no obligation, just a friendly gesture.*"

"I don't want it."

"He stays here a lot," the waitress said. "It's fine. He just likes to let beautiful women know that someone is admiring them. It doesn't mean anything."

Jenna pushed the glass to the edge of the table. "Please take it away."

"Lighten up. All you business gals are the same. He's friendly. Can't a guy buy a drink for a pretty woman without it causing some imagined offense?"

"You don't understand," Jenna said.

"I understand more than you know."

The muscles in Jenna's neck tightened. She didn't want some guy in the corner noticing her, didn't appreciate the waitress categorizing her with such a condescending tone. She picked up an egg roll and bit through the crisp wrapping. The vegetables were surprisingly full of flavor. Chewing slowly, she adjusted her position so she could get a better look at the man in the corner.

"Anything else?" the waitress said.

Jenna shook her head.

"Do you want me to take away the wine?"

"No, it's okay." There was no point in fighting it, she'd only draw more attention to herself. She picked up her glass and took a sip. She shouldn't have wavered. The minute the waitress walked away, Jenna knew she'd made a mistake, but she hadn't wanted to act superior. The waitress would be thrilled to have a man look past her sallow skin and limp hair, noticing her legs, which were long and lean. But Jenna didn't care how meaningless the glass of wine was. Nothing ever came without a string of some kind, an expectation, even if it was a smile or a gentle nudge to let down her guard, to speak to him if he walked past her table and greeted her.

She moved the unwanted glass closer to the edge. When the waitress returned, she'd insist that it be removed. She'd have a second glass in her room.

"Hi there."

Jenna startled. The wine splashed up the inside of her glass. She took a quick sip to steady herself.

"I didn't mean to scare you."

The man was at her side, but she couldn't see his face without turning and looking up. "You didn't scare me."

"Mind if I sit down?"

She picked up the second, untouched glass of wine and held it up. "I won't be able to drink this. I hope you'll enjoy it."

"Don't be that way. I'm not hitting on you."

She still couldn't see his face. He stood near her elbow so looking at him would require violent twisting around in her chair, and that much effort would give the impression she cared what he looked like. "I'd rather be alone," she said. "I've had a long day."

"If it's that bad, wouldn't it relieve some stress to tell it all to a stranger. Then you can go on your way. Absolved, as it were."

His words created a split in her mind. It was nothing like she'd expected, praise for her appearance, a sob story about his own problems, a flirty and pouty complaint of loneliness. He'd managed to avoid all the clichés and hit her right where she had an open wound. There was no one to talk to. The thought felt like a betrayal of Devon, but it was true. She and Devon told each other everything. They were truly best friends. But his drug selling had gnawed silently at her bones until this faceless man told her it might make her feel better to dump it all out on a stranger. It hurt, more than she'd wanted to admit, that Devon had a secret.

She drank the rest of the wine too quickly. She set the glass to the side and pulled the second one close to her plate of egg rolls. The stem was wet, and the bowl of the glass looked drippy. She patted it with her cocktail napkin and took a sip. It was still cold.

"No, it wouldn't help. But have a seat."

He was actually quite good looking. Dark hair, neatly trimmed, longish in the back, almost touching the open collar of his white shirt. He wore a black suit and no wedding ring. Forty, she guessed.

He set his cocktail napkin and drink on the table, something pale gold with lots of ice. He extended his hand across the small table. "Brent," he said.

She gripped his hand and let go. "Jenna."

"So what are you in town for, Jenna?"

"Quarterly sales meeting."

"What company?"

He must have noticed a narrowing of her eyes because he said, "Never mind. It's not important."

"Today was the last day, I head home tomorrow morning. It went really well," she said. "What are you here for?"

"Wining and dining clients for a few days."

"Why aren't you with them now?"

"I think we wore them out with a day of golf in the desert sun. And a late party last night. Tomorrow is golf again."

"Don't you get tired of it?"

"Golf? Never." He laughed. "It's addictive."

Jenna had heard that, but she didn't see how. If you wanted to be outside, enjoy nature, why not something challenging, exciting, like sailing? Especially when you were young.

"So what did you want to tell me? I seemed to catch your attention when I said I could absolve you." He laughed again.

"I don't want to tell you anything."

"It's hard to strike the right balance with you."

She sipped her wine. "You're a little pushy." One minute she thought it was best to stand up and walk away, but a moment later he would smile, and she knew she was being paranoid. He was a business traveler, unwinding after constant contact with groups of people, just like she was. There was no harm in talking. He hadn't said anything that set off a major alarm.

"Sorry." He picked up his drink and shifted his chair a few inches further away from the table.

"Sometimes life gets to be too much, you know? You're going along, and you think you have things more or less under control, and then ..." Jenna said.

He nodded. He set his glass on the napkin, moving it until it was centered precisely over the damp ring that had formed there.

"Someone betrays you or shakes your confidence. You realize things weren't what they seemed." Everything in her wanted to blurt out the truth about Devon's lapse. She sipped her wine, once again aware of the noise around her, aware of the pinch of her shoe on the baby toe of her left foot. She remembered the foot massage Devon had given her in New

Mexico, stroking the muscle and pressing his thumbs into the arch, rubbing her feet until every knot was smoothed out. He was so good to her. Yet, he'd broken the law. Was still breaking the law. She couldn't tell that to a total stranger. Entertaining clients? What did that mean? For all she knew, this guy was in law enforcement or knew someone who was. She had no idea what she'd been thinking. There was nothing else to talk about. She wasn't going to tell him they were in debt up to their eyeballs. Tell him her friend was missing, and they'd lied to the police. Some things you couldn't talk about, no matter how enticing the promise of anonymity. There was no such thing. Six degrees of separation and all that.

"What were you going to say?"

She picked up her glass and took several sips of wine. Shifting the glass to her left hand, she picked up the last egg roll. It was cool now, but still tasty, and easy to bite without fear of burning her tongue. She chewed and swallowed. "Nothing."

"You'll never see me again. Relax and let it go, it'll make you feel better."

"I doubt it."

"You're wrong."

She set her glass on the table. "You don't even know me. How can you possibly know how anything will make me feel?" She took one more bite of the egg roll, then pushed the plate to the side. "Thanks for the wine."

"You haven't finished it."

"I've had enough. I need to get some rest. I have an early flight." She was annoyed that she'd succumbed to the need to let him down easily. If there were nothing alarming about his demeanor, she wouldn't be making excuses. She stood. "Nice talking to you. And thanks again for the wine."

"It's a waste not to finish it."

"I've had enough." She turned toward the bar. "I'll ask the waitress to put it on my bill."

"That's not necessary."

"Well, I don't want to offend you, by not finishing it."

"It's a waste no matter who pays for it."

Jenna smiled. "Enjoy the rest of your stay." She turned quickly, walked to the bar, and asked for her bill. She had that exposed feeling that crawled up her spine when she knew someone was watching her. She never should have invited him to sit down, never should have let the waitress guilt her into keeping the wine glass on her table. Now, she wanted to pay and get to her room and crawl under the covers where there wouldn't be any eyes on her.

After she signed the receipt, she kept her back to where he was presumably still seated and walked to the opposite end of the bar. She still had the sensation of being watched, but it was surely her own self-consciousness. He'd probably already left the bar.

At the end of the row of slot machines, she turned. She couldn't help letting her gaze wander back to the cocktail lounge. The table was empty. She wound her way around blackjack tables and slot machines. The hum of voices and clang of jackpot bells vibrated in her ears. The entire casino sparkled with light from chandeliers and blinking machines, and yet it was still filled with shadows. Her eyes and ears ached equally by the time she reached the relative quiet of the alcove that housed the elevators. Eight elevators and none of them were on the casino floor. She pressed the call button and stepped back so she could see all the overhead lights as she waited for one to descend.

"I hope I didn't offend you." Brent's voice was quiet but quite clear.

Jenna's hands twitched. She turned. He was taller than she'd realized, six foot three or four, and as good looking under the brighter lights of the elevator area as he'd appeared in the darkness of the lounge.

"I'm not offended. Enjoy the rest of your evening." She turned to the elevator, staring at the arrows overhead. It wasn't checkout time, it shouldn't be taking so long for one of them to arrive.

"I'm calling it a night," he said.

The elevator behind her chimed. She was forced to turn to face him as she moved toward the opening doors. With a sweeping gesture, Brent stepped to the side and indicated she should enter first. Jenna stepped into the elevator and positioned herself in front of the panel of buttons.

Brent followed her and moved to the back.

She pressed the button for the seventeenth floor, then

realized her mistake. The doors slid closed. "What floor?" she said.

"Seventeen."

The elevator raced upward. Jenna tucked her hands in the pockets of her jeans.

"How strange that we're on the same floor," he said. "All these floors, all these rooms. Maybe we're right next door to each other."

She shoved her hands further into her pockets although there wasn't much more room. She pinched her elbows close to her sides. There was no way in hell she was getting off the elevator and letting this guy see where her room was located. He felt larger, somehow, inside the narrow steel box. A mirror covered the entire back wall, reflecting the low wattage bulbs that made the interior glow as if they were underwater. Or maybe it was the rapid rise of the elevator, or the thick feeling in her head, drinking the wine too fast, that created a submerged feeling.

Brent took a step forward. She could feel the heat of his body, closer to her bare arms. Yet, the air inside the elevator was cool. She shivered. He ran his finger down the back of her upper arm.

Jenna turned. "What are you doing?"

"You look cold."

"I'm fine. Please don't touch me."

He held up both hands. "Sorry."

The bell chimed, and the doors slid open. Neither one of them moved.

"After you," he said.

"I'm not getting out, I forgot I need to check back with my colleagues. To make sure everything's wrapped up since I'm leaving so early." Her voice was thin, rising to an airless squeak from speaking too fast without taking a breath.

The door started to close.

Jenna stuck out her hand and pressed her arm against the rubber edges.

Brent didn't move.

"Aren't you getting off?" she said.

"I'll ride back down with you and keep you company."

"I don't need company. Good night."

"I should cash in my chips now. There's no spare time in my schedule tomorrow."

Jenna moved away from the doors and let them slide closed. She pressed the buttons for the mezzanine and the casino. She couldn't force him to get off. Now she was trapped in her lie. The room where they'd managed registration and other details was locked for the night. She had no idea what she would say if he followed her. At the same time, she was angry with herself. She should tell him to leave her alone, or she was calling security.

"I get the feeling you're trying to dodge me," Brent said.

She turned to face him. "I'm not interested in spending any more time with you."

"That's the trouble with chicks like you."

The bell dinged. Jenna turned as the doors opened, but they looked out on a floor of rooms. No one was waiting. The doors remained open for several seconds, hoping for another rider before they slowly closed.

"You're so hot, you think you're too good for a regular guy."

Jenna laughed. She regretted it. He would interpret it as an invitation to continue, but she couldn't help it. Originally she'd thought he was good-looking, but that impression had shifted as it became clear that something wasn't quite right. He definitely wasn't a regular guy. Did he realize he was scaring her?

"I don't think anything. I'm tired, and I'm married

"Tired of being married?" He chortled like a derelict cowering in the back of an alley filled with trash and empty liquor bottles. "Well someday you'll be old and saggy, and a guy like me won't give you a second look. I tried to be respectful and sensitive to your mood, and you blew me off like I'm a low life barfly."

The bell chimed for the mezzanine level.

Jenna stepped out.

Brent stepped out and waited.

She walked quickly to the stairs down to the casino.

"Where are you going?"

"I'm going to ask security to escort me to my room."

"Don't get all freaked out. I'm just being friendly."

"You're too friendly. Go away, or I'm calling security."

He held up his hands again. "So sorry to offend. Have a good night. Bitch." He stalked to the staircase and hurried down the steps.

When she finally closed the door to her room, she turned the deadbolt and stumbled toward the bed. She flopped on her back and let her shoes fall off her feet. A sob rose from deep inside her chest. This wasn't only about being trapped in a steel box with a strangely behaving man.

Since she was twelve years old and her stepmother told her she could lose her pudginess if she started jogging, promising that she'd buy Jenna new clothes and take her to a spa for pampering once she'd lost twenty pounds, Jenna had been focused on looking good. Christine made it clear what looking *good* could get you – Christine had gotten Jenna's father, for example. Now, Jenna couldn't comprehend why that had ever been her goal.

The appreciative looks from men had always pleased her. When they came from strangers, when the men looking her way were drunk or overtly leering, she'd either been with Devon or her friends and brushed it off as harmless.

Never before had she felt like her looks were advertising something she wasn't offering. It had never occurred to her that her long, thick hair and tight jeans would put her in a situation that left her hands trembling, even now. And it could have been worse.

More than anything, she wished Devon was lying beside

her. She loved him so much, it felt like massive hands pressed around her throat, turning her love into a physical ache for oxygen.

Twenty

BETH DROPPED HER satchel on the hall table and went into the kitchen. Six hours with thirty-two second-graders had been more exhausting than usual. Despite her flat, sole-hugging sandals and her ever-present water bottle, her feet and throat ached equally. Her arms felt as if they were filled with liquid. It wasn't the kids, really, making her limbs swollen and heavy. It was the constant whisper of certainty that Allison was dead, brutally murdered. Perhaps cut into pieces.

Beth's stomach convulsed. She opened the refrigerator door. For the past few days, she'd experienced an intense cold in the center of her bones. At other times, she wanted to cry. Would they ever know what had happened? Could a woman disappear off the face of the earth? Of course she could. You heard about it all the time. Well, not all the time, but often enough. That's why there were TV shows about unsolved crimes – real and fabricated.

It was unbelievable that the police had no leads, at least as far as she knew. They hadn't been able to find Allison's bike, and they hadn't determined whether anyone had seen or talked to her after Craig left for the gym. She'd vanished into thin air. They didn't even know where to look. Now that there'd been an article in the local paper, there was a steady flow of calls to the police station. Apparently, that happened all the time when someone went missing. It meant nothing, and most of the callers were so clearly cranks or delusional, the police followed up on only a very few.

She filled a glass with ice cubes and took the pitcher of orange juice out of the fridge. She poured juice over the ice, soothed by the popping as the ice changed shape. She was glad to be doing something that didn't require mental effort, concentrating on nothing but the sound and sight of juice and ice adjusting to each other's presence.

The police had been by to talk to her and Michael again on Wednesday. Their questions were repetitious and simplistic – *When was the last time they'd spoken to Allison? Was it possible Allison was having an affair? Did they know of any problems in her life with money? Gambling? Drugs? Was Craig violent?* That last question made her angry. She'd snapped at the officer, telling him the questions were out of line. Why did they assume it was Allison's fault that she was missing? The detectives assured her that it wasn't their intention to give that impression. Right. Then why were all the questions about possible hidden vices in Allison's life? How could they think a man like Craig would ever be violent? He was a doctor. And not a high-strung specialist, but a GP, the gentlest man she knew, aside from Michael. It was cruel the way their questions created ugly scenarios, stirred up doubt. Could you really live an admirable life, then have your integrity questioned because someone you loved was abducted? It was outrageous.

Craig said he'd been answering questions on a daily basis. Beth hadn't spoken to him since Monday, but they'd exchanged a few text messages. She felt his friends, herself included, were failing him. Craig's brother had come to stay with him, but that wasn't enough. His friends should be getting together and eating dinner with him every evening, supporting him. Michael didn't agree. He said it was morbid and they'd drag each other down. Craig insisted he didn't feel like eating, or socializing. Devon and Jenna were behaving as if they didn't even care, as if they hardly noticed their friend had been missing for almost a week. Jenna had flown off to Las Vegas. Beth realized that wasn't a very fair criticism since all of them were going to work, even Craig was seeing a few patients. But somehow "working" in Las Vegas seemed more of an affront.

She sipped her juice and went into the living room. She slid open both glass doors and checked that the screens were locked. Behind the house was a greenbelt filled with oak trees and grass that was fading as summer approached. She'd always loved the wild look, the lack of human interference, a space free of houses and power lines. Now it looked like a place where a faceless predator might hide, watching. There was nothing to fear, it was light out, she lived in an exclusive area. Until a week ago, she'd never felt unsafe in her house, but now she wasn't so sure. How did someone grab a woman off her bike? Unless Allison had stopped that afternoon, too comfortable, not acknowledging the reality of a dangerous world. Beth set down her glass and closed and locked both doors. She fastened the security locks. Michael would be home in a few hours, then she'd open the doors and enjoy the lazy breeze and the scent of the gardenias clustered in large blue-glazed pots on the patio.

She picked up her glass, went into the kitchen, pulled her mobile phone out of her bag, and pressed Craig's number. While she waited for the call to connect, she wandered back to the living room and drank a few more sips of juice.

When Craig answered, his voice sounded rough, as if he'd been crying or yelling, or simply talking too much, his vocal cords strained by abnormal use.

"How are you doing?" Beth said.

"Tired."

"Did you sleep last night?"

"Maybe for an hour or two."

"You said that last time. You should ask your ..." She laughed, then immediately felt insensitive for finding anything funny right now. "I was going to say you should ask your doctor for something to help you sleep. Can't you prescribe something for yourself?"

"I don't want to sleep. And I don't want to dull my mind.

In case I think of something. Or in case the police get even more aggressive."

"What happened now?"

"They still can't find anyone who saw her. So guess what that means."

"I don't know."

"I was the last one. And I say that with air quotes. It seems the last one to see her means something sinister. It pisses me off. Obviously, they can't find the person who actually saw her last, because that would be the person who abducted her. Or worse."

"You can't think that way." Her words rang false, especially since she thought *that way* every ten minutes. Still, she felt compelled to say something reassuring.

"There's no other way to think. She's been gone too long." He coughed. "This time the questions got really ugly."

"What did they ask?"

"I don't even want to say. They asked how I felt about her career, whether I was jealous of the men she worked with, of their power. They wanted to know about our sex life, whether we did role playing, tied each other up. Used strangulation. They asked questions that made it sound as if they thought she might have died accidentally and I hid her body."

A sob that was half bellow, half screech blasted from the phone. Beth went back to the kitchen and set her glass at the center of the table. The front yard was covered with shade. The sky was still a pale, watery blue, but the large fir trees cast shadows, and even though light filtered between the trees, those narrow spaces were invisible on the lawn as the darkness ran together into a large inky pool.

She let Craig cry softly for several minutes. If there were anything worse than Allison's disappearance, this would be it. Being accused of aberrant behavior that had caused your wife harm, possibly death, must be unbearably painful. There was no way to defend against that kind of suspicion. The accusing words had been said, the thoughts already passed into being. No matter what happened with Allison, no matter what they discovered, Craig would have to live with that stain. It was cruel.

The phone felt too small and slippery in her hand. If only she could hold onto something larger. Sometimes she hated smartphones with their cute bodies, so convenient for sliding into your pocket, but so difficult to get a grip on without ending up with cramped fingers. "I wish I could do something." She didn't honestly expect him to respond, but she had to keep speaking. "The police talked to us again."

"What did they ask? Did they say anything about me?"

"It was mostly the same questions. It felt as if they were trying to catch us contradicting what we'd said the first time."

"I know how that is."

"General stuff about how long we'd known you." She hesitated. She could lie, not tell him everything. It wasn't required, and he might not ever find out. She didn't want to treat him as though he were fragile, in need of protection. If she did that, it was only for herself, so she wouldn't have to face his despair. "They asked about your marriage."

"What did you say?"

"We told them you seemed very happy as a couple, that you ..."

"*Seemed?*" Craig said.

"Let me finish. We said you were devoted to each other, supported each other's careers, that it was obvious you're in love not just infatuated."

Craig sighed. "It sounds so trite. They manage to take good things and twist them into something unflattering, at best. Evil, at worst. They probably took a word like *infatuated* and thought it meant I'm looking around for someone more exciting."

"I don't think so. I think I said something about infatuation being juvenile. Like Devon and Jenna." The moment she said it, she wished she hadn't. They didn't need to turn on each other, despite that scene in the driveway — Devon's rough, nearly violent treatment of her. And when Michael had called him on it, Devon acted as if she were the one with a problem, laughed it off that she'd over-reacted. It was upsetting that Michael had let that pass. She was sure Devon had made her out to be an over-sensitive female. He used to be so kind, so easy-going. Her lower back was stiff from sitting at the table, leaning on her elbows. She walked back to the living room and sat on the sofa.

"I haven't heard from Devon," Craig said. "The cops

must have talked to them."

"Jenna's in Vegas, for a sales event."

"That wouldn't stop them from talking to Devon."

Beth leaned back and stretched her feet toward the coffee table. She pressed her toes against the edge. "Do you think Devon and Jenna know something about Allison?"

"What makes you ask that?"

"Devon got angry at me."

"For what?"

"I stopped by the other day because I saw his Jeep in the driveway. He was in a panic that I was making him late for work, and he grabbed me. He scratched my arm with his keys. Hard enough to make me bleed."

"Really."

"And they both seem, although Devon mostly ... he seems disconnected from everything. As if he doesn't even think there's anything scary about her disappearing."

"Something happened when I was over there. Sunday," Craig said.

"What?"

"I smelled Allison's perfume."

Beth tried to digest this. There could be an explanation. She wasn't sure how long a strong scent might linger.

"I mentioned it, and they brushed it off. They tried to make me think I was imagining it. But I wasn't."

"Did you tell the police?"

"What are you saying?" Craig said.

"Not that. Not anything terrible. I would never even think that."

"Then why would I tell the police?" Craig's voice was eager, giddy almost, as if he was anxious for her to tell him what to do. He sounded like he hoped for a specific answer, one that echoed his own reasoning.

She wasn't sure what to say. She knew what was in her thoughts, what had been eating at the back of her mind since Monday. The unbalanced feeling she'd had when she was at Devon and Jenna's last Sunday, the sense that they wanted her to leave. Something had been off. Their steady re-direction of the conversation. Maybe that wasn't it either. All she knew was she'd felt their reactions hadn't rung true. Once she said the words though, once she spoke out loud to anyone other than Michael, what she'd felt, it would be too late. It was the same as the questions the police were asking Craig, implications. After the words were said, they would never go away. They'd linger forever in their collective memory. Her suspicions would transform themselves into something solid, like an egg full of liquid, boiling and turning into a dense, new object. But Craig had smelled Allison's perfume. She supposed that could be written off as fear, his longing to have an answer. Then why hadn't he "smelled" it somewhere else? Why not in her living room?

Jenna and Devon were like family. She shouldn't be thinking this way, and she wasn't even sure what her subconscious was hinting at. Critical thoughts floated around in her head, vague and half-formed.

"Why do you think I should tell the police?" Craig said.

"Because I'm not sure perfume lingers for weeks. A few hours, possibly overnight."

"Maybe they were right, I imagined it."

"If you really believe that, why did you mention it?"

"I can't stop thinking about it."

"Then you should tell the police."

"They'll think I'm trying to change the subject. Divert their attention from me, and then they'll crank up their focus on me. I can't do anything right. If I get choked up, they think I'm over-wrought. If I'm calm, they think I'm cold."

"How do you know that?"

"They stare at me constantly. The very fact that they're talking to me every other day, saying things I would never even think, is making it worse."

"You're probably being paranoid. Because you feel uncomfortable," she said.

"I don't think so."

"Well, you have to put that out of your head. You have to tell them. What if Allison was at the Porters that day, and for whatever reason, just pure self-absorption because they don't want to be involved in helping to find her, they aren't saying that they saw her. If they know where she was going, or even know what mood she was in, it could help. You have to tell the police."

"I'll see how it goes next time they ask questions."

"No. Call them." The more she thought about it, the more convinced she became. Twice in two months, Devon had nearly assaulted someone. After he got in Craig's face at her shower, the party had been uncomfortable for a while. And he'd scared her the other day in the driveway. He didn't really hurt her, that was true, but she'd been terrified, all the same. There was no doubt in her mind now that Craig had smelled Allison's perfume. On Sunday he'd still been in denial, so he'd written it off as something with a reasonable explanation. It was obvious Allison had been at the Porters. The last time the whole group had gathered there was right after the holidays. There was no way Allison's perfume would have clung to the carpet and furniture all that time, hovering in the air like an unwelcome ghost.

"What are you saying? Do you think they know where she is?" Craig said.

"I'm saying there are no leads. They can't find her bike, they can't find anyone who knows about any dark secret they keep insisting she has." She rushed on, "they have nothing, and this is one sliver of information."

"It would be like turning wolves on my friends."

Beth gripped the phone. A cramp ran down the back of her hand. She loosened her grip and nearly dropped it. "Your wife has been missing for six days! Tell them you smelled her perfume. I'm sure Devon didn't do anything to hurt her, but they must know something. Maybe Allison does have a secret, and they know what it is. Doesn't that make more sense than her disappearing into thin air?"

"Yes."

"Look how Devon attacked you at my shower. Way back then, it seemed like they were hiding something. Didn't it?"

"He was a little off."

"So maybe there was something going on between Allison and him."

"Do you mean she was cheating on me? With Devon? No way. He's obsessed ..." He stopped abruptly. He coughed. When he spoke again, his voice sounded deeper but quieter. "Allison would never do that."

"That's not what I meant. Something. Maybe about money. Devon and Jenna are having money problems. Who knows how far that goes? Anyway, it's not our job to figure it out. You need to call the police and tell them about the perfume."

"Okay."

After they said *good-bye*, Beth cradled the phone in her palm. She rubbed her finger across the screen to remove the film that built up on the slick surface. The sky outside the living room window was still as blue as mid-day. The presence of bright sunlight when it was time to fix dinner unnerved her in the early weeks of spring. She supposed her body was still adapting to the time change – yet another example of how human beings were more tied to the natural world than most people in developed countries recognized. That's why Craig was both suspicious and self-doubting about the lingering odor of Allison's perfume in the Porters' house. His body told him he smelled his wife's scent, but his civilized mind wanted to be polite, trusting of his friends. She hoped he'd follow through and call the police. If he didn't, she would.

Twenty-one

JENNA UNLOCKED THE front door. It was only eleven a.m. She'd made good time from the airport. Highway 101 was nearly congestion-free in the middle of the morning. She yanked her suitcase up over the threshold and carried it up the stairs and wheeled it into the closet. After the dry air of Nevada and the airplane cabin, she desperately needed a glass of water. Maybe two. Unpacking could wait.

She walked downstairs. The small metal door that closed over the back end of the mail slot built into the wall in the entryway was stuffed. Had Devon not emptied it the entire time she was gone? She pulled open the door and shoved her hand against the contents so everything wouldn't slide to the floor. She pulled out the mail and set it on the hall table. As always, most of it was junk. There was a flyer with local ads, several glossy cards with smartphone and TV offers, a few credit card solicitations, and a Pottery Barn catalog.

Stuffed in the center of the pile was an envelope with a

return-address logo for a contractor who claimed to specialize in wine cellars. It was addressed to Devon. She poked her finger under the tab and tore it open. A single sheet with lists of square footage and pricing. She went into the kitchen and pulled open the drawer under the cabinet where they kept their wine and scotch. She groped around for the key to the basement. It wasn't there. Proof that Devon had been down to the wine cellar recently, possibly, shown the space to a contractor. Was that why he'd been so distracted on the phone, going on about the taxes? Maybe he'd been getting estimates while she was out of town. She slammed the drawer closed and went into the office. The file cabinet behind the desk contained a rack with their duplicate keys. She found the one to the padlock that secured the basement door.

She stood outside, staring at the weathered oak door to the basement, and remembered she'd been thirsty. Her throat was even more parched from breathing hard through her mouth the past few minutes. She needed to calm down. She was rushing to conclusions. It was possible the contractor got Devon's name off a mailing list for a catalog, and the price list meant nothing. On the other hand, maybe Devon felt his drug sales allowed him more freedom to spend cash, continuing to let all the debt sit there like a boulder crushing their backs.

She inserted the key into the padlock. The door lifted easily. The single bulb hanging from the basement ceiling was turned on. So he had been down here recently. If he'd left that light on months ago, it would be burned out by now. She walked down three steps, ducked her head under the frame of the foundation, took another step, and stumbled. It smelled of dry earth, making her throat tighten and her desire for water increase tenfold. There was something else. In the far corner was a pile of blankets and towels. Nearby was a half-empty bottle of water and a power bar wrapper.

She walked slowly, holding her breath. It felt as if her blood had stopped moving through her veins. Her eyes processed what was in front of her, but her mind was afraid to acknowledge what she was looking at. The pile of blankets moved. The edge of the top one slipped down, revealing a strand of light brown hair.

She felt her pulse in her neck and along the backs of her hands, pounding, pushing her to move closer, to find out what she was looking at. She took another step forward, bent down, and pulled back the blanket. A strand of hair, filled with static from the wool blanket, clung to the back of her hand. She shrieked, jumped back, and clawed at her skin as if a large spider had leaped on to her wrist. The hair was no longer touching her, but she rubbed her hand furiously.

Finally, her mind caught up with her eyes. Allison. She wasn't dead. Jenna shoved away the thought, not wanting to consider why her first instinct had been that this was Allison's body on her basement floor. But what the hell was Allison doing sleeping down here? She pressed Allison's shoulder, turning her onto her back. There was no movement of her eyelids to indicate she was waking up. Jenna pulled the blanket down further. Allison had her arms extended with her hands shoved between her bent knees. Duct tape circled her wrists. Rough, fibrous-looking cord was wound around her ankles several times and tied in a large knot that pressed against her Achilles' tendons.

Jenna's legs felt as if the kneecaps had slid out of the space where it belonged. She lowered herself to the ground, wondering how she could be looking at this, yet thinking about how the grit of the basement floor would tear at her jeans, requiring an immediate washing of the clothes that had been clean that morning when she got dressed in Las Vegas.

She coughed from the chalky odor of dirt. The light formed a circle around Allison's head, creating the effect of a spotlight. Jenna picked up the water bottle. She wanted a drink, but Allison's lips were dry with flaked skin and crusted scum at the corners. The thought of putting her own mouth over the same opening erased her thirst. Now that she was sitting, her mind was slowly adapting to what she was looking at. Devon must have put Allison down here, wrapped her wrists with tape, and tied her ankles. But why? What had happened last Saturday? For an entire week, a woman had been held captive in their basement while Jenna slept peacefully in her bed, flew to Las Vegas and back, and Devon went to the office every day. In fact, while the police had knocked on the door and questioned him about when he'd last seen Allison.

She pulled her knees up and rested her forehead on them. She closed her eyes so she wouldn't have to look at Allison's sleeping form. Hopefully, Allison would wake up soon. Jenna was not going upstairs until she asked a few questions. She didn't want to think about what was going on in Devon's head. She shivered. The chill ran through her body, but after it subsided her arms continued to shake.

When Jenna and Devon first started dating, she'd been jealous of his closeness with Allison. He and Allison had a connection that went beyond words, exchanging smiles and quick glances that made it obvious they were thinking along similar lines, mentally departing from the group while conversation and laughter flowed around them. It wasn't that Jenna doubted his love, doubted his absolute devotion to her, but that friendship had always been a part of him that she'd never possess. Two days before Devon and Jenna were married, he and Allison had gone on a bike ride. It was the last thing they'd done without Jenna or Craig joining them. They were gone all day. When he returned, Devon couldn't get enough of Jenna, clinging to her, telling her he felt a void when she wasn't with him. Yet, he never said what he and Allison had talked about, why he felt the need to spend all that time with her. It wasn't that Jenna worried they were having sex, nothing like that. It was only that lifelong connection, almost like siblings, knowing each other in a way that no one else ever could.

She had guessed what they'd talked about on that bike ride. Before that day, Allison had seemed to judge her. Allison tried to prove she was smarter than Jenna, which she was, so the competition seemed pointless. Allison made snide comments about Jenna's attention to her appearance as if that proved she was shallow. She was dismissive of Jenna's job, calling it a waste of a good education. After the bike ride, all of that stopped, but lately, it had changed again. Jenna couldn't be sure if the refusal of her credit card was the first time it had started up, or if Allison had been whispering behind her back for years, and Craig's thinly veiled criticism at the shower was the first time Jenna had felt the disapproval resurfacing. Now that she thought about it, there might have been a slight shift around the time Devon began supplying Allison's cocaine.

None of this explained why he would tie her up, essentially kidnap her. If Jenna had thought the debt would destroy them, that drug sales were risking their lives, what was she supposed to think about this? Could he be experiencing a mental breakdown? Or was it some kind of game? That thought made her feel better. She'd misinterpreted the whole thing. Maybe something was wrong between Allison and Craig. It could be that Allison wanted Craig to worry about her, that she wanted to prove some kind of point, that she ... Jenna lifted her head. It was wishful thinking. She'd find out when Allison woke. She pulled a blanket off Allison's feet and spread half of it on the floor, leaving half so she could wrap it around herself. She lay down and curled into a ball.

THE BASEMENT SEEMED colder, despite the blanket. Jenna rubbed her eyes and felt mascara smear across her cheekbone. She sat up. Allison's eyes were wide open, staring at her as if she'd asked a question and was waiting for Jenna's response.

Jenna sat up.

"My feet are cold. You have to take my blanket? After all this?"

"What happened?" Jenna lifted her hips off the floor and pulled the blanket out from under her. She spread it over Allison's feet.

"Aren't you going to untie me? Why haven't you already? You two are sick. Sick. Sick. Sick." Allison's voice was rough, her words running together without all the consonants, so it sounded as if she'd said *sig, sig, sig.*

"How did this happen?" Jenna said.

"So you're not going to untie me. Are you going to shove more Vicodin down my throat, too? You're as bad as he is."

Jenna wasn't going to give Allison the satisfaction of watching her turn on Devon. Despite the duct tape, the blankets, Allison's half-drugged state, she couldn't believe that Devon would do something like this without an excellent reason. "Devon tied you up and put you down here?"

"Who else?"

"Why?"

"Because he's obsessed with you. Because he's turned into a horrible person that I don't even recognize. Every year, every month, he moves further and further away from who he was."

"I don't think he's changed," Jenna said.

"How would you know?"

"What happened?"

"I was teasing him, and he took that ridiculous statue on your bathroom counter and hit me with it. He's lucky he didn't kill me."

"What were you teasing him about?"

"Are you going to sit there and talk like we're in a coffee shop, or are you going to untie me?"

"I have to get scissors to cut the tape."

"Then get them."

"I want to know why he did this."

"Ask him."

"I'm asking you. Devon never hit anyone in his life. What were you talking about?"

"You. What else. I told him the statue couldn't possibly look like you because it would be sticking its ass out, wiggling it at every man that walked by."

Jenna pushed herself to her feet. The movement was too fast. Her eyes blurred and a high-pitched tone rang in her ears. She bent forward and pressed her hands on her knees. Part of her wanted to smack Allison. Another part of her, a very large part, was pleased that Devon had defended her.

She never looked at other men, never *wiggled her ass* at them.

When her father had chosen Christine over her mother, she'd quickly learned that women who made the most of their appearance got what they wanted, even if it belonged to someone else. There was power in beauty, and it had nothing to do with sex. Well, maybe it did, but not overtly. It made her heart ache when she thought about how her mother had let her husband slip through her fingers, a woman too ethereal, too delicate to fight for what she wanted. Her mother was never made for this world. She was sensitive and had the kind of fragile beauty that made you want to take care of her, but not the kind that gave you power. There was nothing wrong with looking your best, knowing that men, a man, would do almost anything for a beautiful woman. Of course, after that creep in Las Vegas, she was no longer sure that was a good thing.

Once the dizziness had cleared, she straightened and looked down at Allison. "Is that what you think of me?"

Allison stared at her. She shifted under the blanket, rolled onto her back, and bent her knees into an inverted V. This had the effect of pulling the blanket tight around her neck. She squirmed, trying to loosen it. "I think I'm going to throw up."

Jenna took a few steps back, moving closer to the stairs.

"Where do you think you're going? Get this blanket off my neck and untie my feet. I'll go with you to get scissors."

"Why should I?"

"Devon is already in a shit-load of trouble. If you don't do something right now, you are too."

"It sounds like I already am." Jenna slid her fingers into her pockets. It was so cold down here. Without any natural light, she'd almost forgotten it was early afternoon. She had no idea what to do. Once Allison was let go, Devon would face ... what? Arrest? Prison? She wasn't sure what Allison would say. Until a moment ago, she thought Allison might protect her childhood friend, her drug supplier. After all, if Devon was arrested for keeping Allison in captivity, why wouldn't he tell them she was using cocaine? Because then it would be even worse for him, that's why. Her mind spun around the possibilities. Nothing seemed like a good outcome for Devon.

"You've ruined him," Allison said. "He was sweet and fun."

"He still is."

"He was a sweet kid, and he grew into a nice man. One of the nicest guys I knew." Allison coughed. She rolled onto her side. When she spoke again, her voice was louder. "He was there for his friends. Now, he ignores us most of the time. All he does is think about money and how he can buy more shit for you so you can feed your bottomless vanity. You're disgusting, and you've destroyed him. The old Devon would never have done something like this." She thrust her taped wrists forward, so she looked like a trapped animal writhing underneath the blanket. "All he cares about is making you happy, buying you this house you obviously can't afford, trying to get promoted so he can feed your desires. You've taken every good thing out of him and turned him into a freak."

"He's not like that at all." Jenna didn't want to shout, but couldn't stop herself. "And I'm not all those things you're saying. You think you can say whatever you want because you assume you're smarter than everyone else and whatever you think must be right. You don't know anything about us. No wonder he tied you up."

"Let me go."

Jenna turned and ran up the stairs.

"Come back here!"

Jenna pushed open the door and stepped outside. The sun was bright. Her eyes filled with tears. She let the door fall back into place and fastened the lock. She walked to the edge of the pool. Her hands trembled so she could hardly keep control of the key. Part of her wanted to toss it into the swimming pool. She slipped it in her pocket and sat down on one of the patio chairs.

How had this happened? She felt a warm, although shameful, glow that Devon had defended her. At the same time, she had no idea how they were going to get themselves out of this. Their lives were careening down a hill, slick with mud, and they were picking up speed with no trees or shrubs to grab onto. The entire day felt surreal. She should be going into the office, but now that it was mid-afternoon, on a

Friday, there was no point. She couldn't focus, couldn't even think what she was supposed to be doing at work right now. The whole world had tipped sideways. Nothing looked the same.

She went into the house and locked the door behind her. If Allison started screaming, would the noise carry into the house? Most likely not, or she would have heard something before now. She would have heard shrieks last weekend when no one but Devon knew Allison was down there. Although it looked like Allison had been kept limp with drugs, so maybe she hadn't tried to scream. She had to think about what she was going to say to Devon, and what they were going to do.

In the kitchen, her phone vibrated. She'd left it on the table, and as it danced across the wood surface, the rattling made it feel as if the whole house was vibrating, shaking in a tangle of nerves. She picked it up and looked at the display. Beth. She slid her finger across the screen.

"Are you still in Las Vegas?" Beth said.

"I just got home."

"Did Devon tell you what he did to me?"

"He told me you over-reacted."

Beth sighed. For several minutes, she didn't speak. "The police are questioning everyone about Allison. Have they talked to you yet?"

"I just got here."

"Did they talk to Devon?"

"Yes."

"What did he tell them?"

"There's nothing to tell."

"I think there is. I think Allison talked to one of you and you know something about where she might have gone."

"Why would you think that?"

"Craig told me about the perfume."

"He's imagining the perfume," Jenna said. "You know how that is."

"No, I don't."

"Poor guy," Jenna said. "I'm sure he's frantic."

"Of course he's frantic. We all are. Everyone but you and Devon."

"That's not fair."

"Then why did you rush off to Las Vegas when your friend is missing?"

"I had to work, Beth."

"In Las Vegas?"

Jenna walked to the window, trying to take a long, slow breath. She wasn't going to get dragged into explanations. She had enough problems, and Beth was being catty, making it into something it wasn't. "What do you want?"

"I want to know what you two aren't saying."

Jenna swallowed. How had Beth hit so close to the mark? She wondered how much force Devon had used when he grabbed her, how much he'd frightened her. And now, it made sense. Of course, he'd been far beyond annoyed, he'd been terrified Beth would discover Allison in the basement.

God, she still couldn't believe it, that while she casually talked on the phone, a woman was tied up in her basement. She felt like some kind of medieval witch. "Everyone is keyed up because we're worried about Allison." That was the truth. "No one is acting normally, whatever that is."

"Something doesn't feel right. And Craig knows it too."

"The only thing that's not right is that you don't know where Allison is." Jenna walked to the sink and turned on the faucet. Something about the words she'd just spoken stuck in her throat. She moistened her fingers and moved the phone away from her face. She patted water on her cheeks and turned off the faucet. She took a juice glass out of the cabinet and went to the fridge to fill it with filtered water. *You ... you don't know where Allison is.* Had Beth noticed? The phone had been silent for several seconds. She couldn't imagine what Beth was thinking. "Allison might be in some kind of trouble with her drug habit," Jenna said.

"What are you talking about?"

"You don't know?"

Jenna waited. It felt good, letting the silence expand, knowing she was in charge of the conversation instead of defending herself against Beth's certainty that she had an enhanced sensitivity to the world when all she really had was a heavy dose of paranoia. "Allison ..." Jenna took a breath. She had to say this carefully, make sure she didn't use the wrong tense or pronouns or anything else to hint that she'd seen Allison recently, or that she had anything more than a vague guess about what might have happened.

"Allison, what?"

"She uses cocaine."

"I don't believe that."

"Believe it."

"She wouldn't. She's smart … her career, it would damage her career … her health. She wants to get pregnant … Craig would never allow it."

"Craig doesn't have to *allow* it. He doesn't even know."

"Then how do you know?"

Jenna realized she hadn't planned this as carefully as she thought. She'd been too anxious to divert Beth's attention. There had to be a way around it, to keep Devon out of it. She was treading on dangerous ground, but she couldn't change direction now. "I found it in her bathroom."

"When?"

"I don't want to say."

"How do you know it was cocaine?"

"I asked her, and she didn't deny it."

"I don't believe it. You want to change the subject, or something. This is what I mean about you. Devon too."

"I don't want to change the subject. I didn't want to say anything earlier because she was using it at your wedding."

"She wouldn't do that."

"Haven't you noticed how hyper she's been? How fast she talks?"

"She's a high-energy person."

"Not like this. She can't stop, she hardly breathes."

"She wouldn't go against everything we wanted the wedding to be." Beth's voice was thin, breathless, resisting tears.

Jenna drank the entire glass of water. She pressed the spigot to refill it. She was desperately thirsty. Hopefully, Allison had been given plenty of liquids down there. If all she'd had was that half bottle of water, she might get dehydrated, collapse. She'd said she was going to throw up. It had sounded like drama, but now Jenna was worried.

She checked the time – two-thirty. Devon wouldn't be home for nearly four hours. She had no idea what she was supposed to do. All she wanted was to end this phone call and take a nap. A nice long nap would be good. She wouldn't have to think until Devon got home.

"I need to do some work," she said. "Shouldn't you be in the classroom right now?"

"It's recess."

"Well recess must be almost over, so I'll let you go."

"I'm not sure I believe you. Just so you know."

"It doesn't matter whether you believe me," Jenna said.

"Have you told the police? It might give them something more to work with."

"I told you, I haven't talked to the police."

"Well did Devon tell them?"

"I have no idea. I've been out of town, remember?"

"Right. I hope they find her soon." Beth sniffed. "It can't

be good that she's been gone this long." Her voice was quiet, lacking assurance.

"No, it can't," Jenna said.

Twenty-two

ALTHOUGH IT WAS still nearly full daylight outside, the entryway was filled with gray light when Devon stepped inside. The only word from Jenna had been a text message that she'd landed, and then a second text mid-afternoon that she hadn't slept much in Vegas and was going to take a nap. She must still be asleep.

He really should check on Allison. She'd been drugged and unwilling to eat or even sip water when he'd left that morning. He needed to get down there, but it was risky right now. He stood in the center of the entryway, uncertain. He'd thought about coming home at lunch but then realized Jenna was likely to be getting home right about that time. Allison would have to wait. She had been fine last night. She'd eaten a pear, a power bar, and half a bottle of water with the Vicodin. He'd helped her pee, so he knew her body was functioning properly. She hadn't spoken a word the entire time he'd been down there.

His stomach clenched into a hard knot. This had to be resolved. Tomorrow. He'd face himself and be a man and find a way to put enough fear into Allison that they could come up with a believable story as to where she'd been. She wouldn't throw away twenty years of friendship. Not to mention a good, safe supply of cocaine, or her career. He'd force some pragmatism into her. They'd plan together how to fix this.

He went into the family room and flicked on the TV. A talking head droned on about the stagnant housing market and the unemployment rate. Devon hit the mute button. The whole country was in debt, he shouldn't feel so bad. Their mistake had been trying too hard to hide it from their friends, worried that they'd look foolish, or unsuccessful, or whatever else it was they worried about when their problems were as minor as a little credit card debt and some overweight loans. It was a mistake to assume he and Jenna were the only ones with a significant imbalance. Look at the federal debt, the state debt, the out-of-whack home loans, student loans, and car loans. The whole world was sinking in a tar pit of debt.

The makeup-coated dude on TV was still moving his mouth. Devon went into the living room and opened the back door, hoping no mosquitoes or flies came in with the fresh air. He sometimes missed having screened doors, but Jenna loved the authentic look. She was probably right, she usually was about most things. Screens would cheapen the style, and a fly or two was a small price.

"We need to talk."

Jenna's voice startled him. He jerked his head around. Her hair, mussed from napping, hung over her left shoulder, clinging to her breast. He hadn't heard her footsteps descending the stairs, or felt a change in the air when she entered the living room. She wore a tight-fitting running top and navy blue nylon shorts that hugged her hips and thighs. Her feet were bare.

"Are you going running?" He loved it that she ran, but he hated that she ran without him. Of course, he didn't have the body of a runner, and he found running awkward and tiring. The few times he'd gone with her, he was certain he'd looked like Frankenstein's monster, lurching along beside her, and, if he was honest, a little bit behind. She'd had to cut her time short because his stamina wasn't even close to hers. Lifting weights was the only sports-like activity that made him feel competent. He was slim enough, and he wasn't overly bulked up, but he just didn't have the fluidity required to run well. If he ran with her, they could merge together more completely, into their own private world, a single being. When she ran, he felt shut out of her life. It was irrational in the extreme, but he felt as if she was running away from him, hanging on to a private part of herself where she didn't need him, didn't need anyone. She loved being alone. That desire to separate herself from everyone else was incomprehensible to him. How could you be all alone, what did she think about, why didn't she crave conversation, or at least the companionable silence of her mate right by her side?

"Sit down," Jenna said.

She knew. She must know. Why had he let this go on so long? "What's wrong?"

She walked into the room and sat on the sofa. "I saw Allison."

He closed his eyes. For a moment he thought he might pass out. Or puke. He felt disconnected from his body. "Why were you down there?"

"Are you insane? There's a woman drugged and tied up in our basement, a woman the police and her extremely upset husband, not to mention her other friends and co-workers are looking for. And the only thing you have to say is *why was I down there?*"

Devon sat on the armchair. He wrapped his fingers around the tight curves of the arms, clutching them like the sides of a boat that was slipping beneath the surface of the water. If he held on tightly enough, maybe it would right itself. Maybe he would be okay. They would be okay. "I don't know. I don't know how this happened. Things just … escalated."

"You hit her."

"I know. I didn't mean to. It was an accident."

"How is smashing someone with my sculpture an accident?"

"Did you talk to her?"

"Of course."

"She was awake?"

"Not at first. But ..."

"How did she seem?"

"Pissed off."

"Really." If she was in that state, he needed to give her some more Vicodin. Soon.

Jenna snapped her fingers at him. "So what is your plan? To keep a woman tied up in our basement for the rest of our lives?"

Devon swallowed. He felt like his whole life was stuck in his throat, strangling him, squeezing tighter, cutting off oxygen to his brain so he couldn't think. There wasn't any plan. It had all unfolded without a single identifiable moment when he clearly knew he could correct his course. One thing led to another, he took each successive step and now, here he was — about to lose the only thing that ever mattered to him. "Are you angry?"

"I don't think anger describes it."

"I'm sorry. I don't know what to do."

"So you have no plan. As usual."

He felt like a piece of shit. He wanted to make her happy, prove how much he loved her. There was no plan because there was no way out. He couldn't put his finger on where he'd gone off track. Trying to hide the cocaine from Jenna, Allison begging for a hit, enjoying that first rush, and then her vicious comments about Jenna. It made him crazy. Jenna was as close to perfect as any woman would ever get. It didn't matter if he and Allison had been friends forever, she had no right to say those things. And they weren't true. Vain. Trying to seduce other men. Allison was jealous and bitchy, like lots of women. Another thing he adored about Jenna. She had confidence. She didn't need to tear down someone else to make herself feel better.

His life was dissolving around him, nothing was working as he'd expected. See, there had been a plan. Getting his MBA, buying this house so they could start building a beautiful life, having kids at some point in the not too distant future. She looked so gorgeous sitting there, her feet tucked under her hips, her arms folded across her bare stomach. His pulse pounded in his ears. His scalp throbbed, pushing blood into the spaces behind his eyes. He coughed. "It just happened. One thing after another and I didn't know what else to do. I was afraid if she woke up on our bathroom floor she would run to Craig, they'd call the police."

"Well, what do you think she's going to do now?"

"I know. I didn't think it all the way through. She was unconscious, and I had to do something. Fast." He stood and walked to the center of the room. Despite the widened appearance of her eyes, the lack of any hint of softness in her smile, she looked absolutely edible. He took a step closer, unsure whether she would get off the sofa and meet him halfway.

"You had to do something? How about not hitting her? How could you have possibly thought that tying her up was a good solution? I can't even believe it." Her voice trembled. "Every time I think about it, I get the feeling this must be happening to someone else."

"I know."

"So you sat here all week and thought of nothing?"

He stepped closer. He had to hold her. If nothing else, reaching out to touch her, making the first move, would tell him whether she was still on his side.

Her body seemed to shrink on the sofa. She pulled her legs closer, curled her toes, and squeezed her hands around her elbows, hiding that silky, warm skin of her stomach. By curling in on herself, her breasts pressed close together, and for a moment, he forgot what he wanted to say, forgot what he really needed from her. He moved closer and touched her shoulder. There was a coolness to her skin. She didn't flinch or pull away. He ran his hand down her arm and tugged gently on her elbow. He needed her to hold him, to let her body fold into his so he'd know she wasn't going to abandon him.

Although she didn't pull away, and she let him run his fingers along her upper arm, she didn't yield to the pressure of his attempt to pull her to a standing position. She sank back further as if she preferred the sofa's arms around her.

"I'm sorry. I'm so sorry, I don't know how this happened. I've done everything I can to screw up our life. This, the coke, not getting promoted."

"It's not your fault you weren't promoted," Jenna said.

"I never wanted to hurt you. Things somehow went ... wrong." His voice shook, weak and thin as if there was no oxygen left in the room. God, he wasn't going to cry was he? That was not the way to convince her he was in control, that he would take care of her, that everything would work out. Snot collected in his nose, and he snuffed it up.

Jenna leaped to her feet. She slid her arms around his waist and pulled him toward her so hard that he stumbled and stepped on her toe. Despite her bare skin and the feel of her hair against his throat and the softness of her breasts pressing against him, all he felt was relief.

"Don't cry," she whispered.

"I'm not."

"I know what Allison said, I know you were defending me, even if it was stupid and macho. It feels good to know that you'd do anything for me."

"I would." He rested his cheek against the top of her head, sliding his face so her hair stroked his skin. It was soft and smelled sweet. He could lose himself in her. He wanted to crawl inside her and forget everything. He would die without her. And he'd been right, she was perfect, she loved him. She'd stay with him. They'd find a way out of this.

Jenna's voice was muffled against his chest, but she didn't try to pull away. "We have the upper hand. I can't believe she'd want everyone to know about her coke habit. Right?"

"You would think."

"You know her. And she'd do anything for you."

"Maybe."

"Have you even asked her?" Jenna ran her hand up his back. He felt her fingertips gliding over each knob of his spine.

"Not really."

"She thinks you've changed."

"I know."

"Why would she say that?"

"I don't know." He sighed. He didn't want to talk about it. He wanted to release his grip on her shoulders, take her hand, and lead her up the stairs, slide her nylon shorts over her hips and down her legs, and make her forget that she was dressed to go for a run. "Can we not think about it for a while?"

He moved away from her but kept his hands on her shoulders. He tilted his head so he could look directly into her eyes. "It's all I've thought about for six days. I haven't slept. I had to field all those questions from the detectives. And Beth. I need a break. Maybe if I stop thinking about it, the solution will be more obvious."

"You can't keep ignoring it!"

He didn't like that she said *you* instead of *we*. Weren't they in this together, wasn't she behind him a hundred and ten percent?

"Only for a few hours. I need to sleep. I'm so tired."

"I hope you didn't act edgy with the police."

"I don't think so."

"You know Beth called, bugging me about Craig smelling

Allison's perfume. And you grabbing her. Why did you do that?"

"Please. I'm begging. I need to sleep. Will you come to bed with me?"

"I was going for a run."

"You can do that later."

"In the dark?"

"Tomorrow. I need you right now, I missed you. My head's been going in circles all day, all night, all week, trying to figure out how I would let her go, trying to decide what story we can construct, even if she does agree to keep this a secret. Trying to think of so many things, I can't think at all anymore."

"What about dinner?"

"I just want to hold you. And sleep." He put his hands on her hips and pulled them tightly against his own. No matter how he looked at the situation, there was no way out. "I'm so sorry, babe. I fucked up our lives, and I'm so sorry." His upper back convulsed. He couldn't start crying. All his screw-ups were bad enough. He couldn't break down in front of her. But it seemed the more he thought about it, the stronger the force inside compelled him to cry.

Jenna squeezed her arms more tightly around him. "I love you. It's okay." She burrowed her face in his chest and ran her hands up to his neck, pulling his head toward hers. She stroked the back of his neck. It felt good. And more than her fingers on his skin, it felt good that she somehow, maybe, didn't blame him. How did he get so lucky?

"We'll get through it together," Jenna said. "We'll figure out something. You're right, we're both exhausted. We'll be able to think clearly in the morning."

Devon moved away from her, took her hand and led her out of the living room and up the stairs to their bedroom.

The only problem was, he'd thought clearly for several mornings now, and nothing had come of it. A soft voice pricked at the back of his mind. The only way things could go back to normal was if Allison disappeared. He stumbled on the carpet as he entered the bedroom. With the implications of that thought whispering deep below the surface, beneath his awareness of how he'd screwed up, he was sickened to realize the possibility of getting rid of someone had even entered his conscious mind. A girl he'd known as a little kid. When he was a little kid. A friend. A close friend. At one time, his best friend? He wasn't the kind of person who would ever think about doing something like that. He wasn't. But the thought had been there, and now, he could never go back to being that person.

Twenty-three

DESPITE MAKING LOVE, despite her assertion that they were both exhausted, Jenna hadn't slept more than three or four hours. At five a.m., she'd woken for the third time, hungry, all her muscles twitching. She got up at five-thirty to go for the run she'd desperately needed the night before.

After a cup of yogurt and a glass and a half of water, she ran her normal weekday route, five miles around the curving, tree-lined streets of their neighborhood. She left her iPod at home so she could quiet her thoughts, but nothing productive came of it. Near the end of her route, her mind emptied itself, and she enjoyed the pounding of her feet on the road, the thudding of her heart, and the deep gulps of air, letting those sensations wipe out thoughts altogether.

At home, she made a pot of coffee. She and Devon each drank three cups and ate toast. They didn't talk. What was there to say? If they managed to persuade Allison to "reappear" and say nothing, tell everyone she'd gone off partying for a week, would that story be believed? And how could they be sure Allison would stick with that for the long term, over weeks of Craig pestering her for details, and then for months, years? The rest of their lives.

Jenna didn't want to say these things, but there was simply nothing that guaranteed they could return to a normal existence. Maybe the solution was to escape. Disappear to a country where it was easy to get lost. There was a certain appeal in walking away from everything. She used to think she wanted nice things, money, security, but did any of that really matter? After twisting around in bed half the night, feeling Devon's breathing, knowing he wasn't sleeping either, she'd seen clearly that he was all that mattered. And running, she loved to run, which could be done anywhere. It wasn't as if his job was headed in the direction he'd expected. For all he knew, the company would withhold the promotion again this summer. The odds were higher on that side than on the side of him getting it.

Was it really possible to disappear? Could you walk away from credit cards and jobs and a mortgage? And a woman bound in the basement. Don't forget that, she reminded herself.

She looked at Devon. He stared blankly at the window, not really looking out at the yard that was a burst of color – daffodils and tiger lilies in bloom all along the edge of the front patio. She'd adored this house from the moment she first saw it, but now it felt like a prison. In more ways than one. Devon's eyes were red, the lids puffy. His lips were pale but still looked soft and profoundly kissable. His shoulders curved forward as if he was trying to wrap himself around his coffee cup. All of this had happened because he loved her. She knew that would sound delusional if she told anyone, but it was true. Past the fear flickering at the corners of his eyes, past the crease at the center of his forehead, she knew that all he wanted was to build a perfect world for her. All she needed, though, was him, not all that other stuff, not when she really stopped to think about it.

The idea of escaping was appealing. Starting over. There was nothing holding them here. Her mother. She couldn't leave her mother. Maybe they could take her? But how would they get money? Everything was over-extended. They could cash out their 401k accounts. Would that be enough? And could you truly escape and never be found?

She reached over and put her hand on Devon's arm. He didn't move or seem to notice she was touching him.

The doorbell rang.

"Shit," Devon said.

Jenna pushed back her chair. "Why did you say that?"

"Because the doorbell ringing is no longer a good thing."

"Maybe it's just a religious group. Or someone soliciting contributions."

"At eight on a Saturday?" He stood and walked to the window. "It's your mother."

Jenna realized how deeply she'd escaped into her fantasy,

considering something they couldn't really do, but feeling good that at least she was weighing options. When she thought of Allison, her brain stopped abruptly as if it had run into the face of a cliff, towering hundreds of feet above them, smooth granite, impossible to scale, even if they had the right equipment.

She set her mug on the center island, went to the entryway, unlocked the deadbolt, and opened the door.

"I'm so glad you're home." Hannah took a step forward, caught the front edge of her sandal on the threshold, and stumbled toward Jenna.

Jenna grabbed her mother's upper arm to steady her. "Why wouldn't we be home? What's wrong?"

"Someone broke into my house."

Jenna pulled her mother inside and closed the door. "When? Were you there? Are you okay?"

"I don't know when. I noticed this morning when I went to put on my wedding rings." Hannah's voice caught. "I took them off because I worked in the garden all day yesterday, and then I went out to dinner with that couple I met at the Farmer's Market. Remember?"

Jenna remembered, but she was more focused on her mother's wedding rings. Devon was right, when was she going to let go? Her father had been married to Christine for seventeen years. Yet, Hannah still wore her wedding rings. Jenna would give anything for her mother to let go of the past and live a real life. She blamed herself for that. She'd been too willing to let her mother lean on her. But when could she have done it differently? Was she supposed to just cut her off, tell her to start over, to consider getting a job, find more friends than the woman who lived five doors down or the couple she met at the farmer's market? Her mother wasn't a fighter. Even her physical appearance hinted that she was a creature designed to be taken care of, her slender arms, her pale skin, her soft, wavy hair. She looked like someone from another century, a woman suited to embroidery and pouring tea, with a staff of people to cook and clean for her, never having to spend a moment thinking about taxes, insurance, retirement funds, or anything else beyond the flowers and vegetables in her yard.

"So I guess it happened then. When I was out to dinner."

"Are any locks broken? Windows?"

Hannah shook her head. "I didn't want to tell you about that part. That's why I waited so long before I came over."

Waited so long? Jenna glanced at the grandfather clock in the far corner of the entryway. Eight-forty. "What didn't you want to tell me? Come in the kitchen, I'll make you some tea."

Devon had disappeared. He must have fled to the office. Or maybe he'd gone down to the basement to check on Allison. A wave of nausea washed through her stomach, pushing its way up into her esophagus. She grabbed the edge of the counter to steady herself.

"Are you okay?" Hannah said.

"Yes. Fine." She reached across the counter and picked up the teakettle. "So what didn't you want to tell me?" She put the kettle under the faucet and turned on the water.

"I can't believe my rings are gone! My pearls, and those dangly diamond earrings your father gave me when you were born." Tears filled Hannah's eyes and splashed over her lower lashes. Even crying, she looked delicate, no big gulping sobs or an angry red nose, just sparkling tears clinging to her lashes and trickling over her cheekbones.

"How did they get in?"

"They didn't technically break in."

"What do you mean?"

"I checked the dining room, but they didn't take the silver. They took jewelry and the coin collection. Tom's coin collection."

"Is that really worth anything?"

"It is to Tom."

"If it were, he would have taken it when he moved out, Mom."

Hannah shrugged.

"How did they get in?"

"Why did they have to take my rings?" More tears spilled out of her eyes. She patted her lashes with her fingertip. "I wasn't thinking. Remember those tree trimmers?"

"What about them?" Jenna had a feeling, but she wanted to hear it. She couldn't believe her mother was so naïve, and yet, she was. She trusted everyone, even her ex-husband. It was endearing, in some ways, but she didn't manage well as a single woman, in a world full of people looking for an easy mark.

"After I showed them the trees that needed pruning, we were in the backyard. They needed to use the restroom, and I had to write the check. Instead of going back to the front door, which made no sense since we were standing right there, I got the key out from under the mat. I'm sure they noticed."

Jenna laughed. Her mother looked hurt. The sound of her own laughter echoed strangely in Jenna's ears. She realized she hadn't laughed since she'd walked in the door after her trip to Las Vegas. And before that, how long had it been? Of course, this laugh wasn't true pleasure, more a cry of despair over her mother's vulnerability to the world; and Jenna's own vulnerability to the woman imprisoned in her basement, and their debt, relentlessly pressing down like a mountain of damp earth. "So presumably they came back and got the key and went into the house."

Hannah nodded.

After a few minutes of silence, the teakettle whistled. Jenna turned off the gas and set the kettle on another burner, took a cup out of the dishwasher, and pulled a teabag from the basket.

"I can't stay there."

Jenna knew better than to ask whether her mother had money to get the locks changed, but she and Devon surely couldn't manage that right now. She filled the cup with steaming water, dropped in the tea bag, and swirled it around for a few seconds. "We can ask Tom to help with getting the locks changed."

"Oh, I don't want to tell Tom. He'll think I'm foolish."

Jenna pressed the tongs around the tea bag, squeezing hard to release the excess water as if she was trying to squeeze the life out of the limp bag. She tightened her grip, pressing harder. She lowered the bag back into the steaming water. It was all too much. Her mother had to get over her deference to what Tom might think. Jenna couldn't handle it. Not now. "No, he won't."

"Yes, he will."

Hannah was right, but there was no choice. "We can't help right now, Mom. We have too many other expenses."

"It doesn't cost that much. Or I could stay here until you have enough money."

"We're not going to have enough money in the foreseeable future!" Jenna picked up the cup. Her hand shook. She gripped her wrist with the other hand and walked to the table. "You can't stay here."

"Why not? I could help. I could make dinner for you two, so you wouldn't have so much pressure."

"It's not pressure, we don't need you to fix dinner. We …"

"You have to let me stay here. I can't stay there, knowing my key is out there floating around in the world."

"Well, they got what they wanted. I doubt they'll come back."

"You'd let me stay there, knowing thieves have a key to the house?"

"No. I'm tense, I didn't mean that. We'll call Tom. He can help with the locks, and you can stay with him until they're fixed."

"I don't want to go all the way to Marin. I'll feel trapped up there. I hate driving on the bridge, you know that."

"Have a seat," Jenna said. She pulled out the chair, and her mother sat like an obedient child. Jenna sat across from her. She put her hands on the table and folded them, looking at her fingernails. The white on her French tips was worn at the edges, harping at her that she'd need a touch up soon.

"Tom will understand. He'll arrange for the locks to be changed, you can stay there a few days. How long has it been since you've had time alone with him? You haven't seen him at all since Christmas."

"He's been traveling a lot. He's busy."

"I'm busy too, Mom. You know I'd do anything to help you, but it's really difficult right now."

"You and Devon aren't having problems, are you?" Hannah's voice shook. Then she steadied it. "Make sure you give him enough attention. Don't make the same mistakes I made, thinking that you can stop flirting with a man once you've settled into married life."

Jenna squeezed her hands together until her fingertips

turned white. Was she really having this conversation right now? Her parents' divorce had not been the result of her mother's failure to keep flirting once she was married. Her mother had been no match for Christine. The woman had swept into her father's life with a brassy laugh and aggressive sexuality. Christine's independently wealthy status allowed him to pursue all his ventures, no matter how questionable, without worrying about a financial mistake affecting his family. He could pay spousal support and child support and still be true to his gambling style, all thanks to Christine. "My marriage is fine, Mom." She pushed back her chair. "I'm calling Tom."

"Please don't. He'll think I'm stupid."

"You're his mother, he loves you." Jenna went to the tiny built-in desk and picked up her phone. She wasn't sure if it hurt or made her angry that her mother was so concerned over what Tom might think. Those concerns never factored into Hannah's relationship with her daughter. Jenna supposed she should be pleased that her mother felt close to her, that she felt loved, that she didn't have to hide parts of herself in fear that Jenna would think poorly of her. Everyone should have one person who loved them with all their ugly, uninteresting, shameful parts. Jenna had that with Devon, her mother had no one. Except Jenna. But that didn't mean she wouldn't call Tom. She couldn't have a houseguest, especially not one as curious as Hannah. Had she even mentioned to her mother that Allison was missing? She didn't think she had, but it would have to wait. There was no way to pass on the information now without a tremor in her voice or her facial muscles betraying her fear. Her mother could be quite perceptive.

She pressed Tom's number and waited for the call to connect, impatient as always that mobile phones often took such an extended amount of time before they even began connecting a call. Wasn't this supposed to be more advanced technology compared to a landline? And yet, everything about it was sub-par – the connection speed, the quality of the sound, the ability to hold on to a call. Smartphones did all the things you didn't need, like taking photographs and tracking your location. Her fingers spasmed as she clutched the phone. Surely Devon had turned off Allison's phone. And dumped it somewhere? Could they track it when the phone was off? She was almost certain that wasn't possible. He hadn't said anything about Allison's purse, or that sneaky phone. Of course, he would have taken care of all that. If he hadn't, the police would have been here already. Still, she hated the racing, hammering, jittery feeling of her heart, the tightness of breath caused by a simple thought.

"What's new, Jenna? It's been a while." Tom's voice was even-toned as if he wasn't surprised she'd called on a Saturday morning after weeks of silence.

She ignored the question. Her words rushed out, explaining what had happened.

"When is she going to grow up?" Tom said. "I can't

believe the brainless things she does. Like that time she thought she smelled gas and took it upon herself to turn it off so that PG&E had to come out and re-start it."

"She's having a cup of tea, I thought we could drive up there in about an hour." She hoped Tom would pick up on the fact that now was not the time to chastise her mother when Hannah was sitting right here, terrified that her beloved son would think less of her, would consider her dumb or foolish. What her mother didn't realize, was that Tom already thought those things, and any misstep Hannah made was a simple confirmation of the opinion he'd held for years. Perhaps that's why her mother worried about it so much. She must sense his condemnation. It wasn't that he didn't love her. He was as devoted as any son, but he clucked like an old woman over her behavior.

"Why does she have to come all the way up here? I'll call a locksmith, and you can meet them at her house."

Jenna smiled at Hannah who was staring at her, clearly trying to decipher what Tom was saying. Jenna moved closer to the table, patted Hannah's shoulder, then turned and walked out of the kitchen, through the entryway, and up the stairs. Once she was inside her bedroom, she closed the door, holding the knob so it didn't click and then slowly releasing it without a sound. "I have a lot of stuff going on. I'm always taking care of Mom, and you need to help me out."

"It makes no sense to drive her all the way up here."

"Then come get her. In fact, that's even better. You can

deal with the locksmith and stay over to help reassure her."

"I'm not spending the night with my mother."

"I can't do this right now, Tom."

"She needs to stand on her own two feet."

"She does. Most of the time. Have a little compassion. She's your mother."

"I know who she is."

"If you don't come down, I'm driving up there. I'm dropping her off, and if you're not there, you can be responsible for the consequences." She knew she would never do it, but she had to say something to force him to do his fair share. Any other time, in any other situation, she would drop everything to help her mother. And not out of obligation. No matter how dependent or needy Hannah was, Jenna loved spending time with her. But not now. She and Devon had one day to get this horrifying situation resolved.

"Fine," Tom said. "I don't have time to drive down there today. I have a golf tournament this afternoon. I'll leave the key under the pot of tulips on my back patio. I should be home by five. Or six."

"So I'm just dropping her off?"

"You can either wait until later, or she can stay by herself. Those are the choices."

Why did he always win? She sat on the edge of the bed, a pile of twisted sheets, the comforter hanging off the end. She kicked off her flip-flops and laid down. The ceiling was a sea of texture, plaster whorls, and peaks that looked like frosting on a cake. She closed her eyes. The sheets where cool. She could smell Devon's skin. She rolled to her side so she occupied his half of the bed, pressed her face into his pillow, and inhaled deeply.

"Are you there?"

Maybe that was the way to get Tom to recognize that he wasn't the center of the universe – silence. He sounded unnerved.

"Jenna?"

"I'm not your underling. You don't get to dictate the terms and conditions."

"I'm not dictating anything. I have plans, you can't drop in out of nowhere."

"Well mom calls or drops in out of nowhere all the time, and I take care of her. And I don't resent that for one minute. I like helping her out. But right now, I need you to step up."

"I said she can stay here. I'll come down mid-week so the locksmith won't gouge us for weekend work. We'll come by your place after it's done and we can all have dinner together."

"No."

"That was harsh. Don't you miss your big bro?"

"There's a lot going on. That's why I'm asking you to help."

"What big thing is going on that you're completely unavailable?"

"I didn't call to get in a debate or explain my life to you. I'll bring mom by around eleven, and she can wait until you get home, although I feel a little cold dropping her off like a package that was miss-delivered."

"And dinner." He paused. "Tuesday?"

"I said no, and I don't want to talk about it right now." She'd figure out something later to explain her behavior. She didn't have time or the creative energy for that right now. Maybe she'd think of something on the drive to Marin.

"Is everything okay?" Tom said.

"There's a lot going on."

"You already said that."

"Under the tulip pot, right? You won't forget to put it out?"

"It's already there."

Tom lived in a multi-million dollar home, but he left a key under a flowerpot?

After she said good-bye, she dropped her flip-flops on the closet floor and slid her feet into flat chocolate-colored sandals with wide leather straps and heavy buckles. A seventy-mile drive would make her feet ache if she wore flip-flops. She went into the bathroom, brushed her hair, pulled it back from her face, and wrapped an elastic band around it, folded the length of her hair in half, and pulled it through the band again, so her hair hung in a loop between her shoulder blades.

She told Devon they were headed out, leaving him in the office, brooding over the computer.

AS SHE DROVE across the Golden Gate bridge, water

sparkling on both sides, one of those days with a crisp, cloudless sky that made the water a rich blue shade, rather than its usual green or gray, Jenna realized she couldn't leave her mother sitting alone in Tom's house. She called Devon and told him not to expect her until close to eight. It wasn't as if hours of time talking about Allison would help anything. They'd already done plenty of talking. She'd figure out a plan on the drive home when her thoughts were able to roam freely, and then she'd tell Devon what they needed to do.

Twenty-four

AFTER HE SPOKE to Jenna, Devon grabbed his keys and ran down the hall to the garage. He felt like a kid who had been let out of class, allowed to freely wander the empty corridors. It wasn't that he needed to escape from Jenna, it was the constant thought of Allison, tied up, lying on the dirt floor of the basement, the increasing darkness at the edge of his mind, whispering that there was no way out. He might have been able to juggle bills to keep their finances somewhat liquid, and he might have been clever enough to make a few coke deals to prevent all the money from flowing in a single direction, but his utter screw-up with Allison was hopeless. He might as well be duct-taped and locked in the basement with her.

It had taken Jenna and Hannah forever to get out of there. Once they decided Hannah was going to Marin, they talked about how many nights she'd stay and what she needed to pack. Jenna made sandwiches and filled a bag with bottled water and two hard, green pears. After they left, he'd collapsed on the sofa. He'd slept until Jenna's call woke him to tell him she'd wait with Hannah at Tom's house until he got home.

All he wanted to do was forget. Jenna wouldn't be home for hours. Sleep had been nice, but there was no chance he'd get more of that now. He didn't even care what condition Allison was in. Probably quite alert since he hadn't been down there since yesterday morning, and probably hungry. Definitely pissed off. He would deal with her after he had some time to calm down. Hannah showing up with her motherly intuition made him worry, irrationally, that she'd want to go to the basement, or that perhaps she'd smell perfume and know it wasn't Jenna's. He was even jumpier than he had been for the past six days. Had it really been six days? Seven, now. God.

He needed a movie. Something violent on a big screen with blaring surround-sound. Candy, popcorn, an over-sized soda. He would watch and listen and feed himself into a stupor so that when he went to bring Allison dinner, and try to get her to take another Vicodin, he'd feel in control. His hands would stop shaking, and his brain would stop trembling inside his skull.

HE EMERGED FROM the theater, two movies and four hours later. His stomach ached from all the crap he'd ingested. Not such a good idea after all. His hands were steady when he inserted the key in the ignition, but his brain still wobbled as his thoughts raced like gunfire, ricocheting off bone, making it impossible to settle on a single train of thought. The only thing that was stable in his mind was a steady string of profanity directed at himself, at what he'd done, at the universe in general.

He drove to Safeway and waited while a cute teenaged girl made two roast beef sandwiches. He'd be ravenous once his body absorbed the chocolate and junior mints and popcorn. The sandwich girl's skin was scrubbed and clean-looking, her eyes round and innocent, her smile free of trouble, as if she was gliding through life, not yet having experienced so much as a nightmare. Once he had the sandwiches, he cruised down the liquor aisle and picked up a bottle of scotch, priced more moderately than what he normally drank. His usual vintage wasn't sold at supermarkets, but the way he was feeling now, he didn't want to waste the good stuff anyway. All he wanted from this bottle was some numbing and a good night's sleep, if that would ever be possible again. The taste, the aroma, the entire experience was irrelevant. Besides, he couldn't really taste anything.

Outside the store, the sun was gone, but the sky still glowed dark blue. It was already six forty-five. Allison was going to be spitting mad. He should have thought to get some candy for her. Something to pacify her. In cryptic language, clearly phrased to avoid her mother's curiosity, Jenna had assured him when she called that she'd think of a plan during her drive home. He knew, deep in the center of his brain, that this wasn't possible, but still, he hoped. She was smart, she was always thinking about the future. There was still room for a shred of optimism.

He pulled the Jeep into the garage and hit the remote. He went to the kitchen and put his sandwich in the fridge and grabbed two bottles of water. He left the other sandwich and the water on the table while he went up to the master bathroom to get more Vicodin. Suddenly he wished he hadn't taken all the coke to his office. Why hadn't he thought of that earlier? If he brought a snort or two down to Allison, she would be more willing. More willing to what? Agree to keep his horrid mistake a secret? Agree to figure out some fantastic story that would make everything turn out okay for him? He shook four capsules onto his palm and shoved them in his pocket. He walked down the stairs. His pace slowed as he got closer to the bottom. The unopened bottle of scotch was on the table next to Allison's sandwich. He took two glasses out of the cupboard and loaded scotch, sandwich, and water bottles into a grocery bag. Carrying the glasses in one hand, the bag straps looped over his arm, he went through the living room and out to the backyard. The air was warm, the scent of jasmine heavy. Doves cooed from the roof of the pool house. The water was still. It looked inviting, but he had stuff to do.

In direct contrast to the backyard, the cellar smelled musty and maybe a little bit like piss. Had he forgotten to empty that bucket the last time he was down here? Or had it been so long, she'd peed in her pants? She would hate him for that alone, would never forgive him, never in a million years agree to make up a story to cover for him, if only for the humiliation of having to relieve herself in a bucket while he held her.

"Who is it?" snapped Allison. "It doesn't matter. You are so dead, whichever one of you it is. You can't keep me here forever, and when I get out, you're screwed."

"It's me," Devon said.

He closed the door behind him and made his way down the stairs to the center of the room.

"You're a monster," Allison said.

She'd tried to wriggle out of the towels and lay with her body twisted like a giant moth trying, and failing, to escape its cocoon. Clearly, the Vicodin had worn off. Should he give her some scotch first, or would that inflame her rage? It was a difficult call – figuring out whether a person moped or turned angry when they drank. He tried to remember the last time he'd seen Allison drunk. Women were different, men went one way or the other, but women were cagey. No matter what their mood, they didn't always let it show right away.

"Hey," he said. "Calm down. I know you're upset, but I thought we could have a drink. Talk about things."

"Are you out of your fucking mind?"

Allison's voice was loud and shrill. The earthen walls absorbed sound, but he still worried. Although she'd probably screamed earlier and he hadn't heard anything inside the house, so he supposed he was safe.

He set the bag on the ground. "Are you hungry?"

"How would I get hungry? All I do is sleep and have twisted, confusing dreams."

He peeled the plastic off the top of the scotch, pulled out the stopper, and poured some into each glass without even looking to consider whether it was a shot or two shots, or more. It made no difference.

"I'm not having a drink with you. It's macabre."

"It'll make you feel better."

"The only thing that will make me *feel* better is getting out of this hell hole."

He set the glasses far enough away from her that she couldn't kick them over. He put his hands under her armpits and tugged her to a sitting position. Surprisingly, she didn't fight him. Her body was light, thinner than ever. She was probably sore from lying on the ground. There weren't enough blankets to overcome the hard-packed dirt and the chill. He reached behind him for one of the glasses and held it to her lips. Again, she didn't resist. Still, at any minute she might spit the stuff in his face.

"If we're going to pretend this isn't some sick alternate universe, are you going to un-tape my hands so I can hold the glass, or are you going to feed me like an infant?"

"I just want to talk to you."

"Then get this shit off of me. You have no idea how

badly it hurts."

"I can't."

"I don't know who you are anymore. What has she done to you?" Allison's eyes filled with tears. Her nose was red and glossy. A week without bathing had turned her hair oily. It clung to her head so that he could see the shape of her skull. "This is my fault, not Jenna's," he said.

"Yes, but she's the one who made you into something inhuman. When you look at me, or any of your other friends, you look right through us. We might as well be dead for as much as we matter to you anymore. Since you met her, you look like a man under the spell of a siren. She's sucked the brains and all the personality right out of your head."

"Don't say that! I'm the same as always."

"Then admit that you've done something terrible and fix it right now."

"What will we tell people? I'll go to prison."

"Let me go, and we'll figure it out."

Devon held the glass to her lips. She took a sip and coughed. He wiped the scotch from her chin and the corner of her mouth.

Allison laughed. "That does feel good. Aren't you going to have any?"

He held the glass to her mouth again. She tipped her head back, stretching her neck and forcing his hand to follow so he wouldn't spill it all over her face. When the glass was empty, she kept her head back, letting it hang like a lead weight between her shoulder blades. She ran her tongue over her lips. The surface of her tongue was pale. A pasty substance coated the edges.

"Do you need some water?" Devon said.

She shook her head. "More scotch. Since you're never going to let me go. Just more scotch."

"Do you need to pee?"

She shook her head again.

"I'm worried you're dehydrated."

She raised her head and laughed, a short, harsh sound, like a seal barking. "You're worried? There are a lot more things for you to worry about than my state of hydration."

Devon reached behind him and picked up his own glass. This really was quite relaxing. He liked the idea of sitting here in limbo, not thinking. He'd been thinking forever, his brain thrashing like a lawn mower – *What to do? What to do? What to do?* That was the beauty of scotch, that warm numbing elixir soaking into your brain and shutting up those racing, chattering words. He tossed back the entire contents of the glass. He put both glasses on the dirt and leaned over to get the bottle.

It wasn't long before he was well on his way to wasted, drinking too fast, but there was nothing else to do, so why not keep filling his glass. The bottle was nearly half empty. Allison had grown quiet, content to let him feed her tiny sips, not complaining about her taped wrists or tied ankles. Her eyelids were half closed, with a hazy expression, which made her look as if she was gazing at him with adoration, thinking of forgiving him.

The last time they'd gotten drunk together, just the two of them, was before he'd met Jenna. It was their first year at Stanford. He'd been walking from the gym across the main quad, feeling relieved after his first round of exams, confident this whole college gig wouldn't be quite as grueling as everyone made it out to be. Allison was sitting on a bench, alone in the dark, pouring shots for herself from a bottle of Johnny Walker. It should have been obvious then that she had the potential to be a substance abuser. But at the time, it seemed like nothing more than normal college partying, kicking loose after sleep-deprived nights and a fear of failure that had turned into the first hint of the success waiting for them.

Allison had lifted the bottle toward him and demanded he join her. They'd talked for hours, remembering friends from high school, laughing in disbelief that they were Stanford students. *Fucking Stanford!* They'd repeated the phrase until they were hysterical. Although they'd been confident they would get into good schools, had studied their asses off in high school, sitting there at the famous university, knowing they had the chops to survive, was surreal.

He shifted his legs. The dirt was like concrete. He splashed a bit of scotch into each glass and set the bottle between them.

"Please at least untie my ankles. Look how torn up they are."

She moved slightly, turning her feet. She wore those low socks that barely showed above the edge of her athletic shoes. Above the anklebone of her right foot, the skin was an angry red. Hair-like scratches from the rope ran across the red spot, and a few had bits of blood on them.

"Why did you move around so much?" He felt worse, if that were possible.

"Have you ever tried lying in one position for however long I've been here?" Her voice was meek, defeated.

She didn't sound as if she was accusing him of making her uncomfortable, worse than uncomfortable – miserable. Her eyes were still half closed, her lips glazed from licking.

"I'm not going to go anywhere." She lifted her hands. The upper part of her hands and the skin above the tape looked puffy. She sat with her legs straight, her feet only a few inches from his knee.

He uncrossed his legs and knelt slightly so he could get better leverage on the knotted rope. When he untied the rope, she immediately drew her legs up until she was sitting with her knees bent, pressed close as if she wanted to hug them. But of course, she couldn't.

"That feels better," she said.

He held the scotch glass to her mouth. As he tipped the glass, she turned her head, and a few drops dribbled onto her cheek.

"What are you going to do to me? You can't keep me here forever."

"I know."

"So is Jenna leaving you?"

"No." There was a sharp pain in his chest. Had Jenna said something to Allison? She hadn't acted as if she was done with him. In fact, she'd assured him they were in it together, no matter what *it* consisted of. "Why would you think that?"

"She was pissed off when she found me."

"She's not now." He felt warm, just thinking about it. "She could see how I was defending her. She knows it was an accident."

"Defending her?" Allison snorted. Her eyes were wide, staring at him, challenging him.

"The three of us can put our heads together and resolve this."

"There's nothing to resolve. I hope they lock you up. Evidently, that's the only way to get you away from her. She's poisoned your soul." She shivered violently, her body continuing to tremble as if the press of hard packed walls, dry and airless, blocking out all sound, was making her so cold, even the blanket across her shoulders couldn't stop the trembling. "You're going to kill me, aren't you."

Devon stood. "No! How can you even think that?"

"She's not only poisoned your heart, she's made you stupid. Think it through. You have no other choice."

"She hasn't poisoned me. She's the best thing in my life.

She is my life."

"Oh, barf." Allison coughed as if to punctuate her words, but her cough turned into wheezing. "I need some water," she said.

Her voice was thin and strained. Devon unscrewed the cap of one of the water bottles. He sat down and held it to her mouth.

She gulped it down and shuddered. "It tastes horrible after the scotch."

She parted her lips, and he held the bottle up close again. She took several small sips then turned her head to the side. "You're stupid. And blind."

"Stop saying that."

"You never knew I was in love with you."

Her face was suddenly soft, her mouth partially open, her eyes still droopy, but without the glassy, staring look she'd had earlier. A section of greasy, darkened hair fell across her brow. She tilted her head to move it away without taking her eyes off his face.

Devon laughed. "Really?"

"When we were kids. And in high school."

He laughed.

"And in college."

He coughed. "You certainly hid it well."

"But once she came along … " Allison said softly.

"You never said anything."

"I wasn't sure you felt the same."

His neck was hot. The scotch burned in his throat. He needed another shot, but it would be awkward to turn and grab the bottle now. He picked up his glass and tipped it back. A single drop slid down and touched his tongue, not enough to swallow. The drop stayed on the end of his tongue, stinging as if a bee had found its way into the basement.

"So you didn't."

"Didn't what?"

"Don't play games. You didn't feel the same, so I never told you."

"It was a long time ago. You love Craig, you have a great marriage."

"Had."

"Is something wrong with you two?"

"No. But I'm not with him, am I. And you're changing the subject. Aren't you going to ask when I got over you?"

"It doesn't matter anymore. I'm sorry I never noticed, but …"

"I got over you this week."

He reached for the bottle. He felt for the cap, but his fingers touched only moist glass. He hadn't corked it a few minutes ago, or many minutes ago, he wasn't really sure how long it had been since he'd poured the last shot. He splashed some into the glass. Had Allison been in love with him since they were kids? All this time? Through college, through grad school, weddings, vacations, parties, dinners. It wasn't possible. He took a swig of scotch. He had no idea what he was supposed to say. Unless she was making it up, driven by no other desire than to make him squirm. Allison liked to make people squirm. That must be it. The way she grabbed on to something and wouldn't let go, like she'd dogged them about the money they owed, like she couldn't let go of her desire for cocaine. No wonder she needed it. She had to have something to smooth out that tight brain. Although coke probably had the opposite effect, winding it tighter, at least it did with him.

"Aren't you going to say anything?" Allison said.

"I think you're full of shit."

"Thanks."

"I would have noticed. And you're married to Craig. That guy's crazy about you, and you love him."

She nodded. "I do. But there's a huge piece that holds on to you."

"Why?" He turned for the scotch, poured some into his glass, and set the bottle by his knee.

She shrugged. She looked uncomfortable, straining to pull her taped wrists closer to her pelvis, making her look as if she was slightly off balance, in danger of tipping sideways. Without setting his glass on the ground, he reached for the bottle even though he hadn't taken a drink.

She leaned over further, her head to the side as if her whole body wanted to fall into him.

He put his hand on her shoulder. When he'd first lifted her, she felt light, but now, the weight of her body seemed too much for one hand. What good were all his bench presses, which should have provided the strength to support a hundred pound woman? The scotch jiggled in the glass. Allison was collapsing against him. As she leaned harder, not trying at all to right herself, she swung her leg. The toe of her athletic shoe slammed into him right at the side of his kneecap. His leg exploded in pain. Scotch splashed onto the back of his hand. As he tried to regain his position, the glass slid out of his grip, hit the dirt, and broke into three neat pieces. "Stop!"

She flung her upper body backward and kicked him again. His knee was killing him. He wondered whether he'd be able to stand. He inched away and managed to knock over the bottle of scotch. It thudded on the ground and rolled away from him, spilling scotch. It didn't matter, it wasn't the good stuff, but the waste oddly annoyed him. He couldn't believe a woman with her hands taped together had kicked him into submission. He couldn't manage to brace himself to get into a standing position. He slithered away from her, moving like a wounded crab on his hands and one foot, dragging the other foot across the dirt. God his knee hurt. She must have hit it in precisely the right spot to do some damage. He grabbed the bottle and set it upright.

Allison rolled across the dirt, her legs cycling furiously, kicking his knees and lower legs. She reminded him of that witch, before she became a witch, in the *Wizard of Oz*, furiously pedaling her bike, in that curiously sped-up film clip, trying to out-run the tornado. As if that were possible.

He needed to pull himself up, fast. It would be easy enough for her to climb the stairs to the backyard, despite her taped wrists. Then she'd be off to one of his neighbors, screaming for help before he could catch up. Operative legs were better than arms in this situation, and his knee refused to function. It seemed as if he could actually feel it growing larger, pressing against his pants, the fabric so tight it prevented him bending his leg at all, growing watery and puffy, completely useless. He rolled onto his right side and pushed himself up.

She threw her whole body at his feet, kicking, sometimes at the air, but landing a few well-placed kicks on his ankles. He moved sideways further and tripped over the scotch bottle, sending it rolling across the dirt again. It made a hollow thud as the speed slowed and it came to a stop near the stairs.

In her all-out pursuit of him, Allison had managed to catch a piece of the broken glass on the back of her hand. A wide red line ran across the fine bones. Blood spread across her skin without really pumping, just appearing and covering her knuckles, dripping toward her wrist. She lifted her shoulders off the ground and hurled herself forward.

He jumped away from her, tempted to rub his ankles that ached almost as much as his swollen knee. He wasn't sure it was really swollen or if he was hallucinating, feeling sorry for himself in a haze of scotch and a roiling stomach from all the junk he'd eaten during the movie marathon. The afternoon seemed like a lifetime ago, everything did. His whole life was distorted so that he couldn't remember when things had been normal. His adorable, beloved wife was right now driving back home, plotting on his behalf. He'd done nothing but cause trouble for her.

Allison shoved her shoulder against his ankles, and he stumbled back. The pain in his knee as he landed hard on his left foot, forced him to double over. What had she done to his knee? If she'd screwed it up forever … He had to get control of her. The alcohol seemed to have had no effect, and any lingering sluggishness from the Vicodin was clearly eradicated.

"You're not getting away with this."

She was shrieking, and the sound was more intense, painful against his eardrums. He glanced at the door to remind himself that he'd closed it securely when he entered the basement. "Calm down."

"I'm not calming down until you let me go."

The problem was, she wouldn't calm down if he did let her go. There was no way out. *No way out. No way out.* He couldn't count how many times that phrase had echoed through his head this past week, even when he was sleeping, half-dreaming, it pounded against his skull. He limped sideways to dodge her feet, marveling that she was still going, an endlessly circling loop of rage and strength. She would out-match him. She had nothing to lose. Pent-up infatuation, or love, suppressed for nearly twenty years fueling her.

He grabbed the chunk of broken glass and held it down near her face. "Stop. This isn't helping anything."

She laughed. "So the boy I loved wants to kill me now. Is that really your plan? Or is it Jenna's? She told you to get me drunk and kill me?"

"Don't talk about Jenna anymore."

She laughed.

"There is no plan," he said.

"That's obvious."

"Stop shouting so we can talk, figure out what to do."

"There's nothing to figure out, Devon." She hurled herself against his ankles.

He sat down hard. *No way out.* Although his mouth was open, he couldn't breathe for a moment and felt his chest grow tight. Finally, he gasped, sucking in air.

Allison turned and kicked at his hand. She missed, and he yanked his arm out of her way, still holding the piece of glass. As if he was watching a movie, he saw his arm fall. No, not fall ... slice through the air with as much force as he could gain from a sitting position. The glass ripped across her neck to her throat, and before he could think again she was covered in blood, he was covered in blood. He lifted his hand. The piece of glass was red. He thought he'd intended to do something with it, but now he couldn't recall what. He wanted to stop up his ears to block the sound of Allison's gagging.

The chunk of glass was slippery in his hand. After a moment, his fingers relaxed, and it fell to the ground. The thud was the same sound a golf ball made when the guy who lived behind them accidentally hit one over the fence as he practiced chip shots in the backyard. He couldn't believe he was thinking about golf balls. Nothing seemed real. A low, dull tone rang in his ears.

Allison's eyes were closed, and he couldn't be sure whether she was breathing. He turned away. With her neck like that, how could she breathe? He wasn't a killer. This wasn't at all what he'd wanted, but she wouldn't stop kicking. She'd done real damage to his knee. He wasn't sure he could walk up the stairs. Jenna. What was he going to tell Jenna? She was racing home to him, formulating a way to get their lives back, and now he'd really screwed it up. Irrevocably.

There was a strange smell. Allison's blood? He wasn't sure. This was not his fault. She attacked him. She shouldn't have said those things about Jenna. It was even sort of Allison's fault that he'd sold cocaine. If she hadn't been such an easy customer, such a safe customer, he might not have considered it. And her constant pressure on Jenna about the check. She had no patience, no ability to go with the flow. Lawyering had taken over her entire life.

His stomach heaved, and he turned quickly, but not before all the scotch and candy and popcorn erupted out of his mouth, some of it splattering on Allison's limp arm. One of her fingernails had a large chip. He felt bad about getting vomit on her, but it wasn't as if he could stop himself. It was a gut reaction. He laughed at the absurdity of that expression in this situation. If he had something to wipe off the vomit, he would. Although there was all that blood. He should get a shovel right now. Bury her on the spot. But he didn't feel well. His stomach was still unsteady, his mind fuzzy, and his knee was wobbly and hurting. He kicked his right heel at the dirt. It was packed hard. California clay. He picked up one of the extra blankets and wiped at Allison's arm. Vomit smeared across her skin and seemed to melt into the fabric of her shirt. The texture of the blanket was too rough, he needed a damp cloth. He needed a lot of things. For now, it was best to leave her here, think through the right course of action so he would be sure to avoid any further mistakes.

He dropped the soiled blanket on the dirt and picked up one of the others that had formed her makeshift bed. He placed it over her, pulling it up so her hair was completely covered. He turned out the light, walked to the stairs, and climbed slowly, dragging his left leg behind him like something dead. It was a terrible thing, leaving her on the basement floor, covered in blood and vomit, her life still lingering, for all he knew. But she wouldn't be aware of that. At least he was fairly certain she wouldn't be aware. There was no other choice. It was peaceful down there, quiet, she wouldn't be exposed to any rain or dew, insects or rodents. He really needed a drink. The good stuff, this time. As he closed the basement door, he glanced at the swimming pool.

Maybe it was better not to have any more to drink. He could go for a quick swim so he'd be in decent shape when Jenna returned, not a disgusting mess of puke and blood. He pried off his shoes, pulled off socks, jeans, and shirt and dove clumsily into the water. The cold hit him fast, but it felt good as if he was sharpening his senses, rinsing off all his mistakes.

Twenty-five

THE HOUSE WAS devoid of light when Jenna pulled into the driveway. Devon must be watching a movie. Television viewing with a few lights was okay, but he liked to watch films in total darkness so he could lose himself in the experience.

She pressed the remote. The garage door opened, revealing his Jeep. Seeing it made her feel as if life was normal, which of course, it was so far from normal it was laughable, although not actually funny. Her mind was so twisted and anxious she couldn't even find a word to define her life right now, any word she chose was off balance, ludicrous in its irony. She pulled into the garage. She'd promised to think of a plan on the drive home, and of course, she'd done no such thing. When she assured Devon there would be plenty of time to work it out in her mind, knowing a long quiet drive outside of her normal routes always spurred fresh thoughts, she'd believed it herself. It hadn't worked out that way.

First, it had taken her a number of miles, all the way to the bridge, to shake off the sadness she'd felt leaving her mother at Tom's. The look on her mother's face was one of accepting her fate, no matter how distasteful. It wasn't that her mother didn't adore Tom, wouldn't love a brief stay with him, but the anxiety of knowing her house was unsecured, of knowing that Tom would make her feel, even if he didn't say a single word, as if she was completely incompetent, didn't make for a pleasant visit. It wasn't only the look on Hannah's face, but also Jenna's sense that she was making her mother feel like a burden. Alongside that, was the yearning to pour out the whole sordid story to her mother's sympathetic ears. And Hannah would be sympathetic. There hadn't been a single time in Jenna's life when her mother hadn't been understanding and encouraging. Even after Christine took Jenna to a spa for the first time, Hannah didn't act jealous that another was trying to usurp her place. She accepted with equanimity Jenna's bonding with her stepmother.

Jenna was confident Hannah would be understanding of the horror of this situation as well. Even though Devon wasn't always as warm as he could be, Hannah loved him. She believed he was the perfect man for Jenna. But if she told Hannah about the mess with Allison, the drug sales, their debt, Devon would feel betrayed.

Driving through the city from the bridge toward the southbound 280 freeway had taken all her concentration, so she hadn't really given focused thought to the immediate problem until she was sailing along at seventy again. And nothing had come to mind. Absolutely nothing. No matter what angle she'd viewed it from, they needed Allison's help to pull it off, and Allison was not going to agree to that. Maybe Devon had been able to persuade her to go along with him in the past, but all the rules had changed.

She went into the house. "Devon?"

All that came from the living room was a faint glow, meaning the floor lamp next to the armchair was the only light. The house was cold and she wasn't sure if it was nerves or the temperature had actually dropped. It was almost drafty as if all the doors along the back of the house were open. She walked toward the living room. It was empty. She'd been right, the brass floor lamp with molded leaves and vines trailing around the pole was the only light in the room. She stepped back into the hall. The office, TV room, and workout room were all dark. The entire second floor was also dark. Of course. Why hadn't she thought of it immediately? He was in the basement.

She walked through the living room to the back doors. She pressed down on the handle. It was unlocked. She stepped onto the patio and paused. The last thing she wanted was another encounter with Allison. The backyard was dark, and she couldn't tell if the basement door was open. Although if it were, she would have thought she'd see the light from the bulb.

The sky was partially overcast and the moon only a sliver,

vague behind thin clouds. Light from the neighbors' houses was mostly blocked by trees, shrubs, and fences topped with lattice, woven with bougainvillea and jasmine. The privacy was nice, but right now she wished for glaring spotlights. Or maybe not. She reached back inside and flicked the switch for the patio light. After being in near darkness from when she'd first entered the house, the light was too much. She squinted and walked a few steps to the center of the patio. The sound of water lapping at the sides of the pool seemed louder than it had a moment earlier. She walked closer. Devon lay sprawled on an air mattress, floating at the center of the pool, his boxer shorts plastered to his hips. She couldn't tell if his eyes were open and she didn't want to think why he might be floating in the pool as if the weather was so hot he had to cool off.

"Dev? What are you doing?" She walked to the side of the pool. "Devon?"

He didn't move. It seemed as if her heart had stopped. Her body felt like a block of ice had formed around her. He wasn't … there wasn't something … there must be something terribly wrong. She knew, but she couldn't think. "Why are you in the pool? Are you awake? It's not safe, falling asleep in the water. In the dark like this. Get out."

The only sound was the slosh of water, so he must be moving slightly, or the water would be still, wouldn't it? "Devon!" She raised her voice but didn't want to speak too loudly, didn't want the neighbors thinking there was a domestic disturbance. No, this was something far uglier, and she knew why he was floating in the water, not speaking. "Oh, God," she whispered.

The silence was so intense her ears created their own sound, a buzzing that came from inside her head. The clouds around the moon appeared to be muffling everything, and it was getting darker, more difficult to see. "Get out of the pool."

The raft moved slightly so that Devon's knees pointed in the direction of the rocks where the waterfall was supposed to splash into the pool. She stepped back from the edge and turned toward the basement. She didn't want to go down. Maybe he had secured the padlock, and she wouldn't have to. She walked slowly along the side of the pool, past the picture window in the office, to the door leading to the basement, the part of her house she'd come to hate. A part that she wished didn't exist.

There was enough light from the porch to see the padlock, looped through the hook, but hanging open. She lifted it out, pulled back the metal bracket and stuck the arm of the lock back through the metal ring. She opened the door and stepped back. It stank. Alcohol and vomit and something else she couldn't identify. She put her hand over her mouth and nose and used her left hand to feel her way slowly down the steps. She should go back for a flashlight, but something was driving her to keep going, to find out what she didn't want to know. Yet, she knew.

She waved her arm in the air, trying to make contact with the nut at the end of the string. Finally, it bumped her knuckle. She grabbed the string and pulled. The light came on. A blanket covered Allison. "Oh. Oh, Devon. No." She whimpered, longing for the sound of another person. She couldn't run away, she had to look. Scotch and vomit and the inexplicable smell of roast beef forced their way through her hands, into her nostrils, no matter how hard she pressed her fingers together. She forced her breath through her mouth, bent down, and lifted the edge of the blanket. The gash, the blood, the dirty hair, and the smell of Allison's body rushed at her, and she dropped the blanket. Bile heaved into the back of her throat.

Her feet made a dull thud on the dirt as she turned and ran to the stairs. She raced up, two at a time, and out the door, flinging it closed behind her. She'd left the light on, probably knowing she'd have to go back. Tonight. She jogged to the shallow end of the pool. "Devon." His name came out of her mouth with a huffing sound as she kept her voice low.

She sat down and unbuckled her sandals, then stood, pulled off her jeans, and wriggled out of her hoodie. She stepped into the pool. It wasn't as cold as she'd expected, but then her skin was cold and hard from the chills that had been racing through her for the past several minutes. She walked down the steps. When she reached the bottom, the water tugged at the hem of her shirt. She walked as far as she could and then swam, her chin lifted above the surface until she reached the air mattress. She grabbed the corner and pulled it toward the shallow end. Once her feet could reach the bottom again, she moved around to the other side and pushed Devon close to the steps. "Get out," she said.

He raised his head slightly, looking at her as if he wasn't quite sure who she was. She sighed. It wasn't clear whether he was being deliberately obtuse or if he wasn't capable of responding. He smelled of scotch. She pushed the air mattress close to the top step. Water splashed around them as she tugged him off the mattress. She hoisted herself up onto the side of the pool, put her hands under his arms, and dragged his shoulders and upper back onto the concrete. By the time she'd rolled his whole body onto dry ground, she was gasping for air. She wriggled back from the edge and leaned forward, breathing deeply, hoping he was now going to stand up and walk into the house.

He groaned. As the sound rose up from his chest, the volume increased. Jenna leaned over and pressed her hand over his mouth. "Shhh. Get up and come in the house." She stood and backed a few steps away from him. "Come on."

Slowly he pushed himself onto his hands and one knee. He stayed in that position for a minute or two. Finally, he stood, stumbled, and fell against her. She pressed against him to prevent them both from falling. With Devon leaning on her like a man who had been pulled up from a near drowning, they walked to the back door. He dragged his left leg, moving with an awkward limp. Usually, they went in through the side door to the hallway bathroom when they'd been using the pool, but there was no time and no reason, now, to be concerned about water on the carpet. It flashed across her mind that later she would have a great deal of concern if the police came searching and testing, but right now she didn't care.

Slowly, they made their way up the stairs, pausing on each step, until they reached the landing. She helped him into the bedroom and eased him onto the bed.

She went back outside to pick up their discarded clothes. The water was silent again. Their jeans were stiff and cold. She folded the clothes in a bundle around their shoes and stood for a moment wondering if she should put the air mattress away. It could probably wait. Any other day of her life, if she'd gathered up clothes from the side of the pool, it would have been after swimming nude on a summer night when the air was still warm and dry. That would never happen again, at least not for a very long time. It was part of another life that was as unreal as this one. All of which made her feel she had no life at all. She existed on some disembodied plane, not human, not dead.

She went into the house, locked the door, set the alarm, and turned off the patio light. She carried the clothes to the laundry room and dropped them on the floor.

Upstairs, she sat on the bed. Devon was on his side, his back toward her side of the bed. The sheets were damp around him. She sighed, feeling heavy, as if she was still in the pool, water soaking her clothes, making it hard to move. The rest of the night and everything after stretched ahead, promising nothing but physical labor. "What happened?"

"I'm so sorry." Devon's voice was gravelly, coming from someplace deeper than normal. "I've ruined our life."

She put her hand on his shoulder. "Tell me what happened."

"Not just Allison, not just ... she's dead."

"I know."

"The debt. The coke. Always thinking things will get better. They never get better." The bed shook as sobs took over his body. His feet trembled and his back heaved as he cried.

Tears swam around her eyes. She had never seen, never heard a man cry before. It was terrible, a horrifying thing that scared her more than Allison's bloody, torn body on the basement floor. She went around to her side of the bed and laid down. She folded herself around him, sliding one arm around his waist and slipping her other hand under his neck, trying to hold his head, trying to hold him together, to make him stop those awful, guttural sounds that ripped through her like knives.

She wanted to go back, back, back. She couldn't remember where. Back before Allison came over that day and Jenna had been so eager to escape with her mother, back before the wedding, the shower, before they bought this house. Their dream home. She tightened her arms around him. He continued to sob, although the sounds weren't as loud and frightening as they had been a moment ago. No matter what waited for them in the basement, she knew she couldn't live without him. They were in this together. The dampness of their clothes and the sheets had worked its way into her bones, and she felt they were colder than they'd ever been, no matter how tightly she held him, no matter how she pressed her body against his.

"Why did you kill her? We would have figured out something."

"I didn't. I didn't kill her." His voice was fierce, hard. "I'm not a killer. It was an accident. Please don't think that, don't say it. Please."

Jenna pressed her face against his back until it was difficult to breathe, but she didn't turn her head. After a moment she moved, rolling onto her back. "How was it an accident?"

Devon turned and buried his face in her hair, pressing the wet strands against her neck. "She was kicking me. She ..."

"Why does it smell like the basement is soaked with alcohol?"

"It spilled. I thought if we had a drink together, she'd listen. That it would be like old times and if I let her go, she'd keep it a secret. Where she'd been."

Jenna could guess how that conversation had gone.

"But everything went the wrong way. She said she was in love with me."

"When you were kids?"

"Always. In high school, college, now."

"What?"

"I don't know. I don't think she meant she doesn't love Craig. I don't know what she meant. But then she started kicking me. She said terrible things about you."

"What things?"

"I don't want to say."

"Tell me."

"That I love you too much, or you poisoned me, or something ..."

"You can't love someone too much." Jenna wriggled closer, she slid her leg between his and gripped his waist. She pressed her jaw against his shoulder, wanting to push her whole self inside of him. She would never let go of him. Never. He wasn't a killer. "How did her throat get gashed?"

"She kicked me, and the glass broke, and she fucked up my knee. I don't even know. It just happened. But I didn't go down there thinking I would kill her. I didn't mean any of it to happen."

"I know." She rubbed her cheek across his shoulders.

"What am I going to do?" He moaned and tugged at her.

"We."

"I don't deserve you,"

"Don't say that. Besides, she was already destroying her life with the cocaine. Craig would flip if he knew about it. He wants kids desperately. It doesn't seem like she does. Maybe their marriage would have ended anyway."

"There's a huge difference between divorce and being dead."

"I know. But it was an accident," she said.

"I should turn myself in."

She felt as if a boulder slammed into her chest. "No! You can't."

"But I …"

"It won't bring her back," she said.

"But Craig."

"Isn't it better for him not to know? To not know that his wife was damaging their future child before it was conceived? That she loved another man all these years? Not knowing is better." She waited, wondering why she was persuading her husband to hide a brutal crime. At the same time, she insisted to herself there was no crime, just an unfortunate series of events that veered out of control. Devon was a good person, no one would even believe he'd done such a thing. Allison was angry, combative, argumentative. She'd provoked him. And Allison had loved him all this time?

"You might be right," Devon said.

"Of course I am."

They wound their arms and legs around each other until it was difficult to tell which was hers, which belonged to him.

Twenty-six

BETH WOKE ON Sunday morning determined to do something to help Craig, no matter how insignificant.

She turned on her side and put her arm around Michael. She ran her fingers across his belly, feeling her ring finger dip as it crossed his navel, a reassuring marker of life. He let out a deep sigh. She wasn't sure if it was the sound of pleasure or of something passing from the dream world into the daylight spread across the pale green carpet.

"You should wake me like that every day," he said, turning.

Beth scooted close and wrapped her arm around his waist. "We should have Craig over for dinner tonight."

"He won't come." Michael's voice was rough as if he wasn't fully awake and had decided he didn't want to be awake after all.

"We have to make him. Or maybe go over there and bring him dinner."

"Leave him alone."

"I can't. It seems as if his friends have abandoned him."

"There's nothing we can do. You're projecting your own feelings onto him. Don't pester him to make yourself feel better."

Beth rolled on to her back. That wasn't fair. He made it sound like this was about her, and it wasn't, she wanted to help. And she knew Craig wouldn't admit he was lonely or scared or felt let down. They had to assume those things were true and take charge. He'd be grateful; later. "That's harsh. I don't think that's what I'm doing. He's all alone in that enormous house, every day, wondering what happened, not knowing where she is." Beth found it easy to imagine how she would feel in a similar situation, the complete lack of answers. The realization that your own life had stopped and the rest of the world was moving along without you. At least they could let him know that they noticed his life had turned inside out.

Michael put his hand on the side of her head. His fingers were warm, and she thought she could feel him flowing into her, softening her brain, melting the thoughts that spun themselves in spirals. They lay quietly for several minutes.

"I'm not saying I don't want him to come over," Michael said. "But I don't think he will. Sure he might feel abandoned, but doing something normal can be disorienting."

"So we do nothing?"

"Sometimes there's nothing to be done. If you want to try, it won't hurt anything, but don't be upset or think we're failing him if he says no."

At ten-thirty she called Craig. She was certain her invitation would make him feel cared for, supported. As it turned out, Michael had been almost right. It took her nearly fifteen minutes to convince Craig to accept a *low key* dinner invitation. *Very low key*, she promised. He said he'd be terrible company, that he couldn't look at food, that he wasn't in the mood for talking. No matter what he proposed as an excuse, she countered with, *that's okay*. Finally, he relented and agreed he'd be there at five.

The rest of her day was consumed with going to the supermarket and baking chocolate chip cookies, large and soft, with two extra handfuls of chocolate chips. No matter how *not hungry* he was, she knew the cookies would help. It would be therapeutic, forcing him to keep up his strength by offering an enticing meal. He probably had no appetite because he was eating fast food, or something prepared from a box with a packet of chemical-laden seasoning. Or not eating at all. She knew exactly what he needed.

Craig rang the bell at quarter to five.

Beth grabbed Michael's arm. "See?" she whispered. "He's terribly lonely. He came early, he's so hungry for human contact."

"Craig's always early," Michael said.

"He needs us."

Michael slipped his hand under her loose blouse and rubbed the small of her back. "I'm not disagreeing."

She smiled and let her muscles relax into the gentle pressure of his fingertips. She set the deep ceramic bowl on the counter. It was painted with vegetables in mustard, gold, and cranberry. She'd filled the bowl with greens, as well as the same vegetables depicted on the sides. For another moment, she let Michael stroke her skin, then she moved away. Her blouse fell back into place. She hurried to the door. She didn't want Craig thinking he wasn't welcome, second-guessing his grudging acceptance.

The flesh under Craig's eyes was puffy and dark gray. His lips were pale, and his neck looked thinner than she remembered. She couldn't decide whether he'd lost weight or she hadn't been all that observant. Who was? People drifted past each other every day. Subtle changes were unnoticeable. You didn't see someone for two years, and the shock was sometimes so sudden, it was hard to maintain your composure, to keep from blurting out something rude about deep lines in the skin or a much thicker waist. She opened the door wider so Craig could enter.

"Who else is coming?" he said.

"No one. I told you there wouldn't be any pressure to be sociable."

He stepped into the foyer.

Beth hugged him. Despair flooded out of his pores and into her arms and shoulders. "We'll find her," she whispered. She stepped back.

Craig looked at the floor.

It was the wrong thing to say, but she had to say something to take that expression off his face. She wanted to make him feel better, even though it wasn't possible. "Come into the living room. What do you want to drink?"

"Water's fine."

Michael shook Craig's hand. Beth felt disconnected — it was so formal, highlighting everything that was wrong — as far as she could recall, she'd never seen the guys shake hands.

"How about a Mojito?" Michael said.

"I don't want any alcohol," Craig said. "After dinner, I'm going over to the Porters. The more I think about it, the more I know I'm right. I smelled Allie's perfume. They know something about where she went, and I'm not leaving until they tell me the truth."

"I thought you were going to tell the detectives about that," Beth said.

"I didn't get a chance. They usually have their own agenda," Craig said.

"Are you sure that's a good idea?" Michael said. He leaned against the post that split the opening to the living room. His shirt, slightly too small for his long torso, slid up. The edge of his boxers showed over the waist of his shorts.

Beth suppressed a smile. It was nice to know she could still notice and think about normal things, despite the everything-but-normal world they were living in right now. Conversation, the food they ate, the weather, were all slightly out of tune, obnoxious in their commonness.

"Why wouldn't it be a good idea?" Craig said.

Michael shrugged. He ran his hand across the top of his hair. "Let the police handle it."

"They're not. They ask me rude and offensive questions. I'm going to do the same thing. I was too nice to them, didn't want to seem like I was doubting their integrity."

Michael turned and walked into the living room. Craig followed.

Beth went into the kitchen. Craig could really use a drink, it would help him relax. Looking to alcohol for relaxation might not always be a good thing, but in this case, it was necessary. Maybe she should open a bottle of wine and serve two glasses. Craig wouldn't refuse if it were placed right in front of him. Or beer. That would be better. If she opened wine, she might be tempted to have a glass, and she didn't want to do that. She couldn't do that. She rubbed her belly.

The baby had been there, barely a whisper, at their wedding. Any day it would start showing. All of this should not be happening when their child was developing. It wasn't right. Her fears for Allison were trickling through her bloodstream to the baby. She and Michael had done everything right — the spiritual atmosphere of the wedding, knowing their child was there with them, starting out their family in such perfect harmony. And now this. She rubbed her belly more slowly, then let her hand rest over her navel. Getting angry would only make it worse. She took a long, slow breath, then let it out. She smiled and closed her eyes, thinking of Michael's love, of how they were nurturing Craig, generating positive energy. Of course, life couldn't be perfect. The point was to keep your own mind in a cocoon of love and goodness.

She opened the fridge, pulled out two beers, closed it with her hip, and twisted the caps off the bottles. She put them on a round tray with a tiny rail around it that kept things from sliding over the edge. She opened the fridge again and took out the pitcher of lemonade. She poured half a glass for herself and carried the tray to the living room.

Dinner was light and simple – Satay chicken, jasmine rice, and sautéed green beans with a hint of cumin, and a large plate of cantaloupe. It was sliced into spears and arranged around a pile of raspberries. There was a pitcher of water with sliced cucumbers floating among the ice cubes. Craig talked about work. As he steered the conversation to the children who were his patients, his face lost some of the gray tinge. He actually smiled once.

It wasn't until they started nibbling on the chocolate chip cookies that Craig switched, without warning, back to the topic of Allison.

"The police questioned Devon, but they won't tell me anything about it, of course. So I can't get any information there."

"Even if she was over there, and they knew where she was going, would that really help anything?" Michael said.

"I don't know. Probably not. But every little piece of the

puzzle gets us one step closer. It sure doesn't help not knowing."

Beth rubbed her belly. Then, because she didn't want to tell Craig, not right now, she casually moved her hand to her opposite arm and scratched as if she was attacking a mosquito bite.

"I have to know. And if she was there … I know she was there … why are they lying? That's what bugs me. There's no reason to hide that fact unless they know something bad."

Beth swallowed a piece of cantaloupe without fully chewing it. She coughed.

"Are you okay?" Michael half rose out of his chair.

"Fine. I'm fine." She loved how he watched over her body since the day he'd learned she was pregnant. She picked up her glass and sipped some water. She set it down carefully and looked at Craig. "What do you think they're hiding?"

"Who knows. I smelled her perfume, and they insisted I didn't. Do they think I'm that easily manipulated? Devon's been different lately anyway. You saw how he was at your shower. I thought the guy was going to punch me for a second. Must have hit a nerve, the way he got in my face, made a fist, everything but haul off and smash it into my mouth."

"Then why are you going over there?" She thought about the scrape on her arm. That had been the least of it. Worse, had been the grip of his hand, his fingers like iron clamps around her wrist.

"I have to know," Craig said.

"I think you should let the police handle it. Like Michael said."

Craig took a swig of beer, the third one, after all. He took a long swallow. "They're taking too long. I'm only asking the question." He picked up another cookie. "I have that right."

AFTER CRAIG LEFT, Michael went back into the dining room. He came into the kitchen with the fruit platter. He set it on the counter, picked up a piece of cantaloupe, and bit off half.

"I'm nervous about him going over there." Beth pulled open the door of the dishwasher, then turned and opened the cupboard full of stacked plastic containers. Inside was such an array of shapes and sizes, she stared for several seconds – a shallow, circular container, or something deeper? Something small for the raspberries. There were only a few left, she should eat them while they cleaned up the kitchen. She grabbed the container closest to the front.

"Why?" Michael said.

"I don't know. That they'll get in a fight, that someone will get hurt. I have a bad feeling, that's all."

Michael reached around her arm and grabbed a slice of cantaloupe.

"If you want to eat something, finish the raspberries." She pushed the plate toward him.

"You have bad feelings because you're trying to suppress

the thought she might be dead. It magnifies every little thing out of proportion."

"She can't be dead."

"But we all know that when someone is missing this long, it's likely she's dead."

"Don't say that." Beth cupped her belly, wanting to press her palms over the baby's ears so she wouldn't hear such ugly words, wouldn't come into a world of fear and death. Allison couldn't be dead, she refused to believe it. "We have to stay positive until we know for sure."

"I guess it doesn't hurt anything to be hopeful." He ran his hand down the back of her head, threading his fingers through her hair.

"I'm going to call Jenna. So she knows Craig is coming over." She set the plastic container on the counter and went to the breakfast nook where her phone lay on the bench near the window.

"What's the point of that?" Michael said.

"They have to know that they can't hide anything."

"What do you think they're hiding?"

"I don't know. But Craig is so fragile."

"No he's not."

"Okay, unstable. Vulnerable."

"What is it, do you think the Porters know where she is and aren't saying?" Michael said.

"I don't know."

"Come on, Beth. That's highly unlikely."

"Then why are they lying?"

"How do you know they're lying?"

"You didn't see how Devon was with me that day. Rough. Angry," Beth said.

"He fell all over himself apologizing. He said you might have ..."

"Don't. Do not make this about me being a female. Or pregnant."

He walked to where she stood. He wrapped his arms around her disappearing waist and pressed his head against hers. "I'm not." His breath smelled of cantaloupe.

"They're lying about Allison being over there the day she disappeared," she said.

"That could all be in Craig's head. He wants something to hang on to. It could have been Jenna's perfume or even her scent on his own clothes."

"No. Something is wrong."

"You're upset. I know you think you sense things," he said.

She struggled against his arms. "I don't *think* I sense things, I know."

"Okay, sometimes you do, like when you knew your sister was going to change her mind at the last minute about moving back to California. That was unnerving. And I guess there was the time you knew I'd get that extra stock grant. But I still don't think you should get involved. Let the police do their job. If either one of them is hiding something, the police will figure it out."

"It's taking too long." Her voice caught in her throat.

"What if you're wrong? You'll destroy a friendship."

"It's already ruined." Tears swam into her eyes. "I don't really like Devon anymore, after the way he treated me. And Allison … I have to do this." She wriggled out of his arms. She turned and walked out of the kitchen, around the corner and into the living room. It would make her feel too awkward if Michael listened to her call. She needed to be alone. He didn't know what she knew. She wasn't sure why she hadn't told him, why she felt she couldn't tell him right now.

It was loyalty to Allison. Even though the specter of death hung over everything, even though they were all trying so hard not to believe it was too late, she had to keep her friend's secret. Because if Allison wasn't dead … she wouldn't want everyone, the police, the Porters, most of all Craig, knowing that she'd loved Devon all of her life. It would destroy Craig. She touched the screen, tapped her finger over Jenna's name, and waited for the call to connect.

Amazingly, Jenna answered. Sometimes Beth felt like no one answered their phones. They reverted to texting. It was easier and required less interaction. Efficiency seemed to be the focal point of most relationships lately.

"Beth."

"How are things?" Beth said.

"Okay. What's up?"

"Craig came over for dinner tonight."

"That's nice. I'm sure he needed that."

"He said he's planning to stop by your place."

"What for?"

"He's beyond upset."

"I know. So why is he coming over here? And why wouldn't he let Devon know?"

"It's about Allison's perfume."

Jenna heaved an extended sigh.

"Maybe you should tell me if you saw her the day she disappeared," Beth said.

The phone was silent. For a moment, she thought Jenna had hung up, or the call had been dropped. Both possibilities were equally likely.

"Why can't he let go of the perfume?"

"Would you?"

"He's imagining it."

"So you have no idea where she went that day?"

"Why does everyone keep asking that? And even if I did, why would it matter? She could have gone a hundred places. And they've already checked out those possibilities."

"Why did your living room smell like her perfume?"

"I have no idea."

"Maybe Allison dropped by to talk to Devon. When you weren't there."

"Not likely."

"Have you asked him that question?"

"What is this, are you helping the police now?"

"Why does it feel like you keep dodging the question?"

"I don't know. Because you're imagining things? Because Craig is so freaked out, he's imagining things? We all feel helpless, it plays tricks on your mind."

Beth leaned back in the chair. It was big and soft. The chair was a cheerful presence in her life, white with enormous pink and lavender chrysanthemums splashed over the fabric. She put her hand on the back of her neck and massaged the muscles. The more Jenna evaded the question, the more it seemed likely that Allison had visited the Porters the day she disappeared. After all, Craig hadn't imagined smelling perfume when he'd been inside Beth's house. "I don't want Devon to assault Craig. Like he did to me that day. If he provoked Craig, it could get out of control really fast."

"He didn't *assault* you."

"He hasn't been his normal self since Allison disappeared. Not the day she went missing, and not when I saw him on Monday."

"He's under a lot of pressure at work, it has nothing to do with you or Allison."

"Maybe it's just the opposite," Beth said.

"What?"

"Maybe there's something going on between him and Allison. He knows where she is, and that's why he's behaving so strangely."

"There wasn't anything going on between them. Don't ever say that again. You have no reason to think there was."

The phone started to slide out of Beth's hand. She gripped it more tightly, but her fingers cramped. Suddenly, she wanted to end the conversation. Something was making her uncomfortable – the total picture of Jenna and Devon, the excuses about job pressure and the shoulder-shrugging insistence that there was *nothing they could do*. Of course, there wasn't anything they could do, but most people still felt the urge to take action, and both of them seemed to be lacking in any desire or any curiosity, for that matter. They didn't express fear that Allison might be dead, and they seemed unsympathetic to the horror Craig was living with.

"Are you still there?" Jenna said.

"Yes. I guess I'll hang up now. I wanted you to know Craig is coming by, and I hope you'll be kind to him, that you'll think about what he's going through."

"Of course we will," Jenna said.

The tone in Jenna's voice had shifted from terse, to thick and syrupy. She didn't sound false, but neither did she sound genuine. Beth said good-bye. She tapped the phone to end the call and slid it into her pocket. She wanted it nearby in case she heard from Craig, or, hope against hope, defying all odds of rational expectation, if Allison tried to contact her.

She went back to the kitchen. Michael sat at the table, playing *High Noon* on his iPhone. The dishwasher hummed softly, the counters glistened, still damp. Two mugs sat near the stove with tea bag strings dangling over the sides.

"Thanks for cleaning up. I didn't mean to abandon you."

"No problem."

"What do you think is wrong with them?" she said.

He twisted his phone, tapped his thumb faster.

She didn't repeat the question. He wouldn't know the answer, no one knew the answer. A cup of tea would be nice. She put the kettle on the burner, turned the knob to light the gas, and studied the side of Michael's face. It was something about Allison and Devon. She'd thought Jenna didn't know anything about Allison's feelings. How could she? Devon didn't know, and Allison wouldn't have told Jenna, of all people. Yet, Jenna's response was definite as if she hadn't been surprised by the question. The words had barely escaped Beth's lips when Jenna said, *there isn't anything going on between them*. A response so fast it was as if she'd been waiting for the question, that she'd prepared in advance.

Twenty-seven

JENNA'S STOMACH WAS queasy when Beth said good-bye. Even if Beth hadn't noticed the slip-up while they were talking, surely once she thought back over the conversation, something would sound off base. Jenna had no idea why she'd used the past tense when she tried to suppress Beth's suggestion that there was some kind of secret relationship between Devon and Allison. It was a childhood crush that Allison had never grown out of. There was nothing on Devon's side. Nothing. He hadn't even known about it until yesterday. She couldn't have Beth hinting things like that to other people, to the police.

It only lasted for a moment, barely a passing thought, brushed away as soon as it flickered in her mind, but for that single instant, she was glad Allison was ... gone.

The doorbell rang. Rather than walking to the door, she sat on the closed lid of the toilet. While she was talking to Beth, she'd walked back and forth along the upstairs hall.

Near the end of the conversation, she'd settled in the master bathroom, staring in the mirror, watching herself talk. The movement of her lips as she spoke was riveting as if she was observing a stranger. The air in the bathroom was cold, the tile icy on her bare feet, the lid of the toilet as hard as concrete against her bones.

The bell rang again. She heard the front door open. She leapt to her feet. She should have let Devon know about her slip-up. If it was Craig, and surely it was Craig, she and Devon had to be on the same page, now more than ever. She glanced in the mirror. Her eyes were too bright, her face pale as if she'd just woken up and the blood hadn't returned to the surface of her skin. She tugged her belt to settle her jeans on her hips and walked into the bedroom. Everything seemed out of place, as if it belonged to someone else, things that she saw several times a day looked new – the antique dresser with the marble top, the 8x10 photograph of her and Devon from their engagement shoot, leaning against each other in front of Yosemite Falls. Strangers peered back at her, living in a scene from a different life. Her life now consisted of evading questions. Ever since that creepy encounter in Las Vegas, she felt as if she was being watched, followed, that she had to consider every step, every word. It was exhausting. She walked slowly down the stairs.

"… and I'm tired of your bullshit," Craig said. "You aren't going to bullshit me into thinking I didn't smell anything. I know she was here, and you need to tell me, and the detectives, everything you know. If you don't, and something happens to her, it's your fault."

Jenna hadn't realized she'd been holding her breath, but now she let it out slowly, a thin stream, her lungs settling down into a soft, relaxed state. It wasn't as if Craig suspected them of hurting Allison. He simply thought they were hiding information about where she might have gone. This was the problem with guilt, she was magnifying everything and imagining people suspected far more than they did. She did feel guilty, but loving Devon was so much bigger than guilt.

"I'm not hiding anything," Devon said. "I really don't know what you're talking about. It's in your head."

"It's not in my head." Craig's voice filled the entryway as if his voice was a solid presence standing there with them. Beads of sweat clung to the side of his face. His skin was red, making his hair, short and shaved well past his ears, looking paler than usual, almost silver. He moved closer to Devon, his gray *San Jose Sharks* tee shirt sagged at the neck, the folds of the fabric covering up half the logo so that the only visible part was the exposed teeth of the shark, biting the hockey stick in half. It was difficult to tell whether that shark was leering or fierce. The sagging shirt revealed the base of Craig's neck and his collarbone, as red as his face.

Devon limped backward into the archway leading to the kitchen. "Hey, settle down."

Craig glanced at Jenna then back at Devon. "Is that what you'd want to hear if Jenna disappeared into thin air? No contact for over a week? Out there alone, lying in a ditch, or suffering something unspeakable?"

"No. But I ..."

"Then tell me where she is."

Jenna was thankful for the clarity of a moment earlier. Craig didn't really think they knew where Allison was, he was crazed, half-mad with grief and fear. Devon might not realize that, he might say the wrong thing, might protest too strongly. It was so difficult to strike just the right note in all of this. She shivered at the coldness of her thoughts. No one could help Allison now, but Jenna could still help her husband. The most important thing was to make sure Devon was safe. Once they were past all this, they needed to find some new friends. Dealing with Craig's grief was too much. It consumed the room, had the potential to consume their lives. Even if he knew Allison was dead, started to move toward acceptance, he would dominate everything from here on out, his feelings so large they couldn't be absorbed by a small group of people. The most important thing right now was to get him out of here.

She moved closer and put her hand on Craig's arm. He jerked away from her. "We want to help," she said softly, "But we can't. Attacking us won't bring Allison home."

"You two are lying. I know she was here and you need to tell me right now why, and what she said, and where she went."

Devon leaned against the inside of the archway. "Do you

want a beer or something?"

"No! I don't want a damn beer! If you don't answer me now, I'm telling the cops they haven't asked you enough questions." Craig stepped back. He teetered on his heels, lunged forward, and grabbed Devon's shirt.

"Hey!" Jenna put her hand on his arm again. "That won't solve anything."

Craig shook her off and yanked Devon's shirt, stretching it away from his body. The threads broke apart from the fabric, snapping like someone had stepped on a beetle. "You're a smug little prick," Craig said. "But that one detective, Madrone, will make your life hell. Trust me. I know." He slammed the heel of his hand into Devon's chest.

Devon stumbled and smacked against the doorframe.

There was a crunching sound and Jenna wasn't sure if it was plaster or the cartilage in Devon's shoulder.

Devon winced and bent over, grabbing his knee.

"Don't. Please," Jenna said.

"Stay out of it, Jenna." Craig twisted Devon's shirt around his hand as if he was trying to staunch a flow of blood. Suddenly he let go and turned. "Or maybe not. Maybe it's you."

"You have to let the detectives do their jobs," Jenna said. "You can't blame us just because you don't know what else to do." Her head ached from trying to form sentences that weren't lies, that would persuade Craig to back off. She wasn't sure why she was so concerned with not lying. The things

Devon had done, that both of them had done, were far beyond simple lies. And she was lying anyway, by suggesting the detectives would do their jobs and find Allison or at least discover what had happened to her. Jenna didn't want that at all, so wasn't that a lie? Her brain felt as if it was cracking, splitting into pieces, floating around inside her skull.

"Good suggestion," Craig said. He walked to the door. He opened it and turned to face them. "You don't know how rough they can get. We'll see how you stand up under that. They start from the premise of guilt and work forward from there, or in circles. They act as if I killed and dismembered her."

"Oh, that's horrible," Jenna said. "I'm so sorry."

"You think? They asked me about everything from kinky sex to who I thought she might be sleeping with behind my back. They make wild swings from assuming I'm a sicko to accusing Allison of being a prostitute." He laughed. "You think I'm exaggerating? And since I was the last *known* person to see her, that automatically equates to guilt. But if you were the last ones … well, we'll see what they do with that."

"We didn't see her."

"I'll let the detectives figure that out." Craig stepped onto the front porch. He turned and walked to the edge, then sauntered along the path. He got in his car and backed out of the driveway without pausing to buckle his seatbelt.

The door stood open, inviting the scent of jasmine and cut grass into the entryway. Jenna closed it and turned the deadbolt. "I have to tell you about my conversation with Beth. I kind of screwed up."

Devon's eyelids drooped. They'd worked until four in the morning, digging a hole for Allison's body in the hard clay of the basement floor. Each shovelful had been a monumental effort, not really shovels full, but little bits that came out in powdery flakes. Devon had used the pick, and even with that, it had taken hours to dig down three feet. She'd been amazed at their lack of horror as they worked side by side, knowing what they had to do, numb from the exertion. They wore gloves, but still, their palms were red, and a few small calluses had appeared. Craig hadn't noticed, but she couldn't believe the police would be that blind. If they decided to search the house ... the basement still needed work ... they had to do something with Allison's bike. There was a faint smell of urine, and Jenna wasn't sure if it was her own disgust, picturing the scene, or whether it would be noticeable to an investigator. They'd slept a few hours and woken again at seven to spend most of the day scraping areas where blood had splattered and dried, packing up clothes and their set of china, and stacking the boxes over the disturbed dirt. Hopefully, there were enough boxes remaining in the garage that could be carried down to the basement so it would look as if they'd always used the area for storage. That had to be done next, but they'd finally stopped for a sandwich when Beth called.

First, she had to tell Devon about her slip up. Before she

could speak, Devon limped toward the living room. He bumped against the small table near the stairs. The dark green ceramic bowl teetered. He kicked at the table leg, turned, and hobbled into the living room. He went to the doors, yanked open the one on the left, and leaned on the handle. He bent over and pressed his hand against his forehead. He slid his hand through his hair, stopping and clutching at the hair so it stood up in waves between his fingers.

Jenna went into the living room and stood behind him. She wrapped her arms around his waist and leaned the side of her face against his back. He seemed to stiffen, but he didn't pull away. He stumbled forward, pushing the door open wider.

"Can we sit down?" Jenna said.

"We have work to do."

"I know. But we should talk first."

"About what?"

"Beth. It sounds like she knows Allison had a crush on you. She implied, well, more than implied, that you two had something going on. And I was so upset that I said there wasn't anything going on between you."

"So?" Devon shifted slightly. He closed the door.

"I said *wasn't*, as if it was all in the past."

"That's pretty subtle."

"I'm still nervous."

He turned. "It doesn't really matter."

"It might. If she thinks about it. For sure it will make her more suspicious."

"I'm going to the police and telling them what happened."

"No! They won't see that it was an accident."

"I don't care. I can't destroy your life."

"You'll go to prison. For years. Or worse."

"This is worse. Can't you see how all this will turn into its own prison?"

She squeezed her arms more tightly around his waist. She felt the press of his spine against her face and his butt against her pelvis. Something inside slipped like liquid running from her neck, down her back and through her knees until she wasn't sure she could remain standing. "I won't let you."

"I wanted to give you everything, and I might as well have poured gasoline on our lives and lit a match. I'm not going to have cops crawling around here asking you questions and sending you to prison for helping me."

"It's too late for that. They don't know anything, and they can't find out anything because we'll stick together."

"What if they search the house?"

"Why would they do that? Besides, we have the … the spot … covered up."

"Do you have any idea what cops do when they search a house? Who knows what fibers and hairs Allison left in the living room, the master bathroom, in the basement."

"Maybe we should hurry and build the wine cellar. Right

now. Once the floor is put down, would they really find anything?"

Devon laughed. "We can't afford it."

Jenna smiled. The awareness that her smile was lingering sickened her. She let go of him and moved around to face him. "We shouldn't have buried her at our house."

"I know. As always, I keep doing what seems easiest at that moment. What's the saying, *sin in haste, repent in leisure?*"

He looked so defeated. She wanted to put her hands on his jaw and mold it back into the face she was familiar with. "You're not turning yourself in. We could gut the 401ks, build the wine cellar, maybe move her body. I'll do anything." She wound herself around him again, pulling on his neck, pressing herself so hard against him it was difficult to breathe. His body gave her strength, made her feel like she was alive, that nothing could happen to her. "I'm not letting you go."

"I killed someone. I killed my friend."

She pulled back. "It was a terrible accident. We both know that. Allison wasn't a saint. She pushed you, and you lost your temper." One half of her mind was disgusted with the words she was saying, trying to explain it all away, acting as if murder was nothing. But the other half of her knew the truth – Devon wasn't a violent man. No one would believe that about him. He was generous and fun loving. A good friend. Things had gotten out of hand, and Allison had an equal part in that. Devon wasn't a killer.

Twenty-eight

ON MONDAY MORNING the police arrived. The only surprise was that it had taken them so long. The minute Devon saw there was a uniformed cop with the detectives, he knew this was different from the casual conversation he'd had with the guys who chatted him up when Jenna was in Vegas. At that time, they sounded as if they were reading from a standardized questionnaire. *When did you last see her? Was she in any trouble? What is her marriage like? Did you witness any violence between her and her husband?*

All thoughts of confession were sucked out of his brain as if by a vacuum cleaner as he watched the three men emerge from the car. The reality of answering questions, sitting in a police station, not to mention going to prison, looked completely different on a perfect spring morning. He should be headed to work, driving with the canvas top stripped off the Jeep, thinking about what he'd accomplish once he had the expanded authority of his new role. He didn't like to admit it, even to himself, but what he really meant was the increased power that a Director wielded.

Survival mode kicked to the surface from some place deep inside, something far deeper than his desire to do what was best for Jenna, far beyond his logical consideration of what would bring the least painful results. This would be a battle of wits. He wasn't the average dumb criminal. Guys that got caught weren't very bright. They couldn't think fast, and they let nerves take over, or made mistakes because they couldn't remember what they'd said. If he handled this right, there was no reason they would ever consider getting a search warrant. That way, Allison could stay buried in the basement forever.

Eventually, Craig would accept his loss and move on. He was better off finding someone who loved him with her whole heart. Devon believed that now. Craig was into doing the right thing. He didn't care about prestige or money or any of that. He and Allison were a mismatch of epic proportions. Craig would find someone new, the pain would heal, and he'd eventually realize his life was better.

By the time Devon re-filled his coffee mug, walked to the entryway, and turned the deadbolt, he felt composed. He hoped he looked that way.

The lead detective was the same guy – Hank Madrone. He introduced the uniformed cop – Bob Argyle. It seemed like an odd name for a cop, but everything was out of sync lately, and what was a cop's name supposed to be? Was it supposed to conform to some guideline? And why was he even thinking about this?

"We'd like you to come with us, Mr. Porter," Detective Madrone said.

"What's up?"

None of them smiled at his attempt at casual friendliness. In the upstairs bathroom, Jenna's hair dryer had gone silent. It seemed as if the whole house, his whole life, was standing behind him, waiting to see what would happen.

"We need to ask you some more questions about the disappearance of Allison Watson."

It made no sense for Madrone to be so officious. Of course it was about Allison, and they didn't need to repeat her last name either.

"I need to get to work. I have a staff meeting this morning."

"We'll wait while you let your office know you won't be coming in."

Shit. Craig must have done a number on them, they were very intense. He'd have to call in sick, he sure wasn't telling his team he had cops breathing down his neck. Telling Jenna would be bad enough. "Can you wait here for a minute while I make some calls?"

"You can call your office. Any other calls can wait."

"I need to tell my wife."

"We'll come inside while you do that." All three of them stepped into the entryway and moved forward, forcing him to take a few steps back. They didn't speak, they simply stood, not making eye contact with the arched openings leading to the kitchen and living room, or even glancing with genuine curiosity at the dramatic rise of the staircase.

As he climbed the stairs, he leaned hard on the rail, trying to hide his limp from the knee that seemed permanently altered by Allison's ferocious kicks. The force of the cops' presence followed him up the stairs. The front door stood open, a breeze rising with him to the second-floor landing. He had no idea how Jenna would react. Yesterday she'd been a hundred and ten percent in his corner, but as he'd already experienced in his own visceral response, the reality was much different. Hadn't he just done his own about-face?

The minute his reflection appeared in the mirror, Jenna lowered the brush she was using for her eye makeup. He glanced at the sculpture. The figure's eyes were closed, a tiny smile on her lips, one of her long, slim legs bent slightly. It used to be a metallic shadow of Jenna. Now when he looked at it, all he could remember was Allison laughing and pinching the nipple, and then what happened after that. He still sometimes felt it hadn't really been him. It was a bad dream. If only he'd …

"What's wrong?" Jenna said.

"The cops are back. They want to take me to the police station to answer more questions."

"Oh God." The makeup brush fell out of Jenna's hand, hit the edge of the counter, and dropped to the floor, where it left a black smear. She leaned on the edge of the sink. After a minute, she bent down and picked up the brush. She put it on the counter. "I don't suppose I can go with you."

"Not likely."

"Call me," she said.

Her eyes were glassy. Her lips looked soft, juicy. He wanted to kiss her, but he didn't want to make her cry. He kissed her forehead. "I will."

"Hold me."

"I can't," he said.

She lifted her arms and wrapped them around his neck, pulling his head down so their foreheads touched. She put one hand on the back of his head as if she was trying to mix their brains into a single entity.

After a moment, he put his arms around her and held her as tightly as he could without making himself choke on the fear that was rushing out of his throat, heating his breath so it was too warm on his lips.

He left the bathroom. Neither one of them spoke. He was glad she didn't whisper at him what he should say, what traps to watch out for. She trusted him, and he wouldn't let her down. He would manage this like it was a meeting with the top executives. He'd stay cool and in control of his game, not allow them to back him into a corner.

Deep inside, something whispered that the best thing for Jenna was for him to confess. He should take responsibility and make sure she wasn't dragged into this. Isn't that what executives did? Isn't that what a man did when he loved a woman more than his own life?

THE POLICE STATION was just as Devon had imagined it would be. Perhaps there were no surprises in the world anymore since everything could be experienced first on TV, or at least mocked up with an enormous degree of authenticity. Two cops in uniforms sat behind a counter, one answering the phone and the other greeting people that came in the door. You wouldn't think a police station needed greeters, but maybe that was required here more than anywhere. People had to know where to go and what to do without breaking unknown rules.

He followed the detectives through a door and down a hallway to a small room that contained a table and three chairs. There was no window, and no additional furniture, not even a trash can. In the corner across from the door was a video camera mounted just below the ceiling. Somewhere along the way, Officer Argyle had disappeared, and it was just Devon and the detectives and the four off-white walls and those chairs that looked like they'd make your bones ache after twenty minutes.

Detective Madrone gestured at the chair on the far side of the table and closed the door. He remained standing.

"Tell us what you did on Saturday, March 26th," Detective Madrone said.

They sure weren't going to waste time. And the tone was

a hell of a lot different than the last time. Devon's stomach felt as tight if he'd just finished two hundred sit-ups, pushing himself to double his usual number of reps. He hoped he wasn't going to sweat. But thinking about sweat wasn't going to help. Best to take a small breath, answer the question, and know that if he answered the easy ones quickly, it wouldn't seem odd if he took longer on others. "Hung out at home," he said.

"All day?"

"We ran errands in the morning."

"Who's we?"

"My wife and I."

"Did Allison Watson come over to your house that day?"

"No."

"Was your wife there with you all day?"

"Yes. Or, no. She went out with her mother."

"How long was she gone?"

Devon shrugged. They didn't know a damn thing. This was all the result of Craig's imagination.

"Please provide verbal responses," Madrone said. He leaned against the wall and crossed his arms and ankles as if he was watching a sporting event.

"Are you recording this?" Devon said.

"We need a direct response."

"I don't remember how long she was gone. A few hours, I think."

"What time did she leave?"

Devon lifted his shoulders, remembered the directive, and kept them hunched around his ears for a minute. Then he realized that probably made him look creepy and uncertain. He spoke quickly so they wouldn't notice. "Four."

"PM?"

"Yes, 4 p.m." It was difficult not to roll his eyes. This could take forever.

"Ms. Watson didn't come by when your wife was out?"

"I said, no."

"You didn't see her at all that day?"

"No."

"What about the night before?"

"No."

"Where do you think she went on her bike ride that Saturday?"

"I don't know."

"She didn't ride to your home, Mr. Porter?"

"No."

"Her husband thinks she did."

"Why would she do that?"

"You and Ms. Watson have been friends since childhood, is that correct?"

"Yes."

"Would you still consider her a close friend?"

"Yes. Her and Craig."

"But you were closer to Ms. Watson."

"I …" Devon coughed. "I've known her longer." His

back was damp. He couldn't believe how close he'd come to saying *I knew her longer.*

"Do you need a glass of water?"

"Sure. That would be great." He hoped his tone was casual. Normal thirst, that's all, not a sudden case of nerves that elicited coughing, an effort to distract from the barrage of questions. How long was this going to go on?

The spare detective pushed back his chair and left the room. Madrone hardly missed a beat. "Do you tell Ms. Watson things you don't tell your wife?"

"Uh. No."

"You hesitated."

"The question surprised me. What does it have to do with …?"

Detective Madrone held up a finger. Apparently, questions were uni-directional. Devon waited.

"How close are you and Ms. Watson?"

"We're good friends."

"Does she tell you things she doesn't tell her husband?"

"How should I know?"

The other detective returned and put a Styrofoam cup of water on the table in front of Devon. It appeared that they used the term "*glass* of water" loosely.

"What is your opinion?"

"I really don't know."

"Mr. Watson seems to think his wife often had conversations with you, exchanged text messages with you, that he wasn't privy to."

"I don't know why."

"When was the last time Ms. Watson was in your home?"

"I don't remember."

"What happened to your knee?"

Devon picked up the cup and drank the contents. Instead of calming him, buying him time, it was so icy he had a brain freeze.

"What happened to your knee?"

"I was working on the waterfall in our swimming pool. I tripped over the pool cleaning hose and landed right on a rock. With my knee."

"Have you seen a doctor?"

"No. I've been icing it. That's all the doctor would tell me to do."

"Where do you think Ms. Watson went that day?"

For another two hours, the questions continued in the same weaving pattern. Devon's neck began to ache. His eyes burned. The room had a serious lack of ventilation. They probably did that on purpose. Despite the repetition, they never came right out and said that Craig had smelled Allison's perfume. Yet, they clearly didn't believe Allison hadn't been at his house that day.

WHEN THEY FINALLY drove him home, he had a feeling he might be taking another trip in that enormous sedan. It might not be this week, but he could tell they would be relentless. His own questions had gone unanswered – *Did they have any leads? Did they think she was okay?* Nothing but silence.

As soon as the front door closed behind him, he pulled out his phone and saw three missed text messages from Jenna. Reading backward in time, they said:

Text me the MINUTE you can.

Call me as soon as you're done.

I'm going into the office, it's making me crazy sitting here worrying about you.

Devon smiled. He was so damn lucky. He was also tired. Too tired to go into the office. It might provide a good distraction, but he was nervy, jumpy, couldn't imagine having a coherent conversation. Besides, he'd told them he was sick.

He went into the living room. He flopped on the sofa, pulled off his shoes, and texted Jenna that it had gone okay. Her next message said she was coming right home. He called her. "I'm really tired. I'm going to try to sleep."

"I want to be there with you."

"I'm fine. You need to be at work. We need to look normal until this is over."

THE DOORBELL WOKE him. Not the detectives again. Already. He grabbed his phone off the coffee table. Six o'clock. Why wasn't Jenna home? He couldn't believe he'd slept all that time. Four missed text messages. The bell rang again. He shoved himself off the sofa, limped across the room, and opened the door. "Hey, Beth. What do you want?"

He looked down at his phone and clicked to the text messages. All from Jenna. His shoulders relaxed.

"I need to come in," Beth said.

"Why?"

"I know about Allison being in love with you." Beth stepped up so close he could feel her breath on his face. She smelled like chocolate. "She told me."

"She had a crush when we were kids, that's all."

Beth nudged him with her shoulder, and he moved back. She stepped into the entryway and pushed the door closed.

"I don't remember inviting you in."

"I'm going to find out what's going on. There are things the police won't know to ask because they don't know she was in love with you. I don't want to hurt Craig, but I'm not going to sit back and pretend there isn't something weird going on here."

"Whatever you think you know, you're wrong."

"You don't even know what I'm going to say."

"I know you're bugging me and you're sticking your nose in where you don't belong. You've changed since you got married. All that money makes you think you're in charge."

"That's not true."

Devon shrugged. He looked at his phone. Jenna's last text said she was picking up tacos for dinner.

"Look at me," Beth said. Her eyes were damp. "Allison told me she'd been in love with you her whole life."

"I told you it was just a crush, and it was a long time ago."

"I think you've seen her."

"Nope."

"If you know how she felt about you, that means you've seen her, because she told me a few days before she went missing that you still had no clue."

"That's quite a leap."

"Maybe I'm doing the wrong thing, trying not to hurt Craig by not telling him." She turned back to the door. "I can imagine how much better their investigation will proceed if they know about this."

Devon grabbed her arm and yanked her toward him.

"Let go of me!"

He relaxed his grip but didn't let go. "You don't know anything. It would kill Craig if he finds out."

"This is already killing him. Let go of my arm."

He twisted her arm behind her back.

"Is this what happened with Allison? Did you grab her, push her around, and it got out of control?" Beth said.

"No."

"I think it is. Either that or Jenna found out and did something to her."

"What are you saying?"

"I don't know," Beth said.

He let go of her arm. He shoved his phone in his pocket and grabbed her shoulders. He felt as if he was standing outside his body, knowing this was yet another huge mistake, knowing he was scaring her, making her more suspicious, but he couldn't stop. Her eyes bulged. The flecks of brown in her pupils swam like tiny pieces of ash in hazel pools. He squeezed hard until she whimpered, then moved his hand over her mouth. He wanted to put it around her neck. "Stop making things up. I could kill you right now. You're fucking with our lives, and you don't know what you're talking about."

Beth moved her mouth and made a sound, but the pressure of his hand prevented her from speaking. Tears filled her eyes, and she suddenly went limp.

He dropped his hands.

Beth backed up. She was full on crying now. "I'm pregnant! If you hurt my baby, I'll never forgive you. You've turned into the scariest person I've ever known." She flung her arm out, groping the door behind her until her hand landed on the doorknob.

"If you're so scared, why do you keep coming over here?" He folded his arms across his chest. He'd blown it. He could see that now.

Beth opened the door and scurried out. He heard her car start and the sound of it in reverse as she backed slowly to the end of the driveway, then a long pause, while she waited to make a safe turn into the street. He closed the door.

He got the key to the basement padlock and went out to the backyard. The pool no longer looked inviting. In fact, the sinking sun glared into his eyes, making him squint, tinting the water with a reddish glow, so it looked like an enormous pool of blood. He opened the padlock and went down the stairs, feeling his way along the wood handrail. When the light was on, the boxes they'd stacked over Allison's grave looked staged. There was nothing to indicate this had been used regularly as a storage place. For some reason, the boxes looked like they hadn't been there very long, or maybe that was his fear whispering.

This house had truly been for Jenna, to show her how much he loved her, to build a life together. Instead, he'd dragged her into covering up a murder. The key slid out of his fingers and made a soft tap on the dirt. Everything was silent as if he was closed in a tomb with Allison.

Twenty-nine

JENNA OPENED HER eyes. The bed was empty. She sat up. The previous night was a blur. All she remembered was Devon trying to convey the series of questions the detectives had asked. They all sounded inane. She hadn't been able to understand why Devon was so concerned. Finally, he'd told her he was done. He didn't want a drink, and he didn't want to talk. He'd insisted they go to bed and he'd made love to her. It had been so different. She couldn't say why. Slower, maybe? Or only because her senses were in a constant state of alert? Now, she looked at every object, every gesture in the changed light of knowing a woman was buried under her house. She closed her eyes. Where was Devon? She wanted him.

She pushed back the sheet and climbed out of bed. The room was warm, the breeze through the open balcony door was soft on her skin. She went to the closet and grabbed a pair of jeans and a white tank top. After she'd tugged on her clothes, she walked down the stairs, her feet still warm, somewhat sticky on the hardwood. She smelled coffee, not fresh, but brewed several hours earlier, kept warm for too long.

One of the living room doors stood open to the patio. Devon sat on a chair with his back to the house. She went to the door. "Hi. Aren't you going into the office today?"

Without turning, he spoke. "If I tell them it was me, that I pressured you into helping, maybe they'll leave you alone."

"No!"

"I can't do this to you. Sooner or later, I'll be headed to prison."

"I want to be with you."

"That's the thing. We'll be separated no matter what. They're going to figure it out. Eventually, they're going to search our house. Knowing I'd put you in prison would kill me. But I can survive anything, knowing you're out there, free."

"You're not going to jail. They won't find out." She went to him and settled herself on his lap. "I can't live without you."

"Yes you can."

She started to cry.

"My mind's made up. If you love me, if you ever loved me, you'll trust me that this is the best thing for us.

Now she knew why making love had been so different, so filled with significance in a way she hadn't realized.

THEY SHOWERED TOGETHER and dressed. There was nothing left to say, after all the weeks of talking. Jenna felt as if her head was filled with dense, spongy clouds. Her thoughts moved lethargically, unable to consider anything beyond her present activity. As she brushed her hair, she noticed each strand as it passed through the bristles. Every motion swelled out of proportion until it seemed both the most important and the least important thing in the world.

Without discussing it, they got into Jenna's car, the silence grew heavier because they both knew it made sense to take her car. She'd be driving home alone. The house. The bills. The things she'd have to manage swam in her head, but she couldn't talk to him about that. Not now. Not with what he was doing for her. If he could submit to arrest and a trial and years in prison ... Would they believe it was an accident? The fact she and Devon had disposed of the body, tried to hide everything, wouldn't help support that conclusion. But initially, it had been an accident. They had to see that. She needed to find a lawyer. How the hell would they pay for a lawyer? If she sold the house ... but the economy. She closed her eyes. These were their last minutes together. She had to think about Devon, feel him sitting inches away, the warmth of his presence, the energy that radiated from him. The Devon-ness that would be ripped out of her arms. When would she touch him again?

Before she could finish her thoughts, they were at the Palo Alto police station. He parked the car. She started to cry again, so many tears this time that she couldn't see his face. They stood on the sidewalk, not caring whether the people strolling past noticed or what they thought. He held her so tightly she could hardly breathe. She didn't care. She didn't know when she'd take a full breath again, if ever.

"Don't go," she said.

"I have to."

IT WAS ELEVEN-THIRTY when she walked out. Alone. She'd waited on a chair that had the back sloped at too much of an angle to be comfortable. She'd waited while they took his statement and then took him away.

The air was warm and smelled of jasmine. She felt as if her skin had been peeled off her body. Instead of walking to her car, she turned in the opposite direction and started toward University Avenue. People would be outside, sitting at coffee shops, even on a weekday morning. The birds would hop from branch to branch in the small curbside trees. Cars would roll slowly down the street in no particular hurry because it was spring and life was good.

As she walked, she felt the sidewalk, hard and unyielding through the thin soles of her sandals. It brought back the sensation of Devon's fingers on the bottoms of her feet last night, pressing out the tension that collected in those small muscles. She hoped the memory of his hands on her body wouldn't fade. She could do this. It was a cleansing. Everything washed out of her life except wanting Devon. Worry about money, work, their careers, fear of their friends finding out about their debt, lying, blackmail — all of it — vanished as the noise of life swept across her.

A plan began to form in her mind. She would downsize her life – sell the house, move to a studio apartment. Spend her days working, eating simple food, drinking nothing but water. She'd run ten miles every day. The bare essentials. There was nothing left but Devon and waiting for him.

LETTER FROM CATHRYN

Thank you so much for choosing to read Buried By Debt . Your support is greatly appreciated and I hope you enjoyed the book as much as I enjoyed writing it. I especially hope you enjoyed this unusual love story. If you enjoyed the book, I would be extremely grateful if you could take a few moments to leave a quick review on Amazon. It's always great to hear what readers think and it can also help others discover my books. Any recommendations to friends and family are also very welcome! I love hearing from readers so please feel free to let me know what you thought via my Facebook page or Twitter. You can even contact me directly through my website. To make sure you don't miss out on my upcoming releases and more, you can sign up to my mailing list at my website link here: CathrynGrant.com/contact

Thank you again for all your support – it is greatly appreciated.
Cathryn